The Winds of Change sweep across the Empire. . . .
The Clan War is over, but the struggle for the throne goes on.

Toturi has united the Clans and brought peace to Rokugan, but a taint infects the land, threatening to corrupt all that he has fought to build. There is only one way to cleanse the realm, but his final sacrifice may destroy everything he holds dear.

Legend of the
Five Rings

THE
STEEL
THRONE

EDWARD BOLME

THE STEEL THRONE
©2002 Wizards of the Coast, Inc.

Cover art by Stephen Daniele
First Printing: March 2002
Library of Congress Catalog Card Number: 2001089468

9 8 7 6 5 4 3 2 1

UK ISBN: 0-7869-2732-1
US ISBN: 0-7869-2712-7
620-88553-001-EN

U.S., CANADA,
ASIA, PACIFIC, & LATIN AMERICA
Wizards of the Coast, Inc.
P.O. Box 707
Renton, WA 98057-0707
+1-800-324-6496

EUROPEAN HEADQUARTERS
Wizards of the Coast, Belgium
P.B. 2031
2600 Berchem
Belgium
+32-70-23-32-77

Visit our web site at www.wizards.com

For the fans, who made all this possible . . .
I hope I meet your expectations.

ACKNOWLEDGMENTS

I would like to thank Ryan Dancey, who hired me—apparently on instinct more than anything else—as well as the rest of the team, who accepted me without question (you know who you are, and there are too many of you to list for fear of accidentally leaving someone out). Accolades need to be given to Paul Allen Timm and Luke Peterschmidt for working above and beyond. Finally, special thanks go to Peter Archer and Rob King, who were willing to help me rebuild the bridges I had burned.

1 FLIGHT OF DRAGONS

The
Fourth
Year
of the
Reign
of
Toturi I

In the blink of an eye, the dragons returned.

For four years, they had sequestered themselves. During that time, some of the samurai in the Empire had begun to wonder openly if all of the kami—all of the gods and spirits—had abandoned the ancestral lands to the mortals, if indeed the Age of Man had dawned with the ascension of Toturi, the Ronin Emperor. For four long years, not even the most enlightened shugenja could sense the dragons' presence, hidden beyond the immortal veil. In those four long years, the people of the Empire began to turn their back upon the dragons and upon the other kami as well. Perhaps that was part of the plan of the Unspeakable: turn the people away from the myths and legends and traditions that guide them and leave them rudderless in a world where their only duty is unto themselves.

No more. The dragons ripped across the stained skies of Rokugan at astonishing speeds, bringing terror, raw power, incomprehensible magic . . . and hope.

The dragons had hidden themselves from the Unspeakable

long enough. It was time to fight. Across the continent, the Unspeakable was tearing at the fabric of the world itself, and even the dragons feared what might happen.

The Dragon of Air parted the winds for the others. The Thunder Dragon roiled in its wake, keeping the path clear. Above, the Celestial Dragon illuminated the way for its siblings, while below the Dragon of Earth shook the world to announce their arrival—a deafening, horrifying sound of the lands themselves being beaten as drums. The Water Dragon guided their course as creation itself threatened to collapse, and the Dragon of Fire left a glimmering trail in their wake, an arc of blinding dragonfire for the entire world to see. And, of course, at the center of it all was the Void Dragon, calm, empty of thought, as pure of action as the falling snow.

They moved across the Empire, each dragon a storm unto itself, all seven together nothing less than an apocalypse. Mountains trembled in fear. The oceans withdrew from the dragons' power. Trees broke their own backs to bow before the great spirits. Those humans unfortunate enough to be in the dragons' path prostrated themselves, stammering out desperate, fearful prayers of thanksgiving and fervently hoping that they would remain beneath the dragons' notice.

Of a sudden, the flight of dragons burst apart, each going its separate way, each with its own duties to perform. They had announced themselves. The Empire knew now that they had returned. Still, there was much to do.

The Water Dragon spiraled down into a river, merging with the waters. Once in its own element, the dragon knew no limitations. To the small mortals nearby, it seemed the river itself erupted along its entire length to the sea as the dragon moved through. Fishing boats abruptly soared skyward on the van of a river-long geyser, then dropped again to the suddenly placid water, filled to the gunwales with flopping fish. By the time the fishers could cry out a prayer of thanks to the glassy waters, the dragon was already moving through the ocean.

The dragon turned landward again, following the course of a small stream and sending its contents erupting out of the streambed. Then, abruptly, it surged out of the water and surveyed the land around. This was the right place.

There was a village just off the stream's bank. The dragon looked at it carefully. It was a small village, simple, quiet. The Void Dragon would approve. At the center of the village was a shrine to the ancestors, carefully tended. Feng shui radiated from its rustic construction. This was no immaculate wood shrine, no religious structure so perfectly rendered and polished that it had become sterile. This shrine had been hewn by hand, carved, rubbed with oils, and, above all, revered. Its rough and irregular exterior proved that it was alive to these villagers, a part of their intimate life and not an empty ritual. This was indeed the right place.

The dragon narrowed its focus and saw the villagers, face down in the dirt. It chose one and gave him a nudge, spirit to spirit. He gasped and leaped backward, his face drained of color.

Look at me.

Trembling uncontrollably, the villager looked up helplessly. It seemed as if the stream itself had risen out of its bed to flow into the air, curving elegantly upward. The surface of the water rippled in the breeze, constantly shifting and refracting the light of the sun.

Higher.

The villager craned his neck back, following the arc of the stream as it curved over his head. He saw a pair of forelimbs clasped delicately together, the folds of the liquid skin confusing his mind. Above that, the water formed a dragon's head with long, wavering watery whiskers gracing the muzzle. Water dripped from the whiskers, making the sound of falling rain. He couldn't tell if the dragon actually touched the sky, or merely seemed to.

Look at me.

At last, the villager met the dragon's eyes. Though made of water, they seemed to reflect the light of the sun itself. The villager gave a small, strangled cry of fear. Surely he was about to die. It was not right for anyone in the Empire to look a superior in the eye.

You are the samurai of this village.

It did not seem like a question, so the samurai chose not to reply.

All must serve the Empire in their own way. Your way is to obey the dragon.

The samurai, cringing, nodded.

The dragon reached one of its forelimbs into itself, water merging with water the way a stream enters a river. It drew forth an egg-shaped ball, made entirely of water. There was something inside, but its image was distorted by the surface of the watery egg, and he could not tell what it was. The dragon held it for a moment, then reached out and placed it upright on the ground in front of the samurai.

I have carried her long enough. Now you will care for her as one of your own.

The watery egg suddenly lost its form and splashed about as if some invisible skein had been abruptly slit open. There sat a woman, trembling uncontrollably. She was pretty and looked rather young, except for the deep, haunting emptiness in her eyes and the hair that had turned as white as snow. She was curled into a fetal position, clutching her kimono tightly about her body.

The samurai noticed that although she had come from the water-egg, she herself was dry. Momentarily forgetting his station, he turned toward the water dragon to ask, but the dragon was already gone, vanished as if it had never been. He was at once startled but also profoundly relieved.

Still too shaken to stand, he crawled over to where the woman sat. She took no notice of him, but stared vacantly into space. Slowly he reached out his hand to hers. As soon as his skin touched hers, she started and gasped. Her head jerked toward him, but not quite all the way, and again, she did not appear to see him.

He took her hand, gently but firmly. He pulled softly, gradually, coaxing her up. She rose, seemingly an activity she had almost forgotten.

Gently he led her to his hut. She followed, taking timid, tiny steps, shaking her head slowly from side to side, with her free hand always clutched across her belly.

2 | SOUL OF THE EMPIRE

The
Fourth
Year
of the
Reign
of
Toturi I

Kaede stood at a window in the Imperial Palace, looking at the streets below with her dark, knowing eyes. It was cold—far colder than was ordinary for this time of year, and she adjusted her thick robes to seal off a persistent draft.

The people in the streets below moved quickly, almost furtively, heads down so that they would not see the uncomfortable color that the sky had become. Even here, in the heart of Otosan Uchi, the eternal capital, proper face and decorum had fallen prey to fear and isolation. One does not need to be the Oracle of the Void, Kaede mused, to sense that the Empire itself is in grave danger.

Even were the sky not that unnatural hue, even were the world not seemingly less colorful to the eye, the air not somehow less substantial, Otosan Uchi would still be a worried city. Spirits walked the streets, unable to find their rest in Jigoku. The voices of the ancestors were dimmed, the welcome weight of their approval fading, leaving an emptiness behind. The Empire's past was fading like a dream.

And there were rumors crackling through the streets like a storm. Fear flashed like lightning in listeners' eyes. Hearts thudded like thunder with trepidation. Rumors of faceless fiends, rumors of darkness and shadow, worst of all, rumors regarding Emperor Toturi the First . . .

The Emperor was the soul of the Empire, the pinnacle of mortals, beloved of the gods, ruler with the authority of the heavens. His word was law. Furthermore, this was Emperor Toturi, the hero of the Day of Thunder. Known in those days as Toturi the Black, a dishonored ronin whose family name had been struck from history, his army of samurai, ronin, and peasants had been instrumental in the salvation of the Empire. Now he ruled as Emperor, and when Toturi the Thunder ruled, what harm could befall Rokugan?

That was what worried the citizens. The rumors said Toturi had lost his mind. The rumors said he had slaughtered the Imperial Court, butchered the courtiers, aides, magistrates, and servants in a twisted frenzy, scattering their spirits about the castle as they looked for the way to the afterlife. The rumors said that anyone who saw him might be showered in praise . . . or ordered to commit seppuku.

Kaede knew these rumors were true, yet they did not tell the whole truth. The truth was darker still . . .

She turned away from the window and crossed the floor toward a door leading to the Emperor's antechamber behind the throne room. She could hear the Emperor struggling, the hiss of his breath cutting cleanly through the rice paper walls of the palace.

She feigned not to hear, as did the servant who opened the door for her. All hope would be lost if the Empire knew how far the Emperor had fallen since the Day of Thunder. This she could see clearly. She foresaw the complete destruction of the Empire and everything in it. That was the curse of her destiny, to see everything that she could not change.

She had been called by the Oracle of the Void four years ago, on the Day of Thunder, and was thus spared the carnage her Clan had suffered on that noble and sorrowful day. Of the Elemental Masters of the Phoenix Clan, only she, the Mistress of the Void, survived, and only because she could not resist the Oracle's call. She had left her compatriots to die on the battlefields while she sought her destiny elsewhere, far from the gathered armies. She found the Oracle of the Void and accepted the dragon's soul into hers, opening her mind to whole new realms. The Oracle then left this world, leaving his seat and his title to Kaede.

Yet on that day, she had resisted taking the final step and sitting upon the Oracle's seat. Though the dragon's power coursed through her veins, enticing her with its cloying wisdom and insight, still she held tightly to her humanity, so that she could fulfill her duties and vows as a member of the samurai caste. This she did for the sake of her husband, chosen for her by Emperor Hantei XXXVIII, shortly before his death. She resisted taking the final step so that she could serve her husband, and also because she loved him.

The rice-paper door whispered shut behind Kaede, and those in the antechamber, save only Emperor Toturi himself, bowed deeply in greeting, touching their heads to the floor where they knelt. The Emperor did not appear to notice her arrival.

She knelt beside him. He sat on his heels, knees slightly apart. Sweat ran freely from his shaven brow, dripping on his well-muscled and battle-scarred chest. He held his arms out in front of him, hands tightly clutching his katana, held upright and sheathed in its beautiful polished saya. She could see his brows furrowed with the force of his concentration, focusing his whole being upon the katana.

The katana was the symbol of the samurai caste, an elegant curving sword of razor's edge. It symbolized the samurai's duty to wage war, just as the smaller wakizashi companion sword symbolized the samurai's duty to die. The katana was said to be the soul of a samurai; how fitting that Toturi was using it to focus his thoughts in the battle for his own soul.

"I . . . I am . . . in control," hissed Toturi. He began to breathe a bit easier. "I am the Emperor. I answer to no one but my ancestors."

Toturi glanced up at Kaede from beneath his furrowed brow, and Kaede dropped her eyes. It was hard, very hard to look back at him.

"How are you, my husband?" she asked.

"I can feel the Unspeakable sapping my soul, draining it. It wants me. I can keep it at bay, even push it back during the daytime, but every night it creeps back in, steals away my ... my ... it ... it steals me away, Kaede. It steals, and I can no longer find the words."

"You are strong, my husband. You can keep yourself pure until we discover how to fight this."

The Emperor sniffed sharply and looked at the three other figures in the room. These were his most trusted servants. They sat, attentively, awaiting his orders. Matsu Hiroru, outcast from the Lion Clan, trained as a ninja; dressed all in white, he even covered his face as would a Scorpion. Akodo Godaigo, a legend thought dead and gone for several centuries but still moving, although only the skeleton of his body remained in the ornate antique armor. Toku in a simple kimono—brash, but in whose heart no fault could be found. Such excellent samurai. How could he possibly betray their trust, their devotion?

Toturi looked back to Kaede. "Tell me what you see," he said quietly.

Kaede quickly dropped her eyes to the floor. "My lord—"

"Tell me," he repeated sternly, "what you see."

Kaede closed her eyes and opened her mind to the void, as she had been taught by the Phoenix shugenja those many years ago. Her vision expanded, peace settled comfortably around her. Silence reigned. She was as a still lake at sun's rise. Then she felt the dragon's blood lift her chi, and, carrying it forward, propel her into the void and beyond. Emotion left. She was the Oracle.

Kaede stopped breathing, an effect that had always unnerved Toturi, then she opened her mouth, and it seemed as if she spoke without breathing, her voice strangely deep and resonant, echoing out of her throat.

"I see darkness approaching. I see a land with no sky, no heavens above. I see a people with no face. I see a present with no past and a future with no hope. I see Nothing."

"Where am I, Oracle?" he asked, wiping the sweat from his brow. "Where is Emperor Toturi the First?"

"You are the fall of night. You are the pebble that announces the avalanche. You are the rivulet that breaks the dam. You are the one who leads us Nowhere."

"And if someone else leads the people, Oracle? What then?"

"Who can lead but the Emperor? Who can command but by the will of the gods? None can defy the Celestial Order, and none can surrender the Jade Throne."

"You are my wife, Oracle. You are my Empress and my heir. We have no children. If something should befall me and you should lead the people, then what?"

"I can see all ways but my own, for I walk backward in the night."

"By the blessings of the Kami," Toturi said, "I thank you for your insight."

Her oracle finished, Kaede studied the void with a passive spirit. All was in balance, for she was at the center of nothingness. She was focused, pure, enlightened, satisfied. Yet somewhere, the mortal blood in her struggled, discordant in this place of peace. It pushed her, giving rise to desire. She grasped that desire as a drowning sailor grasps a thread. Desire became hunger, hunger became pain, and pain became duty. The thread pulled her back, out of the void and into the world of mortals once more. Kaede's eyes fluttered open, and she took a deep, gasping breath.

"My Emperor, what does it all mean?" asked Toku. He was ever the eager warrior, always ready to cut through the careful dance of etiquette and strike at the heart.

"It means, samurai, that if he who sits upon the Jade Throne does nothing," said the Emperor, "the Unspeakable shall win and the Empire shall fall.

"My shugenja tell me that the very gate to Jigoku is fading," Toturi continued, "erased by the touch of the Unspeakable. It separates us from the afterlife. Those who die may not ever be able to reach Jigoku. Our ancestors in Jigoku cannot speak to us. If a thousand ancestors guide our every step, what shall we, as samurai, do when those voices are cut off from us entirely? Our steps shall become weightless, and we shall no longer be able to touch our world. The living will walk the lands like ghosts, unable to touch . . ." Toturi took a deep breath. "Our duty is service to our families, our Clan, our Empire. Yet how can we perform our duty if we cannot change anything? Our honor is found in how we serve those who came before, and how our descendants serve our memory. What will happen to honor when we are cut off from our ancestors, when we cannot hear their advice, and they cannot see our actions?

"Yes, my friends, a shadow falls across Rokugan, blotting out not only light, but honor, action . . . everything."

Toku waited two full breaths before interrupting. "But, Great One, you are the Emperor. None can stand before you. You defeated Fu Leng and his legions. You can defeat this, and I will follow you to the pits of Jigoku to give my sword and life to your cause."

"You are right," said Toturi. "Nothing can defeat the Emperor. I was raised among the Akodo, the greatest generals of the Empire. I was tutored by the monks of Shinsei, who taught me the strength of weakness and the weakness of power. With these studies in my heart, some say I am the greatest tactician who has ever lived. I have the gods behind me and the Empire at my feet.

"Now look at my eyes, all of you."

There was a sudden, uncomfortable shifting of silk kimonos. Toku started to raise his head but didn't. Hiroru narrowed his eyes to slits and looked at the bridge of the Emperor's nose, refusing to meet his gaze directly and hoping he wouldn't notice. Only Godaigo raised his head and looked at the Emperor's face squarely from his empty skull's sockets.

Toturi glanced at his samurai. "Look at my eyes!" he shouted.

They did. Toku trembled noticeably. To dare to look into the Emperor's eyes was punishable by death. And death was what Toku saw.

The eyes were utterly black, so black they did not even shine in the lantern light. No hint of the piercing deep brown he had known when they were both ronin, no white at the edge. Just an empty, flat black. They were like holes punched in Toturi's face, holes that vanished to nothing.

"The same shadow that falls upon Rokugan falls upon my soul," Toturi said quietly. "The Unspeakable tries to take my soul from me. If it succeeds, I will belong to it, and I will lead the Empire into ruin. None, as you said, shall stand before me, and it will consume everything."

"This, then, must be what the Oracle meant when she said you were the pebble that heralds the avalanche," observed Hiroru. "Whe—er, *if* you fall to the shadow, you will bring the Empire down with you."

Toturi smiled a thin smile. "There is no 'if,' Hiroru." He leaned his head forward and rubbed his forehead idly on the engraved pommel of his katana. The cool metal touch eased his fever somewhat. "You have seen what is happening to me. Do not deny it. I may win battles, but I am losing the war. It is only a matter of time. In all of history, an Akodo general has never known defeat. I will not be the first. Even if I no longer bear that name, I owe it to the family that raised me, and to the Empire."

Toturi drew in a deep breath through his nose, turned it over in his stomach, and expelled it forcefully out his mouth. He felt his strain leave with the air. Twice more he repeated this, clearing his heart and mind.

"Duty," he said. "Honor. Glory. What is left to me now is duty."

Toturi took his katana and held it horizontally in front of him, with the handle to the left and the blade's edge, still safely inside the saya, toward him. He held it out toward Hiroru. "You will be my second," he said simply.

Hiroru started. Toturi could see his jaw working beneath his white hood, trying to find a reply. "My lord—" he stammered, "what—? You can't be—! That is, I assume you speak in jest."

"If I continue to live, Hiroru, the Empire will fall. My soul is failing. There will be no sound when the Unspeakable wins. You may not even know it has succeeded. But whatever it is, it must not be allowed to sit upon the throne. Be my second."

Hiroru bowed his head to the floor. "Yes, my Emperor, as you command." He scooted forward on his knees and took the proffered katana, rolling the blade over in his hands so that the edge pointed toward himself. Hiroru's eyes looked over the hilt, freshly wrapped in bright green silk, the aged handguard beautifully wrought with a celestial lion. The saya itself was easily a few hundred years old, wood polished so thoroughly that its luster seemed as deep as a lake. It was a beautiful sword, heavy with age, heavier still with responsibility, yet in his hands it seemed as light as a feather. "When?" he asked quietly.

"The time to strike," said Toturi, "is always now." He stood slowly, and added under his breath, "While I am still in control."

The others bowed and stood as well, keeping a respectful distance as Toturi walked to the throne room. Servants opened the rice-paper doors quietly and smoothly, and Toturi walked into the very heart of the Empire. He knelt on the floor in front of the throne, pulled his wakizashi out, and set it on the floor beside him.

Hiroru followed and stood a few paces behind Toturi, holding the Emperor's sword as if it were a fragile butterfly. Toku, apparently still confused by the turn of events, stood to one side. Kaede moved to her place at the side of the Jade Throne and looked at it forlornly.

Of the group, only Godaigo seemed to have anticipated what would happen in the throne room. He knelt in front of Toturi and offered a piece of parchment, a brush, and some ink.

"Thank you, old friend," said Toturi solemnly. He stirred the ink with the brush, then, with bold strokes, composed his final haiku.

> *Grasping bushido*
> *to cut the dark from my soul*
> *I serve the Empire*

Toturi set the brush down and picked up the wakizashi. He drew the blade forth slowly, then set its saya aside. Carefully he rolled the wakizashi into the parchment, leaving only a hand's breadth of the blade exposed. He picked up the blade and turned it toward himself, gripping the handle in one hand and the paper-covered portion of the blade in the other. He set the blade in position at the left side of his abdomen, and he felt the razor-honed tip already starting to slide into his skin.

Behind him, Hiroru drew the katana with the sound of a perfectly tuned chime. "This is a beautiful blade, my lord," Hiroru whispered in amazement.

Toturi heard the blade slice through the air as Hiroru tested its weight and balance. It sounded like a hawk in flight. "It is yours," he said simply.

"My lord, it is far too fine a blade for the likes of me," protested Hiroru. "I would dishonor it by carrying it."

"You are a samurai, and you will carry it proudly and honorably. It is yours," repeated Toturi.

"My lord, this is your sword and it should go to your heir," answered Hiroru. "Give it to Kaede."

"You have earned the right to carry that blade by the service you perform now," said Toturi. "The two of you will be the better together than separate. It is yours."

"As you wish, my lord. I am honored to accept." Hiroru hesitated. "One thousand pardons, my lord, but I have nothing—"

"The gift you give me with that sword is gift enough. You will, I hope, forgive me for not refusing the gift the first two times you swing."

Hiroru smiled in spite of himself. "As you wish, my lord."

Whispering to herself, Kaede called for the void to embrace Toturi in this final moment, and for the Kami to see him safely to Jigoku . . . if it were still possible for his spirit to enter.

"Hiroru," said Toturi. "This . . . this thing that plagues me . . . it has caused great pain to the Empire. It has caused me great pain. Stay your sword until I straighten my neck. I want it to suffer for all it has done. I want it to feel the pain for as long as possible. I want to show it that in the end, I am the stronger."

So saying, he plunged the wakizashi into his abdomen. He exhaled slowly, then drew in another sharp breath through his nose. Then, as slowly as a thunderhead, he drew the blade laterally across his abdomen, slicing through muscle and viscera. Blood gushed from the wound, but Toturi neither hurried nor slowed down the cut. When the blade reached the other side, he exhaled again, and inhaled, steeling himself. Behind him, Hiroru waited, blade held high, quivering slightly in his fear and amazement.

Toturi moved the wakizashi back to his navel—what was left of it—and turned the blade up. A grim smile stole across his face, and he slowly raised the blade, making the final cut. As the wakizashi reached the bottom of his rib cage, Toturi paused. His hands were quivering. The grin slowly distorted, twisting into a grimace. Tears formed at the corners of his eyes.

Hiroru waited.

At last, Toturi's eyes cleared, turning a rich brown color. He stiffened his spine, raising his head to give Hiroru a clear target.

With the sweep of a hawk's wing, Toturi's life ended.

Kaede sagged against the throne, unnoticed by Hiroru, Godaigo, and Toku, who stared in awe and reverence at the decapitated body lying on the throne room floor, surrounded by an expanding pool of blood.

Hiroru looked down at Toturi's blade—his blade, now—and sagged to the floor.

Toku at last spoke. "Can you name me any other Emperor in history who would do such a selfless deed as this?"

Godaigo could only shake his head.

3 | FACING YOUR DEVILS

The
Fourth
Year
of the
Reign
of
Toturi I

Toturi awoke with a start.

He had been sleeping on his stomach, a very uncomfortable position for him, especially on the open ground. He rolled over and looked about. The Spine of the World Mountains stood to the south and west, rosy with the dawning sunlight against the deep blue western sky. Judging by the terrain—rolling hills and scattered copses of trees—he'd slept somewhere between the lands of the Scorpion Clan and the Crane Clan, perhaps near the Lion holdings.

A pall of smoke hung in the air, and his warrior's nose picked up the scent of war. There was nothing else that compared to the stench of battle. A samurai cut in half had a raw odor that nothing else could describe. Add to that the smell of smoke, the iron tang of blood, sweat thick with fear and hate . . . it was a smell that all warriors knew, and none spoke of. That smell pervaded the air here. Yet for all the reek, Toturi saw no carrion birds wheeling in the sky. Odd, that.

Toturi stood. The sun had already risen in the east, which

disturbed him. A warrior in the field should always awaken before dawn, and yet . . .

And yet, where was his camp, his gear, his army? He should be surrounded by a thousand of his best troops, hand-picked from the brave warriors of the Lion Clan. His command staff should be attending to the . . . no . . . no, that wasn't right.

He had been a Lion, once, long ago. He had been an Akodo, a general with a proud heritage and a powerful birthright. But that was before. That was before the Scorpion had struck down the Emperor, murdered Hantei XXXVIII, and set their champion upon the throne, Bayushi Shoju, the Usurper.

Here I am near Beiden Pass, thought Toturi, and I seem to have lost my command. How can I strike back at Shoju without an army? It was all so confusing. He couldn't even remember what his plan was. He tried to sort it out, but—

The sudden sound of war cries carried on the faint breeze, followed by the sound of katanas slicing through armor, helmets, people. Toturi started off to the north, following the sound at a jog. As he ran, he could hear the sound increase in intensity. Full melee combat, he thought. Neither side is turning back now.

He came to the crest of a hill and found that the terrain below opened into a wide valley. There, in the center of the valley, he saw the fight. It wouldn't quite qualify as a battle, but it was more than a skirmish. About forty Lion Clan samurai had assaulted a group of about a hundred bandits or ronin.

It should not even have been a contest. The ronin should have been slaughtered, but Toturi could see that these ronin were more than a pathetic cluster of dishonored warriors. They held their line. They fought well and with experience. He could see a few officers yelling orders, yet despite their discipline, they did not see that they could defeat the Lion by giving ground.

For their part, the Lion samurai had attacked in classic Matsu fashion: a head-on charge. They had expected the ronin formation to break and run, but now the Lions were being flanked. If the ronin had given ground, the headstrong Lions probably would have pursued, dispersing their formation in the heat of battle and therewith being surrounded and destroyed piecemeal. Instead, both sides held their position, a set-piece battle, and hacked and slew each other's forces.

Such a waste. A general's duty was not only to win each battle but also to preserve his forces to win the next battle. Preserve enough of your forces and slay enough of your enemy, and the next battle might never even need to be fought. Winning without fighting, that was the true mark of a general. Here, yes, there were officers, but not generals. They sent their warriors headlong into the melee, to kill or be killed.

It was too late for Toturi to interfere now. Even if he could wrest command of the troops, by the time he reached the battle, it would be all but over. Curiously, he wasn't sure which side he would support. He felt drawn to both of them.

Instead, he stood and watched, shaking his head in sadness. Such bravery and skill on both sides. Such a waste of life and effort.

Eventually, the sides tired of the continued slaughter. Seven Lion samurai still stood, weapons at the ready, facing well over a dozen ronin. Both sides were clearly exhausted, and the warriors stumbled in their search for better footing amongst the corpses and gore. Most of those still standing had nasty wounds. A few on the ground tried to crawl away from the carnage and find safety among their fellows.

For a moment, all was still. It looked as if they might part and tend their wounded, but then one of the Lions raised an arm and pointed at one of the ronin. He said something, but the words did not reach Toturi's ear. The ronin officer responded with a howl of anger. He—no, *she* ripped off her helmet, and her long hair cascaded down her armored back. She yelled back at the Lion, a stream of invectives, oaths, and curses foul enough for a Crab sailor. It was going to start again, and for what?

Toturi cupped his hands around his mouth. *"Cease!"* he bellowed, as loud as he could.

He saw both sides falter, hefting their weapons and turning to see who had interrupted their battle, while still trying to keep an eye on their foe. Toturi started down the hill toward them, walking in the brisk, arrogant strut of a general.

Seeing his carriage and gait, the Lions and ronin tentatively pulled apart, unsure what to make of this newcomer. No armor covered him, no banner flapped at his back, no heraldry graced his kimono, yet his gait and boldness proved that he was used to the power of command.

As Toturi approached, he saw some of the wounded who had crawled from the battle a short while ago stand on wobbly legs to wait for him. He walked up to the edge of the battlefield and looked at both sides. "What's going on here?" he barked.

"We are purging the Empire of bandits," said one of the Lions.

"You defy your oaths!" retorted the ronin leader. "You feign to work the Emperor's will when a beast sits upon the throne! We rally to the banner of the one who—"

"All ronin are bandits, fit only to be killed! And we will kill them all!"

"And you are killing yourselves with your lack of tactics," said Toturi quietly. "A true Lion would—"

"Well, well, well," interrupted another Lion, slowly staggering to his feet. Blood dripped down from behind the gold-colored mask that covered the front of his helmet. "Who is this who speaks like a daimyo? Why, it's you, the embarrassment to our family, he who studies with monks. Tell me, what do you know of being 'a *true* Lion,' little brother?"

Toturi blinked, stunned. "Arasou? Is that you? But you . . . I thought you were—"

Arasou pulled off his helmet. The sneering grimace he wore was still the same, but savage hatred only burned in one of his eyes. The other was ruined, and blood and fluids seeped from the socket. "Yes, it's me, little brother," he said.

"Do not forget that I am the elder son, Arasou," said Toturi quietly.

Arasou snorted. "That doesn't change the fact that you are little," he said. He reached for his damaged eye and grasped the small bit of metal that protruded. Toturi watched as Arasou pulled a palm blade the length of his hand from his ruined eye. "While you were off 'exercising your mind,' I was fighting. As you would have been, were you a true Lion. Now get in the ranks, and let's finish these ronin and continue our march to Toshi Ranbo."

"We await your orders, my liege," said one of the ronin. "Shall we dispatch this loud-mouthed braggart or let him live with his shame?"

Toturi turned and looked at the ronin, with his long hair and steely expression. "Mikio?"

" 'My liege?' Ha!" snorted Arasou. "I see you've adopted a scruffy band as your new Clan. Those monks taught you to forget your station, did they? Get in line, Lion cub, and try to pay attention while I show you how to kill vermin."

Mikio moved fluidly to stand between Arasou and Toturi. "No one speaks to the Emperor in such a tone."

Arasou paused for a moment, then laughed loud and long, a booming laugh that echoed among the hills. A few of the other Lion joined in as well, though not all of them. Finally Arasou's laughter trailed off, leaving him gasping for breath and holding one hand over his damaged eye. "Him, Emperor?" the Lion gasped. "Please, no more. It makes my head hurt to laugh so hard." He pulled his hand away and studied the blood on his palm, still chuckling under his breath. "Him—*you* of all people . . . the gods would be mad to allow such a thing. Enough of your delusions, little brother—"

"He is the Emperor," said Mikio calmly. "He led the Lion Clan with grace and honor after you died at Toshi Ranbo. Then the Scorpion used his lover Hatsuko to—"

"After I died?" guffawed Arasou. "I am on my way there now, and I have no intention of falling before measly Crane."

"You have no idea where you are, do you?" asked Mikio. "You are in Jigoku. Toshigoku, to be exact. How many days have you tried to drive us off this very field? And how many samurai have you actually lost in that time? The days are too many to count, and the losses . . . the losses are none. Look at the blade that pierced your eye. It is long enough to have entered your brain, perhaps even scratched the back of your skull. Why do you not die? Simple. You are already dead, as are we. This, samurai, is our doom, for having unfulfilled duties."

Toturi looked deep into Mikio's eyes and saw the truth of what he spoke. He tried to remember how he had died, but he couldn't.

Try as he might, there was a shadow over his memory.

"How did I die, Mikio?"

"I do not know, my Emperor. I gave my life for you on the anniversary of your coronation," he said. Then, abruptly, he asked, "Where is your katana?"

Toturi looked down. His wakizashi was tucked securely in his obi, but his katana, saya and all, was missing. Then he noticed the parchment clenched tightly in his left hand, blood staining one edge of the paper.

"Eh?" he grunted, his brow furrowed in confusion. "How long have I been carrying this?" He unrolled the parchment and read the thirteen words brushed onto it. Then, like the sun breaking from behind dark clouds, memory came back to him, chasing the shadow from his life.

He rolled the paper tightly and tucked it into his belt where his katana should be. "I, too, have an unfulfilled duty," he said to the gathered warriors, Lion and ronin alike. "I cannot complete my work here. I must find my way out. If any wish to join me—"

"Your duty is to help me capture Toshi Ranbo!" shouted Arasou.

Toturi looked his brother squarely in the eye. "You do not understand, and I do not think you will ever understand," he said. "For that, I weep for you, little brother."

Toturi turned and walked away. Arasou watched as the ronin left the battlefield to join him, then as half of his remaining Lions did the same.

When the last of the troops had disappeared from sight, Arasou turned to his remaining samurai. "Come!" he said. "The field is ours. Onward to Toshi Ranbo!"

With a proud cheer, the remaining Lions marched forward.

* * * * *

Two figures stumbled through a dark and barren landscape. A sulphurous stink hung in the air. Mists of yellow and gray did little to obscure the hard pinnacles and fetid bubbling pools all around.

The first figure, tall, wiry, almost like an insect in appearance, sagged against a rock pillar, a katana held limply in one hand. With the other hand, he held a stained piece of silk over his nose. "How can you stand this . . . this stench?" he said. "The sticky heat?"

"It is not so unlike the Shadowlands," came the rumbling reply. The second figure was clearly a Crab—very tall, broadly built, and had the long, unkempt hair of a perpetual warrior. He stood alert and scanned the area, hefting his tetsubo and idly picking away some of the meat and gristle that had accumulated around the iron spikes of the great war club. "I think you can rest for a short while, my liege," he said quietly.

"Rest?" said the smaller man. "Here? How? Where is a futon? Where are the servants? Where is a garden so I can escape this noxious place?" He tried to take a deep breath, but the fumes made him cough and gag. "My bones ache. My muscles burn with every move. This endless harassment, it's . . . I do not even know why I suffer you to live, Tsuneo. You do not even know where we are. Of what possible use are you?"

Hida Tsuneo did not answer. He knew full well where they were. They were in Jigoku, the afterlife, in that portion known to some as the Cauldron of Hate. Undoubtedly this was the place unwittingly built by his companion, Emperor Hantei XVI, through the vile acts of his life. The hate he gave and the hate he received in turn had formed this place over the years, and since the day that the two of them were trapped here, it had only grown worse. But studying religion was beneath the interest of this particular Hantei, and Tsuneo was not about to begin Hantei's instruction.

"Damn this place," said Hantei. "Damn this place, damn those who torment me, and damn you most of all for leading me here! Damn the world and the gods that made it, that all those in the Empire did not have a single neck for me to strangle."

Again, Hida Tsuneo did not answer. In his life he had sworn himself to his Emperor's service. He was the daimyo of the Crab, and the Crab were the right hand of this particular Emperor, who had deemed the Lion too soft for that service. He had given his vow to serve the Emperor as long as he was able. How he wished that death would have released him from the Emperor's presence. Instead, they were both here, where neither could be killed, and where Tsuneo would be bound by his oath for all eternity. Bound to this villain, this broken soul, this brutal madman . . .

Tsuneo's hands clenched tightly around the haft of his tetsubo. If only the gods would grant him one moment's reprieve from his oath. The blink of an eye, that would be all the time he would need, and he could smash this tyrant's skull.

"I want water," said Hantei ruefully. "I should slit your throat to get a drink, but I would not demean myself by touching a stinking Crab."

Just a short reprieve . . . but here, even if he did strike Hantei down, he could not kill him. Truly was there no hope.

"I hear someone coming," said the Crab quietly.

"I ache from killing them," said Hantei. "Will they never learn?"

"No," said Tsuneo, glancing blackly at Hantei as the Emperor wearily regained his feet. "It seems some souls are destined never to learn."

"Then damn those souls for all eternity," growled Hantei.

"By your command," grumbled Tsuneo.

The voices grew closer, some crying, some whispering, some calling Hantei's name, some cursing his eyes. Hantei slowly pulled himself up and clambered up on top of the pillar, which stood a little taller than the Crab.

"I am Emperor Hantei XVI!" he shouted at the crowd of people through the miasmic air. "I rule by the will of the gods! My word is law!"

As the crowd drew closer, a battered woman in a stained kimono stepped forward. Tsuneo could see sparrows carefully painted on the silk, now ruined and stained with blood. "You have always cried like that," she said, "ever since you were a baby."

"Mother!" Hantei spat. "You traitor! You tried to poison me!"

"You killed my other four children," she said sadly. "I wanted to help you finish what you had started."

"I am your Emperor!" he shouted. "Your duty is to obey me!"

"I did obey you," called out another samurai. "What honor did my service do my family? You fed my entrails to the dogs while I yet lived, and sold my children to the Scorpion."

"Impertinent whelp," sneered Hantei, "you have no station. Tsuneo, feed him his tongue. The rest of you," he shouted, scanning the throng of samurai, peasants, courtiers and monks, "leave me to my meditations, and perhaps I shall spare you my wrath!"

With that, the murmur of the crowd grew to a roar, and they surged forward like a wave. Tsuneo worked his tetsubo like a master, spraying blood and brain all about, but the crowd pressed forward. They climbed over the bodies of the fallen, ignoring the Crab and his weapon in their attempt to reach Hantei. The Emperor stood his ground on top of the pillar, screaming curses and cutting frantically with his katana. The bodies continued to pile, forcing Hantei backward on his precarious perch, until he lost his balance and fell.

The crowd pressed the advantage. Some leaped from on top of the pillar to land upon the Emperor, while others ran about the sides to reach him. Tsuneo worked as fast as he could, crippling as many as possible, but the people pushed past him. Hantei scrambled backward, slicing all about with his katana. Rocks, kicks, and blows landed on him. He stumbled blindly backward, lashing out in a frenzy at anything nearby. It was an old habit and one that came easily to him.

But where those of the Empire had feared him, here they did not fear at all. They kept reaching, grasping, attacking . . . they kept pressing in, and Hantei kept having to step back, just to have room to swing his katana.

Tsuneo bellowed a war cry and fought his way through the crowd toward the Emperor who stood tall, regal, and fearful amidst the bedraggled masses. Suddenly Hantei stumbled back into a crater filled with boiling sulphurous water. Tsuneo heard his high-pitched screams as he stumbled through the brine, trying to touch the water as little as possible.

Some of the crowd followed him through the waters, others moved to make their way around the stinking pool. Tsuneo moved rapidly around to the far edge of the pool, there to protect his Emperor from any continued attack. Hantei stumbled out of the pool, screaming with the effort of staying atop his boiled feet. He quickly dispatched those few who'd followed him across the pool, while Tsuneo laid into the remaining people with his tetsubo.

As the last of the attackers fell, Hantei collapsed on the ground at Tsuneo's feet, whimpering and holding his trembling legs in the air. Tsuneo stood, panting heavily, waving his weapon back and forth in an easy swing. Sweat plastered his hair to his face.

"They," panted Tsuneo, "they are . . . vanquished . . . for now."

He scanned the battlefield. Bodies lay everywhere. Some crawled, some simply lay there and twitched. One hapless soul still thrashed in the boiling water, blindly trying to reach any edge of the pool.

Tsuneo saw the silhouette of a woman prop herself up on her arms, on top of the pillar upon which Hantei had stood. She turned her head toward them.

"Villain!" she screamed, and Tsuneo recognized her voice as that of Hantei's mother. "You cannot escape our revenge!"

"We must leave before they can come at us again," observed Tsuneo, wiping his brow with the back of his hand.

"I cannot walk," complained Hantei. "My feet . . ."

Tsuneo stretched, popping his shoulders and neck. He shouldered his tetsubo, and with the other powerful arm, he scooped up Hantei XVI in a rather unimperial fashion.

He took one longing glance at the boiling pool, then turned and walked away into the shifting mists.

* * * * *

Emperor Toturi I now led a sizeable army across the fields of Jigoku. The bulk was made up of those who had died under his command, the remainder of those whose minds were open to his story and his call.

He had a group of shugenja in his forces, wise in the ways of the universe. The Phoenix and Dragon shugenja especially had great wisdom and insight, and Toturi gathered them and his few close advisors together.

"A darkness has fallen upon the Empire," Toturi said. "It drives itself like a wedge between the living and . . . us. It is our duty to fight against any enemy of the Empire. But how can we, from here? In the Empire, the voices of the ancestors are silent. What can we do?"

"We have tried to reach across the veil," said the Phoenix Clan's Mistress of the Air, "but we cannot touch the souls on the other side. We need the means to force our way through that which blocks our voices."

"One standing in darkness can see the fire," said a tattooed Dragon

Clan shugenja, "but the fire cannot see the one in darkness."

"Another Dragon riddle?" asked the Phoenix.

The Dragon looked slightly exasperated. "Even if our voices carry beyond the veil, those of the Empire may not be able to hear them."

"Perhaps, but if we do not try, how shall we know?"

"If we try without knowing, our effort may be wasted."

"We waste time sitting here talking," countered the Phoenix.

The Dragon looked back at the Phoenix and slowly smiled. "Wisely is it said," he said slowly, "that it is better to do than to talk. Why, then, do we plan on finding a way to tell the Empire what to do, when we could be finding a way to do it ourselves?"

"I don't understand," said Toturi. "How could we do such a thing?"

A Fox Clan shugenja spoke up. "Old tales tell of a place called Oblivion's Gate. It is said that this gate is the entrance to Jigoku, and that all spirits must pass through this gate to come here. But gates can be passed in both directions, can they not? And from what you have told us, spirits in the Empire are being prevented from passing through to here; the gate is closed or hidden to them. But if that is so, why do we not open the gate from our side? It may be that we can succeed where those in the Empire fail."

"If we open Oblivion's Gate," said Toturi, "then at least we could communicate. What would happen if we . . . ? Could we pass through, back to the other side?"

"I think so," said the Dragon, "though I believe you would again become mortal, in some fashion or other."

"Then we have a plan and a goal," said Toturi with finality. He stood. "Who can lead us there?"

The Phoenix Mistress of Air spoke. "My Clan brother," she answered timidly. "The Master of Water. Like a river always finds the ocean, he can find the gate."

* * * * *

Hantei lay inside a small cleft—it hardly could be counted as a cave—and cursed the world in a continuous stream of whispered invectives. An Emperor's lot was supposed to be easy, with the whole

Empire waiting to serve his every whim. He scratched at his chin, picking at a flea that hid among his whiskers. Such deprivation was simply not right! He should have a hundred courtiers just to ensure his beard was perfect, every single hair the proper length. He should have long, hot baths, replete with attendants carrying scented soaps and brushes, and he most certainly would have killed them all if they had allowed a single flea to mar his day. Now here he was, lost in this wasteland, with nothing but one taciturn Crab for company. His feet were horribly blistered, his clothes stained, his katana nicked, his hair unkempt, and there was not a drop of perfume to be had anywhere. How could someone be the divine ruler of all he surveyed if he couldn't kill or torture those responsible for every slight flaw in his grooming?

"No Emperor should have to endure this."

The Crab sat at the opening of the cleft, blocking most of the dim light with his superb frame. He leaned against the rock, and although his eyes were open, he breathed the even steady pace of the sleeping. Hantei grudgingly admired the Crab's ability to sleep with his eyes open, although he'd never admit it. Even more he admired the Crab's ability to wake up when something untoward moved within his field of vision.

Thus it was no surprise to Hantei that Tsuneo turned his head almost as soon as the ray of light broke through the hellish air.

The light came from somewhere behind the low formation of rocks at the base of which they camped. It was piercingly bright, and the mists pulled away from its glare as though they were living things.

Tsuneo stood up and climbed the rocks to find the source. Hantei stumbled out of the cave to follow, limping heavily on both feet. As Tsuneo climbed, the ray sliced across the sky, followed by another, and then another two.

"I would almost think a piece of the sun was walking among the trees," said Hantei, wincing at the intensity, "if there were any trees in this damned place. What is it? Can you see?"

"Shh!" whispered the Crab, quite forgetting to append any honorific to the command. Hantei had grown used to such ill-mannered behavior—it was inbred into Crabs from the time they were born—but it still galled him. He was the Emperor, after all; he should be treated with the respect and deference he was due. He started to berate Tsuneo, when he heard it, too.

Voices.

But these were not the voices of those nameless, faceless, impudent hordes of lesser people who continually hunted him down. These were not the hated whispers of his past. These voices were different. They were cheering.

Hantei reached the crest of the rocks and there, somewhere in the distance, was the source. There was brightness there, and color—colors that Hantei realized he had never seen here. And the voices echoed across the wasteland, barely intelligible for all their noise, a continuous chant . . .

"Toturi! Toturi! Toturi!"

Hantei looked up at Tsuneo's face and saw a look of sadness and regret in the Crab warrior's eyes. Sadness and regret were emotions for the weak, for those who made mistakes. They were not for the Emperor nor anyone he allowed to remain in his presence. Hantei's face twisted in a rictus of fury.

"Take me there!" shouted the Emperor, though Tsuneo was within reach of his arm. "Take me there now!"

Tsuneo set his jaw and nodded. He picked up the Emperor and moved out at a brisk pace, almost a jog. Hantei, bouncing uncomfortably on his shoulder, cursed him for a clumsy oaf, but the Crab ignored the epithets and moved on. The two of them moved through the blasted landscape, past bubbling pools of tar and fields of sharpened rocks, gaining upon the source of the light as it moved along.

Somewhere along the way—neither of them noticed exactly when—the terrible landscape that had imprisoned Hantei and Tsuneo for five centuries gave way grudgingly to a smooth, empty plain, and the fetid mists with which they were so familiar fell back before a rising, cold, sharp wind. Though they approached the light, the closer they got, the more diffuse the source became. At some point, they had stopped following the light and started following the crowd that they saw by the natural brilliance that shone all around.

"Put me down, you oaf," snapped Hantei, "and grab one of these people. I will know what is causing this commotion."

The great Crab samurai set down the Hantei Emperor, who stood as straight as he could on his burned feet.

"You!" bellowed Tsuneo, and a samurai, passing nearby to join the jubilant crowd, stopped in his tracks.

"Tell us, samurai, what is happening here," said Tsuneo, and something in his carriage and tone of voice compelled the samurai to answer without hesitation.

"There is great danger to the Empire," he said with a bow, "and he's rallying our forces to open Oblivion's Gate."

"Who is?" asked Hantei quietly.

"Emperor Toturi," answered the samurai, and Hantei's eyes flashed. "You've heard of him, right?" continued the samurai. "He is the greatest Emperor in history! He—"

Hantei's blade flashed out and gutted the samurai where he stood. "Impudent wretch," he muttered.

He looked up at the gathering army and saw Toturi in the middle, gesturing ever forward.

"Look at him, Tsuneo," he said with a sneer. "All that hooting and yelling. No solemnity, no aura of power and fear. You'd think he was a drunken merchant who'd just bought whores for a bargeload of sailors! They should be prostrating themselves before the Emperor, not prancing about like a bunch of silly children!"

"He said they are opening Oblivion's Gate," interjected Tsuneo.

"Yes, he did," Hantei said finally. "Let this self-styled 'Emperor' Tutsuri lead his rabble and try to open the Gate. We shall then slip out and escape, return to . . ." He paused a moment. "It's been a long time, Tsuneo, old friend. Emperor Tutsuri. Pah! The Empire has grown soft and turned their backs upon the Hantei dynasty.

"I will be the hand of the gods, Tsuneo, and you will be my hammer. It's time to pound the Empire back into shape."

* * * * *

The motley army of Jigoku marched to Oblivion's Gate, a gathering of spirits from across a thousand years of history determined to smite the evil that threatened to sever the connection between the Empire and its ancestors. A supernatural storm raged around the collapsing gate, the universe itself writhing as its fabric unraveled.

Outside, a small but dedicated force of the bravest samurai of the Empire also marched to Oblivion's Gate, winding their way across the treacherous Shadowlands and trying to evade those vile creatures that rose against them in blind hate and dementia. These valiant soldiers braved the horrible Shadowlands Taint, for they knew that the safety of their souls was as nothing before the future of the Empire.

The gods smiled upon the desperate venture, and these two forces converged on the afflicted gate at the same time. The darkness gathered around the beleaguered armies and the shadows themselves gathered to strike at the Empire's forces, yet through the magic of the shugenja and the hardened nerves of the soldiers, Oblivion's Gate was prevented from utterly collapsing.

Frantically, the Unspeakable tried to turn the Empire's own people against it, but in the end, true and honorable hearts, both of the samurai of the Empire and of their ancestors now returned through the damaged Oblivion's Gate, freed the Empire from its grip.

There was, however, no time for respite this deep in the Shadowlands. The assembled shugenja petitioned the aid of the gods, and their intervention helped put Oblivion's Gate to rights. This, of course, trapped a huge number of spirits on the living side of the Gate—added help for which the living were quite grateful. There only remained the daunting task of winding their way back through the foul, corrupted and ever-changing Shadowlands to the safety of their homelands. Living and returned spirit alike shared in the battle, the trek, and at last the great relief when they reached the safety of the Wall, marking the boundaries of the Empire.

Once back among the citizens of the Empire, the spirits were welcomed as fellow warriors and long-lost relations. In the wake of this great struggle, those that had contracted the Taint were not shunned, but prayed for, helped, and treated to the best of the Empire's abilities.

And in the great celebration that followed, no one noticed that a wiry noble and a veteran Crab moved joylessly and quietly away.

4 ONE LIFE, ONE DESTINY

The
Seventh
Year
of the
Reign
of
Toturi l

Acry of pain rang throughout the Imperial Palace, screened but not silenced by the rice-paper walls and doors.

Seated on the Jade Throne, Toturi stared vacantly into space. At times like this, he felt the pull of the throne more than ever. He was the Emperor. Tradition dictated that he could not express any concern, could not interfere with matters so trivial to the demands of state, yet his heart told him to do otherwise.

He clenched his fist, and fire seemed to flash from his grasp. He glanced at his hand, and idly watched the flickering golden aura that surrounded his flesh. Three years, and still he hadn't gotten used to the look of it. He opened his hand, turned it back and forth, and always the aura slipped away from his eyes, always seeming to come from a source just behind the curve of his skin, like a thousand fireflies that danced in the shadow of his movements.

Another cry echoed through the palace, this one of both anguish and triumph.

Toturi glanced up. The guards at the doors did not move. The servants to the side did not move. Everyone appeared as if they had not heard that cry, that admission of human weakness, that instinctive and wordless plea for help. They had all heard, of course, it would just be unthinkably rude to admit they had. They all had repressed their reaction. They all had heard . . .

All except one.

Toturi's eyes dropped to the girl in the center of the throne room: Tsudao.

She moved gracefully across the floor, swinging a stick she had found and had refused to part with since. She swung the stick in a butterfly arc, switched hands seamlessly, and mirrored the pattern. She moved back and forth, attacking imaginary oni and bandits, slaying entire armies with her stick, her war cry and the swish of her kimono the only sounds in the room. Such fluid movements, such tireless activity. It was more than could be expected from a two-year-old.

Curious that she did not react to the cries.

Then another scream carried through the Imperial Palace, not a cry of pain as before, but a tiny warbling wail of anger and discomfort from lungs drawing their first breath. Tsudao stopped her movements abruptly and looked at her father.

Toturi rose gracefully from his throne and held one hand out to her. "Come, Tsudao-chan," he said. "Let us go see if you have a brother or a sister."

Gripping the stick tightly in one hand—and carrying it at her waist as though it were a katana, Toturi noted—Tsudao ran up to him and gripped one of his fingers. Together they headed for the Empress's chambers.

* * * * * *

Tsuneo stalked quietly alongside Hantei XVI's palanquin, habitually scanning the terrain about them. Years spent fighting in the Shadowlands, followed by years at the Emperor's side, followed again by five unendurable centuries trapped in Jigoku slaying those who hated the Emperor—an endless task, even if they would have died like mortal people—had honed his warrior's soul to an edge keener than a katana.

Carried by eight burly eunuchs and attended by a score of courtiers too frightened or too fawning to leave, the palanquin moved easily through Lion lands toward the endless grassy plains of the Unicorn Clan's holdings. Small groups of samurai moved ahead and behind, to the left and right. Of all those people, only Hida Tsuneo was allowed to walk beside the palanquin—was required to do so, in fact. Hantei XVI had tested the limits of Tsuneo's vow long ago, and he had found none. Thus, of all the people in the Empire, Hantei XVI trusted only the one called the Stone Crab.

It was, at best, a dubious honor.

Tsuneo's eyes darted to a slight stain on the horizon, a smudge of dusty yellow just beyond the rise of the hill behind them. "A rider approaches," he said, "from the east."

Haneti XVI smiled.

Tsuneo chose to walk backward beside the palanquin, taking large, loose steps that easily kept pace with the bearers. He scratched the back of his jaw as the small dust plume grew closer. There wasn't much to the plume. Even though the sun shone, it had rained in the last few days, and the earth was moist. Nevertheless, the Crab's keen eyes picked up on the slightest changes. Too many times his life had depended on his alertness.

At last a rider cleared the crest of the hill, and Tsuneo's eyes saw that he carried the mon of Hantei XVI on his banner—a chrysanthemum made from a bloom of blades.

The rider galloped up to the palanquin, slowing as he approached. Tsuneo moved to intercept him, and the rider slowed to a walk. The horse sweated freely, and flecks of foam hung about its muzzle. The rider bowed in the saddle and held out a scroll to Tsuneo with a trembling hand, then, as Tsuneo took the message, rolled his shoulders and wiped his brow. He took a swig of water from his waterskin as Tsuneo broke the seal and opened the scroll—just in case there were any scorpions or spiders contained within. The scroll was free of such terrors, so Tsuneo rolled it back up and handed it to Hantei XVI, who trusted no one to read his messages for him. There was as much to be learned by the brush strokes of a message, he said, as there was by reading the characters.

Hantei opened the scroll. "It says that Toturi and Kaede have had their second child, a son. It says that the child has been marked by the gods with white hair and piercing eyes."

"Hmph," grunted Tsuneo. "Marked by a cuckold in the nest, more like. Regardless, now Toturi will have to appoint an heir, and you'll have a clear target."

"No," said Hantei, "a second child does not clarify the target. In fact it confuses the issue. If I were to take the appointed heir hostage, Toturi would simply appoint the other one heir and let me kill the hostage."

"But these are his children. . . ." protested Tsuneo.

"So?" said Hantei coldly. "They're just a couple of mewling infants right now, and later on they'll be scheming little devils intent on his life and his throne. Better to let one die than to allow it to be used as blackmail against you. No, Toturi can always get another wife—a younger, prettier one—and have more whelps. He would let them be killed to protect his throne. He's smart. It's what I would do in his place."

Tsuneo said nothing, but nodded.

"Others may be weak in that regard, but Toturi? No, the more he breeds, the more people we have to kill. Very annoying."

* * * * *

"He looks like a Crane!" giggled Tsudao.

"Do not say such things, Tsudao-chan," chided Kaede gently. "You might start a rumor among the Imperial Court."

Indeed, it was true. As Empress Kaede handed their second child to Emperor Toturi, he could see that the baby's hair was almost pure white, save only two streaks of black that started just above the temples and ran toward the back of the infant's head. A Crane's hair, but for the streaks. Yet beneath his mother's deep, insightful eyes, the baby had Toturi's look. The nose, the chin, the resolute set of the mouth—all were very much the baby's heritage from the Emperor.

"I see he also has the mark of the spirit world," said Toturi, "just like his older sister." He ran his finger across the baby's scalp, watching how his own golden aura melded with his son's.

"Yes, he does," answered Kaede. It was true, but like Tsudao, it only surrounded his head, not his entire body. "Toturi? Do . . . do others . . . do all children of, um, that sort . . . ?"

Toturi laughed out loud. "Three years, Kaede, and you still can't bring yourself to say it. I find that most charming."

"But, my lord, you don't act . . . that is, you're not—"

"Dead? I was, but no longer." When he had crossed back through Oblivion's Gate with the others, Toturi had found himself in a new body. It looked like the old one, but was fresh, whole . . . and healed, even from the grievous self-inflicted wound that had killed him. Toturi rubbed one hand across his navel. "And every spirit who left the lands of the dead has this aura. Maybe it's because our bodies had to be created in the blink of an eye. Maybe it's the touch of the gods, or a curse to mark those who crossed back. I don't know.

"But to answer your question, Kaede, I think all children born of spirits will have that halo. It seems only reasonable to me."

Kaede sat lost in thought for a moment, then smiled as a tear of joy graced her cheek. "It makes childbirth like the rising of the sun after a long night, my husband. It is brightest right before the dawn. Every mother should have this experience."

"Perhaps they do," said Toturi, "or perhaps they could, if they were truly at peace." He unwrapped his son and held him at arm's length, inspecting him carefully. The naked child looked back at Toturi calmly and studiously.

"I see that he is certainly my son," he said proudly.

"The midwife says that boys always look like that when they're newborn," said Kaede, dropping her eyes and blushing slightly.

"Nonsense," answered Toturi with a chuckle. "I am the Emperor, and I say it is his father's heritage." He cradled the child in his arm again and brushed his fingers lightly along the dark streaks in the baby's hair. "Regardless, he has striking looks, doesn't he?"

Kaede looked up at Toturi again. "The midwife says it is the mark of the gods. She says his spirit will be strong and have the favor of the Fortunes."

"*That* I choose to believe," said Toturi. He handed the child back to Kaede and said, "We shall name him Toturi Sezaru."

"Hello, little Sezaru," said Tsudao. "What do you say today?"

Almost in response, Sezaru squealed, just shy of a cry. Tsudao grinned and tromped out of the room, her stick held out in front of her in a challenging manner, chanting, "Says who? Sezaru! Says who? Sezaru!"

* * * * *

All was warm and cozy in the small pavilion. Outside, crickets chirped in the night, and formerly dead Unicorn Clan samurai moved about the camp. Hantei XVI could hear them playing their strange barbaric music, graceless and heavy with drums and not at all the slow, artistic flute or string music of the Imperial Court.

Hantei XVI turned his head back from the tent flap and faced his grandfather again. "And what do these people think of the music of the Empire, grandfather?" he asked. "It is very different from their music."

Hantei XIV tossed back the last of his cup of plum wine. He laughed, a little too loud and a little too long. "I do not know," he said, slurring his words. "I have been traveling with them for over a year, you know."

"Yes, you have mentioned that, several times."

"They are the Lost Clan! They came back! Most wonderful, truly most wonderful. We never had them around when we were Emperors! You . . . they didn't come back when you—" He paused to burp.

"No, they came back much later. That is why I ask you about them."

"Well, I have been staying with them and living as they do—over a year now—and it has been most wonderful. They are most accepting, you know. Not at all suspicious like the Lion and the Crane and the Scorp—the, uh, the Scorpion."

"The music?"

"What music? Oh, the music. They have two kinds of music, you know. The kind they play here, it is most, uh, primitive. They play a lot of drums, you know. You can hear them. They say it is the way of the Ki-Rin Clan. That is what they called themselves originally, you know. It was when they came back that they called themselves the Unicorn. Most unusual.

"But the Unicorn music, that's the kind they play now, you know. The, uh, the living Unicorn Clan, the, uh, members, you know— they have castles and buildings like the . . . uh, like us. Like civilized members of the Empire. Their music is more like ours, most refreshing, but it still has drums and that sort of primitive sound."

Hantei XIV stared for a moment at his empty cup, and Hantei XVI motioned for a servant to pour him another drink.

"These people," Hantei XIV continued, once he had wet his tongue, "those that call themselves the Ki-Rin—that was their original name, you know—these people don't like that music. It's not what they know. Just like they don't like the castles and houses. They say their people have lost their . . . hmm." He drank another large swallow. "Most interesting. Moving all the time, you know."

"So there's a schism between those who call themselves Ki-Rin, and those who call themselves Unicorn?" asked Hantei XVI.

"There is," his grandfather answered. He took another sip. "Well, maybe schismum is too strong of a drink—I mean, word. But it's kind of like there are two Clans here. Most . . . different. Most different."

"Yet they do not fight? There are matters of honor at stake?"

"No!" laughed Hantei XIV. "They might you know—fight, that is. But Emperor Toturi, he keeps a watch on things. He's most wise, you know, most impressive. He keeps the Clans from warring—or the spirits and the mortals. Has done so for, what, three years already? And who knows how many more? Most peaceful."

"What else can you tell me?" pressed the younger Hantei.

"What else? Ppbblflth. Nothing else. I told you everything I know. You just have to live with them. They're a most excellent people. You know, I like not being the Emperor any more. I can live with people. I can keep my own time. I can do whatever I want."

"I always have done whatever I want," answered Hantei XVI.

"Enough about me, grandson," Hantei XIV said. "What about you? Did you do well? We defeated the gaijin at White Stag Plain, you know."

"Yes, you have mentioned that."

"Well, what about you? What did you do that was great? Tell me about it!"

"Let me see," said Hantei XVI sibilantly. He gestured the servant to go and find some more wine. "I grew up under the curse of your spoiled son, who spoke so glowingly of you that none could compare. He turned the doddering, drunken fool I see before me into a veritable legend of might and wisdom. Under that shadow I continually failed to earn his esteem." He looked at his grandfather and saw confusion cloud his bloodshot eyes. "I should have been appointed his heir, but instead he chose his second son, whom he viewed as more stable. I wasn't good enough! I didn't match your stellar reign," he said sarcastically. "My younger brother, who always had me to blame for shortcomings, had an equally spotless image, earned unjustly at my expense, so I arranged for him to have a fatal accident while riding. The pathetic weakling begged for mercy, proving that he was unfit to rule the Empire. Your son—my father—was upset. He did not understand that the ability to wield power without hesitation or remorse is as essential to a ruler as the ability to execute a perfect cut is to a samurai. He did not understand that he had named a mewling, spineless worm as his heir, instead of the son that would rule with a firm hand, keeping the Empire strong.

"Of course I knew that my siblings had learned the lesson. They knew what I had done, and I knew they would in turn try to impress our father with their cleverness and the unhesitating manner in which they exercised their power. I waited for them, of course. Each, one by one, made his attempt to end my life and take the throne for himself. But my steel was the stronger, my mind the faster, my ploys the deeper. Three more times I killed a brother or a sister. And then the throne was truly mine."

Hantei XVI took a small sip of plum wine and studied his grandfather. The words had sunk past the alcohol, and his face had grown pale. His lips started to sputter in shock, horror, amazement.

"Or so I thought," Hantei continued. "There was one more obstacle—my mother, the conscienceless slut you chose for my father's bride. You arranged the marriage. Do you remember? You never liked me, either. You poisoned my mother against me. I know it, for I can remember you playing with my younger sister, but not with me. You had your favorites, too. No wonder I could never do enough to please my parents. You died long before she threatened me, but at last she did, and I can see your hand pulling the strings even now, moving against my life. So I had Tsuneo crush her skull between his bare hands."

Hantei XIV leaned forward with a venomous look, and stabbed the air with his finger. "That—! That's most terrible! You must respect your—! How could you—?" He staggered to his feet. "You are a monster!"

"I most certainly am not. I am the Emperor." Here he paused slightly to gesture Tsuneo to his feet and pointed to the heavy jade writing table by the side of the tent. "The Emperor must be beautiful for all the Empire to adore," he continued, "and ruthless for all the Empire to fear. I am the Steel Chrysanthemum, fragrant as the spring and decisive as a katana." Hantei adopted the slurred speech of his grandfather, mocking him, and added, "The Steel Chrysanthemum. That's what they called me, you know. Most—hic!—most flattering."

"You should never have been allowed to ascend the throne!"

"One is not 'allowed' the throne, you old fool. I deserved it. And I still do. Far more than that impudent upstart who soils it now. Once I understand all that has changed in the Empire in the last five hundred years and how the presence of all these spirits affects how politics works, then I will strike Toturi down."

"No, no," said the aged Hantei, wagging his head. "You can't interfere! I won't allow it! Our time is past!"

Hantei XVI gestured slightly. Tsuneo picked up the writing table, his muscles rippling effortlessly.

"No, grandfather," said Hantei XVI. "It is only your time that is past."

Tsuneo hefted the table and struck Hantei XIV on the head with one corner. He set the table back down by the former Emperor's body where it fell. He clapped three times. Instantly a servant appeared in the tent flap. "Hantei XIV has drunk too much, fallen, and hit his head," Tsuneo said levelly. "Fetch the esteemed one a shugenja, quickly!"

The servant vanished with a patter of feet. His calls for a healer echoed through the nighttime camp.

"Was that truly necessary?" asked Tsuneo. "You could have refrained from telling him your plan, and he would not have interfered."

"He would have," said Hantei condescendingly. "If not now, then later. While you are an excellent servant in your own way, you do not see the whole scene as I do. The throne can only belong to a Hantei, you see. I will therefore unseat this usurper, but before I do, I must ensure no other Hantei survives to covet what is rightfully mine."

*　*　*　*　*

It was a chill morning, and Kaede gathered her kimono about herself as she entered the Imperial Gardens. A heavy fog washed away the details of the artfully arranged plants and stones about her, and the only sound to be heard was the gentle whisper of her kimono trailing along the irregular paving stones. Even the small noises made by the attendants behind her were inaudible. Somewhere out there the sun was clearing the horizon, but here within the walls of the Otosan Uchi, everything was in a gray haze.

It reminded her of her days before becoming an oracle.

Kaede started to cross a small wooden bridge, then paused in the center. The attendants also paused, hovering almost out of sight in the heavy mist. Kaede turned to gaze at the little stream beneath her feet. The stream knew only to move down its path. It thought nothing of the future. It ran blissfully downward, each new bump and turn a new adventure. No wonder little streams like this were said to giggle and laugh. It had no weight upon its shoulders, no foreknowledge of its path, did not even know its destiny was to end up dying in the endless sea. Oh, to have a spirit like a stream again.

But the stream of Kaede's life had already run to the sea and merged with it, the greatest body of water in the world. Now she was one with the sea, knew all shores, and embraced all streams, and though the stream of her life still wanted to run and play, the sea had nowhere else to flow.

Kaede turned back from crossing the bridge and followed a branch of the path through the garden.

She passed a group of guards, who politely stepped aside, bowing deeply to their Empress. One had the telltale glow of a spirit about him, surrounding his clothes and armor where they covered his skin.

t was not quite so noticeable in the dim light and fog, but it was there. A little farther along the path she saw the shape of her husband in the fog. He sat on a small bench in the lotus position, hands held in his lap, meditating upon the new day.

Kaede stopped a respectful distance away, but Toturi immediately spoke up.

"Come sit with me, my wife," he said without turning his head. "Let us enjoy the morning."

She moved forward, bowed to her husband, gathered the folds of her train about her knees, and sat demurely next to him.

"It will be a beautiful day," he said. "When this fog burns off, the flowers will burst forth with color and scent, and the sun shall dance on the droplets and fill the garden with diamonds!"

"My lord," said Kaede, "I think this fog is too heavy. Even if it lifts somewhat, I do not think it will burn off today."

"No matter," said Toturi. "The fog will burn off some time. It always does. And when it does and we share in the beauty it causes, we will have this morning to thank for it. And that makes today a beautiful day."

"My Emperor is always looking for the best in everything," Kaede said with a smile. "I am pleased."

They sat in silence for a time. Somewhere in the garden, it seemed a long way away, a songbird called, tentatively decorating the quiet air of the new day.

"My lord," said Kaede at last, "It is time. You have two children now. The Imperial Court needs to know whom you will appoint as your heir. Will you appoint your eldest child, or your eldest son?"

"I will appoint neither."

"My lord, tradition insists—"

Toturi raised a hand to stop her. "I know what tradition demands," he answered. "I will appoint an heir. It will not, however, be Tsudao or Sezaru."

"Who else can take the throne?" asked Kaede.

Toturi chuckled. "Indeed, my dear, you see all ways but your own." He looked her squarely in the face. "I appoint you."

Kaede's eyes clouded. "But . . . but our children . . ."

"They will serve, Kaede," he said. "Listen. You are the Oracle of the Void. You are the wisest person in the Empire and therefore the most suited to sit in judgment of Rokugan. For a thousand years, we have had a succession of Emperors and Empresses. Some have been just. Some have been incompetent. A few have been—" he paused, pursing his lips and looking for a phrase that would not offend the kami—"somewhat less than ideal. But they have all been mortals in the end, and they have all served their own purposes in some fashion. But the one who sits upon the Jade Throne must care for the Empire for its own sake, not for his own selfish needs.

"Now you, Kaede," he continued, speaking more rapidly as he warmed to his subject, "you are wise and just. When the Clans come to you with their troubles, you will be able to adjudicate perfectly. You will see the truth of the complaints, and you will see the right solution. None would dare bring false accusations before you, for the word of the Empress and the Oracle would outweigh all the testimony in the Empire. Furthermore, the dragon protects you. You will outlive me, you will outlive our children, and theirs as well. Think of the stability that would offer the Empire. A single, wise, just, selfless ruler reigning over the world for a thousand years or more, for as long as your life lasted, and perhaps even beyond. Rokugan would prosper as never before. Not since the children of the Sun and Moon fell from the sky has there been such a harmonious arrangement.

"Of course, as an Oracle, you would not act. Acting is not the role of the Empress. Hers is to rule, and rule alone. The action would fall to our children, and then to theirs in their turn.

"Look at Tsudao. She is proud, confident, obedient, and even more graceful than you are—or at least I believe she will be. She will be your sword. Where there is death to be administered, she would do so. Let the Lion teach her the sword and the fan, and let the Unicorn teach her to ride. And perhaps we can even get the Crab to teach her how to use that stick she loves so much.

"Now Sezaru," he said thoughtfully, scratching his chin, "I think he has a different calling. Where Tsudao is the Empire's sword, Sezaru should be the bell calling them to prayer and purity. Indeed he has the blessings of the Fortunes, for I have not heard him cry since his birth. I propose to send him to the Brotherhood of Shinsei, to the Phoenix temples, and to the Dragon Clan monasteries. There he shall learn all the ways of the unseen world. I hope that he will be able to grasp the strands of those three separate ways and bind them together into a single rope of great power.

"If we are granted a third child, that child shall be your brush and paper. I know you do not need help in matters of the court, but as time passes after my death and you become more the Oracle and less my wife, you will need someone to attend you in that manner. Thus our third child shall apprentice to the Crane and the Scorpion, and learn the yin and yang of voice and silence.

"That is my plan," he said with Imperial finality.

Kaede pondered this for a moment. "But, my lord," she said at last, "I do not think I can do this. I cannot see my own path. I can only be the Oracle for others."

"That is of no concern," he answered. "The Jade Throne is supposed to be above the Empire, not muddled within it. You will not rule for yourself but for the benefit of all. Courtiers will in turn attend your needs. An eternal Empress with the voice of the gods and the wisdom of the dragons! Children raised to serve her in the best interests of the Empire! The Empire will flourish, and you shall be at the center, untouched by the winds of fate. It is a perfect plan, and it will be a glorious new age for everyone."

"As you wish, Toturi, my lord," said Kaede, bowing her head. Then she rose and made her way back through the mists to the palace.

5 | TEACH THE MOUNTAIN

The
Ninth
Year
of the
Reign
of
Toturi I

Five years since the Battle of Oblivion's Gate, and the Empire had not settled down quite as well as Toturi had hoped. The meeting of living and dead, the miracle that had saved the Empire, had not grown into an easy existence. The warriors' bonds forged between spirit and mortal at that momentous battle had held through the celebrations and even some time past, but the very short length of the campaign had not truly unified the realm.

It was true that everyone traditionally thought of their ancestors as being alive in Jigoku and sought for their advice in prayer and meditation, and thus is was not a shock to meet them in the flesh; rather it was a bit of a novelty. But after the first few years, friction began to arise, and no one in the Imperial Court knew why.

Perhaps, some whispered, it was because the spirits simply looked different. It was very difficult to ignore the constant golden glow that tinted the air around them. Perhaps, whispered those who had returned from Jigoku, the mortals were jealous of their new forms, cleansed and purified by their time in the afterlife.

Regardless, almost everyone tried to shrug it off. Thus no one truly expected what would happen when the spring blossoms bloomed with steel.

* * * * *

Toku strode briskly through the halls of the Imperial Palace, one hand resting on the hilt of his katana, the other clutching a crumpled scroll. He quieted his pace as he approached the Imperial Chambers, relieved to see lantern light softly glowing on the rice paper walls. He waved off the guards and leaned very close to the partition, listening intently. He would never admit if he had heard anything, of course, but it was best to ensure that he did not interrupt.

Hearing nothing of concern, he softly asked, "My Emperor? It's me, Toku. Can I talk with you for a moment?"

"Eh? What is it?"

"I got a note from the Imperial Magistrates that you should hear right away." He clenched his fist, adding a few more crinkles to the paper. "It says the Crane are going to fight the Crab."

There was silence for a few moments, then footsteps swiftly crossed to the rice-paper doors. The servants could barely pull them open before the Emperor did so himself.

"That cannot be. Kakita Kaiten would not do such a thing. He knows my will, and he would not lead his Clan to defy me."

"It is not Kaiten, my lord," answered Toku. "It's the spirits. Kaiten tried to stop them, it says, but they say their oaths to some ancestor—their daimyo when they were alive, I think—are their duty. I think maybe they won't obey the regent. So Doji Meihu leads them. They say he was killed during the Yasuki War. He says it is his duty to finally complete his vow of beating the Crab and bringing the Yasuki back to the Crane. He said that the Crab beat him once, and he has sworn a blood oath that it can't happen again."

"That cannot be. . . ." said Toturi, his eyes searching within for an answer.

"If you say so, my lord," answered Toku. "Maybe I didn't read the message right. You read better than I do, so please, you read it and find what I didn't get."

Toturi took the report and read it, then read it again. "You are correct," he said. "And if this magistrate's report is accurate, the Crane armies have already crossed the Crab frontier." Toturi sighed heavily. "He asks me to intervene."

"Very good, my lord. Have the scribes write something good, and I can take it to them and give it," said Toku, ready to serve.

"No," said Toturi, handing the scroll back to Toku, "he wants me to intervene personally. He wants me to go to Kyuden Doji."

"But that . . . but . . . wh-why?" sputtered Toku, affronted that anyone would have the temerity to request the Emperor trouble himself for their sake.

"Toku, old friend, you must remember that these spirit samurai served the Hantei Dynasty. They did not serve the Toturi Dynasty, nor, do I suspect, would they be particularly inclined to obey the rule of one who was not directly descended from the Children of the Sun and Moon. Add to that the fact that it was an Imperial edict that started the Yasuki War in the first place, when the Emperor sought to curtail the more shadowy activities of the Yasuki family."

"Then will you go?"

"No."

Toku paused, then pushed forward. "Can I ask why?"

"Walk with me, old friend," said the Emperor. He called back into the Imperial Chambers, saying, "I shall be back shortly, beloved wife."

The two of them walked in silence through the peaceful halls of the Imperial Palace, eventually winding up on a balcony that overlooked the sea. The moon had risen just above the horizon, scattering a silver light across the waves.

"Toku," said the Emperor, "you were one of the first to join my cause when I was a ronin. I assume you remember what happened to cause me to fall to that state?"

"Yes, my lord," said Toku quietly, venomously, looking at his feet. "You were poisoned by a geisha."

"That's right. Hatsuko, her name was. I sought to evade my duty in her arms. I put my selfish needs above that of my Clan, my Emperor, and my betrothed. Yet even after I had been stripped of my name and refused the chance to honor my Clan with my seppuku, my betrothed never asked to have the engagement annulled.

The Emperor who had arranged it was dead, his son the new Emperor was ill, yet she remained silent upon the matter, and no one else dared bring it up.

"Between the time I was cast out and the time I began to build my army, I had a lot of time to think. Never again would I put selfish desires before my duty as a samurai. Now that I am the Emperor, my duty is to all people, but as with every person, my duty starts at home. A samurai's house, then family, then Clan, then Empire—these are his duties.

"My wife has just had our second son. She is weakened and tired. She needs me, and Naseru needs me. I would like to go stop this war, but I will not abandon either her or my duty here. The dynasty will outlast this war, and I must look after my dynasty first."

Toku pondered this for a moment. "That's probably best, my lord. And you know, if you went there yourself, and the spirits still did not listen to you, your position as Emperor would be a lot worse. I mean, you'd be sort of the Emperor of half an Empire. After all, like you said, they swore an oath to a Hantei."

Toturi stood for a long time, watching the moon rise and the light dance upon the surface of the waves.

"Indeed," he said at last, and turned back into the palace.

* * * * *

At midmorning on a hot, dry summer day, a group of samurai stood on a high hilltop and watched. Most of them were members of the Crab Clan, past and present, and their location afforded them an excellent view of the flatlands of the Yasuki-Crane frontier.

"It is as you told us," said Hida O-Ushi, champion of the Crab Clan. "They are coming."

Indeed they were. The Crane forces, numbering in the thousands, moved like rivulets of water, flowing down the roads and paths of Yasuki territory. The bright blue of their uniforms added to the watery image, and the golden glow of the many reborn spirits walking among them seemed to be the reflection of the morning sun upon the advancing streams.

O-Ushi exhaled bitterly and pulled her long, black hair back from her oval face. She would have been attractive, perhaps even beautiful, had she not the face of a hardened warrior more used to a grimace than a smile. "There," she said. "You see that banner? I don't think their family had formed when you were here last. Those are the Daidoji, who, alone of the Crane, are truly worthy of respect. We call them the Iron Cranes. This is not good."

"Pessimism from a Crab?" asked Hantei XVI in his thin voice. He unfurled himself from his chair, stood, and faced the Crab daimyo. "I would never have expected to hear such a thing."

"Not pessimism, esteemed one," replied O-Ushi curtly. "Realism. After you've stood on the Wall for a year, you get to know exactly how many heads you can crush before you die. Face more than that, well, that's when you balance the loss versus the cost."

She gestured out at the advancing columns. "Here we have a bunch of Cranes moving on Yasuki lands. Now to the west—" she turned and pointed—"Do you see that smudge of smoke on the horizon? That's where the real war is. This attack is a game played by the Crane both in the Imperial Court and here on a battlefield where the whole Empire will see. Over there it's real. Over there our Clan fights to keep the Shadowlands at bay so that over here the Crane can play their pathetic little games." She shook her head. "The Shadowlands have been pressing us very hard these last several years, and our Clan is already strained to its limit. We have no people left to fight the Crane.

"So we don't," she said with another bitter sigh. "Our only other choice is to abandon the Wall, and that is unthinkable. We do not oppose the Crane, they march into Yasuki territory, and they take control of it. We lose face in the Imperial Court, but the Empire will be safe. And if the Crane choose not to give us the grain from these fields . . . well, then, Crab samurai will be underfed. They will die on the Wall, overwhelmed by the enemy, and the Shadowlands will reach into Rokugan. When that happens, we tell the Imperial Court in our 'uncultured Crab manner' that the Crane stole our food and are therefore responsible. Then the Crane lose face, and give the food and wealth from this land to bolster our forces. In the end, not much will change, but it's up to the Crane how many thousands die on the way from here to there."

"Thousands dead . . ." said Hantei with a curious lilt. "So you will let the Crane take these lands, knowing that in doing so, your people will die, the Shadowlands will grow stronger, and thousands of others will die by their hands?"

"I have no choice," O-Ushi said flatly. "The Crane bring this on."

"You have strength," said Hantei, "much like Tsuneo. Perhaps we can help, and in so doing, keep your people on the Wall from having too little to eat."

O-Ushi raised one eyebrow and looked askance at Hantei. It was hard for her to imagine such a thin, weak man being of help, even if he had been the Emperor at one time.

"It's very simple," said Hantei condescendingly. "You need people. There are a lot of spirits in the Empire now, spirits who came through Jigoku with us. Many of them served me. I could arrange to bring many of them here, to your lands. We would not impugn your honor by daring to fight your battles for you. Oh, no. Of course not. We all know that none fight so tenaciously as a Crab, and I'm certain you would entrust the defense of your lands to none but your own Clan."

"Then what use are the people to me?" asked O-Ushi.

"The spirits would work your mines, tend your fields, and administer your supplies. We would tend to all your internal matters, freeing your people to fight the Crane."

"That is an interesting offer," said O-Ushi, running her thumb back and forth across her lip.

"Then you accept?" asked Hantei.

"The answer you provide is not complete," said O-Ushi. "We have barely enough food as it is, with so many of our samurai fighting. How can we feed even more mouths?"

"Ah, that is not as difficult as you might imagine," said Hantei. "Those of us who have returned are clothed in new bodies, purified by our . . . time in Jigoku. We hunger less, tire more slowly, sicken less frequently, and are less prone to whim and emotion. We have been purified as the fire purifies the gold from the dross, as the hammer purifies raw metal into a katana. So not only will we consume fewer supplies than you suppose, but we will work longer hours and be more productive. We will support not only ourselves, but also all of your people who fight."

"You use the word 'we' quite easily, I see," said O-Ushi wryly. "Will you be putting your hand to a pick or plow as well?"

Hantei smiled, a mirthless toothy grin of the front teeth that reminded O-Ushi of a wolf's snarl. She was unsure whether he was amused or offended. Probably both. Served him right. Among the Crab, the meaning of "we" was never in doubt.

"I shall consider it," she said. "If you didn't have the support of a legend such as Hida Tsuneo, we would not even be having this conversation."

Hantei turned to his towering companion. "It must feel good to know your fame has survived the centuries, hmm?"

Tsuneo remained studiously silent.

"A scout approaches!" shouted one of the Crab pickets farther down the hill. The rider dismounted and ran the final distance up the hill, leaving his horse to the care of the picket. He stopped a few strides short of O-Ushi and knelt, bowing his head and placing one hand on the ground, the other holding his katana in place.

"Daimyo," he panted, "the Crane are well supplied. This is no diversionary move. I saw their baggage train earlier today, and they intend to stay. More than half their troops are spirits, although mixed with normal—" Here he abruptly interrupted himself, realizing that almost half of those present were in fact spirits. "That is, they are mixed together with mortals. And, daimyo," he concluded, "they march under the mon of the bird and flower."

One of the guards hissed between his teeth. "The old Yasuki mon. That's bad luck."

O-Ushi's mouth twisted into a grimace. "Bad luck for them," she growled. "How dare they?"

She turned, picked up her warhammer from its resting place and hefted it with one hand. Glowering over its well-used head, she turned to Hantei XVI. "I accept your offer," she said grimly, with a curt bow. "Tsuneo, I install you as regent over the Crab interior. I have a war to plan."

Hantei smiled and watched as she stalked off with her advisors, swinging her hammer from side to side as if she were already cracking Crane skulls. "So do I," he whispered to her retreating back.

* * * * *

The Crane ranks were well formed, resplendent in their sky blue, silver, and white. Ornamental feathers fluttered in the slight breeze, softening the hard edges of samurai armor. Long spears and polearms glistened in the sunlight, a crop of deadly steel, their blades polished to a fantastic sheen. Despite the muggy summer heat, the Crane soldiers looked poised, calm, cool.

Not so their foes.

The Crab ranks were a dark blot upon the landscape, a seething mass of dark blue, with red, brown, black, and the ruddy color of tanned skin. Unlike the Cranes, who stood like ivory statues, the Crab soldiers moved almost like caged animals, shifting their balance from foot to foot, clenching and unclenching their fingers on the hafts of their axes, mauls, and huge swords.

Yasuki Masashi had grown up learning that poise and calm were the keys to creating fear, that the samurai who could kill or die as readily as drink tea (and with equal poise) was truly a samurai to be feared. Now he found that he feared the almost feral appearance of the Crab army. He wondered at the insane courage of the Shadowlands, that they would continually attack fortifications manned by such samurai—and he marveled at the courage of the samurai who would defend the Empire against such savage and horrendous creatures.

Shifting in his saddle, Masashi glanced at Doji Meihu and saw the general's eyes above the iron kabuto mask that protected the front of his face. Mounted astride a beautifully ornamented horse, Meihu's face was calm, the expression in his blue eyes detached, almost bored. Masashi knew that this would not be true for the other side. Even from this distance, he could feel the hate radiating from thousands of glowering eyes.

"A rider approaches from the rear," warned a Daidoji bodyguard behind the commanders.

Meihu's eyes clouded briefly. "Really? What mon does he carry?"

"It looks like the Emperor's mon, my lord."

Meihu exchanged a knowing glance with Masashi.

They waited for the rider to approach. Crane samurai stopped the rider a half bow's shot away, as they had been instructed, Imperial mon or not.

"I am Toku, General of the Imperial Army, and I bring a message from the Emperor!" he shouted.

Meihu answered without turning around. "Emperor Hantei the . . . the what? Which number are we on? Please remind me."

"His Imperial Highness Emperor Toturi the First," answered Toku, "Ruler of the Jade Empire, Slayer of Fu Leng and Undisputed Master of All He Surveys!"

"We swore to serve the Hantei dynasty, beloved of the sun and moon," replied Meihu. "We recognize no other Emperor."

"The Last Hantei is dead, and with him his dynasty!" shouted Toku. "Even the sun and moon fell from the sky and then rose again! These are new times, and Toturi is the Emperor!"

"That may be," said Meihu, "but he is not our Emperor. This is the final campaign of a war far older than your fledgling dynasty. Tell your Emperor that when he has the favor of the gods then, and only then, will we recognize his claim."

Meihu waved his hand, and the Daidoji escorted Toku away. The generals sat together in silence until the hoofbeats of Toku's mount could no longer be heard.

"It is exactly as he said," observed Meihu. The massive war banners behind him flapped limply in the weak breeze.

"That it is," answered Masashi. "Hantei was right, and this self-proclaimed Emperor opposes our Clan's right and our family's heritage. It is . . . offensive. But now to the affairs at hand. Mine is to start the war." His glance turned halfway to Meihu. "Yours is to finish it."

Masashi urged his mount forward. It moved at an easy walk, trained from birth to a relaxed, yet upright gait. Masashi sat astride the horse as if he were touring the Imperial Orchards. At the midpoint between the armies, he stopped.

"I am Yasuki Masashi!" he proclaimed in the beautifully trained tenor voice of a master orator. "I fought the battles you study in your lessons. I masterminded the trade and barter our family uses to this day. I ruled our family until I bravely met my death some nine hundred years ago. I returned through Jigoku to help save the Empire in its moment of need. I remain a loyal son of the family and Clan, but my descendants no longer honor their ancestors, and they cling to the allies of a broken vow. Yasuki Oguri! Honor the vows of the founders of your family, whose name you bear to this very day!"

Masashi sat upon his horse and listened to the whispering silence, the creaks and clinks of the Crab army as it prepared to kill.

"I see you are afraid to answer me with words, Oguri," said Masashi. "But I see that you are not afraid to have others answer me with their lives. Just as your ancestor hid like a cur behind the Crab when he forsook his sacred vows, so too do you now hide behind Crab troops. Today, Oguri, I have come to bring you to heel! I am not afraid to face you! Prove that you are willing to fight for your so-called honor, or prove that you will run from your duty and your honor, time and again, as did your father, and his father before him, and his through the generations! Oguri, I challenge you! Are you a man or a jackal?"

So saying, he dismounted his horse and slapped its haunch to send it back to Crane lines. He stood waiting, his hands folded in front of him, and although his face did not show it, he was pleased. Oguri would have to answer that challenge, lest he lose his face and therefore his command over his troops.

Indeed Oguri came. He stalked slowly across the grassy field with a sheathed katana in one hand and a tetsubo in the other. Masashi noted his gait was slightly stiff, and he smirked that the Crab was showing fear, however subtly. Oguri approached the lone Crane and took his stance just a bit over an arm's reach away.

Keeping his back straight so that he did not appear to be bowing, Oguri lowered himself to one knee. He raised his katana over his head, set the tip of the sheath on the ground to his right, then lowered the katana to the ground with the hilt pointed toward Masashi. It was the most difficult orientation from which to draw your blade. Among friends, it was a sign of great trust. Among enemies . . .

Masashi narrowed his eyes ever so slightly as catcalls and whoops resounded from the Crab troops.

Oguri stood back up, placed the head of his tetsubo on the ground at his left, and let his hands drop lightly to his sides, the left hand gently holding the tetsubo's handle. Masashi dropped his hands as well. For many long breaths they faced each other in silence. Masashi noted that Oguri's breath was somewhat labored. Fear, he thought. The coward!

"You've never fought against Crabs, have you?" Oguri said lightly. Then he went for his warclub.

In the blink of an eye, Masashi had drawn his sword, and in one perfect fluid motion, swept the blade clear of its sheath, into Oguri's body just above the hip, up through his abdomen and through his ribs, and out again just below the collar. He stepped back as Oguri's body stepped forward, barely able to raise his tetsubo before collapsing.

Masashi stood there, blade held high in the post-cut position, and studied the Crab lines. Slaying the general in such a manner, if it could be managed, almost always provoked the Lion into a rash attack that could be defeated. But the Crabs just stood there, fingering their weapons and waiting.

Waiting. They were the mountain, and they would not move.

Masashi glanced down at Oguri's corpse. Three arrows protruded from his back—three arrows fletched in Crab colors. Three arrows, shot there by his companions at his own request. Oguri had walked across the field to enter this duel with three arrows in his back. Masashi had killed no one. He had hacked a dead man. Masashi had not scored a Crane victory. He had merely punctuated a Crab statement, a demonstration of Oguri's resolve and Crab mettle.

Masashi was unnerved. He had expected to die as the Crab army charged in vengeance for this death, but now . . . now his army had to attack. How does one attack a Crab army? They have held off the Shadowlands for a thousand years. Yet he had to attack, and soon, or lose face. He glanced back at his troops and saw the tremors of whispers rippling through their lines, as the soldiers realized what had happened.

Masashi flicked the blood from his blade, wiped it clean, then stepped on Oguri's katana and broke it. He motioned his army forward. They advanced, though not quite in the perfect unison he would have wished.

* * * * *

From a slight rise to the rear, Toku watched the Crane advance. "This is not good," he said. Shaking his head, he turned his horse back to Otosan Uchi.

6   A GLIMPSE OF THE SOUL'S SHADOW

The
Tenth
Year
of the
Reign
of
Toturi I

N o sooner has spring arrived than war is in the breeze," said Toturi.

He stood at a window in the palace, overlooking the Imperial Gardens below. His hands were clasped behind his back, and his head tilted slightly forward as he watched the petals fall from the cherry trees. Despite the beauty of it, his mind was far away—on the field of battle, where samurai would soon be spilling each other's blood.

"I don't understand it," he said, turning from the window. He looked, one by one, at the faces of his guests, the daimyos of the Great Clans—or at least most of them. The Crab and the Mantis were absent. O-Ushi had sent a message that she was too busy conducting a war to attend, much to Kaiten's discomfiture. From the Mantis, no word had been heard.

Toturi gestured with one hand as he continued. "I led the spirits from Jigoku. We fought together to save the Empire against the darkness that had fallen upon it. We died by each other's sides. All of the Clans, each generation, everyone was a single force. We were all Rokugani, even more than we were on the Day of Thunder.

"And since then," he sighed, turning back to the view, "we've had five years of peace, five years of rebuilding, five years of growth and happiness. It wasn't perfect, but now it has . . . crumbled." Last year, in the midst of the summer, the Crane had attacked the Crab, spirits and mortals fighting over the Yasuki family name. Then the Hare spirits attacked the Scorpion for the honor of their broken Clan. "I thought we had reined this in by the end of the year, but clearly I was wrong. Tell me, then, what ill tidings do the blossom petals bring this year?"

"I have already heard that spirits in our ranks are turning their eyes to Toshi Ranbo," said Kitsu Motso. Kakita Kaiten looked at him blackly, and he shrugged. "I will not permit them, of course, but they have some rather hot-headed samurai who drink too much and talk too loudly. I will have to keep a close eye on them all."

"Indeed you'd better," murmured Kaiten.

"Yes, I would be greatly embarrassed were my Clan to launch a war without telling me," replied Motso.

Kaiten shot to his feet.

"Enough!" barked Toturi, before the Crane could say a word. "Is it not enough that the spirits and mortals war one upon the other? Must we, too, fight amongst ourselves? Sit!"

Kaiten bowed his half-shaven pate and sat back down, staring at Motso with steely eyes. For his part, the Lion champion looked more interested in the designs on his heirloom fan.

"I have heard things, as well, my Emperor," said Bayushi Yojiro from behind his mask.

"I would expect that the Master of Secrets would hear a great many things," said Toturi with a pained grimace. He looked at the Scorpion daimyo. Above Yojiro's ornate mask, he had eyes of courage and resolve. Of all the Scorpion Toturi had known throughout his life—including a few he had known far better than he would have preferred—Yojiro was the only one to look directly at someone. All the others habitually looked askance, from under their brows or down their nose. It was never direct. Yojiro was different. He was even called "the only honest Scorpion"—a title he himself used on occasion.

"To my deep regret, I hear that Scorpion mortals are hunting those spirits who failed to protect the Black Scrolls, who'd let them fall into the hands of other Clans. I have issued a decree to stop them, but while our Clan cultivates loyalty and obedience, these samurai believe they are finally executing justice upon those who failed our Great Charge.

"I hear also that the Falcon mortals and spirits are warring over control of their lands and that the Fox Clan is mustering its might. The Fox have always been somewhat closer to their spirits than the rest of us, and perhaps now they feel they have the strength to exact vengeance upon the Mantis. Those are the most reliable whispers that have crossed my ears, my lord."

"After all that we have done together . . ." muttered Toturi.

"My liege," said Motso, "we have all been taught from childhood to honor and revere our ancestors. And yet in the thousand years of recorded history, no one ever said anything about teaching the ancestors to respect their offspring. The issue has usually been avoided when the older generation retires to a monastic life. But these spirits . . . many of them never retired, nor even prepared to. They are still young in their hearts. Perhaps they look upon us mortals in much the same way as we look upon our children. We are much older and wiser than our children, more enlightened to the way of things. Perhaps they see themselves the same way. Who is to say what they experienced during those long years in Jigoku? Perhaps we would be right to defer to them."

"No," said Shiba Tsukune flatly. "Speaking for the Phoenix, we will never bow our knee to the spirits, not if our lives depend on it. To do so is unconscionable. The spirits—may their journeys be blessed, and long may they inspire us—do not belong here. They have died. They belong in Jigoku. It is the way of things. It is the way the Celestial Order was created. The fact that they remain here defies their designated position within that order, which is to guide our swords and watch our paths, but it is up to us to live, not them."

"She is right," said Empress Kaede quietly. "Their destinies have been fulfilled. The living still must fulfill their own."

"So you're saying the spirits have upset the karmic balance?" said

Toturi. He laughed blackly. "Perhaps that is why the Emperor's word is no longer obeyed without question."

"But that still does not answer your . . . well, *our* original problem," Kaiten added. "Why did the fighting start only recently? What has changed?"

* * * * *

Tsuneo sat with his spine erect, uncomfortably positioned in the midst of a pile of soft, silky pillows in a large pavilion tent. "You must appear voluptuously regal," Hantei had said earlier that day. "I shall arrange everything."

An ornate brazier of coals heated the pavilion. To one side a pair of young geisha sat next to a lacquered wooden tray of fine delicacies. Jade chopsticks rested unused in their hands. The scents of rare food filled the tent with a cloying mélange. Behind him, other geisha awaited his bidding. One held a fat bottle of plum wine, which was now over half empty.

The pillows whispered to him. *Relax . . .* they said, and the food tempted him with gross indulgence. Indulgence, indeed; he wasn't even wearing his armor. After years on the Wall, years by Hantei's side in Otosan Uchi, and five gods-forsaken centuries in Jigoku, he'd all but forgotten what it was like. Even after this much time back in the Empire, he still was unable to relax without his armor. Hantei had ordered him not to wear it for this occasion, and he'd relented only because twenty-four of his handpicked Crab spirits surrounded his tent.

His back was sore from sitting so uncomfortably. The pillows beckoned to him. *Lie back,* they urged, *and let the geisha massage you.*

Tsuneo took another heavy pull from his large porcelain cup of wine and absently studied the embers over its rim. It was too sweet for his taste, but the alcohol helped swamp his discomfort.

He swirled the wine and took another sip. He savored the taste for a few moments, then looked again at the food. The delicacies offered something bitter to offset the sweetness, to provide a counterpoint for his tongue. *Lie back and let the geisha feed you,* the odors sighed. He glanced at the young women, two of Hantei's favorites, and saw that one of them had a swollen eye, the bruise not quite concealed by her cosmetics.

With an immense sensation of relief, he finally heard the approaching sounds of samurai leading their horses. The sounds were unmistakable—the clop of shod hoofs, the jingle of harnesses. Every noise shouted the words "dismounted cavalry." The bells and the heavy bootsteps, now those meant the riders were Unicorn. Stupid barbarians had no sense of decorum or subtlety. He was to take advantage of that here tonight. Hantei had instructed him well on what to say and when.

"They are here, General," murmured one of his guards.

Tsuneo drained the rest of his glass in one swig. "Send only one in," he growled. Hantei's first ploy: cut off the speaker's support.

There was some discussion outside. Finally the tent flaps opened, and a single Unicorn spirit entered. She wore heavy boots made of leather, as well as a pair of immodestly tight pants and a jerkin made of quilted fur and studded with brass. Under one arm she carried a small bowl-shaped helmet that came to a point. Barbaric gear, all. At least she had the sense to remove the boots as she entered the tent, though clearly taking them off was harder and less dignified than it would have been had she worn sandals.

The Unicorn knelt and bowed, touching her head to the floor. "Most esteemed Emperor," she began, "I am Moto Shiyun, and—"

"I am not Hantei," came the blunt reply. "I am Tsuneo, called the Stone Crab."

"But . . . you . . . we asked that . . . I am terribly sorry to have disturbed you, my lord," stammered Shiyun. "Please accept my humblest apologies. If you could be bothered to impart directions to—"

"The Hantei will not see you," interrupted Tsuneo. The words slapped Shiyun's arrogance into stunned silence, just as Hantei had predicted.

"Why not, my lord?" asked Shiyun. "I am an emissary from one of the Great Clans. I would have thought—"

"The Hantei has never seen a Unicorn emissary," began Tsuneo.

"Ki-rin Clan, please, my lord," said Shiyun.

"Well," said Tsuneo, "*they* call themselves the Unicorn now. But Unicorn or Ki-rin, your Clan returned after his death. He does not know you."

"But . . . but we were abroad, searching the world for foes and threats," protested Shiyun.

"He knows. That's why the Lion and Crane were allowed to run your lands in your absence. It was a tradition that Hantei continued, to ensure that your lands did not become overgrown with brambles."

"But surely—" Shiyun sputtered.

"You know," said Tsuneo, ignoring her, "the self-proclaimed Emperor Toturi was once of the Lion Clan. Several of that Clan serve him as advisors even today, and he made one of his close friends the daimyo of the Akodo family with but a wave of his hand. At the same time, he was a lifelong friend of the late Crane daimyo, and a Crane still advises him. I wonder if those Clans are vying for his favor. It's just possible that they hope he will reinstate the tradition that they administer the 'vacant lands in the northwest portion of the Empire.'"

"He wouldn't do that—"

"Not if he is forced from the throne, no."

Seeing a new ray of hope, Shiyun asked, "The Hantei would of course support our ownership of our lands. Is that not right?"

"Why should he?" asked Tsuneo casually. "In all the years he ruled the Empire, not once did you or your people pay him respect. Not once did you honor his position with your presence. Never did you honor the anniversary of his birth with an appropriate remembrance. Why should he care for a Clan that ignored his very existence? No, it would not surprise me if he awarded the lands to either the Lion or the Crane, perhaps both, to help sway them from supporting this self-styled Emperor Toturi."

"That's intolerable!" blurted the emissary.

"Such words seal the fate of your lands," said Tsuneo.

Shiyun bowed again, quickly and deeply. "Forgive me, my lord. My tongue speaks hastily and without clarity. What I mean to say is that it would be intolerable for the Unicorn Clan not to rectify this situation immediately and to provide the newly returned Hantei Emperor with the respect and deference that is his due, to overcome the limited experience he has had with our Clan. In this way, he would of course decree that our lands should remain ours. I apologize again if my hasty words were easily misinterpreted."

Tsuneo smirked, an ugly expression on his veteran face. *Hantei knows you too well*, he thought.

"My lord," hazarded Shiyun, "you are close to the Hantei and a renowned legend. You must have great insight, as well as a keen mind for strategy. It was ill fortune that saw our Clan return from its explorations between the Hantei's first rule and his return. Certainly you can see that we meant no offense. But this Toturi feigns to start a new dynasty on the bones of the honorable Hantei lineage, and this cannot be allowed, nor can cooperation with such a man be rewarded, least of all with the lands of other loyal Clans. I beg you, my lord, if you have any ideas on how we can rectify this situation, we would be eternally grateful for your assistance."

Tsuneo twirled the empty porcelain cup in his hands. "First of all, you must understand that the Emperor is the most powerful person in the world, and Hantei XVI is the most powerful of his lineage. It is no coincidence that he is called the Steel Chrysanthemum, nor that he chose the Stone Crab for his right hand. So to attract his attention, you must first demonstrate your strength."

Shiyun smiled, showing perfect teeth, startlingly white within her tanned face. "That, my lord, is not a problem. Our Clan's strength is insurmountable. We have the greatest cavalry in the world, and our steel has been forged by the hardships we have endured as a Clan and as individuals. I myself have ridden across the Burning Sands, explored the vast wastes of—"

Tsuneo held up a hand. "You have, perhaps," he said, "and you need not tell a Crab how a life in the field hardens a samurai. But," he continued languidly, looking at the ceiling of the tent, "your descendants have experienced none of that. They sit in sessile comfort in their palaces and cities, telling tales of how great they are instead of forging those tales with their own actions." He glanced at Shiyun from corner of his eye and saw the emissary's brow was furrowed in thought. "There's nothing weaker than the house-bound child of a long line of heroes, who expects past glories to win the day for him. If Toturi were to give all of your lands to the Lion, would your Clan be able to resist them, or would those city-bound nomads fail in the face of the full fury of the Lion's charge?"

"The spirits would, of course, be insurmountable," said Shiyun, "but of the mortals . . . I had not considered those thoughts. Wisely is it said that a weak ally is worse than no ally at all."

"It's a pity you can't teach the Unicorn the lessons that the Ki-rin learned. . . ." said Tsuneo, half to himself.

"The only way to do that would be to pry them out of those soft cities, where they no longer have walls to protect themselves."

"Stone never serves as well as steel," agreed Tsuneo.

"They have the fire within them, lord," said Shiyun, thinking out loud, "for our blood flows in their veins. They just need the black-smith's hammer and bellows to reforge their indomitable spirit."

Tsuneo pretended he hadn't heard and continued speaking as if to himself. "Not only that, but they're indescribably fond of Toturi. . . ."

"What was that?" asked Shiyun.

"Hm?" asked Tsuneo, as if his concentration had been broken. "Oh, I was just thinking about how the Unicorn Clan was the first to support Toturi when he was dishonored. They let him lead their army at Beiden Pass, and they're likely to keep supporting him, despite his favoritism to the Lion and the Crane."

Shiyun's eyes narrowed. "My lord, I have a suggestion. If the Ki-rin spirits were to strike at the cities that trap our brethren like tar pits, this would serve both of our needs. It would force those who call themselves the 'Unicorn Clan' to face privation and better them-selves with it. It would deny Toturi the help of those selfsame fools. And we would cheerfully gift the Emperor with the riches of those cities to honor the anniversary of his rebirth into the Empire. In the end, he would have great riches, and the loyalty of a newly reformed Clan of the finest cavalry ever seen. Would this, then, ensure our place in the Emperor's heart?"

"That is a very clever plan," said Tsuneo with great sincerity. "It would indeed win the Emperor's favor, perhaps placing you above all other Clans. But do you think you can accomplish this task?"

Shiyun raised her chin. "Our cavalry is insurmountable. With your pardon, my lord, I have much to do." She bowed again and excused herself from the tent.

Tsuneo did not stop her, even though she left without his express permission. He listened to the hushed whispers of the samurai as they led their horses away, remounted, and galloped off. Then he stood up and tossed his porcelain cup aside. He looked around at the opulent furnishings—the pillows, the geisha, and the dinner. With the Moto gone, they once more beckoned, enticed, seduced.

It was all too easy. Too easy to get caught up in the luxuries and the power, the vanity and the manipulation, and to lose touch with what was truly important—honor and steel and loyalty. His lip curled in a sneer. "Guard!" he bellowed. "Bring me my armor!"

His shout had hardly died before his guards ran in with his armor. As they helped him put it on, he growled, "Take this damned tent down. Send everything back to Hantei. I will have no more of this."

Fully armored, Tsuneo moved to an open courtyard and began practicing with his tetsubo, working his muscles hard until the fire of their agony had burned away the last memories of his temptation.

* * * * *

Late that summer, the Ki-rin struck the Unicorn. They moved easily into several key cities along the Clan's frontier—the City Between the Rivers, White Shore Lake, and the City of the Rich Frog. Entering in full battle armor and carrying an assortment of weapons, they were greeted as a parade and welcomed with no hint of suspicion. After all, for a Unicorn to raise a hand against another Unicorn was all but unheard of.

Seizing the cities from unarmed, unarmored, trusting people was child's play. The spirits killed as few as they could and drove the rest into the fields with only what they wore. Most of the harvest had been taken in, and winter would be approaching soon. It was a good crucible to test their mettle.

"Look at them leave," commented Shiyun as she watched the defeated Unicorn move into the autumn fields. "Look at their stance. They look defeated. Did we look so when the floods washed away our camp and we faced winter on the steppes without shelter? I think not." So saying, she felt utterly justified in what she had done, despite the fact that she had raised arms against others of her Clan.

With their border castles seized by the Ki-rin spirits, the Unicorn mortals were cut off from the rest of the Empire. Too proud to look for sanctuary among the Lion or Dragon, the Unicorn vowed not only to survive, but to get their revenge.

Thus, while the Unicorn looked defeated, with hanging heads and heavy tread, Shiyun never saw that her plan had indeed kindled their inner fire, nor that it burned more brightly than she could have guessed.

7 THE WIND'S TRUTH

The
Eleventh
Year
of the
Reign
of
Toturi I

The flames of small wars had run across the Empire, erupting in the wake of Hantei's passage. Now his entourage had wound its way high in the forbidding mountains of the Dragon Clan. Dusk had fallen early, as it always seemed to in the Dragon lands, and now that winter was close at hand, the daylight hardly seemed to linger at all. Servants shivered in the chill, thin air, finding every excuse to linger for a few fleeting moments by one of the small fires that dotted the camp.

The encampment was in a well-concealed ravine, down a treacherous winding path that spurred from one of the lesser roads through the Dragon Clan's mountainous lands. The center of the camp—and the only truly flat portion of the clearing—was taken up by a large pavilion tent. Its gaily colored silk glowed warmly with light from within, drawing envious glances from the guards.

Presently the sound of footsteps came down the path from the road, and a pair of figures entered the firelight. The great armored bulk of Hida Tsuneo moved across the camp, followed closely by a much smaller, stooped figure swathed in thick, billowing robes. The servants bowed deferentially to Tsuneo, then when they saw who traveled with him, they edged quickly away, giving the pair far more room than was actually needed.

Approaching the pavilion, Tsuneo turned to glance at his guest, who stopped and waited respectfully. Tsuneo approached the pavilion, pulled the tent's flap abruptly aside, and stooped to pass through the entrance into the warmth within. Despite the inconvenience, he appreciated the clever mind that had ordered the pavilion's opening to be too small, to ensure that any who entered had to bow, no matter their feelings or loyalties. It also exposed the backs of their heads, to make assassination that much easier. So clever, so functional . . . so brutal.

Tsuneo stepped in and bowed again, though perhaps slightly less deeply than he should have. "He is here, my Emperor," he said.

"Excellent," replied Hantei, sitting at the far end of the tent on a simple, yet comfortable chair. He waited for a while, letting the chill air do its silent work. "You may show him in now," he said.

Tsuneo grasped the tent flap, but before he opened it, Hantei raised one finger, stopping him. "My friend," he whispered, gesturing to a painted cushion, "if he steps past the tiger pillow there, kill him instantly."

Tsuneo nodded and opened the flap.

The stooped figure shuffled in as though in pain, then knelt and bowed deeply, touching his head to the carpeted ground. "I thank and bless the name of Hantei," he said formally. "May the fortunes guide his path and the heavens shower their grace upon him, that he has consented to an audience with a samurai such as myself."

Hantei giggled slightly. "My," he said sweetly, "such a deep bow is reserved only for the Emperor."

The figure, still prostrate, said, "I served him whom I thought to be the last of the Hantei Emperors, may his soul find eternal peace in the celestial gardens. For some of us, it is a relief to find that the royal blood has returned to Rokugan, and the Emerald Empire shall therewith be assured of a ruler of impartiality."

"I see," said Hantei coyly. "And . . . what is your name again?"

The figure sat back on his heels and pulled back the hood that overed his face, though he dared not raise his eyes. Instead, he tared fixedly at a meaningless spot of carpet an arm's reach in front f him, deferentially distant from Hantei's feet. "I am Agasha amori," he said, "and I am the daimyo of my family."

"Oh, yes, that's right," said Hantei, covering his mouth with a fan. Tell me, how is your family these days?"

Tamori pursed his lips and trembled slightly. His right eye started witching. He took a deep shuddering breath, and as he let it back •ut, the rage passed. "They have turned their backs upon their laimyo and upon their past. They are as an unbroken colt, wayward nd foolish. They must be broken anew," he finished, clenching one ist.

"Really?" said Hantei with mock interest. "They . . . they turned heir backs?"

"Yes, my liege. In the midst of our Clan's greatest internal strug-le, my family forsook their oaths to serve our rightful daimyo and led to the lands of the Phoenix. For as long as the moon is in the ky, I cannot forgive them this . . . this betrayal."

"Did you not seek the Emperor's favor?"

"The one who claims to be Emperor refused to intervene. And after refusing our rightful request, Toturi then had the audacity to •rder us to aid his people in the recapture of Oblivion's Gate."

"Oblivion's Gate . . ." said Hantei, feigning ignorance though he knew full well Tamori knew better. "Let's see, that was deep in the heart of the Shadowlands, was it not? My, that must have been dan-gerous."

"Yes, it was," said Tamori slowly. "Many died, others suffer to this day. But for my part, I escaped un—" the briefest hesitation— "scathed. But it was my duty to the Empire and to the ancestors we revere."

"And yet you seem unable to instruct your family in how to respect their ancestors, let alone authority, hmm?"

Tamori, trembling again, simply nodded.

Hantei waited for a long time, watching Tamori clench and unclench his fist, letting the silence grow and swarm, letting the inner whispers have free reign in Tamori's mind. He watched Tamori's eyes dart about the floor, and he saw the man's breathing gradually build speed, then slow as Tamori regained his tempe then increase again. This is too easy, Hantei thought. At last h spoke. "Tell me," he said languidly from behind his fan, "what busi ness brings you to me this evening?"

"*They must—!*" Tamori shouted, then cut himself short, flexe his fists, and tried again. "You are the rightful Emperor," he said, h voice trembling, "and you have the respect of both the living an the returned spirits. I humbly beg that you would intercede on th behalf of my family and *bring my dam*—" Tamori paused, trying control his rising voice by speaking through clenched teeth—"m . . . wayward Clan back under my . . . bring them back . . . to me!"

Over the fan that still covered most of his face, Hantei glanced Tsuneo. For his part, the Crab merely raised one eyebrow. "You as for the Imperial favor to smile upon your family," Hantei repeate "that they may bask in the delight of the Emperor under your right ful guidance."

Tamori nodded.

"So you wish for me to return your family to you, deny th Phoenix any opportunity to save face by right of challenge, and us Imperial troops to enforce this decree?"

Tamori nodded.

"Oh, and one other thing, I assume," added Hantei, smirking "you wish me to undertake all this in such a manner as to restor the honor of a daimyo with no one to rule over, hmm?"

Tamori twitched once, rather violently, and nodded. "Nothing beyond the reach of the Emperor," he said. "Nothing can withstan the will of heaven."

"And," continued Hantei, "in the eyes of those mortals who liv in this time, I am not currently the Emperor."

Tamori remained carefully silent, giving no indication that h had even heard that last comment.

Hantei thought for a moment, then glanced up at Tsuneo. "Yo ask for a great gift," the Crab said in his booming voice.

"I am honored to offer my liege a great gift of my own, in grati tude and admiration for the generosity with which he shall bless m family and my Clan," said Tamori formally. Hantei noticed hi temper was already under better control.

"What gift can compare to the favor of the Emperor?" asked the Crab in a voice like thunder.

"I am the daimyo of my family. I have spoken with those daimyos who went before me into Jigoku and have returned, and they all—" Tamori paused.

"They all . . . what?" asked Hantei, dropping his fan slightly, sensing that Tamori was about to make a disastrous comment.

Choosing his words carefully, Tamori said, "They all voluntarily relinquished their position as daimyo before they died, passing it along to their heir. Therefore everyone recognizes that they have no claim to my position. Yes, they have returned, so now I can speak with them instead of pray to them, and I turn to them for advice as I always have, and their words still guide my hand."

Hantei tapped his fan against his nose, pleasantly surprised that Tamori evaded any phrase that might be construed as judgmental against Hantei's own position.

"In gratitude and honor for the Emperor's favor," Tamori concluded, "I offer a tool to turn Empire's loyalty back to the rightful Hantei dynasty. I offer the Dragon Clan to act as the Emperor's right hand and left hand. Let the two swords of the Dragon drive the usurper from your place in the Celestial Order."

Hantei feigned to hide a yawn behind his fan. "Such a gift is of great worth . . . from one who can actually provide it," said Hantei, at once refusing the gift and insulting its bearer. "I cannot accept an empty promise. It would be an inauspicious event for the throne."

"I have sway among my Clan," Tamori replied, "being a powerful daimyo who has shown no disloyalty to the greater family that raised and taught me. I have spoken with that part of my family that has returned from Jigoku, and we are of one mind. I have spoken to the daimyos of the Mirumoto, the Togashi, the Hitomi, the Hoshi, and the Kitsuki. They seek the honor of the Clan, and they have given me the authority to speak for them. I can and I do offer you the Dragon Clan."

"Really?" replied Hantei, languidly rolling the word off his tongue. "I suppose you might. But then," he sighed, "the Dragon think only of themselves. They remain secluded in their mountain castles and care little for the outside world. Such support would only last so long as the

Agasha remained away, and reach only as far as the borders of the lands." Hantei paused. "No," he said at last, negligently, "I cann commit the favor of the throne to one small portion of the Empire. must think of the Empire as a whole."

Even though two refusals were demanded by protocol, Hantei ha not so much refused as impugned Tamori's family and his Clan. H could see the uncertainty creep into Tamori's posture, wondering he would indeed withhold his favor.

"Great Emperor," he said in a voice tinged with desperation, "th Dragon Clan has changed greatly in the time you were ... away fron your position. Togashi ruled us for a thousand years, awaiting th Day of Thunder. That day has come and gone, and our position i the world has changed as a result of it. The Dragon Clan cannot an will not withdraw from the activities of the Empire. To demonstra our commitment, I pledge you the unconditional support of th Dragon Clan, from the mountain to the sea, from the Shadowland to the Burning Sands. We shall be your swords. Our hands sha strike where you order."

So saying, Tamori turned his palms upward, revealing the inside of his forearms to Hantei. There, just above the wrist on each hand was a tattoo of the Steel Chrysanthemum.

"Unconditional, you say?" echoed Hantei. He smiled behind hi fan, a cold, feral smile. "Very well," he said. "The Emperor thank you for your generosity and your gift. You shall have the favor of th Emperor."

Tsuneo strode over to the side of the pavilion, picked up a small lac quered box, walked over to stand in front of Tamori, and opened th lid. Inside, resting upon a bed of fine rumpled silk, was an old fashioned token somewhat smaller than the palm of Tamori's hand the mon of the Steel Chrysanthemum carved from a single emerald Bowing his head, Tamori reached forward gingerly with both hi hands and reverentially picked up the treasure.

"You know, Tamori," Hantei said, suddenly warm and friendly "in all the years I have walked in the Empire, I have never seen th Dragon come down from the mountains. This is a new and enjoy able experience for me, and I thank you for it." Then all light fle from his countenance, his face becoming as hard and cold as katana. "Your first duty," he said intently, "is to wait. Wait, and plan. I sense there is something in the winds.

"Appoint one of your tattooed monks to be your Imperial liaison. Prepare your best strategy. In the meantime, send a small force to attack the Phoenix lands near the Lion border, where it's flat and the terrain is accessible. Be sure to appoint a spirit from the time of the fourth or fifth Hantei and tell him to use the tactics of the time. Strictly old-fashioned, with no innovation, but of course make a good fight of it and kill as many as you want. He is to win the battle but lose the campaign by virtue of being too cautious."

"But my lord—" hazarded Tamori.

"*Silence!*" bellowed Hantei. "You pledged your unconditional obedience. You have your orders. Why, then, do you stay here and chatter like a monkey?"

Tamori bowed, touching his head to the floor. "Your liaison will be here in the morning, my Emperor," he said quickly, then backed out of the tent into the darkness.

Hantei sat silently, watching the tent flap sway back and forth as Tamori's footsteps retreated into the distance. He waited until the footsteps were no longer audible, and then waited some more. Tsuneo simply stood, waiting. Presently Hantei dropped his fan and closed it. "So," he asked pensively, "what do you think?"

Tsuneo scratched the side of his grizzled face. "I've seen it many times before," he said. "He's got the Taint, just as the rumors said."

"Fascinating," Hantei said, a touch of horror and jaded curiosity in his voice. "So what does it do? Does it . . . eat up the body from within? Is that why he wore such long robes?"

"It corrupts the body, maybe like a mix of bad fever and poison, but it eats the soul, too," said Tsuneo. "It sinks its fangs into a man's spirit and slowly twists him into a slave to evil. This one, Tamori, he tries to deny it, but on some level, he has to know. He's a shugenja, after all, and as smart as he is, he's got to know something's wrong. All the same, he tries to hide it. Honor, pride, fear . . . I don't know. If he were Crab, he'd accept his fate and join the Legion of the Damned, serving the Clan for as long as he stayed sane, because the Taint is also a powerful weapon. When he felt his soul slipping, he'd end his own life. This Tamori, he's more dangerous, because he'll go along like everything is normal until he gets subsumed by his dark urges, and then the Dragon will pay for it . . . or whoever happens to be near. I'd be careful around him."

"How contagious is it?"

"The Taint?" asked Tsuneo, stretching his shoulders. "If you're careful, you'll be all right." He sniffed, thinking. "I'd burn the rug he knelt on. Nothing else is a likely risk."

"I see." Hantei stood up and moved to the back of the tent. He flicked his fan back open, then swept the tines across the silk fabric at the rear of the tent, cutting a long gash in the fabric. He swept the fan again, crosswise this time, and split the fabric again, opening a large diamond-shaped hole in the pavilion's wall. He pulled the opening wider with his hands and stepped through. Once safely outside, he took a deep breath, then turned to look at Tsuneo, still standing inside by the tent's entrance.

"I will not make the same mistake the thirty-ninth of my line made," he said casually. "His soul was never found." He closed his fan and slid it back into his sleeve. "Leave the treasures, Tsuneo. Burn the pavilion." He paused, then smiled a cold smile. "Burn it all."

* * * * *

Empress Kaede smiled as she watched Naseru toddle along the garden path in front of her. A veritable parade of attendants followed behind, silken kimonos whispering like a soft breeze on the grass and the stepping-stones.

Like all two-year-olds, Naseru had a purity of vision that adults forever sought to regain. It was Kaede's opinion that the essence of the void was to be as a newborn babe, taking in everything and ascribing no meaning to anything. Tradition, experience, and anticipation defined so much of every adult experience. Very little was taken simply for what it was. To watch a young child exploring the world was a means to touch that essential awareness once more, without surrendering her soul to the dragon.

She moved serenely through the garden, seeming like a stately Imperial galleon sailing a sea of flowers, with a spry and noisy little dolphin cavorting at her bow.

At the center of the garden stood a large, ornate gazebo, and as the pair approached, suddenly Naseru squealed, "Tsudao!" and ran forward.

Kaede glanced up and saw her eldest child standing near the gazebo, staring into the sky, brown leaves skittering lightly past her feet. Her long, black hair hung like a banner rippling in the late autumn breeze, and she held her hands crossed easily in front. Naseru ran up to her, but Tsudao gracefully turned, moving no more than was necessary to turn her shoulder to her littler brother.

Kaede moved swiftly closer. "Tsudao," she said firmly, "I told you to watch your brother Sezaru."

Tsudao bowed formally to her mother, moving as smoothly as tea pours from a pot. "Yes, honorable mother, I am." She straightened up, and as she looked skyward again, Kaede followed her eyes.

Sezaru stood atop the highest point of the gazebo's scalloped roof. He balanced on one foot, poised on the ornamental ball that capped the roof. His other leg was bent so that his foot rested on the side of his knee, looking almost like a heron. He held his arms to the sky, and worst of all to Kaede's heart, he was blindfolded.

Kaede gasped and instinctively grasped Naseru's hand.

"Sezaru!" shouted Naseru with his shrill child's voice. "You come down! I telling papa!"

"Shut up!" said Tsudao, curling her lip. "You always tell! I oughta spank you!"

Naseru glanced up at Kaede and saw that her attention was still focused on Sezaru. He leaned forward to Tsudao and hissed, "You hit me I pee your futon!"

"You—" barked Tsudao, raising one hand. Kaede glanced back at her children.

"I scared, Mama," said Naseru immediately, artificial tears welling up. "Make Sezaru down!"

Kaede glanced around and spoke loudly enough for the servants to hear. "You children go to the bamboo room and practice your calligraphy. Go!" She ushered them off, and servants adroitly herded the children in two slightly different directions. Naseru took one last opportunity to stick his tongue out at his sister, who pretended not to notice.

As soon as they left, Kaede pulled a windblown strand of hair back from her eyes and looked up at her eldest son. His position had not changed. In spite of the shrieking fears of her mother's instincts, she could see that Sezaru was in no immediate danger, and anything drastic she did would be much more likely to cause him to fall than to provide the boy any help. He was showing a lot of poise for a mere four years.

She closed her eyes and reached out to him with her inner consciousness. Immediately she heard the tinkling of bells, chimes in the wind, the blowing of leaves. She sensed the spirits moving, and the winds circling about this place. And at the center of all this was her son.

She approached.

My son . . .

Mama, please, I'm listening.

Kaede heard whispers in the winds, maddeningly almost intelligible. She could sense her son's attention trying to absorb, trying to understand. She moved closer, to listen, and she felt the winds recoil and swerve away, and the sounds immediately diminished.

Ma-MAAAaaa . . .

They weren't looking for just anyone. They were looking for him.

She pulled back and refocused her chi, sending it out to give Sezaru a stable underpinning—supporting him as he listened, lending him her adult understanding, giving him a familiar foundation upon which to rest his spirit. Much like giving a child a boost into a tree, she hoped her assistance would help Sezaru attain that which he could not reach by himself, though a part of her mind wondered what few things might still fall outside of his reach. It seemed that he, too, had a touch of the dragon.

She heard others approaching, guards and courtiers running to help save Sezaru, but she let none of this distract her. None would interfere once they saw the Empress using her magic. The only one who could rightfully interfere would be the Emperor himself, and she knew Toturi would know better.

Kaede's kimono flapped slowly in the passing wind, and leaves scratched upon the stones as they migrated past. She stood quietly, ands held in front of her navel, thumbs and forefingers forming a ircle.

At last the breeze died down, bit by bit, and Kaede sensed the whispering was over. She withdrew her soul and opened her eyes, linking as the bright sun barged its way into her mind again. mperor Toturi stood beside her, looking up at his son. Kaede lowered her hands and watched as well.

"Well?" Toturi murmured.

"He said he was listening. Air spirits, I believe." She snuck one and over to Toturi's and gave a discreet little squeeze, as much for er reassurance as for his.

"I see," said Toturi. "This should prove interesting."

Sezaru pulled off the blindfold and shook his hair. When he opened his eyes, he started, surprised to find that a crowd had gathered. He looked about uncertainly, slowly dropping his second foot o stand beside the first. When his eyes fell upon Toturi, his face lit up into a bright smile. "Papa!" he shouted.

"My son," said the Emperor, looking around, "it appears you ave summoned the Imperial Court." A nervous titter rippled hrough the onlookers. "I hope your tutor told you that according o tradition, when the Imperial Court convenes, your place is at my ide, not up on a gazebo."

"Yes, father," said Sezaru lightly, and he hopped off the rooftop.

He slid easily down the swooping tiled roof, and when he slipped off the edge of, a sudden updraft whipped the fabric of his kimono kyward and he floated gently to the ground.

"He's giving me so many gray hairs, I'll soon look like him," whispered Toturi to Kaede.

"Shh," urged Kaede, suppressing a smile.

Sezaru discreetly turned his back and adjusted his kimono for a less wind-blown appearance. Then he turned back, approached Toturi, and bowed deeply to his father. "Good day, honored father," he said.

"Your mother says you were . . . listening?"

"Yes, honored father," Sezaru replied.

"Listening to what?"

"The spirits of the air, honored father. They came to me."

"Why were you balanced up there like that, son?"

"I heard them better up there, honored father."

"But why were you standing in such a . . . ?" Toturi paused. He didn't want to burden his son with undue fears, but "dangerous" was the first word that had come to his mind. He searched for a moment, then said, "such an unusual position?"

"I had to balance, honored father. It made me hear better, 'cause I was balanced. The world isn't, you know—it's not balanced."

Toturi glanced at Kaede, and he caught her looking at his golden aura. She quickly dropped her eyes.

"Yes, my son, the world isn't balanced. The smoke of war is on the breeze yet again this year."

"I know father, that's what the spirits told me about."

"Oh?" said Toturi. He squatted down in front of his son and looked him in the eye. "What did the spirits say?"

"They want it to stop, so they told me who was doing it, who was being bad." Sezaru began to fidget.

"Tell me, Sezaru," said Toturi, firmly but gently.

"They said it was the Emperor, the metal flower," the boy said, squirming. "But there can't be two Emperors, can there?"

Toturi's face was grim. "No, son, there can not."

8 THREAT OF WAR

The
Eleventh
Year
of the
Reign
of
Toturi I

Lord Donosu!"

Miya Donosu started, his pleasant reverie broken. His slight jolt disturbed the young woman asleep on his shoulder but did not quite awaken her.

"Yes?" he answered quietly. He knew the guard would hear his reply. It had to be a guard. Only guards would be that aggressive in tone yet use the honorific and deferentially remain outside his chambers.

"Emperor Toturi the First commands your presence," replied the guard with military speed and precision. "I am ordered to honor you with an escort."

"I see," said Donosu as he carefully pulled his arm out from beneath his napping bedmate. It seemed like the golden halo that surrounded him lingered on her skin before sparkling away, but he knew it was just his wishful thinking. There remained a difference between spirits and mortals, and now that the re-sanctified Oblivion's Gate properly kept the dead in Jigoku awaiting reincarnation, she would never have a halo. She could only hold one, and she had chosen his.

She was so young, and he so old, even before he had died a few centuries ago. Perhaps she was the first drop of a rainstorm, the first ray of dawn, the first change in heart that would end the divisiveness between mortal and spirit. Mortals yet to die and spirit returned . . . were they not all samurai? Were they not all ultimately descended from the gods? Were they not all servants of the Emperor?

Donosu dressed himself quickly in his best raiment. He smoothed out his thick, white beard and perched his small, rectangular, black hat atop his shaven head, tying its straps neatly behind his whiskers. Quietly he opened the rice-paper door, slipped through, closed it, and padded to the entrance of his quarters, where two Imperial guards waited. Donosu's brow furrowed ever so slightly as he saw they were dressed in battle armor.

They bowed and without a word led him to the throne room. Not that it was necessary; Donosu knew the palace better than he knew his own home. He had served here for many long years, loyally executing his duties to his Clan and his Emperor.

They approached the main entry to the throne room, which was guarded by a dozen samurai, armored and bearing naginata. Before Donosu could ponder this, two of the samurai swung open the heavy doors to the throne room, and Donosu stepped forward.

The sight he saw made his heart stop, but he concealed his surprise by bowing immediately and deeply, in his most formal manner. As soon as he could muster the words, he greeted Emperor Toturi in his most cultured tones, sensed an acknowledgement, and straightened up again. As he did so he realized that he had no clue what he'd just said.

Donosu blinked involuntarily as he surveyed the scene anew. Emperor Toturi did not sit upon his Jade Throne, but rather stood in front of it. He was arrayed in full battle armor, the same armor the courtiers said he'd worn at the Day of Thunder. It was black lacquered and polished to a mirror shine, with huge gatelike shields protecting his shoulders. His daisho—the long katana and the short wakizashi—was tucked securely into his coiled belt, and he held his war fan in his right hand.

To his left stood his daughter, Tsudao, tall for a seven-year-old,

d honored with holding her father's no-dachi. The giant sword
emed as if it should be too big and heavy for her, but she sup-
rted its heavy saya in her hands with a look of fierce determina-
n in her face.

To his right stood Sezaru, his son, whose eyes seemed to be look-
g nowhere. His eyes were like a lake, and he had pulled one leg up
to his hakama pants, standing like a heron in water.

Behind Sezaru stood Kaede, placid and pretty as ever. Her small
me oozed with power despite her stature. She wore a vague smile
at unnerved Donosu.

Spread out to either side of the Emperor (at a respectful distance,
course) was a wide array of armed and armored samurai. It made
nosu tremble that armed samurai were allowed even to be in the
rone room. Kitsu Motso, the head of the Lion Clan, stood at
turi's right and Doji Kuwanan of the Crane at his left. Bayushi
jiro, daimyo of the Scorpion, stood way to one side, too far in
nosu's peripheral vision for him to be comfortable, yet he could
t look away from the Emperor without causing insult. Diplomats
m the Crab and Unicorn were also present, and the hundred
perial guards dressed in jade green and gold provided a stern
ckdrop.

In front, at once out of place and the perfect summary of all of
is pageantry, Toturi Naseru, not much over two years old, sat on
e floor at Toturi's feet and banged one block on another with a
termination only achievable by infants.

"Most excellent Emperor," said Donosu floridly, "whose face
ghts the land and who wisdom guides the stars, I have come at
ur bidding and joyfully await your command. How may I serve
u, and in so doing, serve the Empire?"

"Miya Donosu," said Toturi. "The histories speak highly of you."

"I was honored to be the messenger of His Excellency the
wenty-Seventh Hantei Emperor, whose soul rests in the celestial
eavens as a beacon to us all. Duty compelled me to serve my Clan
d his word in all things. I claim no merit for myself in so doing."

"Well spoken," said Toturi. He studied Donosu for a moment. "I
now your honor moves you to serve the Emperor, Donosu, yet at
is time I call you to a higher duty: You must serve the Empire."

Bang! bang! went Naseru's blocks.

Toturi straightened himself (if that were possible for one with such a soldier's stance), and seemed to grow another hand's breadth as he held out his war fan and pointed it to Donosu's heart. "Hear now the words of Emperor Toturi the First," he bellowed, "and deliver them accurately to the Sixteenth Hantei and those who follow him!

"Your time is done. You died in ages past, yet you linger here in Rokugan pretending to rule and inciting war among my people! You defy the Celestial Order, you dishonor your family, and you conspire against the soul of the Empire! Samurai do not fear death, yet you, who have tasted it, fear the world you left! For all these dishonorable misdeeds, I should crucify you among criminals!

"Yet the living choose to respect our ancestors, and grant you the opportunity for an honorable return to your proper position in the Celestial Order. The Phoenix shugenja have prepared and sanctified a leaping place that shall return any who pass through it back to Jigoku. All spirits shall pass through that leaping place and leave the lands of Rokugan until the day they are reborn! Thus commands the Emperor!"

With that, Toturi flicked his fan to the side.

Donosu stood for a moment, taking in the scene. Toturi's words seemed to be reverberating still in the room, punctuated by Naseru's blocks. And there wasn't a single spirit in the room, no golden glow, save only his . . . and Toturi's.

Bang! Bang! Bang!

"I shall do as you command, my liege," said Donosu.

"You may leave. If you need anything to assist you in your journey, the guards shall see to it."

"I will not require anything but the clothes I wear," said Donosu.

"No food?" asked Toturi. "No supplies? No change of clothes?"

"I am a spirit reborn, my Emperor, purified by death. As I'm sure you know, I need very little in the way of either sleep or food. I will ride straight through to the Hantei and deliver your message." Donosu paused for a moment, considering, then said, "My liege, if you would please answer me one question, it would put my old heart at ease."

"Ask," said Toturi.

am a spirit, my liege," said Donosu. "You send me to your
[en]my with a proclamation that he—and I—must depart my
[lo]ved Rokugan a second time. Have I failed you, my liege, or
[offen]ded? If so, allow me to—"

[T]oturi held up a hand. "You are honored and respected above all
[ho]lds, Donosu, and I am entrusting you to deliver this edict with
[accu]racy and detail. I would trust no one else."

"[Y]ou are wise in all things, my liege," said Donosu, bowing. "I
[shall] deliver your powerful words and this terrifying sight in my
[mos]t eloquent manner." He turned and left the throne room, fol-
[low]ed by the sound of banging wood.

[H]e did not return to his quarters, for there was nothing there
[that] he would need where he was going. Better to vanish from her
[life] like the morning dew, he thought, than to let the moment wilt
[and] wither in sorrow. Instead, he moved straight to the Imperial
[stab]les, where he found a horse awaiting his arrival, equipped with
[an e]xcellent map, food for the journey, and a half-dozen samurai
[gua]rds.

[A]ll of them spirits.

* * * * *

[W]ithin the throne room, no one moved after Donosu left. Toturi
[stoo]d, lost in thought, and Naseru stopped his play and looked up
[at] his father's face. No one else dared move until the Emperor
[mad]e some sign that it was acceptable to do so. At last, faintly
[aud]ible through the windows, several horses galloped away. Toturi
[bow]ed his head.

"[I] have pressed the attack," he said quietly. "Now the war begins
[in e]arnest."

[K]aede stepped forward slightly. "Perhaps they will agree—" she
[star]ted to say.

"[T]he storm is upon us," said Toturi. "The drops have gathered,
[and] all that is left for them is to fall from the sky and spatter the
[hea]ds of friend and foe alike." He took a deep breath, then let it out.
"[O]ver the last few years we have watched Hantei's words wedge
[the]mselves between living and spirit, until wars rage in almost

every corner of the Empire. He is working to subvert my rule. I have delivered the ultimatum and shown Donosu our resol Leave, my friends, take off your armor and enjoy the day. Winte almost here, and come spring, it may be a long time before you free of your armor again."

The gathered samurai and nobles bowed deeply and filed quie out of the room. Once they were gone, Kaede clapped her han twice. As the servants entered, Tsudao reverently placed her fathe sword on its wooden stand beside the throne and sat down. T servants removed Toturi's armor so artfully that they were nea invisible. They quietly set the armor on its display stand and inco spicuously left the room. Toturi turned and sat heavily upon throne, scowling at the floor, alone with his family and his con dants, Toku, Godaigo, and Hiroru.

Toku pulled of his helmet and cradled it under one arm as sauntered toward Toturi. "That makes me think of a good questi honorable Emperor," he said. "You ordered that all spirits m leave Rokugan. That means you must leave, too."

Tsudao whirled around and leaped at Toku, landing soundly his foot with hers in an arcing stomp. No sooner did Toku start wince than she spun around and delivered a circle kick to the si of his knee, just behind its armor plate, and he crumpled. As he so, she jammed her thumb on the pressure point behind his ear a yelled, "Silence!" one fist cocked and ready for a punch.

"Tsudao," said Toturi quietly, "Toku has earned the right to spe his mind. His insight is one that I have often found valuable ov the years."

Tsudao stepped back, though Toturi noticed she used the thur jammed behind Toku's ear to push herself upright.

Adding insult to injury, Naseru threw one of his blocks, and ricocheted off Toku's scalp. Toturi glanced at Kaede, who imme ately started ushering Naseru out of the room and into the attenti hands of his tutors.

From a safer distance, Hiroru backed up Toku's comment. "I observation . . . has merit, my liege," he said quietly. He walked ov to where Toku was regaining his feet, keeping a careful eye Tsudao. "By your own edict, spirits defy the natural law and mo

utside their position in the Celestial Order. How does the Emperor
mit himself from such a far-reaching sentiment?"

Toturi glanced down thoughtfully at the golden aura around his
allused hand. He turned his hand over and looked at his nearly
eatureless palm.

"Don't think I haven't thought about that, my friends," he said
imply. "If the spirits stay and Hantei leads them to fight, I shall
kewise stay and fight. If, on the other hand, the spirits abandon
Hantei and obey my edict, I shall likewise follow them back to
vhere I belong."

* * * * *

The sudden, loud crack startled Donosu, and he looked up at
Hantei, though thankfully not at the tyrant's furious eyes. Instead,
Donosu's glance locked on the fan held in the spirit Emperor's
ands. It was ancient, that fan—each rib delicately carved from
black marble cut so thin you could see through the creamy veins, the
abric made of parchment as smooth and fine as a young geisha's
kin, and the intricate design on it painted with brushed gold and
ade dust by a craftsman now dead for several hundred years.

Miya Donosu remembered that fan from his first passage
hrough Rokugan, when he served under the twenty-seventh
Hantei. He remembered how very slowly and tenderly the elderly
Dowager Empress had opened and closed that fan and only once a
year, at the opening reception of winter court. He remembered how
courtiers vied for the opportunity to be one of those permitted to
ee the fan in use. It was a great honor, and he had been accorded
hat honor only once, before today.

Donosu was barely able to refrain from gasping as he saw the fan
now shattered in Hantei's hands, a priceless treasure taken from the
Empire in a momentary spasm of temper.

"He . . . said . . . WHAT?" hissed Hantei, heedless of the wreckage
in his fists.

"Emperor Toturi ordered—"

"Do not . . . use that title for a ronin thief like HIM!" spat Hantei,
crumpling the broken bones of the fan in each hand the way a witch

might grind a dove's carcass. If Hantei noticed the flutter of Donosu eye as he did so, he made no mention.

Despite his courtly profession, Donosu was first and foremost samurai. Samurai ruled their tempers, not vice versa. With a ve slight smile, Donosu focused his rage over the fan into words as warrior focuses for a strike.

"The one who sits on the Jade Throne ordered—"

Hantei, his face so racked with hate that Donosu could see clearly in his peripheral vision, hissed inarticulately and held up warning finger.

Donosu bowed again, apologetically, touching his head to th floor, and as he did so, a veteran warrior's calm replaced his ange With surprising clarity, he saw the path that he'd been followir from Otosan Uchi and saw that it was shorter by half than he originally thought. Thus enlightened, he was freed to enjoy the tri He straightened and saw Hantei XVI twisting on his seat. By th Fortunes, Donosu thought with an inward smile, this is fun.

"My lord," he said sweetly, for he had trained his whole life to fi his every word with false deference, "I am sorry that I seem to b upsetting you, for by causing you distress, I find I am unable t repeat the message as you asked me to do."

Hantei ignored Donosu and thought out loud, thumping th armrest of his chair for emphasis. "First he fails to protect m descendant, then he takes the throne for himself, now he turns th people against their own ancestors? By my blood, his entire life is succession of crimes!" Hantei tossed the ruins of the priceless fa aside.

So sweet, thought Donosu, to be able to enjoy the trail's end. " see that I have clearly conveyed the words of Toturi," he said, the added, ". . . the First." He saw Hantei's mouth twist in rage again. "I has been very enjoyable to speak with you," he said with mock sin cerity. "Thank you for your hospitality and the very unique enter tainment."

Then, without Hantei's permission, he rose to his feet. Slowl and deliberately, he raised his eyes to meet Hantei's glare, lookin him in the eye as an equal. He saw Hantei's eyes widen in stunne disbelief, widen to the point of bugging out. "I have done my duty,

Donosu said, "served my Clan in this life and the next. Now it is time for me to respect the Celestial Order and return to the lands beyond death."

"I will have you killed for your arrogance!" said Hantei, his face a rictus of hate.

Donosu nodded casually. "I must obey the decrees of Emperor Toturi I, for the Emperor speaks with the authority of heaven. If you wish, you may help me complete my duty to the rightful ruler of Rokugan."

With a gutteral scream, Hantei leapt onto Donosu, grabbing the old spirit's beard in his hands. Donosu offered no resistance as the two of them toppled to the floor. With his left hand, Hantei wrenched Donosu's beard up to expose his neck, then he began to throttle the life from the smiling herald with the unbridled strength of a frenzied animal.

As Donosu's vision dimmed, he saw the gates of Jigoku open before his eyes. He saw the familiar faces waiting for him, felt the peace embracing him. And with the last of his strength, Donosu smiled.

* * * * *

Tsuneo, seeing that Hantei was fully occupied with pounding the dead courtier's dead head on the floor, bowed to the fallen Miya with great respect.

He straightened from his bow and thoughtfully looked at his own hands, clenching his fists and remembering how the Hantei Emperor had ordered him to kill the dowager Empress with his bare hands. He remembered the feeling, the greasy, unclean ichor that covered his palms scant moments before samurai from the Great Clans cut him and his liege down in the assassination that ended the reign of terror of the Steel Chrysanthemum.

Of old, thought Tsuneo, he let others soil themselves by touching the dead. By his order, I chanced to die unclean and found myself damned to his side. Yet these thoughts brought no anger, no vindictiveness, no braying complaint from the old Crab warrior. He embraced his karma with perfect resignation.

Tsuneo waited patiently while Hantei's fury spent itself on the dead herald. He was pleased he had not had to kill the aging Miya himself.

Finally Hantei stood. "Take that filth," he said, wiping the spittle from his cheek with his sleeve, "and string him up in a tree by his beard so that the crows may pick at his eyes and the ants built a nest in his heart. And slit open the belly of his horse and whip it through the streets. I want to hear the wolves hunting it tonight."

Tsuneo's eyes narrowed ever so slightly. "Why?" he asked.

"You dare question me?" barked Hantei.

"I seek to understand your wisdom," said Tsuneo, passively, though coals burned in his eyes. "Donosu was a respected courtier, with great position and standing. If you dishonor him, the other spirits will wonder why. Fail to explain, and they will doubt you. Explain, and they will doubt you. Unlike before, when you last ruled the Empire," finished Tsuneo tactfully, "they believe there is someone else to follow."

"I will have you killed for that," hissed Hantei.

"My life is yours, and as my lord, you have the right to terminate my life at any time," said Tsuneo calmly. In truth, he not only had no fear of such a fate, but on sleepless nights he hoped for it. "Just remember no one knows what he said here this evening."

Put off balance by Tsuneo's calm logic, Hantei's fury-filled eyes abruptly became as clear as those of a child, and he saw at last the steel in the Stone Crab's eyes and the calm spirit behind them. Hantei dropped his hand, narrowed his eyes, and moved closer to the Crab, inspecting his face very closely.

"You do not fear me," he said at last, furrowing his brow. It was not a question.

"A samurai has no need to fear his lord," grunted Tsuneo, almost apathetically.

"Yet you defy me."

"I speak only the truth. What has any samurai to fear from that?"

Hantei studied the Crab as if he were an exquisite art object seen for the first time. He saw that Tsuneo did not, in the classic sense, defy him at all. Defiance, by definition, involved some portion of fear and rebellion. Fear Hantei understood all too well, nd rebellion, he knew, required both forethought and bravery, which itself also required fear. Yet this nearly emotionless warrior ad no fear whatsoever. To contradict the Emperor was to him as asual and careless as plucking a leaf from a bush. It was incidental o his fearless indomitable character.

All his life Hantei had ruled through fear. All his afterlife Hantei ad suffered for the cruelty he'd inflicted on others, yet through it ll this Crab had been at his side, and for the first time in the five enturies he had known Tsuneo, Hantei was given pause to vonder why.

Then at last the answer came to him, and Hantei began to laugh.

9 RIGHT TO RULE

The
Twelfth
Year
of the
Reign
of
Toturi l

From a wide clearing in the Imperial forest, Emperor Toturi cast off his falcon. The bird circled, gaining height and watching. As it rose, a flock of doves took wing, fleeing the beaters that drove them out of the underbrush. The falcon stooped into a dive, accelerating quickly and slaying a dove in a splash of down.

"Very good, old friend," said Akodo Ginawa grudgingly, as he cracked a nut between his teeth.

"Excellent, my husband," concurred Empress Kaede.

"Bah," said Toturi. "That was too easy. It looked like a weak bird and perhaps not too clever, either. It strayed from the flock."

"Mm," grunted Ginawa. "Maybe. But it's still dead."

Toturi watched the rest of the flock wheel away into the sky and said nothing.

"Shall we send the beaters to the other side of the creek?" asked Ginawa nonchalantly.

"No, I tire of this sport," said Toturi, pulling off his gauntlet. He turned to his servants and said, "Set the bird free. We're going to ride to the hilltop and take in the view. Come," he said to his two companions, and the three of them cantered up the verdant slope.

As they crested the hill, they slowed the horses to a stop, dismounted, and let them graze. Toturi turned his eyes to Otosan Uchi, the capital of the Empire and the center of his life for what seemed an eternity. "So," he said, "the snows have melted and the world is renewed. I understand you have news of Hantei's answer to our ultimatum?"

"Of a sort," said Kaede, nodding. She pulled a tiny scroll from a pocket within her sleeve. "My former Clan has never seen fit to replace me as a member of the Elemental Council, and thus, as the Mistress of the Void, they keep me privy to their secrets."

Ginawa snorted. "The Empress's words are a very pretty way of saying the Phoenix pander to the throne."

"Oh, I see," chided Kaede gently, with a dancing glint in her eye. "And the pressing business of the Lion Clan that bids you to attend to the Emperor's falconry is . . . ?"

Ginawa glanced sidelong at her, and just for a moment Kaede understood how, even when he was unarmed, no one dared assail him. Then he abruptly laughed, loud and long. "Once more the expert in verbal aikido gives this poor samurai a place to lie in the grass with an excellent view of the sky."

"Subtlety was never your gift, my friend," Toturi chuckled. He turned to Kaede and asked, "What do they say?"

"It was sent to me by Tsukune," said Kaede as she unrolled the paper. "She writes, 'He is known to be in Dragon lands. The Dragon Clan hold their secrets as tight as ever, and we do not know exactly what he has been doing there. Donosu must have delivered the message about the time the first snows fell, depending on how quickly he was able to track down the Steel Charlatan.'" Kaede smiled wryly as she glanced at her husband.

"'A few weeks after,'" she continued, steadying the thin paper in the moist breeze, "'a young Dragon general took a force and tried to sneak across our southern border, near Lion lands. He was a spirit—they seem to be flocking to his side—a highly placed daimyo's son from Hantei IX or thereabouts, maybe ten years of age. There's no way he'd had more than a single campaign under his belt. No experience. Waged war like he was reading straight from his tutor's lessons on strategy.'"

"Tactics from the dawn of time?" snorted Ginawa. "The Phoenix must have crushed them."

"Not exactly, no," said Kaede, somewhat defensively. "Tsukune says here, 'Yet not all his tactics seem to have made it into the history scrolls. Most of his maneuvers were stolid and predictable, but a few were very surprising. Maybe they were common knowledge back then and have been lost over time. Plus the spirit samurai aren't plagued by illness and rashes and lice after wearing their armor for a few weeks like we are. Death and rebirth have saved them from mortal hardships. Makes me almost wish . . .'" Kaede's voice trailed off as her brow furrowed.

"Almost wish what?" asked Toturi, absently scratching the memories of fleabites from campaigns past.

"She says, er, 'Makes me almost wish I were a spirit,'" Kaede said, her voice very quiet. She glanced at Toturi again.

Toturi looked back at Kaede and have her a reassuring nod. "Almost," he said.

"What happened to the Dragon's force?" asked Ginawa, feigning not to have heard that last exchange and steering the conversation back to safer ground. Opinions to the contrary notwithstanding, he knew he had some subtlety.

"Let's see . . ." said Kaede, taking a deep breath of the year's early air. "Ah, here she says, 'He fought well on the battlefield but moved slowly on the map. Very cautious. He did little during winter, holing up in Ukabu Mura and launching a few forays to no particular effect. We raided his camps during the winter and made his forces pay. When the thaws came, he struck out again and laid siege to Nikesake—I guess to try to cut off any help the Crane might send. We sent a legion to retake Ukabu Mura and sent a cavalry force to harass his supply lines, and he withdrew back to the border. He still has a sizeable force, of course, and remains a threat. We have our army down to fight him, because his samurai fight very well. Very very well, in fact. It seems every battle we fight we lose many samurai, but we've kept the Dragon at bay.'"

Ginawa turned his head away to scratch his scalp, not because it itched but to hide the fact that he was rolling his eyes.

Toturi, arms loosely crossed, thoughtfully rubbed the edge of his kimono's collar. "How much of the Phoenix army do they have near the Dragon army?" he asked quietly, looking Kaede in the eye.

"Pretty much all of it," said Kaede, scanning the rest of the scroll. "It says she plans to taunt the Dragon out and crush him in a single massive attack. Hmm. According to this, I'd expect news of it shortly. Why?"

Toturi ceased moving, except for one eyebrow, which he slowly raised.

"Why do you ask, my husband? What's the matter?"

* * * * *

Hantei XVI, Agasha Tamori, and Hida Tsuneo stood on a high promontory in the mountains of the Dragon Clan, an excellent viewpoint from which they could survey the impenetrable stone bastion tumbling rapidly down into an empty, dry quarter of the verdant Phoenix grasslands. This particular view seemed almost like the top of the world, although behind the trio, the massive granite bulwarks rose even taller.

"There they are, my liege," said Tamori as he gestured down below, where a thin line of samurai moved through a ravine. From this distance, the collective auras of ten thousand spirit warriors fused into a single golden thread winding its way through the rugged terrain. "The vanguard should be reaching the plain shortly, with the spirit warriors close behind."

"How?" asked Tsuneo. Even from this perspective, he could see that the spirit warriors were still high up in the rocky mountains, and his eagle eye saw only vast, steep slopes of hardened rock. Even with Dragon mountaineers to guide them, he did not think his best Crab troops could reach the valley floor in less than a day, perhaps two, depending on how many soldiers he was willing to lose to accidents and falls.

"Do you see that cliff to the west of the wood?" asked Tamori.

Tsuneo scanned west from the large copse of trees. He saw a dry watercourse leading up to the base of a perfectly sheer cliff that rose to an insurmountable height. The cliff thrust out of the ground, steep and hard, as if the gods themselves had placed a wall to separate the Dragon from the Phoenix. "I see it," said Tsuneo. "It has a sharp notch near the center where there used to be a waterfall."

"That's where our forces will enter Phoenix lands," said Tamori matter-of-factly.

"Do not jest with the Emperor," said Tsuneo, as his sharp vision picked out an eagle soaring on the thermals, no more than half as high as the notch. "I saw that your vanguard brought no rope, and whatever people may say about the Dragon shugenja, I doubt they have the endurance to fly twelve thousand samurai down that far into the valley."

"Appearances can be deceiving, my good lord, and the falls are not nearly so lifeless as one might think," said Tamori with a braying laugh that twisted into a hacking cough. The shugenja pulled a kerchief from his sleeve and daubed at his mouth. As he pulled it away and quickly stowed it again, Tsuneo caught a glimpse of phlegm and blood on the material. Hantei edged slightly farther upwind of the Dragon.

"There!" said Tamori, pointing. "There they go!"

Tsuneo saw a green-and-gold samurai appear in the cliff notch, then, without hesitation, leap out of it into thin air. The Dragon fell rapidly at first, then his descent slowed gradually to much less frightening speeds. By the time his foot hit the naked boulders in the empty caldron below the dead falls, the samurai was drifting down no faster than a feather on the breeze. Quickly he scampered away.

Tsuneo blinked in disbelief. He glanced up at the notch, and saw that a score more Dragon Clan soldiers were already falling to earth, one by one, looking almost like a broken string of green and gold pearls. "I don't belie—" said Tsuneo in surprise, "no . . . I must believe it."

Tamori laughed again, more of a chuckle, which ended in only a few hacks of his tortured lungs. "It used to be a waterfall, of course," he said, "but long ago our shugenja changed it into an air-fall. The Phoenix who farmed here thought we had diverted the river, and he moved elsewhere where farming was easier. Thus we have been able to use this for hundreds of years to slip our samurai out of our lands unnoticed and spy on the Empire in the guise of ronin."

Tamori turned to Hantei, bowed, and said, "Not in the thousand years of the Empire has anyone outside the Clan seen this. Never has any Emperor known such a thing existed. I hope that this shall show to you the depth of our devotion to you and your cause."

Hantei flicked his fan open over his mouth. "It is a good start," he said, "but unconditional support requires unconditional openness. I shall trust the depth of your commitment to the extent you divulge yourselves and shall trust you completely only when you have shown me all of your secrets."

Tamori smiled, though his protesting muscles made it more of a leer. "As you wish, my Emperor. However, the war would long be over before I could hope to show you everything. Now, we should join our forces." He clapped his hands, and tattooed monks ascended to their position, four of them bearing Hantei's palanquin and one other leading mountain donkeys for Tamori and Tsuneo.

The burly, bare-chested monks bore Hantei over the mountainous terrain as smoothly as if he were afloat on the Imperial barge. Tamori rode discreetly behind Hantei, while the narrowness of the path forced Tsuneo to ride in front.

As they moved down the defile, Hantei called back, asking, "This pass you have shown me is excellent. I take it then you have found a way to achieve my ambition?"

"Yes, my liege," said Tamori. "The Phoenix consider this area impassable and believe that the reach of the Dragon Clan ends a few days' march to the west. We will move quickly across the northern portion of their holdings, through the northern edge of the Isawa Woodlands. The Phoenix and Crane spirits with us will enter the Castle of the Faithful Bride, which, with your august presence, we should be able to capture without a sword being drawn.

"We will garrison the castle with a handful of spirits. The bulk of our group will take the 'valuables' you mentioned with us as we march south and take Isawa castle in much the same way. Meanwhile, our second group is striking east from their position. They will move straight to Asako Castle to cut the supply lines to Shiba Tsukune's army. They will use similar infiltration tactics, and then send the bulk of their force and that city's valuables. The two armies should meet at Shiba Castle at the same time. Thus we shall hold the major castles and rendezvous at the capitol with ample . . . persuasion."

"And to the south?" asked Hantei.

"Our army is acquitting themselves well. Their soldiers are making the Phoenix pay dearly for every victory. Too many more of these victories, and the Phoenix will have lost. I believe Tsukune sees that and thus has sent her entire army to face our troops. I have ordered them to withdraw, to lead Tsukune away from the real threat. We shall face no real opposition."

"Excellent," said Hantei, and he laid back and relaxed, watching the stone walls of the ravine glide past his window. He passed the time peacefully, thinking of the horrors he would visit upon all who had opposed him when once again he sat upon the throne. Then the palanquin stopped, and he heard Tsuneo's donkey braying.

"He won't jump," growled the irritated Crab as he dismounted.

"He does not have the discipline of our samurai," said Tamori. We'll have to abandon the donkeys and walk from here."

Tsuneo glowered at Tamori, picked up the animal, and heaved it over the precipice as it screamed in panic. "Walk yourself," he said, as he stepped out into the open air.

Tamori was left standing on the edge of the cliff, listening to Hantei's laughter recede as the monks and palanquin soared to the earth, far below.

* * * * *

"Well," said Shiba Tsukune tensely, "we said we figured the war would be over by now."

"We did indeed, my lady," said her aide.

Tsukune looked about at the plains in which her army was camped, at the wildflowers that bloomed despite the lingering winter chill. "And we were right," she said glumly. "How fitting, then, that it ends here, on the Prophet's Plain." Her stomach growled. Her hair was matted from an extensive campaign followed by a forced march across her Clan's holdings. And for what? She sighed and said, "I must go."

Without waiting for a reply, she picked up her helmet, tucked it under her arm, and began to walk across the plain to the enemy encampment. Golden-ringed samurai pickets stood guard in ancient armor and let her pass without challenge.

In the heart of the spirit army stood a command post that looked like nothing so much as an open-air throne room. Hantei XVI sat upon the Shiba Throne, which had been dragged here from Shiba castle and set on a high stage. Around him stood an inordinate number of attendants, and a score of guards knelt at the front of the stage, long spears leveled at Tsukune's heart. Flags and banners fluttered in the breeze, all marked with the steel chrysanthemum. And, of course, Hida Tsuneo stood at Hantei's right hand, and each of Tsuneo's great callused hands rested lightly on the shoulder of a small child.

She knew the children. One was her own Aikune, the other his friend Yaruko. Tsukune saw that Tsuneo's thumbs rested on the other side of the children's necks. The Stone Crab could kill the children as easily as a farmer kills a chicken.

Tsukune concealed her emotion as she walked up to Hantei. At a safe distance from the spears, she knelt down and touched her head to the ground. "Great Emperor Hantei XVI, I have come to offer my surrender," she said simply. "I ask that the Emperor deal mercifully with my troops, for they have only served the orders of their leader." She sat back on her heels and awaited his judgment.

Hantei paused, savoring the moment, then said, "I do not want your surrender, Shiba," he said kindly, "for samurai need not surrender to the rightful Emperor. I merely want your service."

He reached out and took Yaruko's hand and drew the girl to his side. "I trust that you will have the same wisdom that your subordinates had. It was a very easy choice for them, you know. I entered Isawa castle as a guest, and my simple recitation of facts persuaded them that the future of their family depended upon the Emperor. Is that not always the case?" Here he slid his hand to Yaruko's neck, and pressed his thumb into the pressure point behind the girl's ear.

"Then I went to Shiba castle, and the citizens there agreed that one family cannot pursue their destiny by abandoning the needs of the other families of the Clan. Thus was their future prosperity tied to the future of the rest of the Clan, in much the same way as the different cords of a rope all share the same fate, for better or for worse. So now I turn to you, the rightful daimyo of the Phoenix. Your future is at my side, serving my needs. Is that not always the duty of a samurai? And is it not just and fitting that the future prosperity of your Clan should rise and fall based upon the vigilance and devotion with which you serve the ruler of your Empire?" Hantei's hand tightened even more, and Yaruko gave a little involuntary squeak of pain.

"My Emperor is both gracious and just," said Tsukune evenly as she bowed again. "How may I be of service to him who rules at the delight of the heavens?"

"Excellent," Hantei said. "Even the mortals turn to their true Emperor. I have the Crab, the Dragon, and now the Phoenix. You, Shiba, shall go to Otosan Uchi and prepare my way, for by the time I get there, my fist shall have struck."

10

HIDING IN PLAIN SIGHT

The
Twelfth
Year
of the
Reign
of
Toturi I

Respect," said Toturi. "Utmost respect and perfect etiquette."

"Your judgment is ever sound, my Emperor," said Toku, "but . . . he will try to have you killed."

"Yes, he will," said Toturi, "and so, in his own way, did the thirty-ninth of his line. But we cannot prove his intentions. Not yet. There are only rumors and no evidence, so until he tries, we cannot dishonor him and ourselves with ungrounded accusations.

"We issued the Imperial decree, and it is only proper that a person of his standing should come to Otosan Uchi to accept my order and obey it in person. Therefore, we shall accord him respect, honor, and deference—all that is due to an aged parent, an ancestor, or, well, for lack of better words, a dowager Emperor."

Emperor Toturi paused, and then a knowing smile crossed his face. "See to it, however, that Kakita Yoshi writes the greeting," he said, "for sometimes brush and parchment cut deeper than a blade."

* * * * *

Twenty thousand samurai marched south toward Otosan Uchi under a bewildering array of banners and flags. They were a parade, an honor guard for his Imperial Highness the Emperor Hantei XVI, an escort comprised of spirit samurai from each of the Great Clans. A few brooding Crab stalked along in their dark and bitter blues and reds, artfully placed at a distance from the nonchalant Crane in their pale blue and silver. The war over the Yasuki lands had ground to a bitter stalemate, and both sides hoped to curry favor with the Hantei Emperor so that he would decree for the claims of their Clan.

Dragon samurai in their gold and green made the core of the parade, and tawny Lions were the vanguard. Phoenix and Scorpion were present, the Phoenix in fiery reds and oranges, and the Scorpion in their darker, bloodier colors. Proud and cocky Unicorn cavalry flanked the entire column; in this way Hantei gave them the illusion that they were part of the group, without actually letting them march on the same road. He had never dealt with Unicorns as Emperor, and he had no intention of starting now. All of the various Clans, with their various colors and styles, were gathered together by the force of will of the Hantei and unified by a single golden halo that washed the entire assemblage.

To their great annoyance, the Mantis spirit samurai were not included in this group. Hantei XVI refused to acknowledge "the desperate, weak-willed acquiescence" that had led to their elevation as a Great Clan. If they were a minor Clan when he first ruled the Empire, a minor Clan they would remain.

There were, of course, no mortals. Mortals could not march as far, as fast, or with so little food and water.

The entire entourage moved swiftly and confidently toward the Imperial capital. Even if one ignored everything else suspicious about this escort—their numbers, their weapons, their battle armor, the speed of their movement—the lack of courtiers would prove to any observer that this was no pompous retinue. This was an army masquerading as a procession.

Of course, the spirits in the army knew all this. Rumors circulated among them as they walked, springing primarily from Hantei's Imperial palanquin and spreading among the troops like ripples in a pond. It was of course forbidden to eavesdrop on Hantei's conversations, but he spoke loudly enough that the troops could not help but hear. He intended them to hear. It helped their morale and taught them how foresighted he was. They, in turn, would spread the rumors as "inspired speculation," therewith ensuring that they never admitted that they might have overheard something. As with so much surrounding the Emperor, the proper form was more important than the actual results.

With the sun lowering over the Spine of the World, Hantei's retinue halted some distance away from Otosan Uchi. The steady beats of feet and rumors were quickly replaced with the sounds of troops turning a random piece of roadside land into a well-guarded camp.

"Are we on schedule?" asked Hantei lazily through the slatted doors of his palanquin.

"Yes, my Emperor," said Tsuneo. "We are even ahead of schedule. We are not expected until morning, a day and a half from now. Tomorrow shall be a very easy march."

"Excellent," said Hantei loudly, as he stepped from his carriage. He stood, stretched, then fixed Tsuneo with his steely glance. "Give this order to the cavalry," he said. "Tell them to locate all the scouts sent to watch our movements. Tell them to talk with them, be friendly, and relax. I need to get those stinking, purple, skin-wearing horse-riders out of my camp," he added with a whisper. "They vex me.

"Give the troops here a chance to eat and rest also," he added, looking at the military bustle all around. "Wait until all the glimmer from the sunset is gone and the stars appear brightly just over the mountains. Then we shall ring the gong as our signal. At that time, the Unicorn are to slaughter the enemy scouts without warning. They should have no problem with that; they're a barbaric, honorless, half-bred people, anyway. But not one scout is to get away. I want no word of our doings to reach Otosan Uchi before we do.

"I want the whole army to break camp and be ready to move before the gong stops ringing. We march through the night and reach Otosan Uchi at midmorning tomorrow."

"That will be a hard march," said Tsuneo, "a very hard pace with no breaks."

Hantei turned his head slowly toward Tsuneo and looked at him with haughty disdain. "You trouble me with these mewling complaints for a reason?"

"I do not complain, my lord. I just point out that the army will not be in the best condition for a fight immediately after such a march."

"And here I thought you might have concern for my good sleep as the bearers trot along," Hantei said snidely. He waved a dismissive hand. "No, we shall not need to fight," he said. "We shall simply occupy. By the time we reach Otosan Uchi, we shall be welcomed in."

"How is that, my Emperor?" asked the Crab, genuinely curious. There was also a tinge of concern in his voice, although Hantei misunderstood its implication.

"Not to worry, my dear Tsuneo. The Shiba who thinks she's a Matsu is not the only secret blade at my disposal. Tomorrow morning, the pretender's servants will find him mysteriously slain."

"You mean Toturi?" asked Tsuneo, concern again edging his voice and creasing his brow. "How will this happen?"

"I have sent the very best of the ninja to take care of him and his criminal claim to my throne. Come morning his head will be discovered at the foot of the throne, spiked for display with a tag that reads, FIRST OF THE TRAITORS WHO TURNED THE EMPIRE AWAY FROM ITS GODS. FIRST TO DIE AND MEET THEIR JUDGMENT. It will be arrayed so that his face will be the first I see when I sit upon the throne.

"There will be great panic, of course, and if my study of recent history has taught me anything, it is that the Clans will therefore vie for the throne, and one of the daimyos will move to claim it. The Shiba wench will kill anyone who tries for it. She will also use her intimacy with the pretender's concubine to keep her from claiming it on behalf of their children.

"Then, at that moment I shall arrive with this honor guard. The city shall welcome me, as I shall bring immediate peace to their crisis. Instead of the Great Clans warring over Otosan Uchi to see who shall next steal the throne, I shall present them with the Great Clans unified in support of the true Hantei Emperor. I shall sit upon the throne, I shall see that the people have already presented me with the head of my enemy, and I shall proclaim a weeklong celebration of the return of the true Emperor. This celebration will commence with the capture, confession, and torture of the pretender's children and end with their deaths on the seventh day, assuming they aren't weak little whelps who die sooner."

"Then," said Tsuneo grimly, "all of Rokugan shall understand the power of the Emperor and enjoy the mercy of your rule as they did in days of old."

"Precisely," said Hantei licking his lips with a lascivious smile. "Now see to my orders."

As Tsuneo stalked away, Hantei gazed at the fiery rays of the sunset. They cascaded through the sky like a great glowing silk sliced by the monstrous blades of the mountains. "See there!" proclaimed Hantei loudly, reaching forth with one hand, and all noise in the camp ceased. "The sun sets with the colors of fire and blood, war and rebirth! I say that this is an omen marking the end of a travesty, and that tomorrow the sun shall rise with the golden glow of the spirits reborn and herald a new era for Rokugan! Let fire and blood mark the end of days and steel and gold mark the new dawn!"

So saying, Hantei smiled and listened to the echoes of the cheers roll across the plains like thunder.

* * * * *

It was the darkest time past the middle of the night, and all through Otosan Uchi, only a handful of samurai guards were still awake. The moon shone brightly in the firmament, its light glistening on the ocean's waves. A lone nighthawk swept the sky, its forlorn cry accented by the sound of the distant surf.

A black shadow moved through the Imperial gardens. Human, clad head to toe in soft linen, the shadow was quiet as thought and deliberate as a sprouting seed. Slowly it moved, gliding unnoticed down the paths and across the rocks. The shadow neared the wall separating the Imperial garden from the castle's courtyard and stopped to reconnoiter. So unmoving was it that a small field mouse snuffled and scuttled along its way, not noticing that it passed between the shadow's legs.

Soon a single samurai could be heard slowly walking his post along the far side of the wall, the slight creak and clink of his armor providing counterpoint to the steady fall of his sandaled feet on the fine-grained sand. As the sound of the samurai drew even with the shadow's position, the ninja moved as fast and silent as a tiger.

He sprinted, then tumbled up the wall like a whirling spider and over the other side. In an instant the ninja had landed behind the samurai guard, a garrote around the guard's neck. The surprised samurai clutched at his throat, unable to cry out. The ninja quickly scanned the courtyard for any other guards, arms quivering with the strain of holding the wire taut as the guardsman writhed in agony. It was clear.

Abruptly the ninja struck the guard at the base of the skull just behind the ear, then quickly twisted the guard's head and broke his neck. He slowly lowered the guard to the ground. He uncoiled the garrote with a swift flick of the wrist, and in the blink of an eye it was concealed again.

He scampered across the courtyard in a crouching gait, sideways like a scuttling crab, and all but vanished into a dark corner of the palace's exterior wall. He slid a dart from its place on the back of his glove and placed it on his tongue, ready to spit. As he did so, his other hand pulled three shuriken from his belt. Then, using his feet and his free hand for traction, he pushed himself up the angle of the palace wall.

The ninja climbed easily up until the outstretched eaves of the roof barred his further progress. Being now completely nestled in shadows, he slipped the shuriken back into his belt. His soft-soled boots had a separate notch for his big toe, giving him more dexterity with his feet, which he now put to good use. Holding himself up with just his hands, he kicked at his own ankles with a swift move of each foot, and there, slung between his big toes and secured by knots around each ankle, was a thin cord. Even through the fabric of his boots, the ninja could feel the small spikes imbedded in the cord; they would be very necessary for his next step.

He listened to the wistful *peent, peent* of the nighthawk, and attuned himself to its rhythm, embracing the way of the nighthawk. Then, in one fluid move, he pushed himself up with his arms and kicked out with his legs, extending himself so far that his hands left the wall. As they did so, he swung his arms down and his feet up, slinging the cord over one of the round beams that stuck artfully out from beneath the eaves above him. As his body fell, the spiked cord slipped down the beam, then, just as gravity had the ninja firmly in its grip, the tiny barbs dug into the smooth, polished wood.

With the added weight, the beam creaked slightly just as the nighthawk cried again. The two small noises blended into one. The ninja pinwheeled his arms once to negate his pendular motion, then hung from the beam for a moment like a great black bat.

He saw the guard's corpse several stories below him, but no one else moved in the courtyard. Satisfied, the ninja pulled himself up using the loop around his ankles and peered over the edge of the sloped roof, poking his head to one side and then the other of one of the ornate carved dragons that decorated the palace. He slid onto the rooftop and stowed his ankle loop with a quick flurry of feet and toes.

He slithered to the walls of one of the palace's pagoda towers and drew up in the moon's shadow. He pulled climbing claws from his belt and slipped them over each hand. He started climbing one of the outer corners of the tower, quietly working his way up with his thumbs providing counterpressure for the claws, and his feet gripping froglike on either wall, supporting his weight.

He counted the floors as he climbed and stopped at the fourth. He rocked to the right and left a few times, looking like a praying mantis stalking a meal, then, as he rocked to the right, he lashed out to the right with his left heel. His heel barely caught the sill of a window, and he let his body fall, controlling his speed and angle by rapidly braking his momentum with his hands, right foot, and head. As quiet as a scrabbling mouse, perhaps even quieter, he came to a stop, hanging by his heel from the sill.

Perhaps it was not the most efficient grip for entering the fourth floor, but the window he wanted was the one below him.

He took off his claws and secured them in his waistband, then stretched his arms down toward the ground, pressing them gently on the stone. He released his grip with his heel, let gravity roll him down, and as he completed his flip, his feet landed lightly on the sill below. With preternatural speed, his hands flew forward to catch the underside of the window's top, he thrust his feet through the window, and landed like a cat with shuriken in one hand, a pitch-covered blade in the other, and the poison dart still in his mouth. His head whipped back and forth, but the room was not occupied.

With a flicker of fingers, the ninja reversed his grip on his blade and concealed it behind his sleeve. He flipped his shuriken so that two rested between his second, third, and pinky finger, and the other rested between his first finger and thumb. This left his first finger relatively free to open the panel doors as he moved through the palace.

He scanned the room by the moonlight that filtered through the windows. A low writing table, ink brushes, paper, and other oddments indicated that this was a study. One wall was wood, which was a mark of wealth; the others, as expected, were rice-paper panels. The ninja's expert eye saw that there was only one sliding door to this room. He suspected there might be a secret door in the wooden wall, but he did not have the time to investigate. Even if he did, the chance that a trap or a spell protected the door was a very real and hazardous possibility.

The ninja padded with utter silence across the room. He paused as he heard the noise of a cricket somewhere up ahead, chirping its monotone song to the darkness. He paused and paced his heart to the cricket's song. He would have to be the cricket's rhythm if he were to be able to pass by the insect guardian. He refocused his chi until he and the cricket were one, living in the same world. Then he slowly and evenly removed the dart from his mouth and placed a small whistle between his lips.

He raised the hand with the shuriken to the panel door and slid one deadly blade between the door and the wall. One thousand chirps, he thought, is an auspicious count for us. Is that not right, cricket?

As slowly as a snail, he turned the shuriken like a key, wedging the door open. As the blade reached the limit of its reach, he rolled his wrist into the gap and pressed the door wider, bracing his hand against the wall. One thousand chirps later, the door was open as wide as the ninja's hand was long—just enough room for him to slide through.

He passed through and found himself in the intersection of three corridors. He ignored the hallways that extended to his left and right, for the Emperor always slept in the chambers in the center of the tower. The ninja knew well that Toturi scrupulously followed the dictates of tradition.

The hallway ahead of the ninja was wider than the others, and held a variety of treasures from the Empire's past—gifts to the Emperor throughout the ages. Somewhere among all the priceless artifacts was a small cricket—the ninja's most hated enemy, but this ninja knew the way of the cricket.

He flowed like water across the hallway and slid behind a pedestal upon which rested a water pitcher, crafted by Lady Doji herself, at the dawn of the Empire. As he slid through the small gap between the pedestal and the wall, the ninja noticed that the rear of the vase had been broken open, probably during one of Otosan Uchi's earthquakes, but the display artfully concealed the damage.

The ninja continued, passing behind a rack that held the honored swords of each of the Emerald Champions from Hantei the ninth through Hantei the fifteenth. For some reason, the sixteenth Hantei had not continued this particular tradition, and no one had wished to insult that choice by reinstating the tradition afterwards.

Just as the ninja was leaving the cover of the swords, the cricket stopped chirping, somehow sensing with its tiny insect brain that danger was near at hand. No matter how much a ninja trained to sneak past human guards, nothing a ninja could do could get past a cricket's guard. A cricket's silence was louder to a daimyo's guards than a horn on the battlefield.

The trick, therefore, was not to fool the cricket, but to fool the humans that might be alarmed if the cricket stopped chirping. Seamlessly the ninja began chirping with the small whistle in his mouth, keeping pace with his own heart. He was a cricket, cheerfully chirping away the signal that all was well. He was a cricket, now slipping past an ancient suit of full battle armor. Idly the ninja wondered if the cricket was inside that armor, questioning what this imposter was doing chirping his song. He glanced briefly at the intricate scales on the armor's skirt, then moved on to the Emperor's door, just ahead.

* * * * *

Since he was passing behind the armor, the ninja did not see the skull inside the ancient, ornate helmet, nor the ghastly grin on the skull's face. There was a reason that Akodo Godaigo kept a cricket inside his empty rib cage, and that reason was for moments just like this.

With a speed and perfection born of five hundred years of tireless practice, Godaigo drew his katana in a singing arc, his head turning to guide the blade even as it began its deadly descent. The ninja reacted with inhuman speed, raising his shuriken and lashing out with a backwards slash of his blackened blade, but the poisoned edge merely traced a useless gouge along Godaigo's dry arm bone.

Godaigo's katana struck the ninja where the breastbone meets the collarbone, sliced its way through the rib cage, and cut through the backbone at the lumbar curve. Godaigo stopped the blade a hand's breadth from a three hundred-year-old painted tapestry as the halves of the ninja slumped to the floor. Godaigo could see the ninja's shocked eyes and gaping mouth despite the otherwise all-concealing mask.

Shimmering golden blood pumped itself onto the polished wood. Once he was convinced no other ninja were nearby, Godaigo pulled the ninja's hood off. He noticed that the ninja's skin also showed the all-too-familiar spirit aura. As he wiped his blade on the ninja's hood, the skeletal samurai pondered the ninja's ability to hide his aura.

The Emperor's door slid open, and Toturi stood on guard with his sword, Kaede behind him ready to strike with her magic. Surprised by the sudden motion, Godaigo also leveled his sword toward Toturi but quickly recovered and bowed.

The Emperor looked at the corpse, looked at Godaigo's gold-stained sword, then turned to his wife. "I told you we didn't have to get up," he murmured. "Good night, Godaigo."

The skeleton bowed and closed the door behind his liege. In the depths of his soul, a new haiku joined the thousand of others Godaigo had composed over his existence, haiku that would remain in his heart, unheard and unwritten.

> Death is a secret
> Masks, magic, shadows and lies
> Truth is a sharp sword

11   YOUR LIFE IS MINE

The
Twelfth
Year
of the
Reign
of
Toturi I

Tsuneo raised his eyebrows slightly, for there were no signs of war or panic in Otosan Uchi. It was the first time the Stone Crab had seen a strategic plan of the Hantei do anything other than succeed, and he was determined that no sign of his emotion might leak through his face. Raising his eyebrows was a safe expression, especially as the steady drumming of irritated nails inside the palanquin was clearly audible to him.

Although it was midmorning, there was no noise of fighting in the streets, no thin columns of smoke rising up from any of the buildings, no roiling sound of panicked or worried civilians, and no hint of anything other than slight boredom in the voices of the gate guards on the walls above as they awaited the arrival of an officer.

"I do not like this at all," spat Hantei.

"Perhaps they expected this turn and are accepting the death of Toturi in stride," observed Tsuneo quietly.

"Even so," said Hantei, "their calm robs me of the triumphal parade that is my right! The Empire must see a pageant of power so it will truly understand that a Hantei sits upon the throne again!"

"Most honorable Hantei," called the newly arrived officer from atop the gate, "my name is Toku. The City of Otosan Uchi welcomes you on behalf of the Empire. We will gladly admit your august self, as well as two dozen honor guards of your choosing."

"Two dozen!" hissed Hantei.

"I guess your show of force will have to remain outside," said Tsuneo drily.

"Tell him—" began Hantei, but Tsuneo already knew the request.

"The Emperor has the right to whatever protection he desires," boomed Tsuneo in his powerful voice.

"Yes," nodded Toku simply. His direct answer quite neatly side-stepped the question of whether or not Hantei XVI was the Emperor and therefore put the spirits at a disadvantage. Simply having to argue that Hantei was the Emperor would itself be an insult to the Hantei.

"The Emperor's Guard—" began Tsuneo, gesturing to the army behind him.

"Ah! Yes!" said Toku brightly. "The Imperial Palace Guard stands ready to honor the Hantei's procession to the throne room!"

The throne *room*, thought Tsuneo, not just the throne. This was going to be an interesting day. Having no further honorable grounds for dissent, Tsuneo glanced over his shoulder at Agasha Tamori, who nodded and began choosing his twelve best Dragon samurai. The other spirit samurai stood aside, and Tsuneo and twelve Dragon Clan spirits escorted Hantei's palanquin forward. The gate opened slowly, and the small troop moved into Otosan Uchi.

Hantei's chair moved along the Road of the Most High, an ele-vated causeway reserved for the sole use of the Emperor himself. Tsuneo rode at Hantei's immediate left, also on the Road of the Most High. The honor guard of Dragon samurai walked alongside the palanquin to the right, on the public path that paced the Emperor's Way.

Along both sides of the road, it looked as if the entire Imperial Palace Guard had been turned out. Samurai in the Imperial green and gold stood in a single rank, clad in their finest armor, their long naginatas glittering in the morning sun. They stood as still and silent as stone. Tsuneo nodded sagely. In his day, the Imperial Guard had been a joke. It seemed that the current general had toughened them up. They might almost be able to handle a day or two on the Wall, fighting alongside the Crab against the nightmares that assaulted the great bastion.

Tsuneo heard Hantei's sniff of contempt and the continued drumming of polished nails on lacquered wood. Hantei was not pleased at all. He had wanted to be the returning glory of Rokugan. He had wanted his army to be a symbol of authority, moving through streets fraught with paranoia and fear. Instead, his army waited outside, and the impassive guards stood watch—no cheers, no welcome, no heartfelt swearing of fealty. In fact—

Tsuneo's eyes narrowed. The Palace Guard was standing watch. They were facing the Road of the Most High, not facing away. They were not honoring Hantei by facing outward, protecting him against any threat. They were guarding him, protecting the Heart of the Empire from its latest visitor. It was a subtle difference, one only rarely seen, inasmuch as everyone usually bowed to the ground as the Emperor passed. In times of danger, the guards were not allowed to bow, for bowing made them slower to react. But that order was only used in times of danger.

Or war . . .

As Hantei had foretold, today's sun had dawned on a new era, and Tsuneo had no idea what shape that era would take by the end of the day. He felt the adrenaline pump into his system, felt the tremored edge of impending battle. He began counting the guards they passed. Oh, yes, this would be an interesting day indeed.

* * * * *

The palanquin moved steadily up the Road of the Most High. Inside, Hantei kept the slatted windows closed. Some Emperors opened their window to survey their domain, but Hantei would never stoop to feigning affection for his people. He thought such ideals made weaklings of great Emperors. Like his father.

The small group processed through the inner city and into the Imperial palace grounds. They wound their way through the gardens to one of the many gates. There, according to custom, the Emperor debarked and entered the palace itself.

Hantei looked about and saw that each room and corridor had servants, courtiers, guards, and others of their ilk—nameless and faceless peons in the Emperor's eyes. As he passed, they bowed deeply . . . though not quite deeply enough. I will have to kill them all, Hantei thought, and get a new staff that shows proper respect. But first I must sit upon my throne and show the world that I am the Emperor and I rule all there is to rule.

He stalked through the palace, Hida Tsuneo one pace to his left and a half pace behind, the Dragon samurai fanned out to both sides and the rear. Every juncture had at least two armed guards in it, arrayed as the others in their dress armor. Hantei's haughty eye did not notice that the samurai guarded every hall and turn, nor that pains had been taken to demonstrate their vigilance and thoroughness. The show of force was, for the moment, lost on Hantei.

At last the group reached the Imperial throne room. Hantei salivated with impatience. He had been steadily working toward this moment for eight years, apprehending all the Empire's changes, waiting for Toturi's popularity to wane as his heroic stand at Oblivion's Gate faded from immediate memory. He had undermined Toturi's popularity by insinuation and sabotage, seized control of the Crab wealth, sealed the fate of the Phoenix, and taken the Dragon's soul. All the while he had been building his support among the spirits, wedging his words into the small cracks of misunderstanding, twisting truths and perceptions, until, like him, spirits all over the Empire used "we" and "they" to divide the generations. They began looking on mortals as the enemy, and Hantei fueled the fire whenever he could.

"How can they truly understand us," he had once said, "unless they experience what we have experienced? Killing them is not wrong. It simply educates them as it has all of us. They should consider it a favor."

And it all came down to this moment. He was about to take the throne. His first actions upon the throne would color his rule forever after. He never stopped to reflect on whether he was truly prepared to make the most of it.

The servants opened the doors for Hantei and his retinue, and as they began to swing open, Hantei saw Toturi, in all his Imperial splendor, seated on the throne. The Hantei sneered, baring his incisors like a wolf. "You're supposed to be dead!" he whispered, greatly affronted that his order—to say nothing of Toturi—had not been properly executed.

Toturi glanced at his golden-haloed hand, and rubbed his thumb and fingers together briefly. "I was," he answered quietly.

The doors finished swinging open, and an Imperial courtier cried, "His Imperial Highness Emperor Toturi I, sole ruler of Rokugan, chosen leader of the Clans, righteous defender of justice, soul of the Empire, light of the dawn, and destroyer of the shadow is pleased to open his court and bids welcome to all visitors. The Emperor, who avenged the honor of all of the Hanteis by slaying the vile god Fu Leng, the great foul beast that devoured the last rightful Hantei Emperor thus ending their dynasty for all time, is delighted to grant an audience.

"May the Emperor and his court be pleased, the former Hantei Emperor, the sixteenth of that historic dynasty, who yielded the throne to his son and therewith ingratiated himself with all the peoples of Rokugan, who has since been thrust against his will out of the lands of the dead, and who has toured the Empire and seen firsthand the beneficence of Emperor Toturi, comes now to pay honor and respect to the ruler of this great Empire and to see the palace for one last time before he obeys the Emperor's inviolate decree and travels to the Jumping Place, thereby to return to his proper position in the Celestial Order as a duly revered ancestor residing in Jigoku."

The introductions done, silence fell upon the court, though the courtier's words still rang in Hantei's ears. Hantei stood in the doorway, his hateful hooded eyes locked with Toturi's expressionless gaze. For many long breaths, neither of them moved; neither was willing to make any bow or nod without the other moving first. At last Hantei realized that he had to make the first move. Toturi sat unmoving on the throne, goading him—a Hantei!—

with his puppet herald's slanderous lies. The longer he let Toturi sit there, the more difficult it became to retain the moral high ground.

A slight tremor rattled the palace, causing the rice-paper doors to tremble slightly in their moorings.

Hantei seized the moment, tore his eyes away, and looked at the others arrayed near Toturi the Pretender. To Toturi's right stood a Crane spirit, wreathed in a golden halo and arrayed in a luxurious court kimono—presumably a close advisor. Next to him in turn stood the daimyos of the Lion, the Unicorn, and an arrogant man who flaunted the mon of the Mantis as if it were a Great Clan. To Toturi's left, curiously enough, was the Shiba daimyo, and next to her the daimyos of the Scorpion and Crane. Last on that side stood a Crab diplomat, which so far as Hantei was concerned, meant a Crab who could speak intelligibly of things other than war.

All of the daimyos were in their most ornate battle armor and armed with the samurai's daisho: katana and wakizashi. Of course, no one wore a helmet. To do so in Imperial Court would be unthinkable. Hantei hazarded a second glance at Shiba Tsukune and saw the fear in her eyes. His eyes narrowed ever so slightly with pleasure.

Behind the daimyos and to one side stood the whore who called herself Empress, along with her three bratty children. They would have to die, but first, their father had to surrender his throne and be tortured to death. His very presence and the loyalty for which he bribed the Empire had forced Hantei to live as a common samurai and connive his way, twisting words and stabbing backs, to this place where he could once again take the throne. Oh, the inconveniences he had put up with. He wanted his power, his staff of attentive servants, and a plethora of pretty young men and women to maim when he was under a malaise and needed cheering.

As Hantei finished surveying the room, a look of gracious tranquility came over his features. "The Emperor thanks all of you for keeping this throne room presentable and thanks the steward for guarding the throne so carefully," he purred. "There is no more need for your presence. You may step down now."

"My steward stepped down eight years ago," said Toturi. "His name was Takuan. You may have met him in Jigoku . . . but then again, perhaps not. I have needed no steward since."

"You are gravely mistaken," said Hantei, his voice gaining an edge as he gestured towards Kitsu Motso. "A steward still holds your seat in the Lion Clan. The Emerald Throne, however, belongs to the Hantei."

"The Emerald Throne was destroyed by Fu Leng, along with the last of your dynasty. This is the Jade Throne, which I had carved for my coronation."

"Only a fool crowns himself Emperor."

"Well spoken," said Toturi, with a challenging look.

"I was appointed Emperor by the sun and the moon and their children, the gods," Hantei retorted.

"Neither did I choose this seat," said Toturi. "Your offspring left me no choice, and fate delivered me to this place."

"At times, fate makes grave errors like that, letting a common samurai like you foul the throne with your directionless soul and unwashed hands! Fate has now redeemed its error and has returned a rightful Hantei heir to Rokugan," snarled Hantei.

"I will agree that fate makes grave mistakes," said Toturi.

"Get off my throne, or I shall have you tortured and cast into the Shadowlands to wander forever in agony!"

"No."

"You are clearly a bandit, for no true Emperor would ever allow anyone to carry weapons in his presence," said Hantei.

"I allow it, because there may be need of them," said Toturi levelly. "I trust my people. Do you?"

"Your trust shall be your undoing, vagrant! You! And you!" barked Hantei, gesturing at Kitsu Motso and Moto Gaheris, the Lion and Unicorn daimyos. "Seize him!"

No one moved . . . until Gaheris casually reached up, picked at his teeth for a moment, studied the result, then flicked whatever it was in the direction of Hantei.

Hantei's eyes flashed hot and cold for a few moments. He hated these conspirators and their arrogance. But Tsuneo was one man against five daimyos, a self-proclaimed Emperor, and his witch wife, who, if rumors were true, was a terrifying shugenja. Yes, Hantei had twelve Dragon spirits at his side, but Toturi had hundreds of palace guards. Never before had Hantei been so powerless in this room, and he loathed the feeling. His soul ached to have that power back, yet once before he had been in roughly this same position. He'd had to overthrow his own father and do it without the unstoppable power of the throne to back him up. He'd learned then how to use what he had. And what he had here was his superior intellect.

Hantei's tone became smooth as silk as he glided along the floor of the throne room. "So you . . . what was your name again? Ah, yes, Toturi. You claim to have issued a decree that all spirits should return to Jigoku, hm?"

"I *claim* nothing. I *did* issue the decree."

"And these spirits, what makes you think you can order them around?" Hantei said, twiddling a hand. He glided through the daimyos, between Motso and Gaheris, and noted that they did indeed step aside to let him pass. "They are the ancestors of everyone, and all owe respect and deference to them. Does a child order about his own father?"

"Does anyone defy the Emperor?" answered Toturi. "Even an Emperor's own mother, who bore him and suckled him, obeys his decrees."

Hantei's gait stiffened for the blink of an eye, and he covered the lapse by changing his course to one of the windows of the throne room. He stopped at the sill and gazed out at the city—his city!—with a curled lip.

"My Emperor," said Kakita Yoshi, bowing deeply, "have I completed all the assignments that the throne requires of me?"

Toturi turned to his advisor and said, "My friend, you have done all that the throne has required and more. My thanks for your guidance and wisdom over the years. May you find the peace that you have brought into my life."

How weak, thought Hantei, to be that attached to anyone, especially an advisor. Such limpid affection could slow one's hand when an advisor needed to be killed. Nevertheless, his curiosity was piqued, and he turned to look. Yoshi's spirit halo accented his kimono perfectly. His hair was immaculate. The Crane bowed deeply again, turned, and left the throne room. Hantei saw him pause at the door and bow to Tsuneo, murmuring some courtly platitude.

Tsuneo exchanged a glance with Hantei as Yoshi's kimono swished quietly down the polished wooden hallway.

Toturi exhaled heavily, and turned to Kakita Kaiten. "It is a proud day for the Crane," he said. "Let everyone know that your Clan will not mourn alone."

"I see that even your advisor—a spirit—can no longer follow a mere pretender to the Hantei birthright," said Hantei.

Kaiten glared at Hantei but said nothing. Then Kaiten bowed to Toturi, stepped back, and crossed to one of the windows, one a safe distance away from the window at which Hantei stood.

"You see, my pathetic little ronin," said Hantei, looking out at the sprawling city of Otosan Uchi, "all people owe deference to their ancestors. We ancestors gave you your name, your honor, and a proud heritage to live up to. We sired you, bore you, fed you, raised you, and trained you. And you think you owe us nothing? Quite the contrary."

Toturi stepped off the throne and moved toward Hantei, the daimyos following him closely. "I should think you'd be used to such treatment," he said. "Your own son—the one you didn't have executed, that is—killed you for tarnishing the honor that was his birthright."

"My son did not know what honor was," growled Hantei.

"Then by your argument, if you gave him his name, his honor, and everything else, you had no honor to give. Is that not so?"

Hantei laughed. "Now I understand how you can delude the world into believing that a dishonored ronin should sit upon the throne above everyone. You are excellent at wordplay, for you can turn anything upside-down and make it sound as natural as spring rain."

"And you have yet to give me a reason to turn my throne over to the likes of you."

"Obviously this bandit never learned his history," Hantei said bemusedly. He turned around to face Toturi and leaned back upon the windowsill. "The children of the sun and moon set up the Celestial Order to preserve order in the Empire. Each Clan had its place, and by virtue of winning the contest, Hantei and his descendants were to rule over the rest. I am a direct descendant of the god Hantei, therefore, by the Celestial Order, the throne is mine."

Again a slight tremor rumbled through the palace.

"The Celestial Order requires the dead to stay in Jigoku," said Toturi bluntly. "Go back."

Moving nothing but his eyes, Hantei glanced down at Toturi's hand, the one Toturi himself had glanced at when Hantei had arrived. Then he looked back and met Toturi's eyes with a knowing gaze.

"Since it is clear that logic and tradition hold no sway with this pretender," purred Hantei, "perhaps military truths will make a difference. I do believe the only things that matter to a ronin are gold, alcohol, and force, are they not? And, as I can see that you have already helped yourself to the Imperial Hantei treasury and storerooms, force will have to suffice.

"My dear Toturi, everyone must obey their ancestors. This Empire is filled with spirits, who are the ancestors of mortals. Those ancestors swore to live and die at the whim of my lineage, five hundred or even a thousand years before you were even a prurient thought in your father's loins. They will follow a Hantei, and they will make the mortals follow them."

Hantei smiled his wolf's smile. "You have no Empire." So saying, he glanced at Shiba Tsukune. She immediately dropped her eyes.

"And you are no Emperor. You are a tyrant, and I know that the steel chrysanthemum was more than just your symbol. I know that you commissioned a Kuni engineer to design a device to administer prolonged torture, and that you named that device the steel chrysanthemum. Those who follow me have nothing to lose and everything to gain," Toturi concluded.

At the window, Kakita Kaiten said quietly, "My liege, you wanted to see this."

Toturi walked over to the window at which Kaiten stood, and gestured Hantei to turn around and look out his window. Tsuneo stalked over to stand behind his liege.

Far below and away, outside the city walls, they could just make out a tall, regal man with white hair and a long, pale blue kimono. Even at this distance, the slight glimmer of the spirit's aura could be seen. It was Kakita Yoshi. He moved up the slope of a large rock outcropping that stood like a bastion over the rocky shore.

"I do not remember that rock jutting out like that," said Tsuneo, looking over Hantei's shoulder.

"We had it fashioned by the Mistress of Earth," said Kaede. "She drew the purest granite forth from the ground, and the Master of Fire purified it. Then the Mistress of Water and the Master of Air polished it with the waves and the wind, and the Grand Master blessed and empowered it."

Tsuneo pursed his lips and nodded slightly.

As the onlookers watched, Yoshi ascended the outcropping to the very top, to where it leaned over the crashing surf below. He paused for a moment, his kimono blowing in the ever-present seashore breeze. Then, slowly and properly, he turned to Otosan Uchi and bowed, deeply and formally. Turning back to the sea, he leaped from the top of the rock, and in a flutter of blue and silver silk, he vanished from sight.

"We call it 'The Jumping Place,'" said Kaede. "It will take you back to Jigoku."

"You see, Hantei," asked Toturi, stepping away from the window. "My people are my people, spirits or mortals. We will destroy you if you try to conquer this Empire."

"You dare to threaten me?" said Hantei incredulously. "Is this people so fallen that they could raise a weapon against a Hantei, set above all others by the heavens to rule the people?"

Toturi dropped his eyes for only a moment.

"Very well then," said Hantei, drawing his sword. "Now that I have my answer, I shall have to kill you."

Motso drew his sword and interceded himself between the Emperors. Tsuneo immediately stepped in front of the Lion.

"Oh . . . I see," said Hantei. "Perhaps instead of having the Emperor and the pretender fight, my champion should face your champions, one at a time?"

Tsuneo hefted his huge iron-studded tetsubo. As he looked down upon Motso's graying hair, it seemed a shadow loomed across the room. The Crab flexed his arms, and the tetsubo's wood creaked slightly under the strain.

"Acceptable," said Motso, and Toturi heard the voice of one who has already let go of his last moments of life.

Toturi glanced at Tsuneo and saw the death of six daimyos written on his face. "No," Toturi said. "You want the throne? Here is my answer!" He strode over to the throne, drew his sword, raised it high, and with one mighty pull, he clove the Jade Throne in half.

At that moment, havoc struck Otosan Uchi as an earthquake rocked the city to its core. The floor bucked, and the wooden frames of the rice-paper doors creaked and snapped. Kaede and Naseru together quickly petitioned the lesser kami to keep the throne room intact while the rest of the city thrashed at the whim of the earth.

Screams from the streets were barely audible as the sound of crumbling masonry and splitting wood filled the air. One of the roof beams came loose and crashed down to the floor, crushing the skull of one of Hantei's Dragon samurai. A paper lantern fell from its place, sending burning oil across the throne room floor. Moto Gaheris scrambled forward, wiping the burning oil up with great sweeps of his sleeves, then tearing them off before his flesh burnt too badly. And in the midst of all this chaos, Toturi and Hantei glowered at each other, with both Motso and Tsuneo standing heedless of the catastrophe, guarding their respective Emperors.

The earth's trembling faded like the last tremors of a dying man. Dust settled from the rafters, casting the sunbeams into stark shafts of light.

"There is no throne, Hantei," said Toturi. "I rule by virtue of my authority, and now so must you. Therefore you have no power over us."

"I have more power than you know," the spirit replied and snapped open his fan.

At the signal, Tsukune, who had been standing in a cloud of despair, straightened her shoulders, reached for her sword and turned to face Toturi. Stepping back with her right foot, she drew her sword extending it laterally out at arm's length in a ritual form. Toturi looked at her, dumbfounded. But then Tsukune froze in place. Her face blanched, and she whispered, "Not if our lives depended . . ."

Hantei's face twisted in frustration, trying to will Tsukune to move. Then he heard a girlish war cry break the stunned silence. Tsudao leaped forward and executed a jumping axe kick, striking

Tsukune's right wrist with her heel and knocking the blade from her numbed fingers.

The Phoenix daimyo glanced at Hantei then back at Toturi, fear and self-reproach straining her features. She reached for her wakizashi, but Kaede rushed up from behind, wisps of power spooling around her hands. The Mistress of the Void gently touched the back of Tsukune's neck, and abruptly the daimyo's eyes rolled completely back in her head.

"You see?" laughed Hantei, hiding his anger as Kaede slowly lowered Tsukune to the ground. "You won't be able to trust anyone, Toturi. I do hope not too many of your palace guard were just killed in this earthquake."

So saying, he turned on his heel and left the throne room, the Dragon Clan guards following behind. He strode out of the palace, his eyes wishing death on everyone he saw.

* * * * *

Toturi turned and pointed an accusing finger at Tsukune's unconscious form. "Now her—" he said with a growl.

"My lord," interrupted Kaede. "The Hantei's forces hold the Phoenix children hostage. I felt it when I touched her."

"She turned on me just to save her children?" Toturi asked, his eyes narrowed.

"Not just hers, my lord . . . all of them."

Toturi looked about, mortified, and he noticed Tsuneo still standing there. "Why do you follow that tyrant, Tsuneo?" he asked. "Your name is revered, and his is hated. You know he can only destroy. Join me, return to your family, and help us fight against a return of the darkest days of the Hantei dynasty."

"I cannot, honored Emperor," he said, regret tinging his voice. "I gave my word."

For a moment the two studied each other, then Toturi bowed, deeply. Tsuneo returned the bow, and before he left, he said, "I am honored to have met you—each of you. I regret that we will not meet again." Then he turned and left, his footsteps causing more dust to fall from the ceiling.

Tsuneo caught up with Hantei just as he stormed out of the castle and hopped unceremoniously into his palanquin. "Let's go!" yelled the Emperor. "Move it!"

The tattooed monks hefted the palanquin and began trotting quickly down the Road of the Most High. Tsuneo jogged alongside. "Why not just stay and kill Toturi?" he asked.

"Don't be an idiot," said Hantei. "Yes, Toturi would not kill me. I could see that. I am a Hantei, and he is too honorable. But I could see that damned Lion would have. And the palace guards, they all have this delusion that Toturi is their Emperor, and good samurai will kill anyone to defend the Emperor. Damn it! If I could have just dueled with him, it would have been fine. But that damned Lion had to get in the way."

"But why the hasty departure?" asked Tsuneo.

"Have you gone stupid? Did a piece of roofing fall on your head in there? Look all around you! Do you see the smoke? Do you smell the fear? This! This is what I wanted to see when I got here. I wanted to see a city in chaos, groping in fear and confusion. I wanted to march through the streets and take the city and impose my order upon it. The gate guards wouldn't let me do it when I arrived, but I will do it now before I leave! Get ready, Tsuneo. Get ready to seize Otosan Uchi!"

They marched out of the city, and Hantei had the bearers stop just outside of bowshot of the city gate. "Tamori!" he bellowed, gesturing back to the city. "Get your shugenja and clear that gate!"

He took a few steps farther down the Emperor's Way and spread his arms wide. "Samurai of the ages!" he shouted. "The time has come to destroy the family that claims to sit upon the Hantei throne! Tsuneo! Take the palace and kill everyone within it!"

With a great bestial shout, the army of samurai spirits moved forward. Agasha Tamori and his followers began gathering great power around themselves, and the sky darkened as clouds billowed into existence. A huge, whirling sphere of power coalesced above the circle of Dragon shugenja, and just before Hantei's forces reached the gate, the ball leaped forth like a great cat of lightning, striking the battlements above the gate, shattering the stone and sending the samurai guards to their deaths.

The spirit army poured through the gate and moved toward the Imperial palace, rivers of gold flowing through the shattered streets of Otosan Uchi. The few guards in the outer city were killed where they stood, slowing down the army no more than a sapling slows a gale. The wall to the inner city delayed the invaders for a while until, under Tsuneo's guidance, they forced the gates and scrounged some ladders from nearby houses with which to scale the wall. Guards held them at the palace walls, buying time for their compatriots to seal up the Imperial palace itself.

The spirit samurai gathered wood from the earthquake-ravaged buildings, commandeered some oil, and set fire to the gates. They knew it would take all day to burn their way through the thick wood, but the flames and heat would make it more difficult to defend the gate, as well as weaken the wood for when they tried to force a breach. Other samurai lobbed casks of oil at the gate fortifications, seeking to burn out those who tried to hold back the attackers.

The roof beam of a collapsed house provided the invaders with a battering ram, and they began to pound on the gate. Elsewhere around the wall, spirit archers fired at defending guards, while their compatriots tried to scale the walls directly. From within the palace proper, other guards fired out of the palace's windows, hoping to help repel the assault.

In the midst of it all, Tsuneo stood on the Road of the Most High, surveying the situation and guiding the attack. Crab Clan samurai, who best knew his tactics and methods, served as runners, carrying his orders throughout the city streets. Soon Tamori's shugenja had created a dense, gray mist and set it upon the Imperial palace like a blanket, cutting off those on the palace walls from help from their allies within. As this happened, a single rocket shot forth from one of the high towers in the palace, streaking up into the sky. Tsuneo turned to watch it arc overhead then explode in a brilliant ball of orange.

His eyes narrowed. "That," he said to a runner, "was a signal. Go to the outer wall and report if you see anything."

Not long after, the runner returned. A Lion army was moving in from the northwest, perhaps forty thousand strong. They had evidently been laying in wait, two valleys over, to ambush the Hantei's forces in just this manner. And the Lion daimyo had even gone so far as to place himself in his own trap as bait.

Tsuneo clenched his fist in frustration. Whatever his feelings for his Emperor, he loved warfare, but today was not to be his. It would take him all day to breach the palace itself, but if he remained here, the Lion army would trap him inside the city. He'd be pinned against the palace and the sea, and neither were likely to be more forgiving than an army of Lion samurai.

Reluctantly he ordered the retreat. If the Lion were coming from the northwest, that meant a retreat back into Phoenix lands would be dangerous as best, disastrous at worst. He'd have to pull his forces back to Crab lands for the moment.

Retreat. He hated the word.

His sole solace was the thought that many more such battles awaited him. He bowed one last time to his clever and honorable opponents, unseen behind the magical mist, turned his back on the palace, and strode out of Otosan Uchi.

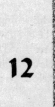

12 FALL ON YOUR KNEES

The
Thirteenth
Year
of the
Reign
of
Toturi I

What supplies do you need?" barked Hida O-Ushi. She pulled her long, raven hair back into a ponytail, and the first touches of gray shimmered in the lantern light. "I must be sure we can spare them. The defense of the Empire is a duty second to none, and it requires much in the line of resources."

"My dear Crab," said Hantei soothingly, "have not the spirits been running your mines and your farms for—let me see—seven years now? Hasn't your Clan's wealth and precious resources grown in that time?"

"Yes," said O-Ushi defensively.

"Then what cause have you to complain about my administration?"

"Your people have pushed my people out of the work and into the field of battle," she said. Hantei smiled happy to see that she, too, had fallen into the "we" and "they" mentality. "Now spirits control all of the mines, all of the farms, all of the smithies."

"Why, naturally," said Hantei reasonably. "They can work longer hours than mortals can."

"If it's all the same to you, I don't like being referred to as a 'mortal.' Spirits can die just as easily as we can."

"But the word 'spirits' doesn't quite convey our unique situation," said Hantei almost conspiratorially. "We are physical beings, you know. But we have also died, whereas mortals haven't. Perhaps you would rather that I referred to mortals as, oh, the un-dead?"

O-Ushi studied Hantei for a moment through narrowed eyes. "Take what you need," she said. "No more." Then she turned and left the traveling house that served as Hantei's home in this area.

Tsuneo waited until her footsteps had faded to nothing. "It's not a good sign when a Crab doesn't answer your question," he said.

"Why?" asked Hantei. "What are you afraid of?"

"I'll go requisition the supplies," Tsuneo said, and left the building as well.

Once outside, he took a deep breath. He hated using his own Clan like this. They were well supported, yes, but they were now also wholly dependent on the spirits. The spirits produced, administered, and distributed. Suspend that support, and terrible things would happen to the Crab . . . and the whole Empire.

Tsuneo pulled a list of needed items from his sleeve. The retreat from Otosan Uchi had not been pretty. Hantei's twenty thousand samurai—well, perhaps nineteen thousand—had streamed out of the city as the Lion army approached. Moving through the streets, the spirit forces had been disorganized. The Lion moved in as Hantei's forces streamed out of the city. Those who exited along the Road of the Most High came through in fairly good order, but those who left by gates nearer the Lion forces scattered at their approach.

The Lion struck the disorganized army, and each Clan's samurai fought largely for themselves. Only the Dragon contingent held firm, safeguarding Hantei as they withdrew from the field. With the aid of the Unicorn and their steeds, the spirit samurai were able to regroup a day's march away. They had expected an easy conquest and to spend the winter in or near Otosan Uchi. Instead, without adequate supplies of food, clothing, and other materials, they ended up having to fight a running series of battles with the Lion Clan just to march across the Spine of the World to the relative safety of the Crab holdings. Fortunately, even with minimal supplies, the spirits could generally out-march the Lion samurai, and the Unicorn spirits were very effective as a cavalry screen.

They had wintered among their people in Crab lands, and the other Clans let them. The Unicorn were fighting amongst themselves, and the Crane were continuing to battle the Crab down south. That left the Scorpion Clan as the only direct threat to Hantei and his troops, and they seemed content to remain uninvolved, and thereby act as a buffer between Hantei and the Lion armies.

Now that spring had arrived, Hantei wanted to return to Phoenix lands and tend to some pleasant business. Once fully provisioned—and loaded down with as many extra supplies as he could possibly arrange—his small force would march northward, re-cross the Spine of the World into Unicorn lands, and cut east across friendly Dragon and Phoenix territory. There he and his favorite general would hook up with the Dragon and Phoenix Clan's mortal armies, and they could once more march upon Otosan Uchi.

He would send a few Crab spirits to ensure that tensions over the Yasuki estates remained high, so that the Crane would keep their attention elsewhere away from the Eternal City. That left the Lion to deal with, and although they were worthy opponents, they would be unable to resist the onslaught of two Clans and legions of spirits—though, being Lions, they would try. Tsuneo had always respected them for that.

But first . . .

"All these supplies," Tsuneo muttered. "It's a wonder any actual fighting ever gets done."

* * * * *

Toturi paused in his calligraphy to greet his wife with a nod as she entered the room.

"My lord," said Kaede softly, "you must do something."

"Eh?" Confused by the abrupt demand, he glanced at his calligraphy, looking for errors.

"Tsukune has not yet forgiven herself. She still awaits your answer."

Toturi set down his brush. "I told you that I was not going to allow her to commit seppuku," he said, shaking his head. "Why does she persist?"

"I told her, and so she waits for you to break her sword and make her ronin," said Kaede. "I thought this might pass with the ending of the year, but it is New Year's today, and her soul is still in winter. I suspect it will remain there without the light of her Emperor to melt the ice about her heart."

Toturi sighed, an irritated tone. "I thought it best not to discuss it," he said, pushing the calligraphy table aside. "Very well, I shall go see her."

"I have already summoned her, my lord," said Kaede, smiling.

"You have?" Toturi grunted. "What if I had said I would do nothing for a despondent samurai?"

Kaede gave him an intimate blink, saying, "I know you better than that."

"Hmph," said Toturi gruffly. He turned to leave, and a servant opened the sliding door for him. Half to himself, he muttered, "How can anyone know an Emperor? His duties are beyond mortal understanding."

"That would mean that an oracle would understand, but a poor ronin would not. Is that not true, my love?"

Toturi stopped in the doorway and turned, inclining his head. "It is bad form to be more clever than your own Emperor."

Kaede smiled, hiding it with a respectful bow.

Toturi strode through the short hallway to his entrance to the throne room. As he entered he was struck—as he always was—by the lack of a throne. Now that it was gone, he longed for it as a ship longs for a beacon among sharp reefs. It was a symbol of permanence, and its absence reminded Toturi all the more that his legacy, even the Empire itself, was being shaped on a daily basis, groping blindly in a war without precedent in the annals of history.

Where does duty lie in a time like this? he asked himself as he entered the room. Thus preoccupied, he strode over to stand where the throne had once stood. It was now his custom to do so.

He took a deep breath, looked up, and faced Shiba Tsukune.

She was kneeling, facedown in a nearly prostrate bow. Her arms were straight out before her, her hair splayed about the floor. Her wak-izashi was at her side, ready for seppuku, and her naked katana—blade aimed away from Toturi, of course—was reverently placed in front of her, awaiting Toturi's judgment. She was dressed head to toe in white, the color of death.

"Did you not get my message?" asked Toturi.

"My lord," cried Tsukune, in the too-loud voice of a samurai giving a heinous confession, "I have dishonored my Clan, my family, and my sword by raising it against you! Please allow me to remove the stain of this dishonor from my people, that you may withhold your punishment from them!"

"I could hardly say you raised your sword against me," he replied.

"I drew my sword to strike!" cried Tsukune. "The daimyos of the Great Clans saw this!"

"Did they? Then why hasn't one of them spoken to me about it?"

Tsukune had no answer but remained in her supplicant posture.

"Tsukune," said Toturi, "you drew your sword, but you did neither raise it nor attack. Had you truly wished to kill me, you would have done so. But you did nothing, so no one can prove that you weren't going to attack the Hantei."

"You know what happened!" protested Tsukune.

Toturi stepped over to her and knelt by her head.

"Yes, I do," he said very quietly, his voice little more than a whisper. "You drew on me, thinking to save your Clan's children. However, your honor prevented you from actually raising your hand against me. You chose to sacrifice your entire Clan's future for me. No Emperor could ask for more."

Toturi reached over and reverently took Tsukune's katana in his hands. Turning the handle to the left and the blade towards him, he held it out to her. "I know you expected to die in dishonor, for the sake of your Clan's future," he said. "That fate has passed from you. I tell you now to take up your honor and live again."

Tsukune looked up for the first time and saw the sword through the veil of hair that concealed her face. "I cannot," said Tsukune. "I will be trusted less than a Scorpion."

"Technically, there is no law against drawing your sword in the presence of the Emperor because, frankly, I'm not supposed to let people have swords in my presence," replied Toturi. "Take your sword and serve your Clan."

"I cannot," she said, "for my shame is too great."

"The Emperor has said there is no shame." Toturi proffered the sword once more. "Take back your soul and serve the Empire," he said firmly. "This is the command of your Emperor."

Tsukune hung her head. With shaking hands, she reached for her sword, took it, and held it across her lap.

Toturi sat down in front of her so as not to leave her alone again, and patiently waited as her tears spattered on the gleaming steel blade.

* * * * *

Shiba Aikune was working up a sweat. It helped him to focus his anger. He was supposed to have gone through his coming-of-age ceremony by now. Instead, here he was, still a "special guest" of the self-proclaimed Hantei Emperor. Still a guest and still a child.

Sure, maybe he was barely ten, but children had become adults at younger ages . . . occasionally. For that matter, Matsu Hitomi had led an army at fourteen. Aikune knew he was ready to be a samurai. Let the others think he was young. He would show them.

He made a cut, advanced, blocked and cut again. Every cut was aimed at the image of Hantei XVI held in his mind's eye; every block stopped a hand reaching for him. Or sometimes he cut at the face of the Stone Crab, because the big man had handled Yaruko roughly. Sure, he had handled Aikune roughly, too, but that didn't matter. An adult didn't cry like a child at being abused. But being cruel to Yaruko was another matter.

Aikune finished his practice form with a butterfly cut, then stepped back, flicked the imaginary blood from the blade of the stripped branch that acted as his surrogate katana, sheathed his blade in the circle made by his left hand, presented himself, bowed, and stepped back.

A smattering of applause greeting the end of his form. He turned and smiled at his friends and cousins, who had watched him with a critical eye. His was a common enough performance in the last—

what?—half year. They had been special guests for so long it almost seemed normal, camped in a small town near Broad Ax Waterfall. The once-thriving town had been emptied by Hantei's spirit samurai so that he'd have a safe place to keep the Phoenix children.

Aikune pushed his stick through his belt as if it were the sheath of a katana and added a smaller stick that he called his wakizashi. He figured it was best to get used to the feel of the two swords of a samurai now, as he would be wearing them as soon as his mother came back.

His mother. He had not seen her since she met with Hantei on the Prophet's Plain. Aikune was not sure whether or not Hantei's people knew he was the only child of the Phoenix champion, but just to be safe, he hadn't told them. To safeguard his secret, his cousins pretended he was their little brother. He just hoped Tsukune came back without Hantei, instead of the other way around.

Suddenly a voice at the edge of the town cried out, "Someone is coming! Coming from the west!"

Aikune turned an ear. Since the spring thaws, a legion of Phoenix samurai had been camped to the east of the town, keeping an uneasy eye on the spirit samurai who guarded the Clan's children. The river ran roughly south to north along the western side of the town, which made the west an unlikely approach for visitors. Perhaps another Phoenix legion had joined the first to embrace the spirit samurai in a clamshell of steel?

He went to the banks of the river along with the other children, all eager for a diversion and the possibility of hope. But as he looked at the approaching army, he saw the all-too-familiar golden hue of their bodies. They were Hantei's spirits, returning to the hostages.

It's just as well, thought Aikune, fingering the stick in his belt. I could use a better look at the Hantei's weasel face. It'll help hone my accuracy.

Hantei rode in a large, open sedan chair at the head of his force, enjoying the fair weather and the chance to look at those lands that he did, in fact, rule. Hida Tsuneo rode a horse at his side, and judging by its size, Aikune figured it was a Unicorn mount. Gelding, of course—the Unicorns never let a breeding horse out of their sight. Aikune started fingering his stick katana again. Speaking of geldings . . .

The procession steered a course for a wide, slow-moving section of the river a ways downstream from the thundering falls. Hantei and Tsuneo reached the bank of the river and the column drew up to a halt. A Dragon shugenja clad head to toe in concealing robes stepped forward. He held his hands together, concealing them in the thick folds of his sleeves, and as he reached the riverbank, Aikune saw why. He pulled one hand free, and the skin was pale, unhealthy, and very thin, with ugly green striations along the back of his wrist.

The shugenja drew forth a small handful of snow from his sleeve, held it out, and blew the snowflakes at the river. They tumbled in his breath, then fell slowly down. Where they struck the river, the surface froze rapidly, spreading out in all directions, until a bridge of ice had formed over the river.

Tsuneo dismounted and made his way across, along with the shugenja. Thus assured of the safety of the bridge, Hantei urged the muscular tattooed monks who bore his chair forward. The four moved easily across the ice in their bare feet, their tattoos almost dancing on their bronzed skin. When they'd crossed the river, they set Hantei's chair down smoothly.

At Tsuneo's command, the town's spirit samurai began gathering all the children together, herding them toward the Hantei, who surveyed the crowd of small faces with a curiously gleeful expression on his face. The children kept their distance, of course, trusting Hantei no more than did his own samurai. At the same time, Hantei's spirit army spread itself along the far side of the river to see what was going to happen.

Once everyone had been gathered round, Hantei uncurled himself from his chair, stretched, and stood up. He walked up and down in front of the crowd, scrutinizing the front rank of children, all of whom lowered their eyes as he passed.

"I have been to Otosan Uchi," Hantei said loudly, surveying the children, "and I saw your over-valued daimyo there. She drew her sword to attack the pretender Toturi." A gasp rippled through the crowd of children, blossoming into furtive whispers.

"However," continued Hantei, "it appears that your vaunted champion could not outfight a goblin zombie. I have never seen someone freeze in panic as she did. It makes me wonder whether the Phoenix have been pacifists so long that they no longer know how to fight. So perhaps your parents need a little extra motivation, hmm? A Hantei Emperor demands the best! Failure to excel results in death! That is the message I will give your parents. And to show that I mean what I say, one of you will deliver the message and its proof."

Hantei paused and looked at the crowd again. He stepped forward and gestured to a pretty young girl. "You," he said, "step forward. You will be my messenger."

"Yaruko . . ." said Aikune as she moved hesitantly toward Hantei. Concerned, the young Phoenix started to step forward too.

"Quiet, you," growled one of the spirit samurai, and he punched Aikune back into place with the butt of his naginata.

Hantei took her chin in his hand, slowly drawing one lacquered nail across her throat. "Yes, I think I remember you. You shall do nicely." Hantei steered her over to Tsuneo and stepped back. "Kill this one," he said simply, "and take her head to the Phoenix."

Tsuneo drew his sword.

"No!" shouted Aikune.

Hantei whirled, his face a rictus of hate. "No?" he bellowed. "You dare defy the Hantei Emperor?" Abruptly he composed himself. "So be it," he said quietly. "She shall keep her head."

Yaruko turned her head to look at Aikune, a mixture of hope and fear in her eyes. Her kimono rippled with the trembling of her body.

Hantei's lip curled into a sneer, and he pulled a dagger from his sleeve. He reversed his grip on the handle, and plunged the blade into the girl's back, just above her kidney. She screamed in agony, and, arcing her back and standing on tiptoe, she tried to reach back to the blade. Hantei's sneer turned into an illicit smirk as he slowly twisted the blade in her back. Yaruko thrashed herself off the blade and fell to the ground, sobbing her last breaths. She tried to crawl to Aikune, but her strength left her.

"Send her head and her organs," said Hantei, "all in one pretty piece."

Horror overloaded Aikune's brain, blasting away all reason, all fear, all choice. With a mighty cry that seemed far too large for such a young man, he drew his katana stick and swung it up at the spirit guard nearest him. The blow struck the man in the larynx, crushing it, and he collapsed.

Heedless of danger, Aikune charged the next spirit he saw. She couldn't lower her naginata in time to stab Aikune but knocked him off his feet with the haft. Filled with fury, he lunged for her thighs, hitting them with both shoulders, his head between her legs. This knocked her off balance, and she tumbled onto her back. Pushing himself up on one hand, he brought the stick down on her nose, breaking it and welting her eye shut.

Meanwhile, two of Aikune's cousins drew the katana and wakizashi from the first downed guard, and moved swiftly through the crowd of children to attack any spirit they saw. This sparked others to action, and the entire crowd of young Phoenix moved to fight or to escape.

Spirit samurai, who one moment ago were herding a crowd of timid and obedient children, found themselves surrounded by little devils, some of whom bore plundered steel. Some, not having been given orders to murder children, fell back. Others, students of Hantei's hate, began ruthlessly butchering everything around.

Seeing the abrupt fighting and the sudden surge of fleeing children, the nearby Phoenix legion immediately launched a disorganized charge into the fray, trying to reach the hated spirit foes as fast as possible while avoiding stampeding their own children. As they closed, the carnage they saw drove them to a frenzy.

At the same time Hantei's army, once it got past its stunned disbelief at events, surged forward across the river, but the ice bridge collapsed beneath the weight of the massed samurai, plunging them into the frigid mountain waters.

The Phoenix army swept into the town, attacking the outnumbered spirit garrison wherever they were found. The spirits moved with great expertise, however, and took a serious toll of the Phoenix. In the confusion, Phoenix servants moved in behind the warriors and shugenja and ushered the children to safety, carrying the smaller ones to expedite their withdrawal.

Hantei looked at his own army slowly trying to ford the deep and icy river and roared in frustration. "Archers!" he shrieked. "Fire! Fire-fire-fire! Kill them all! Kill every damned one of them!"

At their Emperor's command, the army started raining arrows down upon the town. Mortal and spirit, child and adult, samurai and servant all suffered under the deadly rain of wood. Then fire arrows dropped from the sky as well, and the buildings began to blaze brightly. As the fires grew, Phoenix and spirit alike chose to withdraw rather than fight in an ever-worsening environment.

The spirits fell back around their Emperor, who stood guarded by Tsuneo and the tattooed monks at the river's edge. The Phoenix pulled away, and though arrows harried their retreat, their own shugenja whisked the majority of them away on the winds, sending them to impact harmlessly in the fields beyond. The leaders quickly reorganized the troops to escort the children away as speedily and safely as possible, sending riders ahead to plea for reinforcements.

Hampered by the need to ford the river, the spirit army could not press the attack until after the Phoenix army had withdrawn from the field. Hantei considered a pursuit, but at last, ever mindful of the Phoenix shugenja and the Council of Elemental Masters, withdrew his army toward the Dragon borders.

*   *   *   *   *

Empress Kaede and Shiba Tsukune sat in silence in the Imperial garden, sipping tea and watching the water of a small stream flow to the sea. Neither spoke, both stared vacantly into the waters as they trickled on, ever changing, ever the same.

The soft sound of footfalls on grass turned Kaede's eyes upward. She saw her husband walking up to the two women. She bowed her head. Belatedly, Tsukune also looked up, and bowed deeply. She politely readdressed herself to face Toturi but stared into her cup of tea.

"I heard," said Toturi. "I am sorry for the loss."

Kaede nodded.

Toturi looked compassionately at Tsukune's bowed head. "Any word on Aikune?"

"Yes," said Kaede joylessly. "We thought him lost, but he had been knocked unconscious during the fighting. He found his way back to our people two days later."

"Thank the fortunes for that."

"My son lived," said Tsukune, without raising her head, "but his betrothed, the Isawa whom we arranged for him to marry, she . . . did not survive."

Toturi pondered this for a moment. "How many?" he asked finally.

"About half, they say," said Kaede. "Some families were lucky, others . . ."

Toturi took a long blink. "Half."

"More or less," said Kaede. "Exact counts do not describe such a tragedy."

"Such a loss . . ." he said.

Tsukune looked up at Toturi, though she respectfully did not meet his gaze. She pulled her hair back behind her ears.

"Better a beggar's life with honor," she said, "than prosperity with shame."

"But the future of the Phoenix—" began Toturi.

Tsukune bravely raised her gaze to his. "The future of my Clan is in your hands, my lord, as is that of the Empire. Our loss will be a drop in the torrent of blood if you fail to stop Hantei."

13 | THE SOUL OF AKODO

The
Thirteenth
Year
of the
Reign
of
Toturi I

The new year had broken, and though winter's chill lingered, the campaign season would soon begin. Toturi walked into the planning room to survey the situation. The planning room had once been devoted to artwork. Here Toturi and Kaede had practiced their art. Here tutors had taught the royal children the fast, instinctive method of painting that relied on intuition and the expression of inner chi. The walls used to have the best works of their children displayed. Sezaru's was always the most beautiful, but for some reason people always lingered more at Naseru's paintings. And Tsudao? Her paintings were a reflection of her—bold, simple, and unimaginative.

Now the paintings were gone, and the only artwork was an immense map of Rokugan spread upon the floor. Blocks painted in the Clans' traditional colors marked the armies' positions. Small flags, patterned after the back banners worn by samurai in battle, stood on stands atop the blocks and displayed the insignia of specific units and commanders. So much information, thought Toturi, so little knowledge.

Toku, General of the Imperial Guard, sat cross-legged at the edge of the map nearest Otosan Uchi. He bowed briefly to Toturi, and continued studying the map with a frown.

"The emissaries have returned?" Toturi asked, stepping to the center of the map.

"Not all of them, sir," Toku said. "Some are here. Some sent pigeons." Anticipating the next question, he added, "Our shugenja say that none of the pigeons had a forged message. I guess Hantei hasn't interfered with our birds—at least not so far."

Toturi nodded. That was the hardest part—the allies and the enemies were intermixed. Clans, families, even individual marriages threatened to pull apart as the war between mortal and spirits took shape. "So what's the situation?" he asked.

Toku gestured with his left hand. "The Crane and the Crab continue their war. They say Kaiten and O-Ushi both try to stop it, but their commanders keep pressing the attack, so the fighting shows no sign of peace. Maybe both sides want to take the last strike, or maybe they're both too proud to stop. Anyway, we can't get a message from O-Ushi, because she's on the Wall, and the spirits won't let our people see her, so I guess the Crab are on his side, with Hida Tsuneo in charge.

"The Crane are basically on our side—at least the regent and his people are, even if the generals aren't—but they have to keep all their armies down south where they don't do any good. So maybe the Crane and the Crab balance each other.

"The Scorpion have stayed out of things, although it seems there's some . . . um, internal things going on—you know how they hold their secrets. But our emissary says he's heard some things and put a few ideas together. Maybe the Scorpion are waiting to see who wins. Makes me nervous." He cracked his knuckles.

"The Unicorn are split," Toku continued, gesturing to the northwest corner of the map, "and not just down the spirit/mortal lines. They got some 'new traditionalists' who think the spirits were right to drive them into the fields, and they got some spirits who think there were better ways to do things than fighting their own people. So Moto Gaheris supports you, but he's got maybe half his Clan, and they're fighting with the other half. There's fighting all over the place up there, and even some cases where the same side fights itself, so the Unicorn are pretty well tied up until they figure things out.

"The Dragon, they're lost, every last one of them, or so our emissary's ghost told your son Sezaru. No hope there.

"The Phoenix are mostly on our side, and they hate Hantei because of their children, but the Dragon armies have them pretty well bottled up. Hantei tested their frontier last year, and I think he's deciding whether to block them or crush them. Either way, with all the spirits and all the Dragons they're facing, I think they're in trouble."

Toku sighed and looked at the center of the map. "Then there's the Lion. Motso's army harassed Hantei's army after the attack on Otosan Uchi, of course, but those were our people. Since then, they haven't really tried to engage Hantei's forces. There are Lion Clan spirits in his army, of course, and we all know how much the Lion respect and revere their ancestors. And then there's the fact that . . . um—"

"The fact that I was once daimyo," said Toturi, "and failed to protect the thirty-eighth Hantei. Then even when Tsuko gave me the Clan again, half of them fought against me." He rubbed his chin thoughtfully. "That seems so long ago."

"Five lifetimes ago, by my count," said Toku brightly. "Ronin, Thunder, Emperor, Shadow, and Spirit."

"Yes," said Toturi slowly, "but still a painful memory to many of the Lion." He turned a slow circle on the map, studying the blocks, the terrain. "So who, then, is truly with us?"

"The Imperial Guard stands ready to serve, my liege," said Toku immediately.

"My friend, it is not enough," Toturi replied. "We need more than your troops. We need a message. We need a stand. We need someone to plant their Clan's banner beside this dynasty and defy Hantei."

"Well, maybe we could try the Sparrow Clan," said Toku listlessly.

Toturi laughed in spite of himself, then took a deep breath and looked vacantly up at the corner of the room. Looking back down, he turned a slow circle in the heart of the Empire.

"Take a message to Kitsu Motso," he said. "Tell him, 'There is one Emperor. The Emperor has one right hand.'"

"And then . . . ?" asked Toku.

"And then we hope the hand is strong enough to grip the sword."

* * * * *

Akodo Ginawa sat upon a campaign stool and waited. A hundred torches blazed around, defying the darkness and illuminating the large sheets that hung suspended between wooden frames and served as walls in this open-air courtyard. In the center of each piece of gold canvas, the mon of the Lion Clan was rendered in beautiful hand-painted strokes of orange and brown.

Ginawa's force camped on a hill along the Lion frontier nearest the Dragon Clan, vigilantly guarding their general against the Hantei's treachery. Ginawa's courtyard was at the middle of his force, and he was seated near the center of the courtyard, a few aides beside him, facing three empty chairs. A late evening dew had settled on the ground, not unexpected this near the mountains, and Ginawa shivered once as his body adjusted to his stillness in the cool northern air. The world was quiet save for the crackling of a few fires and the occasional call of an owl.

He looked up at the stars and prayed they would guide his words, for truly he found himself in darkness, in an unknown place. The tactician inside him bridled at the lack of experience in such matters—he knew well that knowing the field was winning the battle—but he also craved the intellectual challenge of a difficult struggle over uncharted terrain. Even if the battle was to be nothing more than words.

Presently he heard the approaching sound of horses' hooves, walking steadily up the hillside. He pulled himself into perfect attentive posture. The horses drew to a stop just outside the walls, but the jingle of their tack and harness kept their image sharp in Ginawa's mind's eye.

He heard the riders dismount, heard his guards greet them formally. Two guards drew back the canvas flaps and bowed, admitting them to Ginawa's presence. Three Lion spirit samurai, resplendent in full formal dress and wreathed in yellow halos that stood out against the inky night sky, stepped forward. They walked to their appointed places, and Ginawa and his aides stood. Both sides bowed deeply and formally, starting the meeting off on good terms.

As everyone sat, Ginawa noted that the spirits' golden auras faded almost to invisibility against the pale colors of the canvas surrounding the group. He smiled inwardly, knowing that this was a deliberate stratagem by Motso. The intent was to help Ginawa treat these guests first as members of the Lion Clan, and not as spirits.

"I am glad we were able to arrange this meeting," said the senior spirit samurai. "My name is Akodo Ichihiro, daimyo of the Lion Clan, victor at Golden Sun and defender of Beiden Pass, who slew the Crane Champion and burned Kosaten Shiro to the ground."

"I am Akodo Ginawa, daimyo of the Akodo and general of the Lion armies," he said simply. "I am honored to have such famous and celebrated guests in my camp. Please, let us toast the honor of the Lion Clan."

He clapped his hands, and servants brought in excellent sake. They knelt and poured cups for each of the samurai.

A series of toasts followed. They toasted each other's health, the prowess of the Lion, the bravery of the great god Akodo, the daring of the Matsu family, the genius of the Ikoma, and the wisdom of the Kitsu. They toasted battles won, comrades fallen, and the sun and the moon, who watched over all. Boasts and spontaneous haiku punctuated the camaraderie, turning into an impromptu contest. Finally, after the group had drained their fourth bottle, Akodo Ichihiro stood up and spoke in a loud voice, saying,

> No poetry skill,
> My haiku are imperfect:
> They end with too many syllables.

The six Lions roared with laughter until the tears ran from their eyes. As the hilarity faded, Ginawa decided that the tongues had been loosened well enough and the hearts were warmed.

"Distinguished guests," he said solemnly, "it is time we discuss the business that brings us here tonight."

"You are right," said Ichihiro. "It is time the Lion moved as one. We have our differences, you and I, Ginawa. You have your

Emperor, whom you serve, and I have mine, but that is neither here nor there. I say, let Emperors be Emperors, and let the Lion be Lion!"

Ginawa nodded, neither agreeing nor disagreeing. "I understand," he said. "You have a plan . . . ?"

"Yes!" said Ichihiro. "The Crane are embroiled in a war with the Crab over the Yasuki estates. Personally, I think the Crane are right, but that is not the issue. I say we take this opportunity to strike at our eternal foe! I understand that Toshi Ranbo is in Crane hands. This is not acceptable. We must move now to take it, the entire Lion Clan as one! We shall strike the insufferable birds aside while their attention is on the money to be made in the southlands!"

"We cannot do that," said Ginawa.

"Of course we can! And we will, I order it! Marching side by side into battle, brothers and sisters of the same noble heritage, we shall reforge our Clan into one, spirit and mortal alike! I can teach you such tactics as . . . as have not been seen in hundreds of years!"

"How can you order such a thing?" asked Ginawa.

"I am the daimyo of the Akodo, and the rightful ruler of the Lion Clan. All our traditions place me at the head of the Clan, and you will obey me!"

"No," said Ginawa, "you are no longer the daimyo. That position passed from you when you died."

"And now I am back, and I claim it again. It is my right!"

The samurai seated at Ginawa's left leaned forward slightly. He was very young but well muscled, with the top of his head neatly shaved like an adult. His movements were smooth and perfect, in spite of his youth, and in spite of the sake he had drunk. "This is not about whether you are still the daimyo," he said.

"This is about honor. Shinsei said that honor is not given by your ancestors; it is borrowed from your descendants. This is why a samurai's actions can dishonor his children's children's children but never his ancestors. When you lived, long ago, you borrowed our honor. When you died, you returned it to us intact. Why, then, do you wish take it back once more?"

Ichihiro looked greatly affronted. "Who is this child?" he demanded.

"This is Akodo Kaneka," said Ginawa, "and . . . he *has* come of age."

"Already?"

"He is sometimes called the River's Son," explained Ginawa, looking sidelong at the young man, "because the water dragon left his mother at an Akodo village. She gave birth to him soon after, and tended him for his first three years. She never spoke all the time she lived, and she never seemed to see anyone or anything but him." He paused, and fixed Ichihiro squarely in the eye. "We think his maturity is a gift of the dragons. Since his mother died I have raised him as my own." Ginawa leaned back, crossed his arms, and said, "But he raises a good point. Why do you wish to borrow our honor once again?"

"Who says that I do?"

"You wish to rule the Clan in the place of the one to whom the duty has *rightfully* fallen—rightfully, I might add, by all the traditions we hold sacred."

Ichihiro's brow furrowed. "I seek to restore the honor of the Clan by retaking what is ours—Toshi Ranbo. I have no further concerns than the honor of the Clan."

"Tell me," interrupted Kaneka, "did Hantei tell you to say that?"

"How dare you!" shouted Ichihiro, lunging to his feet.

Kaneka was unmoved. "Will you swear upon your sword that Hantei did not send you to win the Lion Clan over to your authority?"

Ichihiro's mouth twisted in anger, but he did not answer.

Ginawa whistled softly, as Ichihiro's aides dropped their eyes.

"Lord Ichihiro," said Ginawa gently, "please, sit down." He waited until the angry daimyo had complied, and said, "You lived and did great things for our Clan. You died and were revered for hundreds of years as an ancestor of great power. Others ruled the Clan in your stead, always looking to you as an example. I myself prayed at your shrine often, for you were one of the thousand ancestors who guided every move I made, every move our people made.

"Now you are here, in the flesh, and no longer can your spirit guide our arm, except by the actions you take here and now for all the world to see. You brought your name great honor in life, and now that you live again, the only one who can take that honor away is you.

"We all have our duty. My duty is to my ancestors. Your duty is to your descendants—not to do their work for them but to guide their hand and be the shining example that drives us all to perfection."

Ichihiro looked up at Ginawa from beneath his eyebrows and nodded gravely.

"There is a spirit out there, my lord," Ginawa continued, "who seeks to turn the Celestial Order upside down. He seeks to rule from beyond the grave. He seeks to return to the dishonorable acts of his life, and he has already begun to do so. He tried to use you three as agents to turn your own Clan away from its destiny. Anyone who turns Lion against Lion deserves no allegiance. Anyone who tries to take the Lions' ancestors from them deserves to die."

Ichihiro thought about this for a moment, turned right, then left to see if his aides agreed with Ginawa. He thought some more and said, "You are right. A Lion's duty is to help the Clan by fighting while you live and guarding once you die. My time as daimyo is done. You lead our family now. I don't think either of us ever expected to be in this position, did we?" Ichihiro chuckled slightly. "Daimyo, I will gather the spirits in Hantei's camp, and we will abide by the Emperor's decree."

"You are honorable and devoted," said Ginawa. "Although, I must say, these are strange times. An example by my side can be worth much more than an ancestor's whisper in my ear. And I am very curious to see these tactics you speak of. . . ."

Ichihiro laughed. "You are an intriguing man, you know. First you convince me to leave this world behind, then you ask me to stay. Very well! There will be plenty of time to abide by Emperor Toturi's decree." He stood again and threw his arms wide. "But to show all the world that we, the spirits of the Lion Clan, keep our duty to our Clan and the Empire foremost in our mind, we will form a Deathseeker unit! We will fight, and we will die, and we will see the victory of our Clan!"

Ginawa rose to his feet, bowed to the three spirit samurai, and turned around. "Akodo Ichihiro!" he shouted at the top of his lungs.

"*BANZAI!*" came the answering roar, and the cheers echoed all around the camp, a bright spot in the dark night.

* * * * *

A few weeks later, the Lion Clan spirits had slipped out of Dragon lands, and Ginawa and Ichihiro led them back to their ancestral holdings.

Akodo Kaneka rode a horse alongside the column, speaking with various spirit samurai, trying to guess the years they lived and died based on their dress, speech, and tactical knowledge.

"I hear that our unit is to be called Tsuko's Heart," said one spirit samurai, a young woman of no more than twenty—discounting the years she had been dead. "Why is that?"

"During the war against Fu Leng, the Clan was divided," said Kaneka. "That dark god had possessed the thirty-ninth Hantei. Some of the Lion chose to fulfill their vows and serve the Emperor, bound by their honor. Some of the Lion chose to forsake their vows, yielding their honor for the sake of their duty to the Empire. Matsu Tsuko gave her life to try to heal the rift in that Clan, killing herself to try to lift the burden of the vow her people had taken."

"Sort of like this legion tries to heal the rift between spirits and mortals?"

"I guess so."

The spirit samurai pursed her lips and nodded. "I always wondered what happened," she said to herself.

"What do you mean?"

"I was there when Toturi recaptured Otosan Uchi," she said grimly, looking up at Kaneka. "I died of the plague a few months later."

"I'm sorry," said Kaneka.

"Don't be," she said. "I'd give anything to be here right now. I guess in a way I have."

She looked at Kaneka again.

"You know, you look a lot like your mother did when she was your age."

14   STAND AGAINST THE WAVES

The
Fifteenth
Year
of the
Reign
of
Toturi l

In the mountains of the Dragon Clan, steep and barren and forbidding, a solitary figure ran through the low-lying clouds and the insistent chilling drizzle. She ran barefoot, carrying nothing and wearing only short breeches and a sleeveless jerkin laced tightly across her breast. Despite the fact that she ran like the wind and icy water glistened upon her shaved pate, her face showed neither discomfort nor exertion.

As she ran, it seemed her tattoos ran as well. She had many colorful designs over her body—mountain peaks graced her feet, the face of a hawk covered her face, but the largest was the long, detailed centipede that twined its way over her entire body. Bright red in color, it ran up and down each arm, up the side of her neck, around her skull, and down her spine, and could be seen crisscrossing her abdomen in several places. At her speed, it was not possible to locate the centipede's head or tail, and it seemed the crimson centipede itself crawled about her skin.

Her feet made a hard sound against the beaten mountain path she followed, a sound like rock striking against rock, a rhythm as fast as the best drummers could manage. She passed a detachment of guards in an isolated magisterial station (now decorated with the mon of the Steel Chrysanthemum), and no sooner could the guards rise from their seats than she was already past them. They watched her retreating form, then looked with admiration at the faint footprints she had left indented in the rock-hard path.

She had run this way since dawn, without food, water, or rest, and she continued until just after dusk, when she entered Shiro Agasha, where Hantei made his headquarters.

Guards opened the gates and doors for her well in advance of her approach, and she ran directly into Hantei's presence.

There she stopped, bowed, and immediately collapsed, chest heaving, head swaying, water dripping from her monastic clothes. She gestured vaguely with one hand as she fought to retain consciousness. Paper and brush were immediately provided, and she scrawled out her message while she gasped for breath.

"The Lion invade," she wrote. "They marched through Nanashi Mura this morning, heading for Toi Koku."

Hantei looked at the paper where it lay on the floor beneath her quivering hand. "Do they?" he said. "We shall have to pay our respects for their treachery." He looked at the tattooed monk seemingly without seeing her. "Take her," he said, and turned to Tsuneo.

Two samurai stepped forward and lifted her by the shoulders to help her from the room. One of them glanced at her intricate centipede tattoo. Though it was of course motionless, it seemed almost as if it could move.

Strange, he thought, to have such a beautiful tattoo inscribed only in black ink.

* * * * *

The Lion armies marched across the frontier in perfect order. Blocks of warriors a hundred wide and fifty deep moved in perfect unison—stately, majestic, powerful. Wide helmets topped with straw manes waved in the breeze like grain, countless banners rippled with the sound of raindrops, and the sun glinted cheerfully off of the blades of thousands of naginata. Many units sang martial songs. Morale was high, and the golden glow of Tsuko's Heart, the huge Deathseeker legion, swelled the Lion samurai with pride. For their part, the samurai of Tsuko's Heart sang bawdy drinking songs. Having already surrendered to death, they found, brought a curious lightness of heart.

Cavalry outriders patrolled outside the mass of infantry, scouting the best paths and ensuring that enemy pickets could not strike the Lion armies by surprise. Small groups of shugenja were scattered evenly throughout the army. Dispersed in this way they could provide support where needed and did not make a tempting target for enemy archers, or, for that matter, the fire-slinging Dragon monks.

In the center of the army, amid a veritable forest of great banners four and five stories high, rode the command group. At one edge of the group, slightly separated from the rest, Akodo Kaneka rode with his foster father Akodo Ginawa.

"This will be a difficult fight," said Kaneka. "The Dragon mountains are all but impassable, especially once we get past Shiro Kitsuki."

"Ah, but that's not our plan," said Ginawa. "Shiro Mirumoto is our goal."

"But that's north of here," protested Kaneka.

"Yes. First we march west across the lowlands, so it looks like we're going to Shiro Kitsuki. The Phoenix march farther north, curving along the base of the mountains and angling south. We attract all the attention, while they travel under a cloak woven by their shugenja. The Dragon divert their defenses to the south, trying to anticipate our moves. We keep moving west. In this way, we leave our flank open to a Dragon assault. They'll see a chance to strike at our supply lines. When the Mirumoto army moves out, we cut back north. The Lion and the Phoenix attack the Dragon from two sides in the foothills and defeat them."

"Ah," said Kaneka. "The hope is to draw the Dragons out, defeat them in the field, and march on an underguarded castle."

"Yes."

"What if they don't come out?" Kaneka asked.

"Well, the Dragon forces will still be in the vicinity of Shiro

Kitsuki expecting us. We still cut north. And if the Mirumoto army waits inside the castle, we surround it and besiege it, and, since we'll be in the narrow Dragon passes, we should be able to hold off any relief effort."

Kaneka nodded. "And so with this, we hope to smite the Dragon Clan from the clutches of Hantei?"

"Yes," answered Ginawa. "I don't know why they follow him. Maybe he has them terrorized, though it's hard to imagine anything frightening a Dragon. Their own tattooed monks are frightening enough. Perhaps if we can show Hantei's weakness, they will throw off his rule over them. If not," he added, "this could be a long war."

* * * * *

Hantei sat on a stone throne carved for him by the Dragon Clan. It was cold, uncomfortable, and reminded him daily that he was in the mountains of the Dragon and not on the coast where a Hantei should be. He waited in what used to be the throne room of the Agasha daimyo. The location was the best he could find until such time as he captured Otosan Uchi, and if Tamori held any objections to being displaced from his own throne room, he had not voiced them.

The doors to the throne room opened and a spirit samurai entered, clad in old-fashioned robes in the blood-red and black colors of the Scorpion Clan.

"Bayushi Baku," said Tsuneo, by way of introduction.

Hantei sniffed as Baku knelt and bowed to the floor. "I am honored to be in your august presence," the Scorpion spirit said.

"I asked for a diplomat," said Hantei wearily. "Clearly you are not one. Why, then, are you here, and why should you live?"

"We understood that the Hantei Emperor requested an envoy," said Baku smoothly. "I reentered Rokugan from Jigoku some time ago. I have, therefore, more experience with Rokugan than any of my spirit brethren, for I have seen how people behaved when the spirits did not move among them. Thus it was decided that I would be the best envoy to the Hantei, and the most knowledgeable advisor."

"I see," said Hantei. "How is it you managed to slip from Jigoku back here?"

Baku smiled behind his mask. "Scorpions must keep their secrets to themselves, my lord," he said, "or else they are no longer secrets."

"And the Scorpions keep their armies to themselves," Hantei said. "I would prefer that to change. The Lion betrayed me and joined together to oppose my rule. I need a new right hand, for despite their brash statements, the Dragon Clan cannot be both my right hand and my left. I choose the Scorpion to be my right hand, for your sting is far more suited to my taste than the heavy hand of the Lion."

"My lord," Baku said, "we of the Scorpion honor all traditions and revere all ancestors. Forgive me, but we must therefore refuse the honor of being your right hand. Since the dawn of time, we have been the underhand of the Emperor, and we could no more be two hands than could the Dragon. We will not abandon the duty of the underhand, for in so doing, we would disgrace you."

Clever, thought Hantei. He may be more of a diplomat than I thought. But then again, he is a Scorpion. . . .

"You know that I seek to unseat the bandit who has seized the throne of Rokugan," Hantei said. "Does the Scorpion support the traditional claim of the Hantei, or do they oppose the divine mandate given at the dawn of time and favor a ronin?"

"The Scorpion's duty is not to choose the Emperor but to serve the Emperor."

"Then serve me and march to war!"

"My lord," said Baku patiently, "there are many factors that must be considered in such a decision." He held up one finger, his hand held delicately in front of his breastbone. "The Crab and Crane fight along our borders, and were we to weaken out defenses there, our lands might become a battleground." A second finger raised itself. "The samurai of the Hare Clan harass us without mercy, tying up our forces in the protection of our frontier." A third finger joined the first two. "We control the passes through the Spine of the World, and so long as we remain out of the war, your supplies can pass freely." Then the last finger rose up, and Baku's hand looked as if he were about to deliver a chopping blow. "And finally, so long as the other Clans believe we are neutral in this matter, the more easily our agents can move in and out, gathering intelligence and spreading rumors."

Hantei leaned back in his throne and draped one arm over the side. The other he rested on the armrest, and with that forefinger he slowly tapped his lips as he mulled over Baku's words.

"So the Emperor commands you to fight," said Tsuneo, "and you claim to fight best by not fighting. Is that it?"

"A scorpion does not challenge a great predator in the heat of the day," said Baku, nodding. "Instead, he stings the beast in the night that it should die by morning."

"How can we trust you?" asked Tsuneo bluntly.

"I trust I do not have to remind the Emperor, but I shall remind his honorable servant that the one named Toturi personally murdered Bayushi Shoju, broke the Scorpion Clan, and by these actions doomed Shoju's wife Kachiko to be married to the thirty-ninth Hantei. While others may forget, the Scorpion Clan remembers.

"But to show the Emperor's honorable servants that the Scorpion are not a timid people, we shall supply ten thousand spirit samurai to his service. This we offer in addition to intelligence, supplies, and a ready refuge within our lands."

"When will they march?" asked Hantei.

"They stand ready at Soshi Castle."

"Excellent," said Hantei. "Baku, return immediately and march north. I shall provide you with a Dragon Clan liaison. Tsuneo, we'll split our army here between Shiro Kitsuki and Shiro Mirumoto. Let the Lion army continue to Shiro Kitsuki. Follow them with the combined Mirumoto forces at a distance. When the Lion lay siege to Shiro Kitsuki, we shall wait until they are engaged, then we shall hit their forces from both sides. I shall lead half of this army from the north. You shall lead your forces from the south. The Lion will be trapped with enemies on both sides and in their center. I expect that they shall be able to break out, of course, if they focus their force. Then you shall give pursuit as they retreat back to Lion lands, and we shall trap their remnants between your forces and Baku's Scorpions.

"We shall crush the Lion strength in one swift campaign," Hantei said, slamming one fist into the other. "Then we shall see about burning Otosan Uchi."

* * * * *

Lion scouts reported military movement at Shiro Mirumoto, and, believing that the Dragon army had set out to attack their supply line, Motso turned his forces north and east to meet them.

In actuality, the scouts had seen Tsuneo's reinforcements marching into Mirumoto Castle. Immediately after he arrived, Tsuneo reorganized his army in preparation for the campaign. Thus he left Shiro Mirumoto a few days after the Lion commanders thought he had, and with a larger force. For his part, Tsuneo was not aware that the Lion army had turned so sharply back upon its line of march and was greatly surprised when his army encountered them in a matter of a few days instead of weeks.

The Phoenix advance into Dragon territory had been hampered by swollen rivers in the wake of the spring rainstorms, and, informed by a magical message sent by the Kitsu shugenja that the Dragon were on the move, they altered the course of their march. Instead of taking a direct route through the foothills toward their Lion allies, they skirted to the east, across smoother terrain. In this way they hoped to make up the time they had lost fording the fast-flowing mountain runoff. Because they had moved before the Dragon had, the Phoenix were actually slightly ahead and to the side of the Dragon forces, and, thanks to their circuitous route, they failed to contact the Lion scouts.

Thus the Lion and Dragon armies met in a place neither would have chosen, had their scouting been more accurate—a rough and unkind place known as Fallen Ground.

Fallen Ground stood at the base of one of the most severe granite escarpments to be found at the edge of the Dragon mountains. Sheer crags and precipices of solid rock thrust high into the air, the outriders of even higher and harsher peaks beyond. Here the cold, desolate mountains waged an eternal battle with the rolling, grassy plains that ran from here to the Spine of the World. The warm, moist winds of the valley turned the cold insistence of the mountains against them as a martial arts master turns a student's attempts to resist into a weapon. Over the centuries, these warm breezes gently deposited water into the face of the rocky cliffs. The mountains' own winter chills froze that water, and the expanding ice sent gargantuan slabs of primal rock tumbling into the smoothly sloping lands below. It was these huge boulders that gave Fallen Ground its name, and it was the fear of the unannounced arrival of more of these boulders that prevented farmers from trying to till this fertile soil.

Tsuneo's troops moved in two dozen long columns, weaving their way through the massive stones of Fallen Ground. He rode in the center column, a bow's shot from the lead elements, which themselves were a bow's shot from the advanced guard.

"This is fine rock," he said as he trailed his hand along the side of a mammoth chunk. "We should have mountains such as this in our lands. We could build the Wall so high and so thick that even the onis could not pass."

"I have seen the Wall, you know," said Agasha Tamori. "It's impressive. I think maybe you did have mountains like this once upon a time and quarried them down to nothing."

"Perhaps," said Tsuneo, chuckling. "It's as good a way to clear farmland as any."

Suddenly Tsuneo heard a cry of alarm and the sound of a skirmish. He looked all around, but the plethora of granite boulders prevented him from seeing as far as he'd like. "Where is that? What's happening? Damn these rocks, they turn the sounds all around!"

He could see large portions of several of his columns and small sections of several others in the distance. The samurai in each were themselves looking around in confusion. "Damn it!" he cursed again, then he raised his war fan and, at the top of his lungs, bellowed, "ALL HALT!" He heard the order being repeated throughout his army. Another clash of steel and flesh echoed vaguely through the area.

"You! You ten," he ordered, gesturing to the Crab samurai he kept close at hand in his command group, "find out what's going on. We found someone, or something found us! I need to know! Fan out from there to there," he added, gesturing from the front quarter of the army on the mountain side to the rear quarter of the army on the plain side, "and bring me back a report! Move!"

The samurai departed without even bowing, running to their assigned tasks.

Rumors rippled down the columns like fish up a narrow stream, and Tsuneo saw the samurai turning toward the front of the army.

Sergeants began to organize the men, preparing them for battle and sending the detachments forward. Presently one of the Crab runners returned, and panted, "Lion army, met them with our left side to their left, like this," and he placed his fists together offset.

"I see," said Tsuneo. "Go to the four rightmost columns. The column farthest right is to form up. They are our reserves and will wait there in case the Lion try to flank us to the right. The next three columns are to reverse their march and come around behind our army and move onto our left flank. Go!"

As the runner left on his errand, Tsuneo leaned to Tamori. "This is impossible," he said, surveying the field of huge boulders. "I need to be able to survey the whole battlefield. Where can I go that I can see everything?"

"Up there," said Tamori.

Tsuneo followed his outstretched finger to the top of the huge granite cliffs on their right. He grunted. "I see," he said, and clucked his tongue. "I guess we do this the hard way."

* * * * *

Kitsu Motso stood atop the largest granite slab in the area. An ersatz ladder has been improvised using two of the large Lion war banners. Long strips of their cloth lashed the two long poles together, and struts chopped from smaller poles kept the rails separated.

By the time the Lions had assembled on top of their command post, they saw that Tsuneo's forces already occupied a similar position across the battlefield. The Lion command group had formed up, given their foes a cheer of respect, then set about planning a way to crush them.

The late morning and early afternoon had been filled with uncontrolled skirmishing as both sides wrestled to deploy their forces. This sort of disorganized combat bridled Motso, and his temper had worn thin throughout the hours of blind fighting. Across the way, Tsuneo fought defensively. He could afford to; this was his land, and the longer he kept Motso delayed, the closer reinforcements would be.

"If we cannot push them from the field by nightfall, we will lose this battle," said Motso.

"But sir," protested an aide, "we haven't been able to flank them. Each attempt gets counterflanked or cut off. If we try to advance, their archers cut us down."

"I know. Tsuneo has turned these boulders into his fortress," said Motso. "They are as good as one, because they break apart the cohesion of our army."

He folded his arms and scanned the battlefield again. He could see the unit banners of his various formations scattered throughout the rocky plains, their proud emblems standing high enough to be visible even from a great distance. They spread out from his left to his right in a large, irregular crescent, marking the location of his troops. No such banners marked the Dragon army, but Motso knew they were out there. It was frustrating. He knew that Tsuneo arranged his defense based upon the Lion movements, but he could not counteract Tsuneo's moves. They were, to him, invisible. It was as if he were dueling blindfolded. If only he could blindfold his opponent.

Then he saw his error. He turned to his generals.

"Pass the word," he said. "Go to the units at the center of our line. They are to pull back, disengage from the Dragon—all except the Lioness Legion and the Pride, who will maintain an active skirmish line. The standard bearers of all units from Tsuko's Heart to the Steel Claws will move toward the right flank, and those from the House Guard to the Golden Sun will move toward the left flank."

"Ikoma's Double Envelopment?" asked one general.

"Indeed," said Motso, looking at Tsuneo across the way. "It was a new tactic in those days, was it not?"

"I believe it was, my lord."

"Make it happen. And give me seven archers, one for each of the seven fortunes, with arrows of fire. When they fire, all units charge the enemy. Is that clear?"

The generals nodded and passed the word. Within a few moments, the unit standards began pulling back from the Dragon lines, then, pumping up and down to rally the troops, they proceeded toward the flanks. Ikoma's double envelopment sought to engage the flanks of the foe, tying them up and bending the line so that additional troops could move around the ends of the line and strike at the enemy command group. Properly executed, an army suddenly found itself surrounded and without command, and the impact on morale was extreme. Entire armies had been routed and destroyed in this manner.

Motso watched Tsuneo as his orders were executed. Tsuneo studied the movements for a few moments, then erupted into action, barking orders, gesturing to the flanks, and gesticulating to convey ideas that Motso did not recognize but was certain were fiendishly clever countermeasures. Most excellent.

Motso smiled grimly, for his units were not moving to the flanks. Only the standard bearers were. His units, with Tsuko's Heart at the center, waited just behind the skirmish line. He watched as the standard bearers on the flanks paraded around. He was pleased that they spaced themselves apart at such a distance to imply that large numbers of samurai milled around each banner. He waited a while longer to ensure that Tsuneo had enough time to deploy his forces to the flanks.

He turned to his archers. "Fire," he said quietly.

Seven blazing arrows arced through the air. A great roar erupted throughout Fallen Ground, as if the stones themselves went to war. The standard bearers recently sent to the flanks did not surge forward, but those of the rest of the army did. It was a massive charge, involving the whole Lion army. Certainly no one expected a clever general like Kitsu Motso to charge like a Matsu. The units on the flanks served to tie up the Dragon forces, while Tsuko's Heart and the House Guard led a hard thrust right into the heart of the Dragon army, aimed at the command staff itself.

Motso watched the developments. His flank units faltered then fell back as the Dragon counterattacked. He watched Tsuneo, scowling as he noticed that the Lion banners were not moving for an envelopment. He checked the center of his line and saw the banners for the Lioness Legion and the Pride closing on his position.

Motso nodded in satisfaction as he saw Tsuneo's body start in sheer surprise. Arrows began to fly past Tsuneo's command group, striking one of his aides and sending him tumbling from the great stone block. Tsuneo signaled a retreat, then he and his command group rapidly descended from their post.

"Look, sir!" said one of his aides, gesturing to the south. "Phoenix banners!"

For the first time since he had ascended that rock, Motso finally sat down.

"Perhaps they saw the carrion birds circling," added the aide, half to himself.

"Excellent," Motso said wearily. "Send riders to the Phoenix. Have them pursue Tsuneo's army. Take stock of both side's casualties." He exhaled loudly. "We may have won the field, but I am not certain that we won the battle."

* * * * *

The Battle of Fallen Ground was costly for the Lion Clan, which suffered heavy casualties in the massed charge. However, Tsuneo's army of Dragons and spirits fared no better. The Phoenix pursued them aggressively, driving them back to Shiro Mirumoto without a chance to regroup and picking off stragglers wherever they were found. Most of these were, of course, mortals, who could not keep up with the spirit samurai.

When word of the victory reached Otosan Uchi, Toturi's Imperial guard took the field to reinforce the Lion armies. The Lion pushed farther west, leaving the Imperial Guard to watch Hantei's forces at Shiro Kitsuki while Motso's troops sought to cut off the supplies that were working their way north from Hantei's Crab Clan holdings. With the aid of a ragged band of hungry Unicorn cavalry, Motso captured several fully laden caravans, sending strategic supplies back to the Lion capital and burning the rest.

Having expected a move such as this, Tsuneo left the mortal Dragons at Shiro Mirumoto where they were subsequently besieged by the Phoenix. He led the spirit portion of his army on a winding march through the mountainous Dragon lands to Shiro Kitsuki. There they were allowed to rest, although the continued harangues by Hantei drove their morale down. Tsuneo took command of the garrison army from Hantei and led these fresh forces west, leaving Dragon lands undetected and turning south to engage the Lion.

Tsuneo found himself frustrated by the Unicorn cavalry, which acted as Motso's screening force. They rode horses brought back from barbarian lands far to the west, captured during their eight hundred years away from Rokugan. Tsuneo had never fought Unicorn samurai during his lifetime, and he cursed his inexperience. Despite the fact that his spirit samurai were faster than mortals, the Unicorn cavalry were faster still. They expertly evaded any combat and kept his forces safely away from the Lion troops.

Taking his troops on a forced march at night down a river gulley, Tsuneo caught up with Motso at last. The river was low in the wake of the long, hot summer, and at dawn his troops surprised the Lion army encamped on the river's banks. At the Battle of Shallow Waters, Tsuneo's forces won the day, but by then the damage had been done, and Hantei's army had to winter in Dragon lands without the supplies they'd expected to have.

Tsuneo's army, in order to avoid further straining the supply situation, marched south to Crab territory, crossing the Spine of the World amidst the first winter snows. Motso's Lion forces retired in good order to Lion lands and hosted a sizable contingent of displaced Unicorns through the winter.

Hearing these reports in his war room during winter court at Otosan Uchi, Toturi turned, picked up his treasured katana from its ornate mahogany stand, and presented it to Kitsu Motso.

"It is only fitting," he said, "that the right hand of the Emperor should wield the Emperor's sword."

15 WHEN DARKNESS DRAWS NEAR

The
Sixteenth
Year
of the
Reign
of
Toturi I

You have a messenger, General," said Agasha Tamori, bowing as he entered Tsuneo's chambers.

Tsuneo looked up as a tattooed monk entered the room. "Who sent you?" he asked brusquely.

The monk bowed and said, "Emperor Hantei, my lord."

"But the passes are still filled with snow. Spring is weeks away."

"Yes," the monk said simply. He held out a scroll, tied closed with ribbon and sealed with wax imprinted with the steel chrysanthemum. "I am instructed to await a reply."

Tsuneo looked at the monk. He was short but very stocky, his muscles so well defined that they seemed almost cut from crystal. Despite the chilly air, he wore only his thick breeches. The tattoo of a great snowy mountain dominated his chest, and the images of furry goatlike legs projected from beneath his short pants, terminating in sharp cloven hoofs on the tops of his feet. He had a headband tattooed around his head, which Tsuneo thought particularly odd.

The Stone Crab took the scroll, and the monk bowed and sat. Tsuneo unceremoniously popped the wax seal and opened it.

My Servant Tsuneo,

My spies tell me that Toturi is preparing to press his advantage and is already moving supplies south through Crane territory. I expect that he will take the majority of his army and try to destroy your forces while we are divided.

You will defeat Toturi. I am sending a unit of tattooed monks now and will send the Asako Riders and some of our Unicorn allies as soon as the passes clear. I am also taking some other measures that should help.

You failed to take Otosan Uchi. You failed to defeat the Phoenix rebellion. You failed to save our supplies from the Lion's rampage. You failed to keep our army together through the winter. You will not fail again.

Tsuneo crumpled the scroll with a snarl. One hand dropped to his katana, while the other crushed the scroll in his hand, cracking the wooden dowels. He turned his head slowly to his scribe, seated against the wall.

"Write this," he growled. "Emperor Hantei, greetings." He paused, then chuckled mirthlessly. "Your servant is pleased that you order him not to fail, for by following this command he finds he no longer must remind you that your servant, the general of your armies, has been following other orders of yours against his objections. Now he need not remind you that you planned the march on Otosan Uchi. He need not remind you that you precipitated the Phoenix rebellion by murdering a child. He need not remind you that you planned the campaign against the Lion. Your servant is doubly pleased, for he is certain that if he were to remind you of these poor decisions, it would disrupt your mood.

"Your servant finds your most recent message most liberating. He shall pursue this order to his utmost, and any subsequent orders that your servant receives that would prevent him from following this fundamental command shall, of course, with all due deference and obedience to your desires, be ignored. Emperor Hantei is, in fact, welcome to test his servant's resolve by issuing any new foolish instructions he desires that he may witness firsthand the efficacy with which his servant shall not be distracted from the task at hand.

"Your servant shall therefore immediately begin planning to prosecute this order and the war to the fullest degree possible. He shall start by ordering the majority of the northern army to march to the Crab lands and join forces under his command."

Tsuneo paused. "That should do it," he said, leaned over, and signed the scroll. He rolled it up, sealed it, and walked over to the messenger. As the Dragon stood, Tsuneo smacked the scroll sharply into the monk's chest. "Take that to your Emperor," he said rudely, "and make peace with the gods, for you shall not survive its delivery."

The monk bowed, turned, and left the room without a word.

Tsuneo thought for a few moments, then cocked an ear, hearing a commotion beginning outside.

"What could that be?" asked Tamori.

Tsuneo strode out of his headquarters, Tamori close on his heels. A crowd of spirit samurai had gathered around a long pole, from which draped two lengthy scrolls, one on each side, waving in the breeze. A message was inscribed in broad strokes on the parchments.

"Ah," said Tsuneo, glancing at the image of the Steel Chrysanthemum that topped of the pole. "This would likely be the 'other measures' Hantei mentioned."

They moved closer, and the spirit samurai stepped aside to clear their path. The scroll waved slightly in the breeze. It read:

Samurai of Emperor Hantei!

The Great Bandit Toturi has issued an edict. Any spirit killed or captured by his rebel army shall be struck from the family histories. They not only oppose us and seek to drive us from our rightful homes, but now they shall also forget our honor and our deeds, denying us the respect that is our due and condemning us to eternal nothingness! Defend your home, your life, your honor, and your Emperor! Do not let your descendants burn you from their scrolls! You have a right to your privileged position in your hall of ancestors, both in this life and the next!

Toturi's forces are on their way. There can be no negotiation with people such as these, who seek to place themselves above the Hantei and place you below the animals. Every samurai must do whatever it takes to be victorious, casting aside honor for duty, for Toturi leaves you no honor in honorable defeat!

Victory by any means! Victory at all costs!

Tamori looked about at the spirit samurai and saw the anger, consternation, and insult that showed on their faces. "I am shocked," he said to Tsuneo, "that Toturi would resort to such a thing."

"He didn't," said Tsuneo. "He is too honorable. But the lie is spreading like fire among the troops, and it shall never be extinguished."

Tamori looked around again and saw that Tsuneo was right. The fear of being forgotten hung heavy in every spirit samurai's heart.

"So they are coming," said Tamori, "and Hantei has ensured that his troops will do whatever it takes to defeat them."

Tsuneo looked sidelong at the Dragon shugenja as Tamori watched the troops milling and talking. Finally Tamori turned to Tsuneo and asked, "What are you looking at, my lord?"

"I'm just thinking," said Tsuneo absently, but his eyes never wavered.

* * * * *

The Lion army camped outside a small Scorpion village near the Crane border. Amidst the sea of gold and brown, one could see the green of the Imperial Guard, the reds of a sizable Phoenix contingent, and even a smattering of Crane blue and the purple of the Unicorn.

There were, of course, no Dragons, no Crabs, and no Scorpion. It was this last point that prompted Emperor Toturi to accompany the army on this leg of the journey and arrange a meeting with Bayushi Yojiro, the Scorpion daimyo.

The two of them sat at a small table in the finest inn in the village, enjoying a light meal and plum wine. As they were alone in the room, Yojiro had removed his mask, although it lay conspicuously on the table.

"Forgive me, Yojiro," said Toturi, "for following this excellent meal with some unpleasant conversation."

Yojiro nodded, and said, "Whatever my Emperor needs to do is welcome in my house."

Toturi paused for a moment then said, "I need the Scorpion."

Yojiro waited.

"This is a hard war," continued Toturi. "The spirits fight hard, and it is difficult to get the soldiers to fight their ancestors. Thankfully I have the Lion to form the core of my army. But the Scorpion Clan is powerful, and I need your troops so that we can put an end to all this. Now."

Yojiro exhaled heavily. "This is not as easy as you might expect, my Emperor." Toturi's eyes narrowed. Yojiro leaned forward. "No, my liege, this has nothing to do with you or what you have done. Shoju was wrong, and you were right to kill him. I hope I do not have to remind the Emperor that I surrendered to the magistrates on the day of the coup."

"Then tell me why this is difficult for you," said Toturi with a steel voice, "and then tell me why it's easier for the Empire to do without your support."

Yojiro looked at Toturi steadily then, reaching down, he pulled his wakizashi and scabbard from his belt and laid it on the table in front of him. "If the Emperor wishes," he said, "I shall seal the truth of my words with my life."

This time, Toturi waited without responding.

"My Clan is built on unquestioned loyalty," said Yojiro. "For a thousand years we have been the Emperor's underhand, serving for the good of the Empire. We have stained our honor, ruined our name, and sacrificed all that we have to do what was best. As a result, no one now trusts us, not even the Emperors we have served.

"In all these things, we require absolute obedience from our people. You will not find a Lion who will slander his own house and curse his own ancestors in order to complete his mission; he would sooner die than risk dishonor. Any samurai of the Scorpion will do so, for the Lion holds his honor high, and we hold the success of our duty high. I do not claim that one road or the other is superior. Both are necessary, because as the right hand of the Emperor, the Lion must be above reproach.

"Now this Scorpion loyalty flows upward, from the peasant to the samurai, from the samurai to the family, from the family to the Clan, from the Clan to the Emperor. And therein lies the difficulty.

"I swore to serve you and the Toturi dynasty. The spirits swore to serve the Hantei dynasty. The loyalty and obedience of each family runs both through the living, who follow you, and the dead, who follow Hantei. We are a people divided. Divided not between living and spirit, but divided within our own hearts.

"There is a legion of Scorpion spirits serving Hantei. I counseled against it, but the spirits believe that Shoju contaminated all the living with his lies against the last Hantei, so they serve the Steel Chrysanthemum.

"Yet I am not without my resources. Some of those who serve speak to those who serve me. I hear things, therefore, and I know some of the Hantei's moves. Yet I also know that the living who serve me often speak with them. Thus I find myself in a curious position: I do no trust the Scorpion." Yojiro smiled bitterly.

"We are also at the center of the Empire, my lord," he added, "surrounded on all sides. The Hare and Fox spirits press us, and thus our border with the Crab, where Hantei's armies are, has inadequate garrisons. Yet I also cannot move garrisons there from our border with the Lion, for such a move would catch the ear of Hantei and lead to an attack, and in such an attack, I cannot trust the loyalty of my own troops.

"However, my Emperor, I say this: I am playing the part of a neutral leader. I shall assist your supplies, and I shall not impede your troops. Any Scorpion who wishes to join your army may do so, although in light of events, there are not many willing so to do. I fear that if I press my Clan to choose, they shall choose the Hantei. But I am watching, and I am waiting, and I will strike when the time is right.

"And when the Scorpion strikes, my lord—mark my words—on that day you shall behold the power of my Clan."

Toturi sat with his brow furrowed, studying Yojiro's face and mulling over his words. Three times servants quietly opened the screen doors, peered in to see if anything were needed, and silently shut them again. At length Toturi stood.

"I cannot trust an army if its commander does not trust his troops," he said. "I will let you serve in your way." He turned to leave. Servants slid the door open, but Toturi paused as he stepped out. "Keep that wakizashi handy," he said, then turned his back and left.

* * * * *

They called themselves Toturi's Army now, in memory of the bygone days almost twenty years before, when the dishonored ronin had gathered a group of loyal samurai and fought against the legions of Fu Leng. They cut southwest, through the heart of Crab territory, searching for Tsuneo's forces. They marched through the farms and mines of the Crab, once managed by spirits, now apparently devoid of life. Unicorn scouts often saw various gold-hued spirits retreating before the vanguard, and the rearguard occasionally reported seeing them return to the fields once the army had passed. The whole effect was eerie, as if the spirits themselves were truly incorporeal.

"Is Tsuneo going to wait for us at the Wall?" asked Akodo Kaneka.

"Perhaps," said Ginawa.

"That wouldn't make sense. The Wall is designed to defend against the Shadowlands, not to defend against Rokugan."

"It works both ways," said the older man. "But more to the point, if he waits for us there, he gets the samurai who guard the Wall to fight, as well."

"You mean O-Ushi." Kaneka swore. "That's not good."

Toturi's Army continued its march through the apparently deserted fields and hills, knowing that the ever-patient spirit samurai were simply avoiding contact all around them. They bent their path around the armies that fought against the Crane invasion, that war that had bogged down into a series of sieges and relief efforts, a style of fighting in which the Crab were very experienced. Turning more to the south, Toturi's Army advanced on Shiro Hida, the capital of the Crab Clan. Tsuneo could ill afford to hide in his own capital so deep in his homeland without putting up a fight. It would be a great loss of face, and the enemy would control the area's rich resources. Tsuneo had to face his enemies on the open field.

Indeed, in the highlands above Hida Castle, with the great Kaiu Wall barely visible in the distance, Tsuneo's forces and Toturi's Army at last made contact. Motso immediately sent a pigeon back to Otosan Uchi to inform Emperor Toturi of the events thus far, then organized his forces for the battle that would last throughout rest of the day and far into the night.

As dawn broke the next morning, the generals surveyed each other's positions.

The core of Toturi's Army was the Lion Clan, in the very center of which was the heavy golden glow of the massive deathseeker's legion called Tsuko's Heart. On the right wing stood a strong contingent of Phoenix samurai, backed by several groups of shugenja. A small group of Scorpion and Crane samurai stood on the far right flank. To the left of the Lion was the Imperial Honor Guard, and the left flank was held by a restless group of Mantis samurai, their loyalty guaranteed by the donation Toturi had made to their Clan's coffers. Unicorn horse archers screened the army, harassing the enemy with the occasional stray arrow. Tsuneo could also see a small group of lancers held in reserve near Motso's command group, ready to stem any breaks in the line.

Though his force was by far the smaller, Tsuneo knew the burden of the attack was on Motso. Tsuneo's army centered on the spirit samurai, whom he knew tired far less easily than mortals and most of whom had had immeasurably more practice with their weapons. The center of his line was held by Baku's unit of Scorpion spirits, with Crab spirits to their right and Dragon spirits to their left. Tsuneo wished he had some Unicorn spirits, but they lingered near Hantei's forces across the Empire.

Crab mortals under Hida O-Ushi held Tsuneo's right flank, and the Dragon mortals under Agasha Tamori held his left. Scattered Scorpion ninja spirits acted as his pickets, lurking in the tall grass, and occasionally one of the Unicorn riders would go down in a sudden startled flurry of blood and surprise. In front of the Scorpion spirits, the Asako riders, Phoenix cavalry from well before Tsuneo's time, stood ready to countercharge any move the enemy made.

By far the most intimidating were the huge engines of war that stood behind the center of his line. Great catapults, their long arms bent and ready, waited to throw flaming balls of pitch and stone. Though their range was short, the effect was devastating. There were also a couple of siege towers, atop which archers stood, ready to rain death down upon any that approached. It was from the center of these towers that Tsuneo and his staff surveyed the battlefield, above a huge banner emblazoned with the Steel Chrysanthemum.

Motso surveyed the situation. Tsuneo had, in a very literal sense, planted his standard and dared Motso to take it. Motso could not tarry, for this was the Stone Crab's homeland, and to delay the fight would only allow Tsuneo to improve his fieldworks or sneak a few units through this familiar terrain to flank Motso's forces. The key to Tsuneo's defense were the siege engines and towers. If he tried to flank Tsuneo's forces, they would give ground, pivoting around the command tower while the catapults rained death on Motso's troops. In short, Tsuneo was not going to budge from his position. Such immobility could be used. . . .

* * * * *

From his perch high above the battlefield, Tsuneo saw Motso's command group issuing signals. The Unicorn horse archers immediately rode around toward Tsuneo's left flank, and behind the enemy lines, the Unicorn lancers also moved.

"He's committing his reserves early," observed Tsuneo to no one in particular. "Very odd."

The Unicorn archers turned around the left flank, and the Dragon units began yielding the ground, bending the line to keep a strong front against the cavalry. Despite suffering from sporadic barrages of arrows, the units kept good order. The horse archers kept out of range of the Crab catapults, and the lancers formed up behind them for a charge. Tsuneo was not concerned, for although the lancers' speed would prevent the catapults from doing them much harm, the unit was simply too small to defeat the Dragon infantry.

Then Tsuneo saw a surge of magic from the Phoenix ranks. His sharp gray eyes saw the shugenja whirling their hands, gathering power and drawing the winds to them. A unit of Phoenix heavy infantry soared into the sky, carried upon the breezes as fast as a horse could run. They looked like a red waterfall, dropping from one side of the battlefield to the other. Their trajectory would take them to where the Unicorn units had rallied. Tsuneo looked back and saw the Unicorn charging. He saw the intent. Once the Unicorn engaged the Dragon, the Phoenix could move in and drive Tsuneo's left flank back. Glancing back across the battlefield, he saw the Crane and Scorpion units advancing. They intended to hit Tsuneo's line at the bend and break the left flank.

If they think the Crab are slow, Tsuneo thought, they will learn. He ordered the catapults to come about, facing the Unicorn squadron. He knew they would not be able to bombard the lancers, but they could cause carnage as the airborne Phoenix samurai tried to form up for their charge. Once that attack had been stalled, the catapults could easily turn their attention to the rest of the attacking units. Tsuneo watched the trajectory of the Phoenix heavy infantry and gauged the best time to launch his catapults. They were ready, properly aimed, pitch ignited.

A single arrow shot up from Motso's command group, blazing a magical blue fire as it arced across the sky.

"What's that?" asked Tsuneo.

"Some sort of signal," said an aide.

Tsuneo looked over to his left flank. The Unicorn lancers had broken off, veering away from the attack. An updraft carried the Phoenix samurai farther away from Tsuneo's line. He looked right and saw that the Crane, Scorpion, and Phoenix had abruptly turned to their left and were marching parallel to Motso's lines, heading for the center.

"Sir!" said the aide. "Look! It's O-Ushi!"

Tsuneo looked to his right flank. The Crab mortals under Hida O-Ushi were realigning themselves towards Tsuneo's position, each unit readdressing itself into an attack position.

"I feared as much," said Tsuneo. "I saw it in her eyes last year, and now she's done it."

"I don't understand. . . ."

"She's supporting Toturi. Motso feinted left to draw our attention, and now O-Ushi can attack without being hit by the catapults. See? Here they come." Tsuneo gestured to the Mantis and the Imperial Guard. They were marching forward to reinforce O-Ushi's troops, who were already beginning their charge on Tsuneo's now-exposed right flank.

"Well, that's why I put her on the ocean's side of the line. Give the order," he said as he started to climb down from the tower, "retreat to the Wall. Put the catapults to the torch and fire the fields."

Fires rapidly erupted in front of Tsuneo's lines, ignited by troops and ninja alike. The rising flames quickly brought the attacks to a halt. Neither the Mantis nor the guard desired to charge through fire, for they could see a Crab rearguard waiting just on the other side of the flames. With her support denied by the fires, O-Ushi allowed the Crab spirits to disengage, and they retreated from the battlefield, burning the grasses as they withdrew.

* * * * *

Tsuneo's forces angled toward the Wall. Motso pursued in three columns, the center led by O-Ushi. Motso took the right with the Lion troops, and Toku led the Imperial Guard and the other factions on the left. Motso expected that Tsuneo would break north toward Dragon lands, and he intended to harry him with the Lion forces until the rest of the army could join. Toku guarded the left in case Tsuneo made a break for the sea, and O-Ushi kept up the pressure on the retreating forces.

They were all surprised when Tsuneo neither turned away nor stopped at the Wall. He headed straight into the Shadowlands.

O-Ushi sent a message to the other commanders. "We must pursue," she wrote. "He intends to go north outside the Wall, then reenter Rokugan near the Shinomen Forest. These are the Hiruma borderlands, not completely corrupted yet. We should be safe—certainly far safer than if we let him escape." Upon reading this, Motso ordered the pursuit.

The two armies marched hard through the fringes of the Shadowlands. Tsuneo's forces were hampered by the presence of the Dragon mortals, who could not keep pace with the rest of the troops. Additionally, Tsuneo's Crab scouts were hampered by the fact that they had last seen these lands centuries before they fell to the Shadowlands, and the ever-shifting terrain confused them.

O-Ushi's experienced guides knew these foul lands well, having spent their lives hunting vile monsters in these blighted places. Thus Toturi's Army brought Tsuneo to bay against the banks of Black Finger River. This fetid, oozing flow marked the boundary between the marginal Hiruma lands and the absolutely corrupted Shadowlands, and therefore the farthest afield Tsuneo could safely flee. He dared go no further into the Shadowlands, and the three columns of Toturi's Army blocked his escape.

* * * * *

Motso's forces struck at the spirit army immediately, pinning them against Black Finger River. Tsuko's Heart smashed into the center of Tsuneo's line, while the archers poured a deadly rain onto Tsuneo's reserves.

Tsuneo stalked about, shortening his line as much as possible and ordering his lieutenants to take tactical control. "Strategy means nothing here!" he bellowed as he approached Agasha Tamori. "There's nowhere to maneuver! Come with me!" He led Tamori and the Dragon shugenja to the rear, where the reserves were. The rain of arrows had thinned but still continued.

"Gather your power," Tsuneo said to them. "The warriors are doing all they can. They need your help."

Tamori was unnerved but obeyed Tsuneo's command. "Give me your hands," he told his shugenja. "Lend me your power."

"What are you going to do?" asked one.

"I'll . . . think of something. Just give me your power and let me focus." The group joined hands, though those touching their leader were apprehensive. Tamori closed his eyes and concentrated on his breathing. The others did likewise.

Tsuneo waited and watched. He could feel the pulsing energy, see Tamori growing more and more powerful. The green striations in Tamori's hands almost glowed. One of the shugenja was struck just above the collarbone by a falling arrow. She gasped and collapsed to the ground. The two adjacent shugenja quickly joined hands over her kicking body, but Tsuneo saw the ripples of uncertainty moving quickly up and down the line. This was as good a time as any.

He picked up an arrow from the ground and jammed it hard and fast into Tamori's shoulder. Tamori opened his panicked eyes to find Tsuneo's face was towering over his, and the Stone Crab shouted, *"Do something before we're all killed!"*

Panicked, Tamori reached out blindly with his accumulated power, greenish bolts of tainted chi arcing out in all directions. He screamed in agony and power, fear and anger. His eyes widened, and Tsuneo noted that the dark irises were themselves already beginning to fade to yellow—another symptom of the Shadowlands corruption that the shugenja tried to hide.

The ground beneath the group bucked as Tamori sought some way to control the vast power coursing through him. Feeling the sensation, fighting along the front dimmed momentarily, then abruptly stopped. Samurai sensed something was happening. Many turned to look toward the river and gasped in horror.

Black Finger River rose out of its bed, rearing up like a great shapeless watery cobra. For a moment, the only sound to be heard on the battlefield was Tamori's seemingly endless scream, which had twisted beyond pain to where it almost sounded like pleasure beyond his ability to bear.

The river rose, grew, and pulled back along its course, gathering more mass. The two armies began to separate, the samurai seeking whatever negligible safety there might be among their own kind against a horror such as this and unwittingly clarifying the river's target.

The great river spun itself slightly, then lashed out like a striking viper at Toturi's Army, smashing down upon the troops. As the river hit, it seemed to shatter into a thousand roiling coils that thrashed and lunged and pounced and pulled and sucked and drowned anyone within reach. It looked as if a hideous black surf were crashing endlessly on armored, screaming, dying rocks. Toturi's Army broke and ran, seeking to escape the terror. Tsuneo's forces huddled on the banks of the dry riverbed, waiting for the nightmare to end.

When at last the waters settled, they formed into a lake, its shallow bed carved out by the churning waters. Thousands of samurai were visible under the oily waters, drifting in the slight residual currents, eyes and mouths open in fear, fingertips brushing the surface of the water as if they sought to touch the world of the living one last time.

Tamori fell to his knees and looked out at the vile lake. "What have I done?" he whispered.

"Your Emperor says, 'Every samurai must do whatever it takes to be victorious,'" Tsuneo said coldly. "You swore unconditional service. You have done nothing more than what you swore to do, using the peculiar powers at your disposal." He spat on the ground and began rallying his troops, leaving Tamori sobbing in his wake.

* * * * *

Toturi's Army marched in demoralized silence toward Otosan Uchi. The spirits running the Crab lands no longer hid themselves from the troops but raided at night and ambushed foraging parties. As a result Motso pressed his troops to keep moving until they reached Scorpion lands.

"So I guess my first campaign is drawing to a close," said Toturi Tsudao, who rode next to Toku at the head of the Imperial Honor Guard.

"I hope you learned a lot," said the general. "Your father wants you to really be a good general when you get older, as good with your head as you are with your sword."

"I had hoped for a better ending," said Tsudao.

"The first rule of war is: Someone always loses," said Toku.

"But my father's army should never lose."

"The second rule of war is: Maybe nobody wins," Toku replied.

"Huh?"

"You can have two losers, but you can never have two winners."

Tsudao nodded. They rode in silence for some time. "You know what I am afraid of?" said Tsudao at last.

"What?" asked Toku. He was genuinely curious about what Tsudao could possibly fear.

"We don't have the backing of the heavens."

"What do you mean?"

"At the start of time, the sun and moon had Hantei, and they blessed the Hantei dynasty," said Tsudao emotionlessly. "The Hantei Emperors ruled with the power of the sun and moon, and they were even descended from a god."

"That's called a divine mandate," said Toku.

"Whatever it's called, my father doesn't have it. I mean, if he had it, they would have stopped that river from killing all his people. But they didn't. Why? Because he's not a Hantei, because he didn't save the thirty-eighth Hantei, and because he killed the last Hantei himself."

"Only after the Emperor was possessed by Fu Leng," said Toku pointedly.

"So that means he killed two gods," said Tsudao, shrugging. "He didn't get their permission to do it, either. So how can he have that . . . that—"

"Divine mandate?"

"Yeah."

"Well, since then, the sun and moon fell from the sky during the War of Shadows," said Toku, "and now we've got a new sun and moon. So what does that do to your divine mandate?"

Tsudao thought about this for a while. "Maybe that just compounds the problem," she said at last.

16 A SAMURAI NEVER STANDS ALONE

The
Seventeenth
Year
of the
Reign
of
Toturi I

Give me one good reason why I shouldn't torture you to death for your impertinence!"

Tsuneo looked up from his campaign map, cocking his head slightly toward Hantei XVI. Shadows from the paper lanterns fell across his face in unusual patterns.

"My liege," he said easily, "you underestimate the long memory of your servant. Since you entered your servant's camp with the rest of the army last fall, you have asked that question one hundred times. In those hundred times it did not distract your servant from his duty, and neither shall the hundred and first. The Emperor may rest assured that your servant shall do everything to follow your command and direct this war to the fullest of his ability, letting nothing stand in his way, not even your very clever attempts to disrupt his thinking." He nodded his head and turned back to the map. "However," he added as an afterthought, "your other generals are not quite as focused as your servant. You may not wish to ask that question of me in a more public situation, lest your other generals get clever ideas of their own."

"I will kill you when I am done with you," spat Hantei. "You will regret this insolence."

Tsuneo looked up again and blinked. "How could I possibly regret serving you in the fullest capacity? Nevertheless, you are delaying my explanation of my plan. If you would rather I briefed you as I brief the rest of the staff, I shall do so, and you can ask your distracting questions at that time."

Hantei, his eyes burning with hatred, said nothing. He knew that Tsuneo was the only one capable and unswervingly loyal enough to trust with leading his army, let alone safeguarding his privileged life. The man had just become so intolerable when he had realized it, too.

"Very well, then," said Tsuneo. "You need not actually give me your Imperial approval for this campaign, for I know that this is the best plan, and that if you withhold your approval, it must be another clever test to see if you can coax me away from doing my very best to win this war.

"We are camped here," he said, stabbing the map with one thick finger. "We bypass the Crane armies in the south and march to the coast here, at the port of Lonely Shore. That's a thriving Crane port, so we should be able to hire boats with ease. We leave the Asako riders at Kyuden Doji, and they move rapidly north. They draw out the Lion and possibly Toturi's Imperi—uh, *impertinent* personal guard. Meanwhile, our fleet moves up to the Bay of the Golden Sun and lands at White Stag at night. At dawn, we attack Otosan Uchi from the east. With the sea at our backs, we cannot be flanked. It will be bloody, but we can take the capital."

"I do not care about blood," growled Hantei. "I want that damned throne." He stroked his beard absently. "Are you ready if the people rebel?" he asked. "O-Ushi turned on you last year. What if she does so again?"

"We have already moved all the food stores into the mines. O-Ushi can keep her army, and as long as they stay on the Wall, we shall dole out the food they need. If they move against us, they go hungry, and their own stomachs will launch a counter-rebellion. The Crane? We can buy them with gold and the Yasuki lands. We can control the Phoenix by keeping Toturi's wife Kaede alive. We can barter her and her children for the Phoenix children."

"That would work nicely," purred Hantei. "I'd love to have those Phoenix brats back in my hands. And better yet, once we trade Kaede and her brats away, their lives are the responsibility of the Phoenix . . . and I can have them assassinated."

"The Lion," Tsuneo said as if he hadn't heard, "we cannot control. They will attack, but we will be ready by the time they can prepare, and we can hold off their assault until they break their own back. I wouldn't worry about the Unicorn, and the Scorpion you say you have under your thumb. I can think of no other threats."

Hantei eyed Tsuneo narrowly. "Then I guess we'll see how clever my servant is, won't we?" he said.

* * * * *

Tsuneo's army moved north along the smaller mountain range that separated the southern Crane lands from those of the Crab. The army turned east, following a well-traveled road through the low mountains and passing through the lands of the Sparrow Clan. Small and scarcely acknowledged in most Imperial dealings, the Sparrow thought it best to provide Hantei's legions with food, water, and sake to speed them on their way. It was with deep respect and deeper relief that they watched Hantei's army pass by their humble fortress.

Once out of the mountains, Tsuneo turned his army north again, moving upstream alongside the steeply banked river that demarcated the Crane borders—at least, the official Crane borders. They often saw blue-clad scouts in the area riding their white horses, reporting their progress to the Crane regent. The army kept its best pace, making for a large bridge that spanned the river. Built originally to expedite trade between the Crane, the Scorpion, and the Fox Clans, the bridge could accommodate an army as easily as a caravan and would make for a swift crossing.

However, as the lead elements approached the bridge, they found the bridge blocked by a handful of Crane samurai and a single female shugenja. Word was sent back to the command staff, and Tsuneo and Hantei moved forward to see for themselves, Tsuneo on his horse and Hantei in his palanquin.

As they moved closer, Tsuneo saw four samurai with naginata kneeling on one knee on the near side of the bridge, the wicked blades of their weapons aimed at Tsuneo's force. The shugenja stood pleasantly in the center of the bridge. Bayushi Baku, who had been at the army's front, rode back to report.

"Who are they?" Tsuneo asked.

Baku glanced back at the back banners worn by the four samurai. "They are Daidoji. You can see their family mon from here."

"The Iron Crane, huh?" grunted Tsuneo.

"Yes," replied Baku as he turned his horse back around. He gestured toward the shugenja with his head. "I don't know if she is a Daidoji or an Asahina. If the latter, good. If Daidoji, it makes me . . . nervous."

"What do they want?" asked Tsuneo.

"I don't know," said Baku. "They have said nothing. I'm not even sure which side they're on. It's not clear to me whether the Crane spirits fight over Yasuki lands in the name of the Hantei or simply with the excuse of the Hantei. I thought it best to wait for you to arrive."

Tsuneo nodded and urged his horse forward. "You there!" he called, and his voice carried like thunder. "I am Hida Tsuneo, servant of Emperor Hantei!"

The shugenja looked over and began walking briskly up to Tsuneo. As she passed between the four samurai, they retreated across the bridge. Baku directed the army's advance scouts to begin crossing.

Tsuneo watched as the proud shugenja strode over. As she got closer, he saw the gray starting to show in her hair, although her skin still looked quite young. But she was far too frail for him to consider her attractive.

Tsuneo opened his mouth to speak, but the shugenja beat him to it.

"The Crane will never bow to the Crab!" she shouted, and made a swift and sudden mystical pass with her hands. No sooner had she done this than the bridge exploded in a burst of molten rock and fire, ripping apart the stone and flinging shards everywhere. The scouts on the bridge died instantly, torn to shreds by the force of the explosion, and dozens more of Tsuneo's troops were felled by flying chunks of masonry.

The shugenja died an instant later, sliced into three separate pieces by the swords of Tsuneo's bodyguards. Stunned, Tsuneo looked at her, then at his crippled samurai, then across the river for the four Daidoji soldiers. They had already vanished, hiding in the brush and grass.

Baku stared as well, eyebrows raised and fingers steepled together. "The Daidoji are an interesting breed," he said quietly. "She wanted to make a statement to your face."

Tsuneo closed his eyes and rubbed the bridge of his nose. He knew he could march north and cross over the bridge that led to the Hare Clan's holdings, but if he did so, he was certain the Daidoji would blow that up as well. He couldn't move south, because his troops would receive a similar reception from the Crane armies down there. That meant that his only real choice was to build a makeshift bridge here, with those four Daidoji samurai—and probably others—working to sabotage his efforts. With the speed and depth of the river and the treacherous slope of its banks, it could take weeks—and lives.

Not that he had a choice. It would also take him weeks at best to bypass the Crane lands and march overland to Otosan Uchi, and in such a march the precious element of surprise would be irrevocably lost.

Hantei's tattooed bearers padded up silently alongside Tsuneo. The Emperor opened the window to his palanquin and peered out. "Perhaps," he said, "my servant would be well advised not to take on diplomacy in addition to military command, lest it prove more than he can handle."

The window slammed shut, leaving Tsuneo to his thoughts.

* * * * *

After a concerted effort in the face of persistent sabotage, Hantei's army finally forced its way across the river and continued its march to Lonely Shore. The Daidoji made the journey as nightmarish as possible, fouling wells, digging pit traps, weakening small bridges, and creating as much fear and injury as possible. Hantei fumed that anyone would be so dastardly, but Tsuneo took it in stride. Many of those selfsame tactics he had employed during his years on the Wall, bringing down Shadowlands creatures in any fashion possible.

Despite Tsuneo's concerns, the Crane armies never did march north from their battle in the Yasuki estates. The spirit army only faced the continued harassment of the ever-present and never-visible Daidoji.

As they approached Lonely Shore, Tsuneo wondered whether the Crane would try to resist the occupation of the city. In fact, they did not, and Hantei's forces entered the city without incident. The troops moved through the streets and found that they were well received. Teahouses and inns were open, merchants had plenty of wares to sell, and the troops were left with the feeling that they had journeyed through hostile lands to return finally to friendly territory.

Tsuneo billeted his troops in large groups for mutual protection against any attempts at assassination, poisoning, or sabotage. Proprietors had liaisons assigned to them, who never let the Crane merchants out of their sight—the better to prevent any conspiracy against the Hantei's troops.

In spite of these precautions, or perhaps because of them, the short stay was enjoyable, and the citizens of Lonely Shore most accommodating. Fishermen plied the shoreline, bringing in their catch each day. Independent merchant ships, as well as ships from the Crane and Mantis Clans, paid visits to the port over the next few days.

Hantei's staff made arrangements for Crane ships to carry his army north toward Otosan Uchi, and although the captains' fees were rather excessive, Hantei was willing to pay. After the deal was concluded, Hantei's armies cordoned off the docks late at night and began to load their troops onto the ships. Hantei was so concerned about sabotage that he even locked up the captains and crew in their ships' cabins for the duration of the loading.

For hours, the citizens of Lonely Shore watched under a new moon as rowboat after rowboat sculled out to the waiting ships with loads of golden-hued samurai aboard. In perfect stillness, the samurai climbed aboard the ships and disappeared below decks, the utter silence marred only by the lap of waves against the ships' hulls.

It was eerie to observe. The quiet made it seem almost as if the spirits were actual ghosts, incorporeal creatures that neither knew the world nor touched it.

Once the cargo of warriors had been safely hidden below decks, the captains and crew were allowed to take the decks and get the ships under way. The last of the rowboats moved back in to shore, taking with them a few remaining spirit samurai who were to remain behind as a garrison.

In the black of night, it was almost impossible to see the outline of the ships' hulls. Only a few dim lanterns were visible from shore. The ships started to slide out to sea, aided by the receding tide.

As they pulled farther out to sea, a series of splashing sounds reached the ears of those on shore. There were a few shouts, then one by one the Crane ships burst into flames, lighting up the night sky. Suddenly everything could be seen clearly, and the crowd on the shore watched as Hantei's invasion fleet quickly became consumed by flame. Fires roared up the masts and sails, and ran along the beams and decks with amazing speed. Fires even spread out upon the surface of the water, betraying the spilled oil that had started the conflagration, and silhouetting the crewmen, who even now were swimming for the safety of the shore.

Yet in the midst of the blazing infernos, not a sound was to be heard. No spirit screamed, none shouted orders for escaping their immolation, and no one swore eternal vengeance for the betrayal.

The citizens of Lonely Shore crowded the shoreline, strangely entranced by the scene, and they failed to notice that Hantei's garrison was slowly fanning out behind them, sealing off all exits from the city.

Inside a tall warehouse at the ocean's edge, Hantei XVI dispassionately watched the ships burn and die, his fan flapping slowly in front of his face. "You were right, Tsuneo," he said. Tsuneo did not respond. "And you, Tamori," said Hantei, still not taking his eyes off the ships, "your shugenja did their jobs well. The illusions of the troops were so well done I almost believed them myself. I shall certainly have to watch you and your people carefully."

"Doing it at night made it easier, my liege," said Tamori. "Since it was so dark, all they had to do was create the glow."

There was a long pause as the three watched the vessels light up the night. The popping and hissing was clearly audible, even at this distance.

Finally, Tsuneo spoke. "I'll go find the captains of the Mantis ships," he said.

Hantei watched as one of the junks slid under the water until it struck bottom, one of its masts still burning above the waves. "Round up all those who live in this city," he said. "Put them all in this warehouse, then burn them as they sought to burn us."

* * * * *

There was a Mantis ship in the harbor, built for hauling large quantities of heavy cargo over the seas. Its silky green banner fluttered and shone gaily in the rising sun. Even from shore, Tsuneo could see the Mantis sailors watching the city carefully, long pole arms ready at hand.

After waiting a polite amount of time for the crew to eat their breakfast and make their morning prayers and meditations, Tsuneo sent a rowboat sculling out to the vessel. Despite the best efforts of the messengers, the captain refused either to set foot on land or to allow any spirit to board his vessel, a choice that Tsuneo thought very wise.

Since no dignified vessel remained in the harbor after the previous night's fiery debacle, Hantei refused to negotiate with the captain. He did not want to debase himself in any manner and therefore sent Tsuneo in his stead. The Stone Crab rode out in a rowboat and sat in the lurching waves trying to negotiate with a Mantis captain who leaned over the ship's railing, significantly out of reach above Tsuneo's head and silhouetted by the sky.

It was not the most auspicious posture from which to conduct negotiations. Then again, little if anything about Hantei XVI was auspicious. . . .

Tsuneo thought it best to skip the formal introductions. He knew that the Mantis captain knew who he was and which army waited in the port. He also knew that the Mantis Clan had been formed by a wandering Crab many centuries ago and thus, in all likelihood, held most etiquette and social ritual to be hollow posturing.

"I am Hida Tsuneo," he said simply, squinting up at the bright morning sky. He considered standing in the rowboat, but the surf was active, and he wasn't certain he could maintain his balance while staring straight up.

"I know who you are," said the captain. "You are the Stone Crab, of whom legends are told. I am Moshi Shanegon of the Mantis. What can I do for you this fine morning, my lord?"

"We need ships, honorable Moshi," said Tsuneo bluntly, "transports to move our troops north to the capital—your vessel, and perhaps another ten to twelve like it. I trust the Mantis Clan has such resources at its disposal."

The merchant captain grinned, though since his face was in shadow, Tsuneo could only tell by the change the smile made in the man's voice.

"For the right price," he said, swinging his arms wide, "the Mantis has any resources you want."

"Any?" chuckled Tsuneo. "On those small islands of yours?"

The captain pulled his arms back and leaned forward conspiratorially. "True," he said, "many of the Mantis resources we have available for hire or purchase are . . . mm, being stored in Crane lands or Lion lands or wherever, but for the right fee, we'll be happy to retrieve them for you."

Tsuneo nodded, impressed with the man's bravado. "For now," he said, "all I need are those ships, as soon as possible."

"This I can do, though it will take me no less than two weeks to sail home and back again," Shanegon said. He pulled an abacus from the satchel slung over his shoulder and did some quick sums. "Tell me," he said at last, "what compensation does the Hantei offer for this service? We have great needs. Our ships need maintenance, our crews need food and pay, with some extra for working hard to shave time from the journey. I shall have to buy a map of the Bay of the Golden Sun, hire extra rowers . . ."

"Do you mean to tell me a great sea captain like you has no maps that lead him to the shipping port of Otosan Uchi?"

Shanegon shrugged helplessly. "I know where the port is, but I assume you wish your troops delivered to shore, not delivered to a reef or sandbar just off the coast."

Tsuneo stretched his neck and scratched the back of his head. His bargaining position was inauspicious both in physical stature and in financial stature. "Honorable captain," he said, "unfortunately, the gold that we had at our immediate disposal now lies on the ocean's floor in the hulks of the ships whose use that gold was to have purchased. It was a measure Hantei thought would ensure their loyalty. At this moment we have very little at our disposal. However, the Hantei Emperor controls great wealth in his Empire, and he would be more than happy to shower you with tokens of his inestimable gratitude."

"No gold?"

"Not immediately at hand, no, but as I said—"

Shanegon held up a hand. "Please, my lord, let nothing that I now say detract from the honor and esteem in which I hold the Stone Crab, greatest hero of the Crab since Hida Osano-Wo the Thunderer. If there is a lack of esteem, it is because we have heard of how the Hantei has already treated our ancestors, relegating them to a secondary position and ignoring their rightful claim as ancestors of a Great Clan. This insult we cannot bear. Go back and tell the all-powerful Hantei XVI that he has no Empire and that the Mantis have no need for his gratitude." Shanegon raised his voice in a continuous crescendo. "If he wants to take his armies to Otosan Uchi, he can swim there!"

Shanegon gripped the rail for a moment and brought his breathing back under control. "My lord," he said at last, "I apologize for raising my voice. I should have raised it to Hantei, but he is not here. It has been my deepest honor to speak with you, and I wish it could have been under conditions that were more trusting. Please honor me and my house by taking this pendant as a token of my sincere admiration for you." He used a long hooked pole to lower the pendant to Tsuneo.

The Crab general gently took the pendant off the hook and studied it. It was a jade token suspended from a cord of braided silk. Though small, especially in the Crab's large palm, the jade was intricately carved. An image of the celestial dragon twined around a central disk, weaving its serpentine body in and out of itself. The disk had a relief of the Crab mon on one side and the Mantis mon on the other.

"It's older than you are," said Shanegon as Tsuneo turned it over in his hand. "We're not sure exactly where it came from. It's said that it will bring you the favor of the Fortunes, and they will give you what you most hope for."

"I thank you," said Tsuneo, as he put it on, "but I do not think my desires shall ever be realized."

* * * * *

Through the summer, Otosan Uchi remained in perpetual readiness. Crane shugenja and ship captains reported Hantei's movements to Toturi—at least those who survived their efforts at spying. The locations of Hantei's armies were plotted on the map in the strategy room, changing as Hantei's army split and moved south toward the Crane armies and west toward the Scorpion.

The Imperial Guard constantly patrolled the seashore, and their few ships scoured the shipping lanes, while the Lion Clan watched the overland routes, both the northwest route from Dragon lands, and most especially the southern route from Beiden Pass. Beiden Pass was the crossroads of the Empire, starting in Scorpion Lands and ending between Lion and Crane holdings. The Spine of the World Mountains split the Empire roughly in half, and Beiden Pass was the best way to march armies across the mountains. Other ways were possible, to be sure, but all of them were treacherous, narrow, and time-consuming. The Lion could not defend the pass itself, lest the remaining forces in Dragon lands move south and trap them between two armies, nor did they have the strength left to split themselves to guard the both Dragon and the Scorpion lands closely. Thus Beiden Pass remained watched but not guarded.

However, Hantei's troops made no move toward Beiden Pass. Toturi and his generals did not know what to make of this. Hantei was known as a very aggressive person, and he had continued to behave in that manner throughout the war. Toturi was unsure why he did not attempt to cross the mountains in force and seize Otosan Uchi, especially in the wake of the disastrous campaign of the previous year.

With the threat of war hovering and desperate to fill their ranks after Black Finger River, the Lion and Crane had pressed many peasants and farmers into military service. Many long, quiet months passed with these people waiting with spears instead of working with hoes.

As the days passed, the people in Otosan Uchi began to notice fingers of dark smoke clawing their way over the horizon to the south, rising like skeletal hands over the Spine of the World. Their ominous forms drifted gradually westward, dissipating on the prevailing winds and turning the sunsets blood red. Each day new trails of smoke heralded new conflagrations, and each day the dark smudge that smeared the mountain range grew ever longer.

For weeks, Toturi's staff awaited word from scouts, merchants, refugees . . . anyone who could give them information of what was happening, but no news came. No one was sure whether or not Hantei now had a navy, perhaps having captured some ships from the Crab or the Crane. Thus loyal captains were hesitant to investigate, and that there were simply no refugees spoke volumes.

Finally, late in the summer as the time for harvest was drawing near, Hantei's forces did take control of Beiden Pass, and the Dragon Clan began to move. The Lion and Imperial Guard made their defenses near Otosan Uchi—not too close, for it would be unseemly to plan for Otosan Uchi to be attacked. But neither did they make their stand too far, lest Hantei's southern army venture north in ships. However, again to the surprise of Toturi's staff, Hantei's army moved west, across Lion lands, and the Dragon moved east, into Phoenix territory.

One hot and humid night, Bayushi Yojiro found Emperor Toturi I trying to relax by a small waterfall that trickled in the Imperial gardens.

Yojiro was dressed in a pair of full, black hakama pants that billowed about his legs as he approached and a sleeveless vest that was well suited to the heat, if perhaps less formal that ought to be worn in the presence of the Emperor. Nevertheless, the jersey was of excellent quality, and hand-decorated with flowers . . . of a poisonous plant, Toturi noted.

Yojiro bowed formally then knelt down, sitting on his heels to one side of the Emperor, so as not to intrude upon his view of the little waterfall.

THE STEEL THRONE

"I have an answer, my liege," said Yojiro. "I know what Hantei is doing."

"I am distressed that it took so long to acquire this answer," said Toturi with no small concern.

Yojiro nodded slowly and said, "I had to ensure that only those I trust most were involved. Also, it appears Hantei's people are watching the pass most scrupulously. Nevertheless, I have an answer."

Toturi nodded his assent.

"This war has dragged on—four summers of active war against Hantei, plus the additional years of the local wars: Crane and Crab, Fox and Hare and Scorpion, Unicorn spirits and Unicorn mortals. Each year, the fields get trodden under, and the peasants march off to die in fields they should be plowing. Each year the Clans made do with their meager harvest and whatever stores they might have had. The Scorpion has not been damaged as badly as the others, and for the last two years, we've been sending our hoarded stores to feed the armies of the Clans. The spirits don't need it. They eat little compared to us, and they have plenty from the Crab lands." Yojiro paused.

"Go on," nudged Toturi.

Yojiro leaned back and looked at the darkening sky. He took a deep breath and resumed. "Hantei has decided that force of arms is not the best way to turn the Empire to embrace him. He has decided to use food as a weapon.

"He holds the Crab lands, and he has the surplus food for the last twelve years stored in his mines, securely guarded. He knows the Clans have run their reserves dry, so he has burned the Crane fields and storehouses. He did the same to the Crab, so no one can retake those fields. He did the same to the minor Clans, and now he is marching west to do the same to the Lion and the Unicorn, while his northern army moves to the Phoenix. He doesn't want to fight your army. He wants you to march around chasing him while he burns the lands and robs us of this year's harvest. I assume he'll also send saboteurs to poison or foul whatever food stockpiles may remain.

"Come next year, we may have no food. And in the south, Hantei has already issued a proclamation that he will not even feed the Crab on the Wall unless they swear a blood oath to him. Without food, the whole southern half of the Empire could be overrun by a pack of goblins with sticks. But anyone who swears to serve him eternally shall be given food to survive. Soon he will make the same proclamation here in the north."

Toturi rocked back, reeling with the implications. "The Crab will not follow him," he said. "They will go hungry, and the Wall will be breached. Hantei would risk losing half the Empire like this?"

"Better he should have total power over a small Empire, than no power in a large one," said Yojiro. "Besides, he believes he could take it back."

"He is mad," said Toturi.

"History's judgment said that of his first rule," said Yojiro. "There's no reason for it to change its mind."

"What of your farms, daimyo? You said you fed the Clans. How much longer can your people do this?"

Yojiro hung his head. "Our lands have been salted, my liege. The rice withers and dies weeks before the harvest, and the storehouses suffered mysterious fires."

"No . . ."

"Yes," replied the Scorpion. "I am not certain whether it was Hantei's troops or Scorpion spirits working at his behest. We train our children from birth to do whatever dishonorable deeds need to be done in the service of the Emperor."

Toturi shook his head in disbelief. "You must end this, Yojiro," he said. "Do whatever it takes."

Yojiro bowed his head to the floor. "The last time an Emperor said that, my liege, the Scorpion daimyo took his head."

Toturi stood up and stepped forward so that he towered over Yojiro. "If that is the only way to stop Hantei," Toturi said, "then let not the heavens stay your hand."

17 MY ENEMY'S WEAKNESS

The
Eighteenth
Year
of the
Reign
of
Toturi I

Toku, the general of the Imperial Guard, walked slowly down the hall, ushering Toturi's children ahead of him to the throne room. Though they were Toturi's offspring, two of them were children no longer. Both Tsudao and Sezaru had already come of age and undergone the ritual ascent to adulthood, and Naseru's chance was certain to come soon.

Tsudao was now thirteen, tall and slender as she continued to grow. Sezaru paced alongside her, and the two chatted amiably, obviously very close. Though Sezaru was two years younger, he had an unnatural maturity about him that made Tsudao seem the younger and even the smaller, though she very clearly was not.

Naseru trailed behind, and although Toku suspected he felt left out of his sibling's relationship, the general found no hint of dissatisfaction in the boy's face or demeanor. He simply followed idly along, seemingly disinterested by everything.

"Of course Father will pick me for his heir," Tsudao was saying. "I'm older than you. The oldest child gets the throne." She shrugged.

"You may be the *eldest*," said Sezaru, stressing the proper grammar, "but I am the eldest *male*. That means I'm a man," clarified Sezaru teasingly, "in case you weren't clear on that."

"So?" said Tsudao, giving Sezaru a careless bump with her shoulder. "Maybe the Hanteis were almost all *males*, but that doesn't mean the Toturis will be."

"But every Toturi Emperor has been a male," observed Sezaru.

"You are so stupid! Duh! There's only been one!"

"Of such idle chances are great traditions born," replied Sezaru. He stopped and adopted a martial pose as if he were holding a sword. He made a few chops, imitating Tsudao's practice drills. "It is the way it has always been," he said in a gravelly voice. "It is the way it must be."

Tsudao tsked at Sezaru's martial attempts. "Slow and sloppy," she said. "Good thing you have me around. You're so clumsy it'd take you three swings just to hit a paper with a paintbrush."

"That's because I don't always resort to violence," retorted Sezaru. Tsudao bumped him again. "More than that, your calling me clumsy is like a toad calling a sunset ugly. You can't even walk a straight line down a hallway."

Toku cleared his throat loudly as they approached the throne room, and the two fell silent. Servants opened the sliding rice-paper doors, and the four entered the presence of the seat of Imperial power. Toturi stood where the throne would have been, Kaede kneeling by his side. To the left knelt Akodo Ginawa with his adopted son Kaneka, as well as Shiba Tsukune with her son Aikune, and Bayushi Yojiro.

Toku bowed deeply and moved to the right side of the chamber. Tsudao, Sezaru, and Naseru approached their father. They bowed deeply as well, honoring their father and their lord, then knelt down to sit on their heels.

"These are hard times," said Toturi, "and you three must grow up rapidly. Hantei has choked our supplies of food. He controls many farmlands, and those that he does not control he has burned and trampled. He drafts the farmers to support his armies, while we must let many of ours go back and work what land they can, for right now, any food is helpful."

He exhaled harshly, and continued, saying, "This means we must now attack, even though our army is both smaller and hungrier. To attack, we need the best we have out there. You must be the best you can be. Tsudao, I want you to wield an army like you wield a sword. I intend for you to learn attack from the Lion, defense from the Crab, and movement from the Unicorn. Therefore, you will go with Akodo Ginawa to further your training. He will give you a field command. You are to obey him."

"Father," hazarded Naseru, bowing, "Tsudao doesn't like Akodo Kaneka. She says anyone who picks as many fights as he does keeps losing the fight in his own heart."

Tsudao turned and glared at Naseru, while Kaneka narrowed his eyes and watched them both.

"Sezaru," Toturi said, ignoring the comment, "the elements speak to you. Learn to command them as I command the Empire. You will accompany Shiba Tsukune back to Phoenix lands. Your mother the Empress has prevailed upon the Elemental Council to teach you their secrets. You are to obey the Masters as they teach you. When this war is over, you will also learn from the Dragon shugenja and the brotherhood of Shinsei."

Finally, Toturi looked at Naseru. "Second Son, I do not entirely trust the Crane, who are embroiled in a war of Hantei's desire. Therefore I honor the Scorpion with your presence. You have always demonstrated that you are observant and attentive, and I want you to learn the Scorpion's insight. You will remain here at Otosan Uchi with Yojiro's courtiers. This will be a hard year for all of you," he said, looking at his children. "You shall work harder than ever from dawn until dark. Until now, you have had the protection of the Imperial palace. The Empire can afford this luxury no longer. We need everyone involved in this war. Be careful."

Toturi waved his hand brusquely, dismissing the people. He turned to speak with his wife. Tsudao, seizing her chance, leaned over to Naseru and hissed, "You little brat! Why did you have to say that?"

Naseru looked back at her with a dead eye and whispered back, "It's tradition for the Emperor to take a Crane for a bride. You can start a new tradition of taking a Lion for a husband."

Tsudao clenched her fist to strike but managed to stay her hand when she noticed Sezaru's eyes upon her.

"Don't let the brat get the better of you," said Sezaru.

"You'd better listen," said Naseru, seamlessly interjecting himself into Sezaru's words. "He's already ordering his little general around like he's the Emperor." He stood and nodded to the two of them, leaving them steaming in his wake as he walked over to Toku.

He chatted with Toku about inconsequential rumors while Tsudao and Sezaru left the room with their wards. No sooner had they left, than he ended the conversation in mid-sentence and approached Toturi and Kaede. He bowed, deeply and formally, and said, "Father, I want to be the Emperor after you. Tsudao does not think enough and Sezaru thinks too much. Tsudao loves only her sword, and Sezaru spends all day chasing after the Fortunes. I alone follow you. Please make me your heir."

Kaede looked at Toturi and said, "You haven't told—haven't said . . . anything?"

"I was going to," Toturi said apologetically, "but then the war came, and there has been no time since."

"Haven't said what, father?" asked Naseru. "Are you going to make one of them the Emperor?"

"Son," said Toturi, "that is not your concern. Go now, and learn." He ushered Naseru off toward Yojiro, who waited patiently nearby.

Naseru turned and left, and as he did, Toku saw naked emotion flash on Naseru's face like lightning breaking through the clouds, but in the blink of an eye it had vanished behind the mask of his face. Naseru left the room in the same detached manner as he had entered.

* * * * *

The Lion army moved out from Otosan Uchi, intent on striking Hantei's forces, which were dispersed in their effort to destroy the Empire's ability to produce food. The Lion Clan peasants who had been pressed into service were returned to the fields to harvest as much as possible but above all to avoid Hantei's forces and stay alive to continue that crucial work. Without the undisciplined peasant units, the Lion armies were able to increase their marching speed, which might, they hoped, might make a difference, as Hantei's forces still employed some peasants as spearmen.

The Imperial Guard remained near Otosan Uchi, together with the few Crane units north of the Spine of the World. They would safeguard the Emperor and the Crane croplands, which, with the Phoenix lands, were the only secure sources of food.

To the north, the Phoenix armies tested the Dragon Clan's defenses, trying to slip past the castles and infiltrate the mountains. They hoped to tie up the Dragon samurai in defending the homeland, thereby leaving Hantei's armies afield without reinforcement.

Kitsu Motso coordinated the Lion attacks from a central position and left direct command of the armies to Akodo Ginawa, Ikoma Gunjin, and Matsu Ketsui. Hantei's forces were intent on destruction of arable land, and when the Lion forces caught the scent of one of Hantei's units, the spirit samurai evaded the Lion, leading them unwillingly through farmlands. Since the Lion tried to avoid trampling everything underfoot, it took longer than expected to corner the spirits and attack them.

With overwhelming concentration of force—the way all Lions like to fight battles—the spirit units stood no chance when cornered, although they fought with tenacity and skill, costing the Lion far more for each victory than their daimyo had hoped. Samurai were killed and farms plowed under in each battle. After the third such hollow victory, Kitsu Motso summoned Ginawa to his headquarters.

"We are winning the battles," said the Lion daimyo directly, "but we are losing the war."

"How so?" asked Ginawa as he chewed thoughtfully on a straw. "Each victory returns more spirits to Jigoku, where they shall remain. Although we die, too, we can have children. When they breed, they have mortal offspring. We will win in the long run."

"Starvation snaps at our heels, and we are running out of time," said Motso. "As fast as we swim to shore, the tide still pulls us farther out to sea. Hantei is happy to let us chase his troops until at last we either kneel in our hunger or slit our empty bellies. Either way, he gets what he wants."

Ginawa glanced around the tent, and said, "Well, I see there's no one else here. So you called me here not to ask my advice, but to give me new orders."

Motso nodded with a grim smile. "Always astute, you are. And this is a hard task," he said, as he picked up a scroll from his map table and handed it to Ginawa. "We have heard little from the Unicorn Clan for quite a long time. It's been easy enough to ignore them, since they are a long way from Otosan Uchi, and Hantei does not appear to have many Unicorn spirits in his army."

"Whether they are in his army or not," Ginawa said, "the Unicorn spirits seem to be serving Hantei's needs."

"Agreed. That's why we must ignore the Unicorn no longer," said Motso. "Take a look at that scroll."

Ginawa unrolled the scroll and found it was a map of Unicorn territory.

Motso leaned over and pointed as he continued. "We know the Unicorn spirits have taken control of the City Between the Rivers—here, White Shore Lake—here, and the City of the Rich Frog. We hear they also control Shiro Iuchi, but as that is south of the mountains, it makes no difference at the moment. As you can see, the spirits control the river and the borderlands. However, we have not seen an influx of Unicorn refugees, which implies that loyal Unicorn may still hold either Shinjo Castle or Utaku Castle. Perhaps both. If they do, we must contact them and coordinate our battle plans. Take your forces through the less-populated northern route and march hard for Shinjo Castle. I'll cover with the rest of the army."

Ginawa nodded. It was a simple journey fraught with danger. Much like the rest of his life. "And what message do I bring to Gaheris?" he asked.

"I cannot lead what I do not know," said Motso. "You are my general, and I give command of the Unicorn to you."

Ginawa stood and bowed. "Neither can you give what you do not own," he said, "and the Unicorn let no one own them."

"Just get them," said Motso.

"Simple," said Ginawa with a grin. He left the tent, mounted his horse, and rode away.

* * * * *

The Lion troops marched carefully through the very northern reaches of Unicorn territory, the foothills of the mountains known as the Great Wall of the North. After a few skirmishes with spirit patrols, Ginawa ordered them to march at night and stick to the valleys. Granted, not seizing the high ground made them more vulnerable, especially to the frightening thunder of a cavalry charge, but the discreet positioning helped the troops avoid being seen by the ever-present outriders.

Akodo Kaneka and Toturi Tsudao rode side by side in the warm summer darkness. Despite the initial coolness they'd felt toward each other, the weeks of campaigning had built a relationship of respect, if not trust or appreciation. It was easy for the two of them to stay together, as no one else tried to socialize with them. Not only were they both of high rank, they were both children of auspicious parentage—Tsudao the oldest child of the Emperor, and Kaneka given to the Lion by the dragon of water.

It was roughly midnight, and Tsudao finally spoke. "You've never asked me about what my brother said about me and you," she said quietly.

"Yes, my lady, that is true," said Kaneka.

"Doesn't it bother you?"

"The words of a member of the Imperial family are not mine to question, my lady," he replied.

"That's not what I asked," she said.

"My duty is to serve the Empire, my lady," answered Kaneka. "To allow the comments of a child to inflame my emotions is not the way of a samurai. Besides, he said nothing; he reported a rumor. You also said nothing, my lady, rightfully ignoring the attempt to spread slander."

Tsudao rode for a while in silence, thinking about his answer. Finally, she said, "You're very good with a sword. I don't think I've seen anyone who can draw faster than you, not even a Crane."

"I thank you, my lady," said Kaneka, bowing in the saddle. "Your words do me great honor."

"Will you quit calling me 'my lady?' It sounds so stiff all the time."

"I will use the proper form of address when speaking to the daughter of my Emperor, my lady," Kaneka said placidly. "No one shall find fault with me."

Tsudao snorted, almost a laugh. "Why are you always so formal?" she asked.

"I must be perfect and honorable in all that I do, my lady, that I may fill the gap that was left behind for me to fill," he said.

"What do you mean?"

"All a samurai has is his honor and his name, my lady," said Kaneka. "I must live up to and surpass the example of my father."

"You mean Ginawa?"

"No, my lady," said Kaneka shaking his head slowly. "I mean my father. He left me great honor and no name. He is a man above reproach, who made only one mistake in his entire life, a mistake that I must atone for."

"Oh? What mistake was that?" asked Tsudao.

"Me."

* * * * *

One morning, at dawn, a lone Unicorn rider approached the Lion column as they prepared to bed down for the day. She paused, lingering outside of bowshot, and carefully looked over the auburn-clad troops. Ginawa ordered some archers from the rear of the column to move forward and attempt to flank her, so that they should slay her before she could report the Lions' location to her commanders.

These samurai were rather dismayed when they crossed over the hills seeking cover and found an entire detachment of battle maidens on both sides of the Lion column. Upon hearing this, Ginawa decided that a parley was a tactically viable alternative.

"Actually, we've been following you for a few weeks now," said the Unicorn rider. "Following your trail, mostly, and occasionally sending a scout up one of the mountains to keep an eye on you. Once we figured out which side you were on, we concealed your route and laid down false tracks for Hantei's people."

"Then they are serving Hantei?" asked Ginawa.

"Directly or indirectly, it makes no difference. We've found out that those who struck against our own Clan were following his imperious suggestions."

"One other question," asked Tsudao, "if you've been covering our trail, why did you wait so long to talk to us?"

The Unicorn smiled. "One can never be too careful dealing with outsiders," she said.

The Unicorn escorted the Lion troops respectfully to Shinjo Castle. As they marched, Ginawa noted that the farms here had all been trampled as well and the grasslands had suffered from fires. Even the samurai and their mounts seemed less robust than usual. The Unicorn, it seemed, were suffering the same hunger as the rest of the Empire.

Once the Lion arrived at Shinjo Castle, Moto Gaheris granted Ginawa and his advisors an audience, receiving them in the Pearl Room. Gaheris was a bull of a man, large and powerful, and his face bore the broad features of foreign blood. The Unicorn prepared a meal grilled in the traditional Unicorn style, which is to say on a large metal shield over an open fire. The food was excellent, seasoned with wild, unknown spices that the Unicorn had discovered in their centuries abroad, and it at once delighted and appalled the Lions' taste buds. Everyone ate their fill, and the honor being done the Lion by providing so much food was not lost on a single one of them. Once the meal and the traditional pleasantries were concluded, Ginawa cut straight to the point.

"Honorable daimyo," he said, "it has been six years now since we saw you at Otosan Uchi, and even then I wondered that you were able to make it to Toturi's side."

"Nothing can contain the wind," said Gaheris, "and the roar of the hunter cannot be silenced."

Ginawa smiled in spite of himself. "Times are hard in the Empire, lord of the Unicorn. We have heard so little from you that I have been sent to find out how you fare."

Gaheris took a sharp breath. "It started out very poorly for us, very poorly. The spirits drove us into the fields with nothing but the clothes on our backs. Many of our people joined them, claiming that they were right in returning us to our roots as nomads and explorers, but whether they believed or whether they had more hunger than honor I do not know.

"They tried to assault us here a few times the first few years, but they have never even come close to taking our castle. And as time has gone on and more about Hantei XVI has reached our ears, we started to have spirits and their followers leave their side—his side, Hantei's side—and come to my side. Our side, that is. Now the spirits sit in the cities they 'freed us from,' waiting for us to attack. We grow stronger, and soon we shall reclaim our lands. Unfortunately, having more people gives us hardship as well, for the farms have been systematically trampled, and the spirits burn the grasslands before the grain ripens. Nevertheless, all in all, things are going fairly well, fairly well indeed."

"It is the same out there," said Ginawa. "We fight well, although our armies and Hantei's are roughly equal. We lost a lot at Black Finger, but his troops are not concentrated like ours. So we win battles, but, noble Gaheris, my daimyo Kitsu Motso does not believe we have enough time left to win the war."

"Let it not be so!" Gaheris cursed.

"Hantei fights defensively, just as your Clan does, and the Unicorn spirits serve him just as if they were flying the Steel Chrysanthemum. The spirits need less food, and we waste food by chasing his armies down. In time—maybe not a long time—our troops will falter, and if that happens, the Empire is lost and Hantei XVI will begin a new and more horrible reign."

Gaheris leaned back and scratched his neck. "Does Motso have a plan?"

"He could not make one without knowing your disposition," Ginawa said. "However, I have a plan."

"Tell me."

"You now outnumber the spirits who try to trample your fields, right?"

"Yes, but their horses are as good as ours, and they still occasionally slip past our scouts," admitted Gaheris.

"But you can force the issue," said Ginawa. "Attack their cities one by one. Draw them away from your farms and back to defend what they have. Then your people can grow crops for the rest of the year without troubles. You still have enough time to turn a good crop, I believe. Then next spring you can strike forth with enough provisions for a good campaign."

"How exactly do we do all this?" asked Gaheris. "We don't have the strength yet to make a believable assault on one of their cities while still defending our farms from a counterattack. You understand that half of the strength of the Unicorn is our steeds, and mounted troops are less than ideal for siege warfare."

"I hate to state the obvious, honorable daimyo," said Ginawa, "but you have a large force of battle-hungry Lions camping at your doorstep."

"So I do," said Gaheris, smiling slowly like a dawning sun. He clapped his hands for rice wine. "That does change things, now doesn't it?"

18 | THE EMPEROR'S UNDER-HAND

The
Nineteenth
Year
of the
Reign
of
Toturi I

Defeat by action," said Toturi. "Defeat by inaction. For a samurai there is no choice. Still, I am saddened that the Fortunes could do no better than this." He walked slowly from the place the throne used to sit, crossing the room to one of the windows overlooking the gardens.

Toku hung his head. He had hoped to bring better news, but instead . . .

The Lion had spent the last summer and autumn chasing Hantei's troops all over the northern part of the Empire, defeating them in detail and yet still watching farm after farm, crop after crop trampled and burned before their very eyes. The campaign had been a general's victory and a quartermaster's defeat. Hantei's forces north of the Spine of the World had been beaten, leaving the spirits holding only the Dragon lands and Unicorn lands. The Phoenix, Lion, and northern Crane provinces were all now more or less free of threat, but their agricultural ability had been utterly devastated. The spirits had even gone out of their way to slaughter helpless farmers.

Of Hantei's southern forces, little had been heard. Rumors said that he was pressing everyone into service and building his forces for a final assault of Otosan Uchi. Some said overland, some said he was constructing a massive fleet.

Of Ginawa's expeditionary force, nothing had been heard at all. That news was too depressing even to foment any rumors.

Throughout the winter, the Lion, Crane, and Phoenix had tallied their available supplies under Imperial supervision, and now that these figures had been compiled with the first thaws, they were woefully inadequate. There was simply not enough food left to undertake a campaign. Perhaps if Hantei would stand and fight, Toturi's Army might be able to launch an attack across Beiden Pass, but Hantei and Tsuneo well knew the plight the mortals were in, and their evasiveness would add weeks upon weeks to the campaign. Those would be the weeks that Toturi's Army would have nothing to eat.

"If we march, Hantei avoids us and we starve. If we stand, Hantei comes, besieges us, and we starve." Toturi stood at the window looking at the garden and seeing nothing. "Is there a reason, then, not to attack?"

"Perhaps there is another way, my liege," said Toku.

"Really?" said Toturi with a leaden voice. Toku had never seen him so apathetic about an offer of hope.

"It seems there was once an Imperial general who was a peasant in his former life, tilling the soil," Toku said. It was the closest he had ever come to discussing his past, and to do so made his face blush brightly. "If such an activity is not beneath the dignity of an Imperial general, how could it be beneath the dignity of any loyal samurai?"

Toturi turned his head and blinked twice. "Put the troops to work in the fields?"

"I'm sure there's a polite way to phrase that, sir, to not offend—"

"Politeness be damned," said Toturi suddenly showing energy again. "This is a war! They want an example? I'll show them an example. If it's not beneath the Emperor, none can shirk their duty!" He leaned out the window and looked at the gardens again, still spotted with snow. "There," he said, pointing. "Right there. I'm going to plant my vegetables there. I've never liked those flowers much, anyway."

He turned and strode out of the throne room, leaving Toku in his wake, jaw slack with surprise. Suddenly Toku started from his reverie, and trotted after Toturi. "Water chestnuts!" he called after him. "We need to plant water chestnuts! They're my favorites! Uh . . . my liege!"

* * * * *

Bayushi Yojiro moved through the Imperial gardens, Toturi Naseru in tow. The youngest Toturi moved even more gracefully than before, and his face was as impenetrable as any handmade Scorpion mask. It was evident that the Scorpion had been teaching him well. Except for subtlety. If the whispers in court were true, the youngest Toturi preferred to emulate a hammer instead of a feather, much to his mentor's annoyance.

Moving through the gardens, Yojiro felt the buzz of excitement, scandal, controversy. It rippled through the air like a thousand insects, and Yojiro knew at the center he would find the hive, and the hive would be Toturi. Ever unpredictable, that man, and ever intriguing. He had been raised among monks, weathered the storms of a daimyo, and found his destiny as a ronin. Now here he was the Emperor. Emperors were supposed to use divine inspiration for all their edicts, but this man . . . his divine inspiration was liberally seasoned with ronin tang, esoteric monasticism, and a warrior's steel.

As a rule, the Scorpion hated surprises, but somehow Yojiro could never bring himself to hate Toturi. Not that he ever really tried very hard.

They found Toturi near the center of the garden, leaning on a hoe and wiping his sweaty brow. Despite the lingering chill of the recently passed winter, he had stripped himself to the waist, and although he had a small paunch about his middle, he still had the hard muscles of a fighter beneath his skin. Yojiro's eyes widened. Naseru's eyes narrowed.

Toturi turned to them, and they bowed formally. Upon straightening, Yojiro glanced about at the former garden, now thoroughly hoed.

"You set quite an unusual task before the Empire, my liege," said Yojiro, "as well as a hard example for all."

Toturi chuckled. "There will be those who say that to raise more food than the Emperor would insult the Emperor's ability. I want to give those people as much leeway as possible."

"They shall indeed have to work hard before they can use that excuse," said Yojiro appreciatively.

"I have a different task for you, Yojiro," said Toturi. "You've been planting your seeds, it is now time for your harvest."

"My lord?"

"I need the Scorpion, Yojiro. This year, we plant and we harvest. That should give us just enough food to feed our armies. Next year, at the start of the year, we attack Hantei's forces and end this war. We have the Lion, the Phoenix, and some of the Crane. We face the Crab and the Dragon, as well as the spirits of many Clans. We need the Scorpion to fight by our side so that we can end this and so the ending is the one that I would prefer to see. Do whatever it takes, Yojiro. I need your people. I need that victorious 'behold!' you promised me."

Yojiro stood silently for a time, debating a variety of answers, then he bowed and said, "As you wish, my liege."

He turned and began walking away, Naseru in tow.

"Yojiro!" said Toturi. "Some guards say they saw a spirit in Otosan Uchi! What do you know of this?"

Yojiro stopped and turned. Naseru simply stopped.

"I know nothing of it at all, my liege, unless, of course, they were referring to you." So saying, he left Toturi to his work.

* * * * *

Just inside the borders of Scorpion territory, Hantei XVI sat in a large open field, festooned with banners and surrounded by hundreds of his finest spirit samurai. He sat on a makeshift throne, which stood atop a high platform of polished wood built for just this purpose. Hantei thoroughly enjoyed making people slave for his whims. It demonstrated to all that he was indeed the true Emperor—even with that petty creature holing up in Otosan Uchi.

The sun shone on him, and the cool spring breeze added just the necessary touch to make the banners wave proudly without being a distraction. His legions glowed with a soft yellow light. Hida Tsuneo stood on a lower level of the dais at Hantei's right, the iron fist of the Steel Chrysanthemum.

Bayushi Baku, commander of Hantei's Scorpion contingent, approached the throne. He prostrated himself before Hantei just the way the tyrant liked, then sat back and waited. It did not escape Baku's notice that Hantei had erected his throne on Scorpion lands. It simply no longer mattered.

"What news do you bring us this day?" asked Hantei.

"The usurper plans to mount an attack through Beiden Pass next spring," said Baku.

"Is that so? Tell me, how can he manage such a task?"

"It seems," said Baku, "that he has all his samurai planting grains and vegetables to replenish their supplies. As their leader, he, too, works a garden."

At this, Hantei laughed uproariously, and titters ran like foxes among the assembled troops. "Oh, what I would give to see a self-proclaimed Emperor grubbing in the dirt like a common pig," he said, wiping a tear from his eye. "That is simply too much." Then Hantei stood, and turning to one side and the other, loudly said,

> Toturi the First
> Can't escape his ronin past
> Digs for muddy food.

The troops applauded the haiku and cheered for their Emperor. Hantei basked in the praise for a moment, then sat back down. "So," he said, "Toturi comes to fight. Meanwhile, he spends this year farming instead of training. How are his troops taking this?"

"They are less than excited," said Baku, "but they dare not grumble."

"Indeed? Maybe Toturi has a spine after all. But while he crushes the morale of his troops beneath a spade, we will train and prepare. His troops will be weary, hungry, and subdued. We will end this conflict. Just after he crosses Beiden Pass, we will crush his forces and take the capital."

"An excellent plan, my liege!" Baku fawned.

"It is time for the Scorpion to join their Dragon and Crab brethren," said Hantei. "Gather your people."

Baku raised one finger. "I would be remiss in my duty were I not to mention some of our activities," he said. "Per your command, we have been supplying you with all the information you could wish. We located farms, warned you of troop movements, and kept you appraised of Toturi's situation. We even conducted sabotage of food stores, and all of this we accomplished while maintaining our semblance of neutrality. May I suggest, my liege," said Baku supplicatingly, "that for us to cast off our neutrality now might not be the most expedient plan. We are working on some projects that should bear fruit by the end of the year, but the maintenance of our neutrality is necessary for these tasks."

"What tasks?" asked Hantei, leaning forward.

"A Scorpion never reveals his secrets," said Baku, "but—"

"I could make you reveal them under torture," said Hantei.

"But," said Baku seamlessly, "we have an agent at the highest level in Toturi's staff. How else could we get you those extremely detailed reports on their food resources? How else could we tell you the minds of the Toturi household and staff? My liege, give us a little more time, and by the end of this year, you shall have a prize that is beyond measure."

"Or your head on a spike," said Hantei. "Either is fine by me."

* * * * *

Toturi Tsudao sat on a rock in the shade, watching the small spring trickle through the dappled sunlight of the wooded glade. Her unit was on patrol near the City Between the Rivers, guarding against any breakout attempt by the spirit forces. At the moment, however, she was taking advantage of her day off—one came every two or three weeks—to relax. Yes, Ginawa pushed his troops hard, but she was gaining much experience in command, and anything beat hacking at the dirt to raise vegetables.

With a disgusted expression, she threw another rock into the stream.

No wonder Hantei was winning. He was a Hantei, with the gods on his side. History was on his side. On top of that, he made others do the dirty work. Maybe that was why he had the gods on his side. Maybe that was why history remembered him: He didn't grow his own damned food.

She would never dig in the dirt if she were Empress. There were some things that honor required, and one of those was not to demean the throne with the labor of a peasant. She swore again to live her life by the tenets of the way of the warrior. Poetry, yes, a warrior must practice art with both blade and ink, for doing so sharpens the mind and opens the tactician's eyes to new ways of looking at the world. Painting, yes, for creating a singing bird with three fast, instinctive brush strokes taught the warrior to see the underlying truths of the world. But for a samurai, noble and loyal, to grab a tool used by unschooled peasants?

Yet another rock hit the water. It was annoyingly small, and throwing it gave her no release, but all the larger rocks near her resting place had already immigrated to a watery new home. She stood up to gather some more, but when she turned around, she saw an aged woman leaning on a staff, watching her quietly from the edge of the clearing. She wore an old kimono in faded colors of orange, black, and brown, with an intricate insect design crawling all over it. A large satchel sat at her feet.

"How did you get here? What are you doing here? How did you find me?" The questions tumbled out of Tsudao's mouth in a desperate and unsuccessful attempt to conceal her shock at having been watched for . . . for how long, she had no idea.

"I am a shugenja, which, I believe, answers all three of your questions," said the woman.

"Well, you talk just like my brother," Tsudao said, instinctively shifting to an attack, albeit a verbal one. "Your answers don't actually say anything. Who are you?"

The old woman bowed as deeply as she could, a painful process that relied heavily upon her staff for support. "My name is Moshi Juiko, my lady," she said. "Please forgive me for not kneeling, but I fear I could not rise again, and I would not wish to inconvenience you by requiring your assistance."

"Moshi . . . Moshi, that's the Centipede, right?"

"Indeed it is," said Juiko sadly. "For seven hundred years we have kept ourselves secluded, worshipping Amaterasu, the sun goddess. But times have changed since your father took the throne."

"My fath—? You know who I am?"

Juiko looked at the young warrior meaningfully.

"I know, you told me, you're a shugenja," said the Tsudao.

"You see?" said Juiko, "That answer told you more than you thought."

"So why do you want to see me?" asked Tsudao.

"As I said, times have changed," she said, and Tsudao heard the weary grief in her voice. "I am the daimyo of the Centipede, and I find that although I have led my Clan faithfully for decades, we have journeyed far from our path, and I do not know where we are."

"What do you mean?"

"Since our founding, we have supported Amaterasu. We have given her our worship and our adoration to help her walk the heavens with ease and peace. We believed we supported her, kept her in her position, but now, after all that has happened, I wonder if we were too arrogant, if what we worshiped was not her, but ourselves for helping her. That we, a Clan of mortals, could help the One who gave birth to the gods, the One who brought light and life to the world. Perhaps seven hundred years ago, the Moshi sought only to serve, but I think that somewhere along the way we stopped following Amaterasu and started trying to lead her."

Juiko paused for a moment, taking a deep breath as her eyes turned inward, looking into her own heart. "And now what has happened? When the darkness shook the Empire, when the dragons returned and your father committed seppuku, in that time Amaterasu fell from the heavens and a new sun rose in her place. When the armies of the Empire returned from Oblivion's Gate and fought their way through the Shadowlands, my daughter was with them, and the Shadowlands taint infested her soul. Amaterasu is gone. Our purpose has fallen. My child is darkness, and the dark god waits for her to take the throne of my Clan.

"What have we left as a Clan? Nothing but the blessing of Amaterasu. I could no longer bear the burden, but I could not pass it to the hand of darkness, though it is my daughter's birthright. I did not know what to do. Then I had a vision, and Amaterasu herself spoke to me from wherever she is. She said she still watched the Empire she loves so dearly, and she answered my heart's riddle. The only way I could avoid giving this to my daughter is to hand it to one greater than she. In so doing I condemn my Clan to death, yet I have no fear, for my Clan is already dead. We are a decapitated samurai waiting only for our legs to fail so we can fall."

Juiko paused and reached into the satchel that sat on the ground by her side. From it she pulled a belt, woven together of golden threads that glowed like the sun. It was folded nicely, but as she picked it up one-handed, some of the folds slipped out of place. She tried to fix it with the hand that also held her staff, but her fumbling attempts made no noticeable progress. At last, she resigned herself to her own frailties and extended the belt as best she could with a hand and a half. Proper etiquette required her to offer the gift with both hands fully extended, but Tsudao graciously failed to notice the lapse.

"Toturi Tsudao," said Juiko, "please take this obi and receive with it the blessing of Amaterasu."

Tsudao stepped forward and reached out. She stroked the obi. It felt softer than silk and lighter than sunbeams, and its pure glow entranced her eyes. "I cannot," she said as if in a trance. "It is too beautiful. I fear I would damage it with my warrior's ways."

"Toturi Tsudao, you are a samurai," said Juiko, "steeped in a tradition as old as the Empire. None but a samurai can bear this gift. Please accept it."

Tsudao snapped out of her trance, shaking her head violently to clear it. The obi was so beautiful. She could get lost just by looking at it. "I must humbly decline your generosity," she said with surprising formality, "It is far too fine a gift for the likes of a young and inexperienced person like me."

"Toturi Tsudao, you are the eldest child of our Emperor," said Juiko. "At the dawn of a new dynasty, please accept this heritage of the old world that you may remember the divine glory that gave birth to Rokugan."

"A seal of the divine mandate," said Tsudao. Tears erupted from her eyes as she took the obi from Juiko with both hands. "Yes, honorable Moshi Juiko. I shall bear this gift in honor of the One who created the world and all that is in it, and in remembrance of this day in which you gave a poor samurai hope." One of her tears dripped down her nose, landed on the obi, and rolled easily off the side, leaving neither trace nor trail.

"You have made an old woman very happy, young Toturi," said Juiko. She turned, and, abandoning her satchel, shuffled away down the glade's path, leaving Tsudao to admire the golden fabric. Just before Juiko passed out of sight, she turned to Tsudao one last time.

She scratched in the dirt a few times with the end of her stick until Tsudao looked up, then scratched a few more times. "Remember, Tsudao," she said, firmly but kindly, "to be a samurai means one thing only:

"To serve."

*   *   *   *   *

The summer was hot and dry, and despite the best efforts of the samurai, the ground gave up its crop reluctantly. As Hantei had predicted, morale declined among Toturi's Army as the hours of labor under the hot sun seemed all but fruitless to the warriors whose only prior efforts at agriculture were limited to the occasional bonsai.

The Dragon Army and even the Unicorn spirits launched occasional forays to hamper these farming efforts, their heavy infantry causing not only casualties but also more morale problems as samurai watched their hard work go up in smoke or down under military feet.

Tsuneo's Crab forces made a few feints across Beiden Pass, enough to keep a disproportionate number of Lions in armor and out of the fields. The lack of a fight itself proved damaging to their martial spirit.

During this time, the continued reports that trickled in through the Scorpion spy network kept morale high for Hantei's troops. Hantei periodically sent messengers to the capitals of the various loyal Clans, bearing boxes of rotting foodstuffs, a tangible reminder of the plenty that could be had simply by swearing fealty.

Meanwhile, Tsuneo prepared for the final battle, holding strategy councils with key generals from every Clan and era, tapping each of them for their advice and developing a series of grand strategic plans to cover any eventuality. He threw himself wholly into this work, for he found the constant focus of his attention kept his mind off the man whom he served.

Just past midsummer, Ginawa's expeditionary force returned to Lion lands, much the worse for wear but bearing good tidings: the Unicorn and the Lion had retaken several cities from the spirits. There were heavy casualties on both sides, but the Unicorn expected to survive the winter with enough provender for the horses and enough food for the populace. They would send units to aid Toturi in the final battle.

Even better news came in the midst of the harvest season, when a Mantis fleet sailed into the Bay of the Golden Sun, bearing dried and salted fish, dried seaweed, rice, eggs, and chickens, as well as a pledge to provide a legion of Mantis troops for the defense of the Empire—should the Emperor Toturi choose to pay the fee that the Mantis Clan's code of honor required.

This Toturi agreed to do, for the Mantis saw fit to levy an emergency fee of only a single piece of copper. Thus, having saved both their face and their honor, the Mantis agreed to land their army at Otosan Uchi as soon as the winter storms had passed.

Ecstatic, Toturi ordered a feast for the daimyos and generals of the Clans. Since his daughter Tsudao had returned, he wished for his sons to attend, as well. Empress Kaede made arrangements with her former Clan to ensure that Sezaru returned as soon as possible.

But of the Scorpion daimyo and the youngest Toturi, there was no sign.

19 THE WAY OF SHADOW

The
Nineteenth
Year
of the
Reign
of
Toturi I

The harvest, meager as it had been on the north side of the mountains, had come and gone. In the south, fresh supplies came in by the wagonload in the crisp air of early winter. A summer spent drilling had honed skills as sharp as katanas, and every unit had made new banners, each with a steel chrysanthemum embroidered at the top. In this way, when the final battle was launched against Toturi's Army, the division between friend and foe, historically determined by Clan, would be clear.

Hantei sat on a comfortable chair on a battlement of a Crab castle, overlooking a portion of his army as they engaged in a mock battle. Baku stood to one side and Tsuneo to the other. Baku's troops were learning to integrate themselves into the Hantei army. Tsuneo was using these battles to test the acumen of his various subcommanders, determining who would be best suited to lead a portion of the Grand Imperial Army.

A Crab runner approached the trio and stopped at Tsuneo's side. The Stone Crab bent his ear to hear the whispered message. He nodded.

"My liege," Tsuneo said, turning to Hantei, "the Scorpion named Yojiro wishes to see you." Tsuneo no longer referred to Yojiro as the daimyo, because Hantei had officially installed Baku in that position. He thought it better to have spirits running every Clan when this war ended. That the mortal ex-daimyo of the Clan still lived gave Hantei no concern. If Yojiro became a problem, he would die.

Hantei turned his attention away from the battle. It was easy enough to do. Battles were boring without any evisceration or decapitation. "Yes," he said lazily, waving a careless hand. "Bring him here."

The runner quickly departed, and in but a moment, Yojiro approached Hantei, three other Scorpion following in his wake. Hantei turned his head to watch as they approached. Yojiro wore a fine, heavy kimono, and it looked as if his companions were perhaps a small shugenja with a staff, a lithe bare-armed ninja, and an aged samurai. All wore their Scorpion masks—Yojiro a simple drape of cloth, the shugenja a porcelain mask, the ninja a complete hood, and the samurai an armored faceplate that concealed his face behind a stylized animalistic snarl.

They all approached, and as one, they knelt and bowed their heads to the floor.

"I wondered if you would return," said Hantei.

Not when, if. Yojiro ignored the slight. It was the sort of ploy the Scorpion taught their children, and merited no response. "The last time I had the honor of your presence, my liege, I spoke of a project I had been undertaking. I have returned with the project all but completed."

"You haven't finished?" asked Hantei nasally. "How lazy! Why not?"

"Because the final step requires you, my liege, and only you."

Such importance, even in a matter of which he knew nothing, appealed to Hantei's basest instincts. He straightened and, with somewhat more curiosity, asked, "Very well. What is this project that I may judge its worth?"

Yojiro gestured, and the small shugenja stood, leaving his staff on the paving stones of the battlement. His mask was perfectly formed, and the unmoving porcelain glistened in the slanting sunshine. All

Hantei could see that betrayed the life within were the eyes—dark eyes that darted almost up to Hantei's face, then back down. The shugenja stepped forward, and Hantei noticed that with the mask he looked very young indeed.

Hantei looked him up and down. "Who are you that your project should interest me?"

The Scorpion brought his hands up to his face and, gripping the sleeves of his kimono, wiped his face. Hantei's eyes opened wide as he saw that the porcelain mask was actually nothing of the sort, but merely glossy face paint cleverly applied, even down to the illusion of shadows beneath the illusory eyeholes. Although the paint was now mostly wiped away, the man's face—the boy's face, for he was a boy—was still as expressionless as a mask.

Hantei leaned forward, for this boy looked familiar. "Who are you?" he crooned.

"I am Toturi Naseru," said the boy calmly. "I am honored to make your acquaintance. We have met before, but I was only three at the time, and forgive me, my lord, but I do not remember that event well."

Hantei chuckled. "Toturi Naseru, the ronin thief's number two son. Ah, yes. He has coddled you children too long. Time to learn about the real world. I shall take great delight in torturing you, ransoming you, and using your severed head to break your father's will."

"One thousand pardons, my lord," said Naseru, "but the third part can be achieved, if you will but spare me the first two."

"Eh? How's that, brat?" asked Hantei, grudgingly impressed with the poise and calm of this young Toturi.

"Let me be brief," said Naseru, "that I waste not your valuable time. You want the throne of Rokugan. So do I. You are thwarted by my father, who sets an army of samurai against you. I am thwarted by my father, who sired two older siblings before me."

Naseru stepped quietly forward. "The samurai set against you cannot be swayed," he said, "for you are a Hantei and not a Toturi. The siblings set before me cannot be moved for I am a Toturi and not a Hantei. Therefore, I can solve your problem, and you might solve mine."

Naseru stepped forward again. "Take me with your forces beneath the steel chrysanthemum. Those who fight for the name of Toturi shall see that a Toturi rides with the Hantei Emperor. The Scorpion here have been my family for the last year, and they support me. In this way my presence and the support of mortals undercuts the last reason the mortals have to oppose your rule."

Naseru stepped forward again, and began pacing ever so slowly closer to Hantei. "At the same time, you appoint me as your heir, solving the disagreement between the two families. Since many of those who oppose you want to see a Toturi on the throne, they shall be satisfied, eventually."

"Allow a Toturi to take my throne?" said Hantei incredulously.

Naseru paused, then resumed gliding forward. "Think of it as a final insult as you install his heir under your dynasty and on your terms. As the Emperor, you could even adopt me officially, changing my name to Hantei." Naseru, who had by now glided up to Hantei, knelt and bowed his head. "From that day forward, I would be not a Toturi but one who calls you father."

* * * * *

In the west, the sun had just set, and the dark stain of night spread slowly over the sky. Emperor Toturi stood in his quarters, his elbows resting on the windowsill, but he was not watching the flaming sunset of the chill early-winter's night. He was facing east, watching the waves come in from the sea, the whitecaps of the breakers barely visible in the fading light.

He loved the ocean—infinite, unknowable, melancholy, powerful. Much like his own life. Much like his future.

Kaede entered their room and crossed quietly over to where Toturi stood, her long kimono whispering across the boards. Two of the boards chirped like crickets, the intentionally bowed wood rubbing on its rosined support, nightingale boards to warn of intruders. Or loving wives.

Kaede tenderly touched the base of Toturi's neck, focusing her chi as she had learned so many years ago as an apprentice. There was a small spark of pale blue as her energy jumped from her palm and touched her husband, and she immediately saw the tension flow away from his neck and shoulders like incense in the breeze. He reached his right hand up over his left shoulder and took her hand where it rested on his neck. He squeezed her fingers gently.

She sidled a little closer. "What are you thinking, my husband?" she asked softly.

He dropped his head slightly.

"It's Naseru, isn't it?" she coaxed.

"Yes," he admitted.

"Why are you concerned?" she asked. "Surely the letter we received should lighten your heart. . . ."

"We sent for him, and he did not come, nor did Yojiro. I waited until I could delay the banquet no longer. Then, the day after we feast with the loyal daimyos, we receive word that Naseru has recruited the Scorpion, and they will join us in battle against Hantei come spring. It's as if I were forced to disown Naseru and insult the Scorpion, all at once."

"Toturi, love, please don't talk that way," the Empress chided.

"And how would you have me talk?" he asked, turning toward her, though still holding her hand. "All of my children, save only Naseru. All of the loyal daimyos, save only the one who has served me in silence."

"You offered your hospitality, my lord," said Kaede gently. "They did not arrive. Even had you delayed the feast another day, there would have been only a piece of parchment seated at the table. You did nothing wrong."

"I suppose you're right," he said. He dropped her hand and turned back to the window. The moon was rising, and the breakers were taking on a haunting glow in its light. "Still, I feel poorly in my heart. I miss Naseru." He took a deep breath of the ocean air. "I wonder what he's doing right now."

"He is doing as we taught him, which is to act in the best interests of the Empire," said Kaede, "and I'm sure he plans on learning as much as he can about politics, court, and the Scorpion way this winter."

Toturi nodded slowly. "I would feel better if he and Yojiro had been here to share in the celebration," he said. Then he snorted.

"Listen to me," he grumbled. "I'm getting as paranoid as the Hantei. Come," he said to his wife, taking her hand once more, "let us not miss time together with our other children, while they are still here. We shall see Naseru in the spring, when we meet with the Scorpion."

* * * * *

"This is very intriguing," said Hantei to Naseru. He turned to Yojiro. "And you say the Scorpion would support this? Support it openly?"

Yojiro smiled behind his mask, crinkling the corners of his eyes. "Support it, yes, my liege, but not exactly openly."

"What do you mean?" barked Hantei.

"Perhaps I can explain," said Baku smoothly. "Yojiro will lead the Scorpion as their daimyo and swear allegiance to Toturi with a blood oath. The Scorpion forces, spirits and mortals alike, will join Toturi's Army after they march across Beiden Pass. When Toturi's Army has engaged ours, the Scorpion shall betray their erstwhile Emperor, and together we shall crush Toturi's army, with your fist at their front and our stinger in their back.

"We then pursue the defeated Clans into Beiden Pass. They will fall upon each other for the chance to flee the fastest or else surrender where they stand. We then march to Otosan Uchi, smiting whatever defense stands in our way, seize the capital, and impose the will of Hantei upon all the lands.

"All my Clan asks in return is that we receive the respect we are due. For a thousand years the Scorpion have served the throne, willingly offering up our honor to serve the Emperor's needs, and in that thousand years our reputation has become more and more tarnished. We wish respect, and we wish for all of Rokugan to know we are the Emperor's most favored."

Tsuneo looked askance at Hantei, one eyebrow cocked. Hantei stroked his wispy moustache in thought. Then he glanced up at Tsuneo. The Stone Crab did not move—his gesture of assent. Hantei thought some more.

"It is a remarkable thought, but there is one tragic weakness," said Hantei. He stabbed a finger at Naseru. "The weakness is this boy right here! He is a Toturi, and he shall betray me!"

"As I see it, fath—er, my liege," said Naseru reasonably, yet still emotionlessly, "betrayal loses me everything I stand to gain. I cannot take the throne under my father's dynasty. Even were I versed in the arts of assassination, I could remove neither my brother nor my mother without the other one finding out by means of their magic. Once the truth was discovered, I would be killed. My only hope would be for accidents to claim the lives of both Tsudao and Sezaru without my intervention, which is exceedingly unlikely. Why would I throw away my only chance to gain the throne? But if you fear my betraying you after your victory, then make your survival to retirement a condition of my inheritance. I will gladly abide by that."

Hantei stared hard at Naseru's eyes but saw nothing. Nothing but a dead look, which was exactly what he hoped to see there. He turned to Baku and Yojiro. "And the Scorpion would be willing to do this?"

"We are devoted to the throne and he who sits upon it," answered Baku. "Our honor is not in keeping our word but in serving the Emperor."

"Besides," chimed in Yojiro, "Toturi slew Bayushi Shoju. We have never forgotten. It remains an unpaid debt. This seems an appropriate enough payment."

"But you will be breaking a blood oath," observed Hantei coolly, trying to hide that he rather enjoyed that idea.

Bayushi Baku laughed once, with a self-effacing smile. "As the other Clans so frequently mention," he said, "betrayal is our nature."

20 CROSSROADS

The
Nineteenth
Year
of the
Reign
of
Toturi I

The Mantis arrived even before all the ice had cleared from the Bay of the Golden Sun. Hazarding a landing on the seashore outside the bay before the last of the winter storms had subsided, they marched to Otosan Uchi, banners and pennants standing proud in the cold, drizzling rain. Their bright green armor was polished to a sheen, and long arcing spikes adorned their helmets, making them look like a swarm of bipedal insects. This, of course, was what they wanted, both to serve as a reminder of their Clan and to make their armies look implacable and inhuman, unstoppable as a swarm of insects.

The Lion arrived a few days later, rank upon rank of tawny, armored warriors, their helmets maned with straw and their faces covered with armored masks wrought to look like fierce beasts. Gold adornments glittered when the sun broke through the clouds, dazzling the eye. Everything about them was large. The manes made their heads look huge and powerful, the armor plates that protected them were large as walls, and their swords were half again as long and twice as heavy as most katanas. At the head of their army, of course, marched Tsuko's Heart, the spirits' auras enhancing their tawny colors.

A small Crane contingent arrived late that day, clad in pale blue and white, looking as thin and graceful as the Lions looked stocky and powerful. The Cranes had all dyed their hair white, and the feathery ornamentation on their armor added to their elegance. They carried long, lethal naginatas, with blades as sharp as razors and poles twice as tall as a samurai.

Two days later, a Moto messenger arrived from the Unicorn. He had died in the saddle. Arrows fletched in Dragon colors stuck in his torso in several places. In his last moments, he had tied his wrists to the horse's harness and his feet into his stirrups so that he would not fall from the saddle. His katana he had wedged unsheathed into his belt, so that people could see the blood and the flecks of yellow lacquer borne on its blade. His note said that the Unicorn contingent would arrive at the mouth of Beiden Pass in eight days to rendezvous with Toturi's Army, and the Emperor should therefore not await them at Otosan Uchi.

The day after that dawned bright and clear as a force of Phoenix shugenja, clad in the fiery colors of their Clan, arrived on the van of a great wind, together with a few samurai bodyguards. They settled out of the air in perfect order. The last to touch down was very clearly Toturi Sezaru. His white hair with the distinctive black streaks was visible from a long way, the wind flaring it out as though it were a fan. The remainder of the Phoenix army was guarding the Dragon frontier to block that Clan's army from sending additional assistance to Hantei.

From his towers in the palace of Otosan Uchi, Toturi saw the assembled colors of the various Clans and allowed himself a slight smile. No sooner had he walked to the front gate of the palace than the Imperial Guard was ready to march. Toturi and Kaede mounted a large palanquin borne by sixteen strong samurai and led the way out of the city.

As the royal couple left the city through the last gate, the daimyos of the other Clans moved in to flank them. The Imperial Honor Guard followed, and the other Clans fell in behind. Lion cavalry posted itself along either side of the route of the march, keeping watch for ninjas, assassins, and ambush parties.

During the march, word that both Toturi and Kaede were present rippled through the army. The Emperor and Empress would both be on the field of battle. Their eldest daughter was a commander in the Lion troops, their eldest son a shugenja with the Phoenix contingent. Their youngest son awaited them with the Scorpion on the other side of Beiden Pass. In short, the entire Imperial Family would be at the decisive battle with Hantei, commending their fate and their dynasty to the army's success.

Never before had an Emperor attended a battle as anything more than a curious bystander, watching the epic proceedings from a safe, distant, neutral location. This was different. Everyone knew Toturi would lead the army, even fight and die, should his sword be needed. It gave pride to the samurai, and filled their souls with the gravity of the campaign. With these extra lives at stake, the talk around the campfires at night was mostly of how each samurai vowed to perform one act of bravery or another, an act that would turn the tide of battle and attract the attention of the Emperor himself.

Stalking silently through the camps at night, Toturi felt his breast swell with pride. These were his people. These were Rokugani, filled with bravery and daring on the eve of their deaths. In his late-night sojourns, the mantle of his position weighed upon him more than ever before. He could not fail, yet Tsuneo was one of the finest generals history had ever known, commanding an army of spirits purified by Jigoku. How, Toturi asked himself, does one defeat a legend?

After a little more than a week's march, Toturi's army met with the Unicorn forces. Atop their huge war-horses, their strange attire—fur trim and pointed helmets and leather and chain mail, all blended with more traditional Rokugani accouterments—made them seem barbaric.

The Unicorn had already sent a contingent to the other side of the pass, in case the Scorpion had changed their minds or fallen to an early attack by Hantei. With both ends of the pass secured, Toturi's Army began crossing through the narrow, winding gap. So narrow was Beiden Pass in places that the crossing went on all night long, the better to ensure that the army arrived in Scorpion lands in a timely manner. The last thing Toturi wanted was to have to fend off an attack with only half his forces.

The pass was treacherous in areas, as the last of the winter snow still clung heavily to the pass and the slopes above. However, the crossing was executed without major incident.

As Toturi exited the pass, his eyes beheld one of the most beautiful sights he had ever seen: the entire Scorpion army stood arrayed before him on the rolling foothills, huge maroon banners festooned with the black Scorpion waving in the gusting mountain breeze. At the head of the army, though hardly visible at this distance, he saw his son Naseru standing beside Bayushi Yojiro. He saw the tiny figure of Naseru step forward, and turn to face the army. He saw his son raise his arms, and the army did likewise.

A moment later, a "Banzai!" as big as the sea crashed against the mountains like a wave, and rebounded into the distance. Almost immediately his son raised his arms again, the army followed suit, and again silence reigned until the mammoth sounds struck the mountains again. A third motion, a third gap, and a third cheer of admiration. It was a greeting to bring tears to an old samurai's eye, which, in fact, it did.

* * * * *

Toturi spent the next two days in council with his daimyos and generals, giving his troops enough time to exit Beiden Pass, regroup, and get suitable rest. Yojiro informed Toturi that he had issued a declaration of war against Hantei to ensure that none of his people could be tempted to switch their allegiance and also to bait the vain Hantei into attacking Scorpion lands. Scouts reported that Hantei was crossing the Scorpion frontier and would be at Beiden Pass within ten days. The war council agreed with the Scorpion daimyo that Toturi would be best served by meeting Hantei a day's march away from Beiden Pass, so as not to fight with the mountains at his back.

The next morning, Toturi addressed his army. He stood on a pinnacle of rock with a small megaphone to his mouth, that his words might reach all ears.

"Samurai of Rokugan!" he said. "Only twice before in the history of the Empire have the Clans gathered together like this to fight a common enemy. Once was the Battle of White Stag, to save the Empire from evil. Once was the Day of Thunder, to kill the Emperor who was evil. The third time is today, when the Clans gather together to do both at the same time.

"I was privileged to lead you at the Day of Thunder. I am even more honored to lead you today, you who have endured the hunger, endured the confusion, and endured the uncertainty of the times. Now, as on the Day of Thunder, we fight to save the Empire from a terror that defies description and to kill an Emperor who would destroy everything you fight for. The thirty-ninth Hantei bore the soul of Fu Leng, and I say unto you that Hantei XVI has the heart of Fu Leng!

"As we go forth to do battle with those who defy the Celestial Order, remember your vows. Fulfill your duty to the Empire! Uphold the honor of your house! Bring glory to your sword! Let these be your watchwords:

"Duty! Honor! Glory!"

The amassed army immediately picked up the chant, which lasted long after Toturi had stepped down from the outcropping of rock.

It was later said that the noise reached the ears of Hantei's scouts, sounding like thunder from the mountains.

* * * * *

Hantei's army moved across the landscape, legions of spirit samurai covering the hills with their golden aura. Legions of sullen mortal Crab troops followed the main body, looking like the army's shadow. Huge machines of war creaked and groaned as they were hauled across the lands, speaking for their Crab handlers, who were too proud to protest.

The massive army moved across Scorpion lands like a slow fire, and Hantei ensured that they left the castles wrecked and smoldering in their wake. No one could withhold their service to the Hantei for years and escape paying the consequences. The inhabitants of these castles, who welcomed Hantei's troops with open arms, wisely thanked the Emperor for his justice, then began the slow, painful process of rebuilding.

As the army moved, Dragon troops filtered through the lands to join them—tattooed monks, samurai, and shugenja, all of whom had evaded the Phoenix cordon and braved the snowy Spine of the World to reach their Emperor. As they arrived, they were integrated into the Dragon arm of Hantei's army.

Unicorn spirits also trickled south in the aftermath of Gaheris's victories, moving through the wooded margins of Shinomen Forest to link up with Hantei, whom they viewed as their sole remaining refuge. Crane spirits deserted their posts on the Yasuki frontier, hoping that a strong Crane presence at this final battle would move the Hantei Emperor to rule in their favor when the Yasuki problem was brought before the next Imperial court.

Thus, as Hantei's Imperial Legions marched, they grew in strength, swelling with recruits and unhampered by fatigue or disease. As they closed on Beiden Pass, Hantei ordered that wet silks be thrown into the burning Scorpion villages and castles, so that the pall of smoke would remind the mortals of their impending doom.

At last the Phoenix and Unicorn outriders reported contact with the enemy. Toturi's Army awaited them at the far end of the next valley. At this word, Tsuneo left Hantei's side (without asking permission—he was still following Hantei's command in as irritating a fashion as possible) and rode forward to where he could survey the mortals' disposition. Several of his Crab aides ran along behind him, ready to do his bidding.

Toturi had chosen well. His troops occupied a rolling ridge that overlooked a wide valley, flanked on one side by marshy terrain and on the other by a rocky draw. On Tsuneo's side of the valley was another, lower set of hills, neither as smooth nor as tall as Toturi's position. From where he stood, Toturi had a commanding view of the entire battlefield, including, to an extent, Tsuneo's reserves area. Conversely, the best command position Tsuneo could locate was not nearly so impressive. Although he could see the whole battlefield, his staff would not be at the center of his army, nor could he see the reserves Toturi might have behind his ridge. Finally, Toturi's higher elevation gave them much better defense against charging troops. They could even countercharge down the slope.

Tsuneo did not like the terrain. It was clearly of Toturi's choosing, for Tsuneo's position was just barely good enough. Terrain advantage belonged to Toturi, notably so, but the imbalance was not quite enough to warrant further maneuvering. If Tsuneo sought to march around this position, it would dishearten his troops, and in all likelihood the next battlefield would be even worse. In short, tactically the terrain was bad, but strategically, looking for another battlefield was worse.

Tsuneo crossed his arms over his burly chest with both frustration and admiration. Such a shame to have to kill such a subtly brilliant and observant mind, he thought, but a samurai's life is but a string of tasteless duties executed in the name of duty to perfect one's soul.

Tsuneo scanned Toturi's arrangement of the troops. The Lion spirits, as always, occupied the very center, surrounded by their Clan. To Tsuneo's left, he saw the large Scorpion army standing defiantly. To the right, Tsuneo saw the Imperial Guard next to the Lion. Beyond them was a force of Mantis samurai, far larger than he had expected for what he considered a minor Clan. From this distance, he could see neither Crane, nor Phoenix, nor Unicorn. He assumed the Unicorn were held in reserve behind the ridge, poised to strike where they were most needed or least expected. The Phoenix and Crane probably had sent a mere handful of troops. The Crane samurai were likely held in reserve while the Phoenix shugenja were dispersed amongst the troops with samurai acting as bodyguards.

Tsuneo snapped his fingers, and his aides stepped closer. "I will command from there," he said, pointing to the rise he'd looked at earlier. "Arrange the spirit units as we have before. Place the Dragon on the right flank, and O-Ushi's Crab troops on the left, opposite the Scorpion. She has not been happy since hunger convinced her to support the Hantei, and I do not trust her troops." The aides bowed and ran off to attend to the many details that these simple orders required.

Tsuneo tensed as a shadow rose from the grass behind him. He hated this part of his job.

"Honorable general," whispered the ninja, "here is the latest information." Tsuneo sat perfectly still in his saddle, and heard a small scroll being inserted into his saddlebag. Once the noise stopped, he wheeled his horse around rather quickly, but the ninja was already gone.

Tsuneo clenched his fist. He wanted to curse those of the Scorpion Clan and their damned stealth and duplicity, but he dared not. Not while the ninja might still be around.

* * * * *

Hantei's spirit legions primed for battle throughout the day, ever watchful that Toturi's army did not attempt to launch a sneak attack while they prepared. Tsuneo thought an attack unlikely, as it would forfeit the considerable advantage of Toturi's position. Hantei's army took the field, with the Dragon and Crab mortals forming up behind the spirits. Tsuneo did not want to commit his forces to their respective flanks until shortly before the attack. The less Toturi could think about their disposition, the better.

As dusk fell, muting the colors of the mountains and fields, Tsuneo brought a hundred large drums to the front and center of his army. Burly samurai set up the drums, carefully aiming their barrels across the valley. Throughout the long, dark night, Dragon Clan tattooed monks beat a continuous barrage of heavy percussion, drumming martial rhythms from every time and every Clan. Although they played for hours and sweat drenched their pants, the volume of their drumming never waned, and the constantly shifting noise and rhythms kept Toturi's troops from sleeping. Instead, the troops kept watch over the softly glowing spirit legions and tried not to think about how it reminded them of the dawn breaking in the west.

That night, in their command tent, Hantei asked Tsuneo, "What do you think of tomorrow's battle?"

Tsuneo jutted out his jaw as he mulled over the question. "Toturi has good samurai, and they will fight hard. He has advantageous terrain, and his troops are rested, having waited for our arrival. He is an excellent strategist." Tsuneo scratched his neck absently. "Your eyes narrow with distaste, Emperor," he said. "Would you rather I made up some courtier's fluff and dander for you, or shall I continue telling you the truth?"

Hantei waved an irritated hand at him, so he continued. "On the other hand, his troops farmed most of last year instead of drilling. They are not as well fed as he might hope, and they have not trained together as a single army like your troops have. Finally, our spirits are better soldiers one-for-one. Even should the Scorpion promise be empty, we shall take the field. It will be a bloody affair, but the result is inescapable."

"Excellent," murmured Hantei.

"However, the victory will not be an overwhelming one. Even if the Scorpion utterly surprise Toturi, he is an excellent general. I sincerely doubt we shall capture him tomorrow. I believe we will have to pursue him back to Otosan Uchi. Fortunately, our troops can march farther and faster than his, so we should be able to entrap him before he reaches the Eternal City."

Hantei pursed his lips and drummed his polished nails. "The Fortunes confound me at every turn," he snarled, "but for the pleasure of capturing Toturi, I shall wait." He rose and left the tent, leaving Tsuneo alone to listen idly to the drums.

Shortly before dawn, the drumming abruptly stopped. For the soldiers of Toturi's army, the sudden, complete silence was even worse than the noise. The units formed up without being ordered and waited for the inevitable. Across the valley, the sound of marching feet reached through the lingering ringing in their ears. Unseen by Toturi's troops, the Crab and the Dragon were taking their places.

Dawn broke, and to the relief of Toturi's army, it indeed rose in the east, behind the Spine of the World. As it did, the gentle nighttime breeze stopped dead. Nothing stirred. It was as if the world itself held its breath.

Finally, in the center of the spirit army, a surge of magical power whirled into the air, writhing and weaving. It coalesced into the familiar form of Hantei XVI. To the mortal samurai across the field, it looked as if a giant Hantei were wading up to his hips in a sea of spirits.

The Dragon shugenja's ritual allowed the Hantei Emperor to be seen and heard all across the battlefield. He spread his arms wide, as if to encompass his army, and looked down, seemingly inspecting his troops from his heavenly perspective.

"Loyal samurai of Rokugan," he said, and his voice was as loud as the seashore. It even had a touch of the watery, wavy sound to it, due to some strange twisting effect of the magic that amplified it. "Today we face the ronin who calls himself Emperor! We fight the bandit who deliberately destroyed both the Emerald Throne and the Jade Throne to deny the Hantei family their right to rule!

"But today we fight more than just a thief who steals the Empire's honor and destroys the Empire's treasures. We fight the man who seeks to erase the Empire's heritage! His people look not to you, their ancestors, for leadership. They look to him. They do not revere their family. They wish to send you back to Jigoku to be ignored! By sunset, those who wish to forget you will writhe in Jigoku and plead for you to remember them! Forward," the visage shouted like a storm, "to victory!"

The spirit army cheered wildly.

* * * * *

Across the battlefield, Kaede closed her eyes, hung her head, and shook it gently. "What a spate of foul lies!" she whispered. She looked up at her husband. "You must respond. . . ."

Toturi stood beside her, his face impassive, his eyes looking vacantly at the enemy forces. "The best lies are clad in the bright robes of truth," he said.

Across the field, Tsuneo could be seen pointing his troops forward with his tetsubo. The entire spirit army began marching forward.

"It is the beginning of the end," Toturi said. He turned and looked at his wife. "I don't believe we can win," he said, "but we will die with honor."

Across the valley, Tsuneo launched a basic frontal assault. Toturi raised his eyebrows with placid surprise. How simple. How basic. No great strengths, but no great weaknesses.

With a few orders, Toturi deployed his archers on the top of the ridge, where they could shoot over the heads of the infantry. In response, the great Crab war machines began launching huge, flaming balls at the center of Toturi's line.

Kitsu Motso, Toturi's second in command, walked over to Toturi's side. "This is going to be ugly," he observed dryly.

Toturi nodded. "He knows we have cavalry, but if he engages the whole line at once, we won't be able to deploy them," he said. "I wondered if it might not be a mistake to spread the line all the way from the scree to the marsh."

The Lion daimyo chuckled mirthlessly. "It seems he found a small advantage to your choosing the terrain," he said. "Still, I didn't expect this from the Stone Crab. It's not his style."

Toturi shot a glance at Motso. "It's a sumai wrestling match with a whole army," he said.

"Sure," answered Motso. "It may be a Crab thing to do. But it's not a Stone Crab thing to do. He's a brilliant man. It just seems odd. Perhaps he's choosing to rely on intimidation and the superior ability of his troops."

"Only his spirits are superior," remarked Toturi. "He still has Dragons and Crabs on his flanks." The entire command staff reflexively ducked as a flaming boulder smashed into the hillside a short distance below them. A glob of burning pitch, dislodged by the impact, struck one of the banners and ignited the silk, causing it to erupt in flames.

"My liege," said Motso quietly, as a handful of samurai worked to remove the flaming banner, "look over there." He pointed past the burning silk to the left flank of Hantei's forces. "The Crab are holding back."

Toturi watched as the massive spirit army moved closer. The Crab Clan mortals were indeed marching slower than the rest of the army. The adjacent spirit troops were moving perhaps half again as fast, leaving their flank exposed as they kept pace with the other spirit units. As Hantei's forces moved closer, the gap kept growing. If Tsuneo ordered his units to charge, the spirits might not only be flanked, but the units at the gap could potentially be surrounded.

"Fascinating," said Toturi.

"I don't know what blackmail Hantei used to get O-Ushi back under his fist," Motso said. "Probably the threat of starvation, but it looks as if she has found a way to follow his orders and fight against him at the same time."

"No surprise to me," said the Emperor. "She's always been rather, ah, circumspect around authority figures. But we'd best take advantage of her gift while we can."

"I'll see that my people handle it," said Motso. "They're headed for the right end of the Lion section, anyway." He mounted his horse and rode hard for his troops as an errant ball of fire ripped the sky overhead.

* * * * *

Hantei leaned forward on his palanquin. "Higher!" he yelled to his bearers, and as one they lifted him over their heads, supporting his chair atop their upraised arms. Hantei leaned forward further, then quickly turned and glowered down at Tsuneo.

"You said the Crab mortals could be trusted!" he shrieked. "That bull-headed bitch is holding them back!"

Tsuneo glanced over in that direction. "Yes, my liege, she is."

Hantei was momentarily confused. "You . . . you ordered her to do that?"

Tsuneo snorted. "No, of course not," he said with no small amount of exasperation. "If I had, she wouldn't have done it."

"What do you mean?"

"She's trying to sabotage the battle, Excellency," Tsuneo said. "Thus, if I had ordered her to hold back, she would have marched with everyone else, just to thwart my plans."

"Why would she do that?" Hantei asked, affronted and still a little confused.

"Because she hates you, my liege," said Tsuneo. "For that matter, so do I, but I don't let my hatred get in the way of my duty. She does."

Hantei narrowed his eyes to slits of pure fire. It was almost time to rid himself of this increasingly insufferable boor. Almost. "And that, my so-called friend," said Hantei venomously, "is why she is stronger than you. She does not let mystic ideals stand in her way."

Tsuneo actually reached up, grabbed the side of Hantei's palanquin, and pulled it down. Hantei gripped his seat to keep from sliding, and the tattooed monks strained to keep it stable. "You know much about power, little man," Tsuneo snarled, "but you know nothing of strength. I could crush your skull as easily as I crushed your mother's."

"Do not try to intimidate me, weakling," said Hantei. "Over there." Hantei gestured to his bearers. "This man bores me."

The monks looked into Tsuneo's eyes then, without a word, turned and moved to a more auspicious place on the hillock.

Tsuneo returned his attention to the battle. O-Ushi was indeed holding her troops back, just as he had expected her to. She was handing Toturi the flank of the spirit units, as well as freeing up Toturi's right flank to fight other foes. In all likelihood, she would switch sides as soon as the balance shifted. Tsuneo felt her word, loyalty sworn under duress, would probably hold out until then.

But that was all the time he needed.

21 THE BATTLE OF QUIET WINDS

The
Twentieth
Year
of the
Reign
of
Toturi I

As Hantei's spirit samurai approached the enemy lines, they broke into a trot, the Dragon Clan keeping pace solidly on their right flank and the Crab troops lagging behind on their left, leaving the spirits' flank exposed. Heedless of the charge, flights of arrows flew through the sky in both directions, their wicked whispers striking death all around. The great engines of the Crab ceased firing projectiles as the spirit troops drew close to enemy lines. The spirit units' banners began waving, and the troops braced for the final full charge up the hill.

At that moment, the Lion Clan countercharged the exposed spirit flank.

Several Lion units surged forward—three to flank the leftmost spirit formation, two others to engage the spirit units next to them, leaving the flank spirit unit without help. Once that unit was shattered, the flanking Lion units could do the same to the next formation, and roll up the flank of the enemy army, leaving death in their wake. The Lion samurai charged downhill, carried by momentum and the feral war cries of generations of fierce

Lion warriors. Their eyes blazed with anticipation of the crash of arms and armor.

Instead, as one, the spirit units turned and fled.

The Lions continued their countercharge, believing they had routed the spirits before the first blow was struck. They did not notice as a veritable cloudburst of arrows struck their units from the rear, piercing the Lion armor in the back where it was thin. When the second volley of the lethal black rain struck, they turned and saw the Scorpion archers firing as fast as they could, aiming directly at the Lions' hearts. The short range and advantageous position greatly aided the Scorpion treachery. One archer would later comment that it was as easy as shooting a beached whale. Thus distracted by the Scorpion betrayal, the Lion did not notice the spirit samurai stop and turn. Their retreat had been a ruse, and now they surged forward again and struck the disoriented Lion troops hard.

Meanwhile, the Scorpion samurai turned to their left and charged Toturi's archers, neatly lined up along the top of the ridge. The archers with their bows were no match for the fast-moving Scorpion samurai, and katanas spun and struck like palm fronds in a hurricane, leaving a swath of blood behind. Once the spirits engaged the Lion, the Scorpion archers fired their arrows indiscriminately across the length of Toturi's Army, using arrows that whistled or trailed smoke to add to the chaos and confusion they sowed.

In that moment, as the commanders all across Toturi's army came to grips with the abrupt shift of the battle, Hantei's forces charged.

From his vantage point, Tsuneo smiled grimly. His plan had been executed perfectly. Shot from behind and then charged while disorganized, the Lion troops were falling rapidly to the spirit samurai. Toturi's lines were now hotly engaged across the front, preventing the Emperor from maneuvering them effectively. The Crab units on Tsuneo's left flank were now out of combat. Toturi's lines had been flanked, and O-Ushi's troops could clearly see that Tsuneo had already won the field. For her to betray her oath and switch sides now would be nothing but suicidal. Instead, Tsuneo knew, her

oops would continue to follow in a lackluster fashion, but he did
ot care. Just their presence helped Hantei's forces seem more mas-
ve, more numerous.

Tsuneo turned to one of his aides. "New orders for the catapults,"
e said. "Have them fire behind Toturi's army."

"You mean over the hill, general Tsuneo?" asked an aide. "Sir,
ey'll be firing blind."

"I am not worried about casualties," said Tsuneo. "I just want to
ow fear as they look to retreating. A few flaming boulders falling in
eir path of retreat may turn this victory into a rout."

* * * * *

As the Scorpion executed their sudden betrayal, a small detach-
ent of samurai turned upon the Phoenix shugenja assigned to
upport them. They sliced down the samurai bodyguards, who
tood surprised by the cold treachery, and moved for the magicians.
One shugenja unleashed a flaming geyser from his hands, broiling
hree Scorpion and fusing their skin to their armor before he was
ut down. Within the span of a few heartbeats, most of the shugenja
nd their samurai guards were dead.

The last of the shugenja was an acolyte of fire. He turned to the
ast Phoenix samurai and called upon the spirits of flame. The
amurai had been somewhat apart from her comrades, and she
ursed herself as she ran to fight the Scorpions and die. She saw the
hugenja's gesture, saw the sudden eruption of a sword through his
ibs. The shugenja winced, but the pain only caused a brief pause.
He finished his gesticulation and pointed to her. The wind whirled
round her, whipping her hair in her face as wings of fire erupted
rom her shoulders and bore her into the air. Temporarily blinded
by her hair, she did not see the shugenja slip to his knees and die, a
mile on his face.

Against her will the wings bore her away from the treacherous Scor-
ions. When she determined that kicking and writhing availed her
ot, she pulled her hair back from her face and saw that she was drop-
ing rapidly into the Unicorn reserves. They were all looking at her, a
icking, cursing, flying Phoenix samurai.

The wings knew how to fly far better than she feared. They c
ried her rapidly toward the Unicorn, pulled up at the last mome
and deposited her easily on the ground, flaring out of existen
even as they did so. Before anyone could ask anything, she yell
"The Scorpion! They betray us!"

Moto Gaheris looked up just in time to see the Scorpion laun
a volley of smoking arrows down the length of Toturi's line. Rig
teous rage gripped his soul. He drew his sword and bellowed
incoherent war cry, a primal bellow of fury. His horse leaped fo
ward like a bolt of lightning, and the entire Unicorn contingent f
lowed behind, leaving the Phoenix samurai covering her face at t
sudden eruption of thunder, dust, steel, and trembling earth.

The slope did not slow the powerful Unicorn war-horses in
slightest, and Gaheris's troops caught the Scorpion archers on
flank. The archers had time to launch a single barrage of arro
before the cavalry fell upon them like a tsunami, smashing the
beneath spears, swords, and iron-shod hooves.

The cavalry's momentum carried them through the archers, a
into the valley between the armies. Gaheris paused only a mome
blade, horse, and armor spattered with Scorpion blood. He s.
O-Ushi's Crab forces walking across the battlefield in a less-tha
martial fashion, and ignored them. He saw the carnage in the ba
on his left. But most clearly of all, he saw the Hantei command st
and archers ahead. He saw the standard of the Steel Chrysanth
mum, and he wanted blood.

"For Rokugan!" he bellowed, and spurred his horse forwar
leading his troops across the battlefield to kill Hantei and end t
war.

* * * * *

Toturi's army tried to rally under the onslaught of their form
comrades. He sent the Crane to save the archers from the Scorpi
assault and ordered the Lion to pull back to protect the arm
badly mauled flank. He saw the Unicorn reserves lunge forwa
without orders, and he hoped they knew what they were doing.

All up and down the line, he saw his troops embattled, givi

ground, dying, and he saw it was useless. His last hope had been plucked from his hands by the Scorpion and handed to a Hantei demon, decorated with the blood of thousands of loyal samurai. In the thousand years of the Empire, he thought, no Akodo general has ever been defeated. Thank the heavens that the thirty-ninth Hantei stripped me of that name, that I do not dishonor my ancestors with my failure here today.

He turned to Kaede. "Get moving!" he ordered. "Take the children if you can find them, and get to Beiden Pass, now!"

Kaede stared at him in shock.

"We are lost, Kaede," he said grimly, "if I continue the fight, it will only waste the lives of my troops. Go!"

She fled, reaching out with her mind to touch Sezaru's soul, passing the order. She had no idea where Tsudao was, and Naseru was in the clutches of the cowardly Scorpion.

With great reluctance, Toturi began to engineer the retreat. Over protests and under the cover provided by Phoenix shugenja, Tsuko's Heart was pulled from the line and moved to protect the empty gap on Toturi's right flank, where the Scorpion used to stand. He didn't want Hantei to be able to send any cavalry through that gap. The Lion troops at the angle, beset by Scorpion and spirit alike, he pulled back to shorten his line. He ordered the Mantis and the Imperial Guard to begin disengaging, swinging like a gate hinged towards the center of the line.

He hoped his army could hold together as he withdrew. He expected Hantei would continue to attack relentlessly. For him, the carnage would be more important than the victory.

* * * * *

Tsuneo watched the storm of purple and white charging toward his position. "How can they move so fast?" he said in amazement. "It must be magic. . . ."

"Sir, those are the Unicorn," said an aide. "If you have never seen their horses up close, I fear you are in for a very hard lesson. They stand twice as tall as any horse we own."

As the Unicorn cavalry drew closer, Tsuneo could see that the aide was not exaggerating. "Back to the siege engines!" he ordered. "Take the Emperor to safety!"

The command group pulled back as archers launched volley into the oncoming Unicorn forces, felling horses and samurai alike. Tsuneo called up some reserves to reinforce the command staff, and they took up positions inside and behind the huge catapults and other engines of destruction, hoping the great structures would impede the Unicorn assault.

The stalwart cavalry crested the hill and thundered into the defending spirits. Long naginatas, braced against the ground, speared through horses and riders. The mighty Unicorn steeds leaped over defenders smiting their skulls with their trailing hooves. Dismounted riders found themselves surrounded and overwhelmed by defenders, while spirits were crushed to death between the well-muscled chests and haunches of the trained mounts of the mortals.

In the midst of it all, Moto Gaheris swung his two-handed sword like a madman. Its length matched his impressive height, and the reach the weapon afforded his powerful muscles was enough to cleave samurai well before they could strike at him. Though dismounted, Gaheris pressed forward, slaying all who came within reach. "Where is the Hantei dog?" he shouted.

"You can only find him through me," said Tsuneo, as he stepped into Gaheris's path and hefted his tetsubo.

Gaheris found himself looking slightly up as he stared into Tsuneo's eyes. "You must be the Stone Crab," he said. "I am sorry that I shall be responsible for your death."

"Given that you dress like a barbarian dog, your remorse means nothing to me."

Gaheris cocked his head. "Well," he said, "I would not have expected Toturi to speak so highly of someone with such ill manners. I retract my grief, for now I strike for the betterment of the Empire."

Tsuneo dropped his eyes and took a half step back. "No, stranger, I should apologize instead. It seems that I have let my master's lack of decorum rub off on me. I am ashamed. I hope you will forgive me." He looked directly at Gaheris. "Unfortunately, I still have my duty, and that is to kill you."

"No," said Gaheris with a dangerous glance. "Your duty is to try."

Tsuneo whirled his tetsubo around, the spiked wood whistling slightly in the still air. He realized that he had no idea what to do about this strangely dressed fellow. He knew the fighting styles of the Empire, but this man had learned to fight in another land filled with strange, gibbering people. What tactics would he use? Would he know Tsuneo's style?

The two combatants held their ground, studying each other's preliminary moves. All about, samurai fought and died, leaving the two commanders to their honorable combat. Tsuneo took a swing at Gaheris's long blade, looking to break it, but Gaheris wheeled the blade away, whirled it overhead, and came down. Tsuneo dodged aside, although the blade took off half of the armor guarding his shoulder as it passed. Gaheris followed through with an upward cut, but Tsuneo stepped forward and thrust with his tetsubo as if it were a staff. The heavy maul struck Gaheris, but the Unicorn only stepped back a pace, his bulk and his resistance throwing Tsuneo slightly off balance.

Tsuneo gathered himself again and nodded to Gaheris slightly, acknowledging his skill. Gaheris scowled and said, "You are a much harder kill than I thought, Stone Crab. For that I am glad, for otherwise I might never have believed in legends again."

Tsuneo feinted then lifted his tetsubo over his head for a downward smash. Gaheris was surprised but brought his blade up to deflect the blow just enough to the side that the tetsubo dragged harmlessly off the Unicorn daimyo's armored skirts. The spikes, however, nicked Gaheris's finely sharpened blade.

Tsuneo saw Gaheris's eyes narrow slightly, as if he had just decided what technique to use. He thrust his blade forward then slowly pulled it back horizontally across his body. Tsuneo tensed, ready for anything—

Anything, except to see a long spear come from the side to impale Gaheris's neck. The Unicorn samurai grimaced, grabbed the spear with one hand, and tried to turn his head to see who had struck him so dishonorably. The culprit worked the spear back and forth, causing more blood to gush from the injury, then yanked the spear out hard, the narrow blade slicing Gaheris's fingers nearly off as it

pulled out. The Unicorn fell, and Tsuneo saw his hands clawing th
dirt. With a fluid motion, Tsuneo pulled his katana from its sheath
stepped forward, and lopped off Gaheris's head with a mercy cu
allowing him to die as a samurai, without a cry of pain.

Tsuneo flicked the blood from his blade, and turned to the bear
of the spear. "Why did you do that?" he growled, stepping closer.

"Forget him," shrugged the spirit samurai. "He was going to forg
us. He's only a mortal—and a Unicorn, at that. No honor."

With a sharp move, Tsuneo broke the samurai's jaw with the bu
of his tetsubo. The samurai's eyes widened, and he started to brin
the spear up. With blinding speed, Tsuneo struck the man acros
the forearms, breaking them. He then hit the man once more
breaking one of his femurs and dropping him to the ground. H
leaned over the fallen samurai, saw the tears of pain rolling from hi
eyes, and whispered hoarsely, "You will die as you left him to . . . dis
honorably. I leave you your tongue so you can scream."

* * * * *

At the angle of the Lion lines, the pressure was overwhelming
Lion samurai, unused to withdrawing, faltered as they pulled back
The spirits sensed that victory was at hand and redoubled th
assault. Flares of magical energy punctuated the horrid sound o
slicing swords, spilling blood, falling bodies, and cries of vengeance

Seeing that his troops were sorely beset, Kitsu Motso moved for
ward and began rallying the troops, roaring commands and wavin
his war fan, pulling order out of chaos through sheer force of will
His presence kept the troops from breaking, and the units' sergeant
echoed his commands and helped return discipline to the Lion
units caught in the vise. Yet even as the subordinate officers reorga
nized their troops, an unexpected weakness arose.

In the confused fighting, several Lion units had become inter
mingled, and they needed to be separated again if the retreat wer
to be conducted in any semblance of structure and discipline. Th
sergeants saw to this, barking orders and reorganizing their units
in the face of the relentless spirit assault. But as two of these units
segregated themselves, a seam opened up between them, a narrow

corridor of clear ground edged by bloodied steel and fearsome manes.

A handful of Crane spirits saw the opportunity, a fleeting shaft of sunlight in the dark clouds of war. Without hesitation, they charged recklessly between the units. They knew they would not take even seven breaths more before they died, but their names would be remembered forever for the action they took now.

As they charged, Lion samurai cut them down from both sides, but it was already too late. Two Crane passed through the gauntlet between the units. The lead samurai, waving his katana, threw himself on the Lion soldiers who stood between his sole surviving comrade and their target, sacrificing himself to clear a path. The other spirit, holding a long, cruel spear, thrust at Motso, who stood on a large stump to make himself more visible. The spear's blade hit the Lion daimyo's armor at the abdomen, glided up along the lacquered steel plates, and pierced the gap between the plates. Perfectly formed to deflect bows that came down, the scaled armor plates now guided the spirit's weapon upward into Motso's diaphragm.

With the force of his charge, the Crane impaled Motso entirely on the spear, even lifting him off his feet for a moment. Motso fell off the stump, dropping his war fan but not his katana. His momentum pulled the spear and the Crane samurai with him. From his knees, Motso reached out with his left hand and yanked the spear through his body, pulling the stunned spirit even closer. With a great snarling roar, Motso brought his katana over his head and cut the golden-hued Crane in half from shoulder to hip.

His brows furrowed, his eyes threatening to weep from the pain, Motso looked around. No spirits moved within reach. Glancing down, he saw his blood pumping rapidly down the haft of the accursed spear. His legs were already numb; he didn't even know if they would move. There was nothing left but to die with honor and avoid capture. With a flick of his wrist, Motso flipped the katana in his hand so the blade aimed inward, toward himself. He swung his arm out and across in a wide circle, slinging his blade to his left side, then quickly yanked the handle back to the right. The centrifugal force whipped the blade around, and it sliced neatly across Motso's throat, severing the jugular. With his last moment, he forced his face into a calm expression.

The death of their daimyo, the undefeatable Kitsu Motso, brought despair upon the Lion forces. Beset by golden-hued warriors and unable to defend their own daimyo, their morale cracked, and the units started not to withdraw, but to retreat. It was unthinkable, and the sheer shame and shock of it turned the retreat into a rout.

The panic spread through the ranks of Toturi's army like wildfire. If the Lion were retreating, what hope was there? The Imperial Guard broke and fell back despite orders from their general. To save his own honor, Toku stepped forward and attacked like a wild man, whirling and striking about with a speed and accuracy that singlehandedly held back the spirit assault long enough for the Imperial Guard to disengage before he, too, pulled out of the fray. Seeing their employers pulling back, the Mantis routed, having no desire to get pinned against the marsh by a spirit breakthrough.

Hantei's legions were at once exhausted and exhilarated. The flush of victory swept their lines, causing some to abandon their battle fervor and cheer, while others fanatically tried to pursue. The officers rallied their troops, for it was well known that a disorganized pursuit could be turned about by a determined last-ditch defense, and the victors become routed in turn.

Thus Hantei's legions took a few moments to reorganize their troops, and the officers looked to Tsuneo's command post for further orders. The hillock was empty, save for a riderless Unicorn steed, trotting back down the valley.

Precious moments slipped past, Hantei's leaders at once fearful of being inactive and fearful of making an impetuous mistake.

At last Tsuneo and a few of his staff regained the hill from the far side and used their banners to signal new orders to their troops. Tsuneo's signal was clear: the Crab, being fresh, would pursue, and the eyes of Hantei would follow their progress with great interest. As O-Ushi's troops marched forward at a pace slightly faster than might have been expected, Tsuneo and his staff redeployed to the top of the ridge where Toturi had once had his command post.

* * * * *

Guarding the open portion of the line, the samurai of Tsuko's Heart watched as Toturi's army crumbled. The panic was tangible and the fear very real, for thousands of spirit samurai were still eager to fight. Murmurs rippled through the deathseeker spirits as they saw their descendants fleeing. Seemingly without thought, Tsuko's Heart began edging backward, caught by the great undertow of retreat.

Then, amidst all the chaos, a single Lion samurai emerged from the battle, running resolutely toward the Lion spirits. His helmet was missing, his blade bloodied, his steps swift and sure. It was Akodo Kaneka.

"What in the name of the heavens do you think you're doing?" he shouted, and his young voice rang through the battle as clear as a bell. His eyes saw to their hearts, and his words stung their pride. He knew they were beginning to fail, and they could not answer his question.

"The army is routed! The future of Rokugan retreats to Beiden Pass! We must ensure they get there! See! Hantei's legions stall. By columns, at the run, first division leads, form up as a rearguard behind the ridge! *Move!*"

So assertive were his words, so pure his soul, that the commanders obeyed him without question. Within moments the deathseeker unit arrayed itself across the center of the battlefield, inserting itself between the retreating mortals and Hantei's legions. Behind the ridge, they were shielded from Tsuneo's sight and protected from enemy archers.

As the sounds of marching feet swelled, Kaneka shouted, "Not one step back! You are deathseekers! All glory to your name!"

A few spirit units crested the ridge, isolated groups of samurai from up and down the length of the battlefield. As they came into view, they paused, studying the Lion spirits. Another unit topped the rise, and another, and they stopped, too.

"Why don't they attack?" Kaneka asked no one in particular, gritting his teeth.

The sound of marching grew louder, then Kaneka received his

answer. The mortal Crab forces crested the rise, fresh and undamaged. The deathseekers watched as they spread out for an attack. Kaneka readdressed the Lion lines to meet the Crab head-on. With a burly roar, the Crab surged forward, charging the spirits. The samurai of Tsuko's Heart answered with their own feral war cries, and the two contingents clashed together.

After the initial clash, Tsuko's Heart quickly got the better of the fight, slaying Crabs right and left. The Crab morale seemed very low, their troops dispirited. Seeing this, and concerned about being drawn further into a melee when other enemy units were nearby, Kaneka ordered Tsuko's Heart to disengage. Once the order was given, fighting ceased fairly quickly, and the Crab pulled back to regroup, leaving the field littered with their dead.

In this brief respite, a lone rider approached Tsuko's Heart at a full gallop, her long hair flowing from beneath her helmet. She rode up to the commander of Tsuko's Heart and pulled her horse to a halt.

"You have done your job," she said. "Toturi's army has regrouped and marches to Beiden Pass. Pull back and join them."

"Who are you to tell us to retreat?" barked Kaneka.

"I am not telling you to retreat," she said through gritted teeth. "I am *ordering* you to rejoin the army."

"Leave us!" said Kaneka. "We are not afraid to fight!"

Toturi Tsudao whipped off her helmet. "Enough of your tongue, you . . . you . . . orphan dragon dropping!" she shouted. "You will obey me!"

Kaneka casually turned his face away.

Tsudao pulled a fan from her belt and snapped it open with a loud pop. It was a jade fan, emblazoned with the Imperial seal. "Are you defying the Emperor's direct order?" she asked.

"The Emperor, I shall obey," said Kaneka. "Not someone's kid sister."

"I am the eldest!" she snapped, but Kaneka ignored her outburst and set about organizing the withdrawal of Tsuko's Heart.

As the deathseekers withdrew from the battlefield, several units of spirit archers opened fire, raining death upon the Lion. The deathseekers had a desire to die in glorious battle, not as an archery target, so they departed at a fast jog. One of the arrows, however, struck Tsudao's horse in the abdomen. The beast reared, then its rear legs buckled beneath it and it fell sideways, trapping Tsudao's shin beneath its chest.

With another mighty cry, the Crab units charged the retreating deathseekers. Not a full charge at the run, but a more controlled, cohesive charge at a trot. The spirit archers quickly found the Crab units in their way and were forced to cease firing at the retreating Lions. For their part, the Crab saw they were not gaining on the Lion spirits and abandoned the charge.

Tsudao found herself surrounded by Crab soldiers. A tall, powerful Crab samurai approached, with a huge hammer carried idly over her shoulder. As she approached Tsudao, she looked around at the other Crab samurai.

"What in the name of all that's holy are you sodden beggars doing?" she yelled. "Get that damned horse off her leg!"

At once a group of Crab samurai moved in. One clubbed the horse squarely on the forehead to put it out of its pain and to keep it from thrashing as they freed Tsudao. The other samurai heaved the horse off her leg as easily as if it had been a foal.

"One thousand pardons, my lady," said the Crab. "I am Hida O-Ushi. If you please, I ask that you quickly change into Crab armor, that your presence among us may not be known."

Limping badly, Tsudao staggered to her feet. "I will not wear the armor of traitors to the throne," she said.

O-Ushi grimaced. "In that case, my lady, you are now my prisoner," she said. "I only hope Hantei forgets to inquire after you, for otherwise I would not pay a grain of rice for your position."

LEND ME YOUR HAND

The
Twentieth
Year
of the
Reign
of
Toturi I

Toturi's army retreated to Beiden Pass. The units formed into their own column, six samurai abreast, and the army moved like a group of serpents, colored by Clan, winding their way to the safety of the mountains.

Toturi, his wife, and his generals moved among the various units, directing the march and providing aid where needed. Those with moderate to serious injuries were dispersed into the countryside, so as not to slow down the army. Some samurai, injured and healthy alike, volunteered to lay ambushes for the spirits to delay their intractable pursuit.

Tsuko's Heart remained the primary rearguard and suffered repeated attacks by spirit cavalry and hard-marching infantry throughout the day. Each time the deathseekers fought a fierce delaying action, refusing to allow Hantei's troops to trap them in a protracted melee where they could be surrounded and destroyed. Yet each time more Lion fell, mortal and spirit alike, and the strength of Tsuko's Heart grew weaker and weaker.

Unknown to the beleaguered mortals, O-Ushi's mortal Crab

troops continually hampered Tsuneo's pursuit. Somehow their siege engines mired themselves in soft ground, requiring additional troops to pull free. Crab units repeatedly confused their marching orders and ended up in the way of other units, requiring intervention from a commander to sort the trouble out. Certain dispatches became garbled in the transmission, further frustrating Tsuneo, yet he dared not dishonor his own Clan by exposing their sudden incompetence. In part, he understood them and wished he could be in their place.

As Toturi's army reached Beiden Pass, the situation became dire indeed. The Pass was narrow and difficult, and only a handful of samurai could pass through at a time. This slowed the retreat, trapping the majority of the army at the base of the pass. Toturi and his commanders worked to get the troops through in an orderly and efficient manner, but the delay gave Hantei's troops time to encroach and would have been disastrous but for the casually inefficient efforts of the Crab.

Fear and disorder began to rise in Toturi's camp as the army felt the gathering power of Hantei's forces. Night fell, and the army's passage through the pass proceeded even slower.

A Lion samurai approached Toturi, offering a solution. "Disperse the Phoenix shugenja throughout the pass, my liege," he said. "Include the Empress and your son among them. Together they can keep the pass illuminated. Even a little light will help, and their powers may be of immediate use if an accident stops the march."

"What is your name, samurai?" asked Toturi, looking at the samurai's spattered heavy armor, bloodied sword, and damaged helmet with its snarling bestial mask.

"I am Ikoma Kagehiko, my lord," he answered.

"Kagehiko, I have not heard of you before," said Toturi, "but you are now an Imperial advisor. Remain by my side."

"The honor is far too great—" began Kagehiko.

"This is not a gift, Lion. It is an order. Obey. Your first duty is to help the shugenja find their places. Go."

The Lion bowed and left at a run. Soon shugenja and their bodyguards had dispersed themselves throughout Beiden Pass, using means both mundane and magical. They occupied inaccessible ledges and high overlooks, staying out of the way of the marching troops and enjoying a commanding view of the pass. Kaede and Sezaru occupied a high point in the center of the pass, where their superior skills could monitor and assist the entire effort.

A soft glow settled over Beiden Pass as darkness came. In some areas, the air was filled with hundreds of thousands of fireflies, their intermittent glow providing a subtle, shifting light. In other areas, a luminescent haze filled the gorge, and in others the moonbeams themselves were bent into the narrow pass to light the way.

* * * * *

Meanwhile, at the southern end, the rest of Hantei's troops had caught up with Toturi's army. After a few hasty assaults with their leading elements, Hantei's army had taken the time to deploy properly and prepare an attack. Toturi's troops were dispirited and exhausted from a sleepless night, a losing battle, and a day's hard march. Hantei's spirits felt fatigued, though not as greatly, and their energy was buoyed up by their high morale.

"Here we are at Beiden Pass!" cried Hantei, actually addressing the troops in his jovial mood. "The crossroads of the Empire shall be the crossroads of history! Let the final blow be struck here!"

The spirits moved to the attack, and only Tsuko's Heart stood against them.

* * * * *

From his vantage point, Hantei XVI watched the battle. It was difficult to discern what was happening. Only a dim, golden glow could be seen in the dark, punctuated by the occasional burst of magical energy. It didn't matter to him, though. It was carnage, and the sound of dying samurai was music to his ears.

Tsuneo stood quietly beside him, as did Toturi Naseru, Bayushi Baku, Hida O-Ushi, and Bayushi Yojiro. Aside from occasional hoots of glee from Hantei, the group was silent.

At last, as dawn grew in the east, the battle broke. From the movement of the troops it was clear that Tsuko's Heart had fought hard, almost to the last soldier and that those remaining were pulling back into Beiden Pass to continue fending off Hantei's forces within the twisting gorge.

"My Emperor," said Yojiro, breaking the silence as he bowed most deferentially, "Toturi's army is defeated. They flee back to Otosan Uchi. We of the Scorpion Clan are honored and overjoyed to have been the cause of your victory. I beg your favor, my lord, and humbly petition that you grant me the honor of leading the Bayushi House Guard through the pass first, to clear your path to the Eternal City."

Hantei turned to Yojiro, and looked him up and down with a sneer thick with distaste. "You, the cause of my victory? I think you mortals forget your place! The victory is a victory of my people, not yours!"

"My Emperor," interceded Baku, "please forgive the rude behavior of my Clansman. He—"

"And you, Baku!" snapped Hantei. "You have no control over your people if you let a mortal whelp like this make requests of the Emperor without consulting you! This is my victory, not yours! You had nothing to do with it! I brought this moment about, and the honor shall be for my people, not yours! The samurai who have served me all along! The spirits shall march through Beiden Pass and take Otosan Uchi, and if I am gracious, I shall allow you to visit that city before you die!"

Yojiro and Baku both bowed deeply. "As you wish," said Baku, and the two Scorpions backed away and faded into the night.

As they walked back to their troops, they hazarded a subtle glance at each other. Behind their masks, their eyes gleamed.

* * * * *

Hantei's troops pushed through Beiden Pass, ignoring their casualties and overwhelming the beleaguered rearguard. From just north of the summit, Toturi listened to the reports of the fighting. Hantei's troops were hardly even being slowed down. Toturi tried to direct the defense, but the messengers were exhausted and the troops too few.

Toturi's army had disgorged onto the plains north of Beiden Pass, but they were in poor shape to fight. They had already been ordered to march as hard as they could for Otosan Uchi, but with the speed of Hantei's progress, it seemed they'd be caught in the plains and defeated piecemeal.

The faint sound of combat reached Toturi's ears. Considering the tortuous terrain, it meant that Hantei was close. Toturi turned to look for Kitsu Motso, forgetting for a moment that he had fallen, and felt a deep pang of regret when the familiar face was nowhere to be seen.

"I do not know what to do," he said to himself.

"My liege," said Kagehiko softly, "I have another suggestion."

"Your last suggestion worked, although I fear it will come to naught," said Toturi grimly. "Can you make another to save your first?"

"Honorable Toturi," said the Lion, "your shugenja are situated in strategic places throughout the pass. The reports indicate Hantei's spirit troops are swarming through the pass like maggots on a summer corpse."

"Yes . . . ?" said Toturi.

"Collapse the pass," said Kagehiko. "It is the only choice."

Toturi slowly looked up to the steep sides and high pinnacles of Beiden Pass. When they had marched through here the first time, they had been fearful of landslides. How much worse would the landslides be if they were deliberately created, forced into existence? A heavy earthquake would collapse these steep-sided stones, filling the narrow pass with falling rocks. A shugenja of water magics could create a sudden mudslide, drowning those below in thick clay. Nothing could survive that sort of maelstrom.

It had to be done.

He looked up the mountainside to where his wife stood, watching Hantei's progress. "*Kaede!*" he shouted, even though he knew she would never hear. Beside him, Kagehiko pulled a humming bulb from his quiver, an arrow equipped with a piercing whistle in place of an arrowhead. He nocked the arrow, drew his bow, and let fly. The arrow arced through the air toward Kaede's promontory, shrieking its important message.

Kaede looked down into the ravine and, seeing her husband, reached out with her chi and touched his mind. Immediately she saw his plan, saw the inevitability and the decisiveness of the sabotage, saw the defeat that awaited if she refused. All of this took but the blink of an eye, for she was the Mistress of the Void, and the perfection of the idea leaped into her mind fully formed.

She reached out with her soul for the other shugenja, many of whom still lurked, unseen, in their high places, as Hantei's forces passed below them. She reached out and summoned the spirits of the land to heed the call. A webwork of energy began to shimmer between the shugenja, radiating from Kaede and weaving the pass together.

Below, a burst of samurai ran down the pass, and Toturi and his commanders fled with them, Hantei's leading troops not far behind. They stumbled and ran down the narrow, rocky, twisting pass, eventually finding several other samurai readying an ambush, determined to stand against the encroaching spirits.

The approaching sound of running feet grew louder, and the spirit samurai turned the rocky corner and spilled into the defenders. Yet as the sounds of battle erupted, another sound grew beneath it all. The ground began to tremble, and then of a sudden the air split with the sound of a thousand volcanoes, as if the air itself had exploded.

The thundering sound rolled on and on, and a thick cloud of dust rapidly rose to great heights in the pass. So numerous were the spirits caught in that terrible collapse that the dust cloud was illuminated from within by the golden glow of their spilled blood.

The devastation impelled a pause in the melee, and a few spirit samurai moved swiftly back to the corner to see what had happened. The shock that registered on their faces gave Toturi's samurai new hope, and they defeated the spirits in short order, leaving the northern portion of the pass free from Hantei's reach.

Panting with his efforts, Toturi turned to Kagehiko. "It seems your idea worked," he gasped.

"It wasn't my idea, my Emperor," was the reply.

* * * * *

Hantei screamed—a long, monotone, falsetto scream of anger, frustration, shock, and dismay. It lasted far longer than any around him would have expected. It lasted while the billowing dust ceased its swirling movements; it lasted while the last of the loose rocks of the avalanche clattered down from their perch; it lasted until the only noise that disturbed the profound silence was Hantei's voice running out of air.

Where once there had been a mighty army of spirits pressed together, shoulder to shoulder, advancing in victory, there were now only rocks. The sundered end of the column of troops stood in shock in front of Hantei. A few bloodied survivors, some dazed, some crippled, staggered away from the dusty ruins.

Slowly, eyes wide, Hantei turned, seeking someone to blame for the loss of the majority of his army in one cataclysmic event. His eyes fell upon Tsuneo—insolent, capable, indispensable, insulting Tsuneo. Even the Stone Crab stood in shock, teeth clenched with the incomprehensible thought of thousands of samurai struck dead in a single act.

In one fluid motion, Hantei reached into his voluminous sleeve, pulled out a long, wicked knife, and plunged it deep into Tsuneo's belly with a sneer twisting his features.

Tsuneo's attention suddenly turned inward, and he looked down to the red patch rapidly spreading on his abdomen. He pursed his lips and looked up at Hantei.

"Do I understand that the Emperor no longer desires my service?" he asked calmly, though his voice was rather thick with shock and pain.

In answer, Hantei twisted the blade.

"I will take that as affirmation," said Tsuneo through gritted teeth. "Thank you."

Hantei pulled the blade wickedly to the side, slicing through Tsuneo's viscera. Tsuneo drew in a sharp breath, then cocked his huge fist and punched Hantei hard across the face, just in front of the ear where the jawbone connects to the skull, sending the Hantei Emperor sprawling in the dirt. Holding his abdomen together with his other arm, Tsuneo lurched toward Hantei, first one ponderous step, then another.

Hantei scrabbled backward in the dust, fear smeared across his face, but the great Stone Crab settled slowly to his knees, then sat back onto his heels. His eyes still burned with hate for the Hantei Emperor. He bunched up his fist again, but then the fire in his eyes grew dim. He leaned forward, catching himself on his fist. Phlegm trickled from his lip as he wheezed.

At last, he looked up in the general direction of several nearby samurai. "I have completed my duty," he said with slurred speech, "and I have redeemed my honor." Then he fell slowly to the side, and a legend breathed no more.

* * * * *

"Bayushi Baku!" a full, harsh female voice shouted. "Your time has come!"

The Scorpion spirit stood in conference with Bayushi Yojiro and the daimyos of the various Scorpion families. The conversation immediately paused, and he and the others turned to face the speaker.

Hida O-Ushi, her long hair waving in the breeze that only now had begun to blow again, stalked forward, her great hammer ready and thousands of glowering Crab samurai at her heels.

"You have no Hantei robes to hide behind any more, Baku!" shouted O-Ushi. "There are no more spirits to keep my wrath in check. Come now, and let me strike the first blow of vengeance against the Scorpion. I will kill the daimyo for the Clan's betrayal, if you have the courage to face me without your Emperor."

Baku bowed politely, precisely as deep as was required for an inferior when greeting the daimyo of a different Clan. "If you please, honored daimyo of the indomitable Crab, I only serve the Clan. If you wish to kill the daimyo, please challenge him yourself." Here he bowed again, and withdrew, gesturing to Bayushi Yojiro.

Yojiro stepped forward to O-Ushi, hands placidly clasped in front of him. She hefted her hammer to a ready position, but the Scorpion did not acknowledge that he even noticed.

"Honorable O-Ushi," he said, bowing, "the Empire has suffered enough war. I wish to see no more." He turned his head away, looking over his shoulder, and shouted, "The Scorpion surrender!" He knelt before O-Ushi, and at once, the thousands of Scorpion samurai did the same.

"If you wish to begin your vengeance, powerful Hida," continued Yojiro, "you may begin with my head. I ask only that you present it to my liege and Emperor Toturi I before you continue your campaign against the rest of my people."

O-Ushi stood for a moment, then, from her kneeling position, Yojiro saw her feet shift, heard her grunt as she hefted her hammer over her head. For the briefest moment he heard the windsong as the hammer pushed its way brutally through the air—

It struck Yojiro's helmet a glancing blow, and impacted the hard earth with a jarring blow.

"Damn you!" she shouted. "Damn you and your schemes and your twisted sense of honor! Anyone but you, Yojiro, and no one would recognize your headless body!"

With a snarl, she picked up her hammer, and stalked away. In the small crater her hammer had made, Yojiro saw the utterly flattened form of the gold scorpion that had formerly graced the top of his helmet. He closed his eyes and thanked the Fortunes.

* * * * *

Panting with exhaustion, Toturi coughed from the thick dust in the air. He drew his kimono sleeve across his mouth and peered at the rock-filled pass. He looked quizzically at Kagehiko.

Through the ringing of his ears, he heard a noise, and looked up the pass . . . at least what was left of it. A lone samurai was moving out of the thick cloud at the foot of the avalanche. He came closer, and Toturi recognized Akodo Godaigo.

The skeletal samurai moved slowly out of the wreckage. He saw Toturi and bowed deeply, and Toturi noticed a huge dent in one side of his helmet where a large rock had struck him. A dent that size would have killed anyone else . . . anyone but a skeleton.

Toturi noticed that Godaigo was not holding his katana. The sword was sheathed. In his right hand, Godaigo was holding the bones of his left forearm, and he looked at them with expressionless curiosity as he continued out of Beiden Pass toward the plains.

Toturi and Kagehiko stared at Godaigo for a long time, until his shape faded in the slowly settling dust.

Toturi coughed again, breaking the reverie, and wiped his face with his sleeve, leaving streaks of sweaty dust behind.

"Just a moment ago," said Toturi, "you said it wasn't your idea."

Kagehiko reached up and pulled off his great maned helmet. As he lifted it off his head, Toturi saw that he wore a blood-red gauzy mask across the lower portion of his face, where it had been hidden by the fearsome bestial faceplate of his Lion's helmet. A headband secured Kagehiko's hair, and on the front of that headband was the mon of the Scorpion.

"Please forgive me for lying about my identity, my Emperor," he said, "but I was ordered to do so. And I was asked to give you this message." Kagehiko—or whatever his name truly was—reached into his belt and pulled forth a small vellum scroll. He knelt and presented it formally to Toturi.

Bewildered by the rapid chain of strange events, Toturi plucked the scroll from the Scorpion imposter's hands. He unfurled it and read:

Most Laudable and Glorious Emperor Toturi I—
Behold the works of the under-hand of the Emperor! All that I have done, I have done for you, playing even the dissenters of my own Clan as the strings of a samisen.

> *Your loyal servant,*
> *—Bayushi Yojiro*
> *Daimyo of the Scorpion Clan*

Toturi looked up from the scroll, at the immeasurable weight of rocks now filling what had once been Beiden Pass, the hammer that had felled the undefeatable, and the scroll slipped unnoticed from his hands.

* * * * *

O-Ushi turned and slung her hammer over her shoulder. "Come!" she bellowed as she walked back through her troops. "I need my commanders! Now!" The Crab turned to follow her, passing by their erstwhile prisoner, Toturi Tsudao.

Tsudao looked over the thousands of Scorpion samurai kneeling in surrender, and she noticed one samurai still standing. She furrowed her brows and moved purposefully forward. She glided swiftly through the Scorpion troops, neither noticing nor caring about them, honing in on the one person still standing.

"Naseru!" she shouted angrily as she drew closer to her brother. He stood, poised and regal, looking at the dust-choked entrance of Beiden Pass with a faint smile on his face.

Again, "Naseru!" He did not respond.

Confusion warred in Tsudao's heart. The Scorpion betrayed Toturi, then surrendered. She had heard the exchange and knew that Yojiro was . . . still? Again . . . ? Now, at least, was the daimyo. They had betrayed and surrendered, yet now Hantei was defeated and their Clan was whole. And in the midst of this all, Naseru stood defiantly. Traitor? Double agent? Mastermind? Pawn? She did not know.

She stopped a few paces away from him, hand trembling on her sword. Slowly, evenly, he turned his head toward her, and glanced at her from the corner of his eye. She thrust her head forward, eyes narrowed, questioning, trying to see his heart, but his face was as placid as a painted mask.

"Poor Tsudao," he said with a slow blink. "You will never know the truth, for you see only as far as your sword can cut. The game goes far deeper than you know, deeper than even the Scorpion suspect."

COUNTING THE LOST

The
Twenty-First
Year
of the
Reign
of
Toturi I

From the west, a group of samurai approached Otosan Uchi. They were spirits, all of them, two from each Great Clan save only the Lion, and one from each minor Clan. There were also several tattooed monks supporting the weight of Hantei XVI's ornate palanquin. While perhaps the high summer heat would have been more suitable for a sedan chair, the Hantei Emperor did not wish to be seen by anyone. He preferred to brood in the dark, stuffy interior of his conveyance.

All around, the dusty fields struggled with new life. Samurai monitored the peasants closely. They did not pretend to understand farming as did the peasants, but they did ensure the peasants were supplied with food and water, and looked after whatever other needs they had, the better to get Rokugan's agriculture back to its former level of productivity.

As the palanquin passed, the samurai and peasants stopped their work, turning and glaring with open hate at the ornate lacquered wooden box and its guard of spirits. They neither bowed their heads nor bent their knees. In return, the samurai guarding

the last Hantei took no notice of the onlookers, and the latticewo
windows of the stuffy palanquin's box never opened.

Day and night the palanquin moved, stopping for only for
short rest during the darkest portion of the night. The reason f
this hard pace was simple and shared by the Hantei and his esc
alike: the quicker this painful journey ended, the better.

* * * * *

"I still can't believe you actually agreed to see him," said To
earnestly.

"The war is over, my friend," said Toturi.

"Are you sure?" asked Toku. "It started long before you ma
your ultimatum, and he still hasn't made any proclamations of su
render, so why do you think he's going to stop being the vile basta
he's always been? You actually made it a declared war, but if y
declare peace, I don't think that'll change anything. He's not li
that!"

Toturi laughed. "Relax, old friend," he said. "Yes, I agree. He is n
that sort of man. That is why I know the war is over." Toturi gestur
to a scroll that lay upon the low mahogany table against one side
the war room. "He sent a message, asking to see me."

"You mean 'demanding' to see you."

"No," said Toturi. "He asked."

Toku blinked several times, suddenly finding no words on h
tongue.

Toturi laughed again. "Yes, it is a rather dramatic shift of the un
verse, isn't it?"

Kaede stepped forward, gliding effortlessly into the conversatio
"But if you look deeply within, General Toku, you will find that t
truth has been there all along. The Steel Chrysanthemum is obsess
with power, for he believes his power gives him value and securit
There is a hole in his heart, a gap in his soul that he seeks to fill wi
power and blood. When we collapsed Beiden Pass upon his army, v
took his power."

Toku pondered this. After bulk of Hantei's army had died, t
embittered Crab turned upon his remaining legions, as did th

vengeful Scorpion. When Hantei retreated to Shinomen Forest, the Dragon Clan provided no aid. Hantei had wintered in the Shinomen, and the spring found the Phoenix, Lion, and Unicorn guarding against an attempt to reach sanctuary among the Dragon mountains.

Toku nodded his understanding.

"Therefore," continued Kaede, "with his power he has lost his confidence and his security, and therein lies the solution. He can no longer take what he wants by force, so he will negotiate for it."

"But surely you can't let him negotiate for the throne!" objected Toku.

"Of course not," said Toturi with a small chuckle. "He knows he can't have it. He wants something though, some sort of safety or admiration or something. We have to figure out what he wants, sorting out the real truth from whatever he says. Then we give that to him to whatever extent we can, without sacrificing the safety of Rokugan."

"All right," said Toku. "But be careful. He is a viper with a head at both ends!"

* * * * *

Hantei strode purposefully into the throne room, drawing to a stop in the center. He bowed to Toturi, no deeper than he would have to a senior but respected subordinate, thought better of it, and extended his bow a little deeper, as to an equal. Just barely.

Toturi responded in kind, bowing smoothly as to an equal.

Hantei took in the room with his peripheral vision, taking quick stock of the situation. Toturi stood where the throne belonged, the throne that he had shattered nine years before. His wife stood to Toturi's right, with their children lined up at her side. Toku stood at Toturi's left, as did Seppun Toshiken, the Emerald Champion, and Kuni Utagu, the Jade Champion. The Imperial Court, scribes, courtiers, experts in law and tradition, all sat to Hantei's left. The Clan daimyos sat to his right, a group of people he most certainly would rather have never seen again. An openly hostile Hida O-Ushi stared at him with tangible hatred. Bayushi Yojiro appraised him with a cool glance. Even Togashi Hoshi, the Dragon daimyo, sat in attendance, his vacant eyes deliberately seeing nothing.

Hantei felt naked without Tsuneo's looming presence, but he'd be damned before he showed any weakness.

He looked about again, with half-lidded eyes showing disdain for every living thing. His lip curled in the slightest suggestion of a sneer. "I see you feel the need for protection, Toturi," he said, turning his head without looking at anything, "surrounding yourself with guards and sycophants."

"I have survived battles that defy description, Hantei," he said. "I have no need for protection."

"Survived?" Hantei tittered. "Evidence is against you."

Toturi looked at his hand, rubbing his fingers together as if the golden aura that surrounded his fingers were oil. "You would never understand, Hantei," he said.

"I understand the weakness of a man who feels the need for daimyos to bolster his position when dealing with a real Emperor."

Toturi rolled his eyes, ever so slightly, as if the response were beneath his notice. "The daimyos are here neither for you nor for me, but to witness a decision that will affect the future of the Empire, that being so informed they will be better prepared to serve."

"And if I order them to leave us alone?"

"Please, be my guest," said Toturi. "However, by my count, that would make one Emperor telling them to attend, and one telling them to depart. We would then see which Emperor they obey. Such a gesture may in fact tip the balance of this entire discussion, since it would demonstrate which Emperor truly holds sway over the Empire, would it not? After all, the Emperor *is* the Empire, as it is wisely said. So please, command away."

Hantei smiled, a wide smile of mirthless teeth, almost a snarl. "Very clever, Toturi. However, I shall not fall for your ronin tricks."

Toturi waited for Hantei, as if the last comment had never been said.

Hantei looked about again, as if seeing the throne room for the first time. "I thank you, Toturi, for despite your past, you have thus far honored your promise of safe passage for the Hantei Emperor, and you have received me graciously. Let me therefore bypass the standard ceremonial greetings and pleasantries. I would not want to embarrass a commoner by demonstrating his lack of knowledge of such high etiquette. I shall instead proceed directly to the business that brings us to this day, in an effort to appease your less-than-delicate upbringing."

"My past may have been somewhat poorer than your own, Hantei," said Toturi, "but even as a ronin I found petty insults beneath me."

Hantei gave the mirthless smile again. "For a ronin to believe anything could be beneath his station, that ronin must have been upside down."

"The Dragon will tell you that a new perspective is often a blessing," countered Toturi.

Hantei sighed. "I find even to speak with you is wearying, Toturi. Let us therefore be done with this matter. There can never be peace between us while a usurper sits upon the throne."

"I will not yield the throne to a tyrant," said Toturi, "nor will I let the future of the Empire be willfully destroyed."

"I thought petty insults were beneath you," said Hantei, "but no matter. I no longer have the power to defeat you in open warfare, Toturi. I can continue to fight, and I would, but the war would last so long it would destroy the Empire in the process, and I would be left ruling a wasteland."

"Agreed," nodded Toturi.

"I therefore offer you an honorable solution to this dispute, Toturi," Hantei said. It was difficult for him to offer this concession, and everyone could tell he had to force the words out of his mouth.

Toturi waited placidly, quietly, as Hantei gathered the wherewithal to utter the next sentence. The others in the throne room dared not move, dared barely even to breathe.

"Let us . . . tie our bloodlines together," said Hantei through gritted teeth. "It is the only way there can ever be peace between us."

Toturi opened his mouth to respond, but no words came out. Kaede looked over at Toturi with a furrowed brow and pleading eyes.

Toturi's hesitation gave Hantei a surge of calmness and bearing. "I see that the ron—Excuse me, the *Emperor* has no words. You really must be prepared for such surprises if you are to . . . survive on the throne."

"How do you propose we . . . *tie* our lines?"

"One of your children, Toturi, must bear the Hantei name and accept the Hantei blood. Only if our ancestors are honored, and only if a child of both of our bloodlines remains close to the throne, will we cease our war. The Hantei line shall recognize you as the interim Emperor of Rokugan, and I shall abdicate my position and go into retirement as the Imperial father. I shall reside in a villa in the Dragon Clan's mountains, where my grandchild shall visit me yearly."

"The price you ask is too high, Hantei," said Toturi at last. "My children—"

"You think this price is higher than *the destruction of the entire Empire?*" Hantei shrieked. "You do not deserve to rule!"

"How dare you threaten to destroy the Empire just to secure a position for your vanity!" bellowed Toturi.

"Father," a small voice interjected itself. Both Emperors whirled upon the speaker who would have such temerity as to interrupt an Imperial war of words.

Naseru stepped calmly forward, his face a calm expression of reason, compassion, and desire to compromise. "Father, I shall accept the Hantei name."

"Naseru . . ." said Toturi.

"Father, I shall sacrifice my name to end this crisis, just as you did at Otosan Uchi under the thirty-ninth Hantei. Perhaps this will restore the balance of that terrible day. I am the logical choice, Father, for who could better complement the lessons of the Crane and Scorpion than the Hantei Emperor himself?" He looked at the floor. "Besides, as the youngest, I am the least likely to succeed to the throne. Terrible accidents would have to strike down both of my siblings. As an adult, I am free to make this choice. This I now do."

Kaede instinctively began to reach for her youngest child, but Tsudao gently took hold of the cuff of her mother's sleeve before Kaede's arm could rise. Naseru walked over to stand near Hantei, where he turned to face his father. His eyes were dark and empty, even under his father's scrutiny.

"As for my people," said Hantei, deliberately interrupting the moment, "if you swear never to besmirch the honor of those who were righteous enough to oppose you, the spirits under my command shall remain as my honor guard."

That stirred Toturi from his stunned silence. "I would, ah, suggest that all spirits, those who fought for you and those who fought for me, be given the chance to choose whether to honor you as your personal guard, or to honor their house and return to Jigoku through the Jumping Place."

"That is of no importance to me," said Hantei. "Anyone who would prefer to flee like a coward is not a samurai I would wish as a guard."

"Then it seems we have peace," said Toturi, yet he had never imagined that the arrival of peace would weigh so heavily on his heart.

24 THE RISING SUN

The
Twenty-First
Year
of the
Reign
of
Toturi I

Autumn had arrived at last. Hantei had moved into his villa without incident. Toturi had interceded in the Yasuki war and stopped the fighting (although the Crane had neither accepted blame for the war nor waived their claims to the lands). Without the shadowy presence of Hantei goading their actions, the spirits of the Unicorn and Hare Clans had given up their fights, retiring quickly and honorably to Jigoku. Spirits from other Clans had moved along as well.

The Empire was at peace for the first time in many long years, and the first crops were just being harvested. The year was drawing to a close.

It was time for the Lion Clan to go home.

The Lion ancestors had remained throughout the summer, administering aid where necessary, hunting down renegade spirits, and keeping watch for any resurgence of Hantei's subversive power. However, as the last of the spirits—save only the fifty or so that guarded Hantei—had returned to Jigoku, the presence of the Lion spirits was no longer necessary.

Together with the royal house and the daimyos of the Lion

Clan families, Toturi sat in a pavilion erected at the seashore near the Jumping Place. Other Clans' daimyos sat farther back. One by one, the surviving Lion spirits walked to the top of the artificial promontory and turned toward Toturi and his house. They raised their arms and shouted, "Banzai!" then turned to the sea and leaped, vanishing in a flutter of hair and silk and motion.

Toturi gripped his sword tightly as he watched. It was hard. The Lion had once been his Clan, and his heart still bore the burdens of loyalty and love for the Clan. He knew many of those who now saluted him and then embraced their deaths. He had studied their tactics, their teachings, their techniques, and now they voluntarily left this world out of respect for him, he who had once been bypassed for the position of daimyo, who had once been ronin, who had once, like them, died and returned from Jigoku.

He could have remained as stone, but instead, one by one, he wrote their names on a parchment.

The last of the Lion spirits finally jumped off the ledge and departed this world. Toturi took a deep, shuddering breath, and turned to speak to the Lion daimyos. Akodo Ginawa subtly raised one finger and looked meaningfully out to the Jumping Place. There was another figure approaching.

It was the skeletal figure of Akodo Godaigo, wearing, as ever, his ancient armor. His left arm was in place, cleverly tied there by wires, but it did not move with the natural grace of his right arm. Godaigo walked to the ledge and turned to face the pavilion. Ginawa pulled a scroll from his belt as if he were drawing a sword.

"Since he cannot give the Emperor a proper banzai," said Ginawa, "he asked me to read his final haiku." Ginawa untied the scroll and opened it, reading the bold, beautiful brush strokes.

> Life, fragile and short,
> Flutters like a butterfly
> Until my snows come.

Ginawa lowered the scroll and looked at Godaigo. The skeletal samurai bowed deeply, held it for a breath (though indeed he had none), then straightened.

"He never told us the truth behind Matsu Hitomi, did he?" asked Toturi quietly.

"In all those centuries," said Ginawa, "he told no one."

Godaigo reached the edge and drew his sword.

"Fragile and short," said Toturi.

"Mm."

Godaigo leaped from the rock, arcing out high over the water. He did not vanish as had the others, but his bones and armor tumbled apart in midair, splashing quietly into the foaming surf.

* * * * *

The harvest season was in full swing, and across the Empire the twin blessings of peace and plenty made every day a quiet celebration.

In Otosan Uchi, Toturi and Kaede walked quietly through the Imperial Garden, enjoying the changes the season wrought, watching leaves fall to the resting earth on the gentle breeze, and admiring the happy chaos of colors on the trees mixing with the solid unchanging counterpoint of the evergreens.

Courtiers, servants, and guests hovered nearby, sharing the moment and complimenting the Empress on her startlingly beautiful new kimono.

Toturi caught Ginawa's eye, and the two of them unobtrusively moved away from the main body of guests. Toturi paused, reached up, and pulled down the branch of a large fir tree. He smelled the branch, and quietly said, "The Empire owes the Lion a great debt for their service. Of all the Clans, they alone wholly served the Emperor, they alone obeyed without fail, and to them alone belongs the credit for the defense of Otosan Uchi."

Ginawa bowed very slightly, almost as if he was rocking forward on his feet, just enough to acknowledge the compliment but not so much as to attract attention from anyone else. "The Emperor does us too much honor. We are but poor servants who seek to serve our lord in every fashion."

Toturi smiled wryly. "That is true," he said, "and that is why everyone owes you such a debt."

Ginawa started to speak, but Toturi raised one hand. "Please, my friend, we have been through too much together. Despite the fact that I am Emperor, I still hope you also count me as a friend, so please, let us stop the Imperial etiquette."

"It's only these damn Scorpion and Crane that keep me from scratching my itches in your presence," replied Ginawa.

"Really?" said Toturi with a grin. "I guess that means that now even you must acknowledge they serve a useful purpose."

Ginawa chuckled, a self-depreciating noise. "I guess so," he said, looking sheepishly at the ground. "Now you've done it," he added, "every time I get an itch on my backside, I'll think of them."

"Listen, Ginawa," said Toturi, and Ginawa, hearing the earnestness in his voice, looked back up at him. "I know how much the Lion gave. I also know that to acknowledge their service in a manner that they deserve would cause no end of troubles in the Imperial Court."

"Very true. Everyone would accuse you of favoring your former Clan."

"For a start," agreed Toturi. "Others would complain that those who do their duty deserve no special reward . . . even when the complaintants didn't perform their own duty. So I find I must acknowledge your Clan underneath the table. Tell me, old friend, how can I thank the Lion for their loyalty?"

Ginawa started to say something, then changed his mind and turned his face away.

"What can I do?" repeated Toturi.

"I . . . I can think of nothing," said Ginawa.

Toturi pursed his lips for a moment. "Surely I deserve honesty rather than sincerity," he said.

Ginawa remained silent for a moment, thinking, then he took a deep breath and faced Toturi again. "Honestly, my Emperor, I can think of nothing that you can do for the Lion. But there is something you can do for me, and it will help you, and the Lion, and probably even the Empire."

Toturi looked deep into Ginawa's troubled eyes. "What is it, old friend?"

"You could acknowledge Akodo Kaneka as your son."

Toturi reeled, and for a moment, he thought he might lose his balance. "Kaneka?" he whispered. "Kaneka is my . . . my son?"

"Yes," said Ginawa as compassionately as he could. "He is your son by your mistress Hatsuko."

"But that's not . . . not possible. . . . I thought she died . . ." said Toturi. His mind raced across the years. "The dragon," he said at last. "It had to be the dragon who spoke to me from the waterfall. Hatsuko was thought to have killed herself at that same place. He must have taken her."

"Yes, I believe you are right, Toturi," said Ginawa. "A great dragon made of water dropped off a pregnant woman in Lion lands. I think it was no coincidence that she was left in an Akodo village."

"But how do you know she was Hatsuko?" asked Toturi.

"Listen to yourself," said Ginawa. "You grasp at smoke. You know it is true. But to appease your curiosity, one of the Lion spirits recognized Kaneka from his features. He looked like your child would have looked. Ikoma Tsai confirmed her blood with magic, and the Kitsu ancestors confirmed your hand upon his soul."

"It was a dark period of my life, Ginawa," Toturi said, "I thought it the brightest, but it was the first step of my long fall. And it broke Kaede's heart, destroyed the Akodo name . . ." Toturi looked over at his wife. She herself happened to look back at him, and favored him with a dazzling smile. He must have been blind not to see everything that she offered and to throw it all away for the hollow love of a geisha.

"She has never mentioned the subject of Hatsuko, Ginawa," Toturi said. "I think it would be a perilous venture." Kaede started to walk over to the two samurai. "I cannot do it, Ginawa," Toturi said in a whisper. "Perhaps the time will come, but I cannot do it now."

"Do not wait too long, my friend," said the grizzled Lion, "for you of all people know that karma cannot be denied." Then he smiled warmly and bowed as the Empress came near.

* * * * *

The time for Winter Court had at last arrived, and Toturi was making the customary opening speech to the assembled daimyos and other dignitaries.

"This is the first time we have held Winter Court since the war began," he said. "Indeed, it is the start of a new era." Toturi looked meaningfully around the room. "I have learned much in this last war, something that I hope I can pass on, something that I hope shall be a heritage for all who sit upon the throne for all time.

"The Empire has given much for me," he said. "They have given their lives, their service, and their loyalty. They have given their support, their honor, and their homes, fortunes, and lands. I know I do not deserve such unconditional loyalty, but every day I do my best to be worthy of it. Or so I thought."

The room stirred. This was a direction no Emperor had ever taken before.

"I have given the Empire my service, my duty, my honor, and even my death. Now I shall give the Empire my life. No more shall my safety or comfort or prestige be a consideration in those actions the Emperor shall undertake. I allowed the sessile tradition of the Emperor to keep me from intervening when the Crab and Crane went to war, and that war precipitated other wars, which precipitated this last, great war.

"I shall do what needs to be done, for above all, an Emperor must be a samurai, and a samurai's duty is to serve. If the Empire needs my sword, I shall wield it. If the Empire needs my wealth, I shall give it. If the Empire needs my wisdom, I shall teach it.

"I thought I was doing everything for the Empire, but I realized I was wrong. I need to give the Empire my days, each and every day for the rest of my life.

"Furthermore, I need to give the Empire my hope. The Emerald Throne was sundered when the Hantei dynasty began to fall. The Jade Throne was sundered when the Hantei dynasty attempted to return. How could I expect other than great trials when the throne, the symbol of all that is Rokugan, is cut in two?

"Thus I have ordered that a new throne shall be made, the Steel Throne, and it shall be strong enough to withstand even an Emperor as foolish as I.

"I do this in hopes that the Toturi dynasty will last a thousand years and that my words this day shall never be forgotten."

As one, those in the room surged to their feet, shouting "Banzai!" loud enough to wake the gods.

Throughout the winter, the dragons saw to it that the storms were mild, the mountains were quiet, and the fishing was very, very good.

THOSE WHO SHAPE THE DESTINY OF ROKUGAN

Agasha Tamori
: Dragon Clan, daimyo of the Agasha family, learned shugenja and practitioner of magic.

Akodo Ginawa
: Lion Clan, daimyo of the Akodo family, fought alongside Toturi when Toturi was a ronin.

Akodo Godaigo
: Lion Clan, ancient hero thought dead centuries ago; his skeletal remains continue to walk the earth.

Akodo Kaneka
: Lion Clan, orphan, often called "the dragon's whelp."

Bayushi Baku
: Scorpion Clan, returned spirit from times long past, who manifested himself to guide the Scorpion after Shoju's Coup.

Bayushi Shoju
: Scorpion Clan, aka "The Usurper," who slew Hantei XXXVIII in a vain attempt to prevent Fu Leng from returning; he was slain by Toturi when the coup collapsed.

Bayushi Yojiro
: Scorpion Clan, daimyo of his Clan, often called "the only honest Scorpion."

Hantei XVI
: Hantei Emperor, returned spirit, oft called "The Steel Chryanthemum," known for his vile and indulgent practices; he was slain by his own guards.

Hantei XXXVIII
: Hantei Emperor, killed by the Scorpion Clan in their famous coup.

Hantei XXXIX
: The last Hantei, he was possessed by the soul of the dark god Fu Leng, and eventually defeated by the combined might of the Great Clans.

Hatsuko
: Geisha, lover of Toturi, poisoned him at the outset of the Scorpion Coup, jumped from a waterfall when she realized the magnitude of her actions.

Hida O-Ushi	Crab Clan, daimyo of her Clan, known for her short temper, often called "the bully."
Hida Tsuneo	Crab Clan, returned spirit, bodyguard of Hantei XVI; he became a legend in his own time, and was called "The Stone Crab."
Kaede	Empress, formerly held the position of Mistress of the Void of the Phoenix Clan's Council of Elemental Masters.
Kakita Kaiten	Crane Clan, regent acting on behalf of Doji Kurohito, the young child of the late Crane daimyo.
Kitsu Motso	Lion Clan daimyo, took the reins of power when Toturi was unseated.
Matsu Hiroru	Former member of the Lion Clan, trained as a ninja.
Moto Gaheris	Unicorn Clan daimyo, born and raised outside the Empire.
Shiba Aikune	Phoenix Clan, only son of Shiba Tsukune.
Shiba Tsukune	Phoenix Clan daimyo, mother of Shiba Aikune, longtime associate of Kaede.
Toku	General of the Imperial Guard, formerly a ronin, one of the first to follow Toturi after his fall from power.
Toturi I	Formerly Akodo Toturi of the Lion Clan, he was shamed by Hantei XXXIX and made a ronin; in the end, he led a combined army against the last Hantei and was proclaimed Emperor.
Toturi Naseru	Imperial family, the third child and second son of Toturi and Kaede, trained in the art of diplomacy.
Toturi Sezaru	Imperial family, the second child and first son of Toturi and Kaede, trained in the arts of magic.
Toturi Tsudao	Imperial family, the first child and only daughter of Toturi and Kaede, trained in the art of war.

*Change is
on the wind. . . .*

The Four Winds Saga

Prelude
THE STEEL THRONE
Edward Bolme

The Empire teeters on the brink of disaster. To save his beloved realm, the emperor must make the ultimate sacrifice, entering the very realm of death. But in trying to save his people, he opens the door for his worst enemy to seize power.

March 2002

First Scroll
WIND OF HONOR
Ree Soesbee

As the eldest child of the emperor, Tsudao's duty is clear—her life for the Empire, her sword for service, and honor above all. Now more than ever, her courage, her faith, and her integrity will be put to the ultimate test.

August 2002

Second Scroll
WIND OF WAR
Jess Lebow

The forgotten son of the emperor, Akodo Kaneka is the most renowned warrior in all the lands. As the Empire spirals into chaos and the clans bicker among themselves, the forgotten son must find aid among the common people.

December 2002

Sembia

The perfect entry point into
the richly detailed world of the
FORGOTTEN REALMS®, this
ground-breaking series continues
with these all–new novels.

HEIRS OF PROPHECY
By Lisa Smedman

The maid Larajin has more secrets in her life than she ever
bargained for, but when an unknown evil fuels a war between
Sembia and the elves of the Tangled Trees, secrets pile on secrets
and threaten to bury her once and for all.

June 2002

SANDS OF THE SOUL
By Voronica Whitney-Robinson

Tazi has never felt so alone. Unable to trust anyone, frightened
of her enemy's malign power, and knowing that it was more
luck than skill that saved her the last time, she comes to realize
that the consequences of the necromancer's plans could shake
the foundations of her world.

November 2002